MAGIC TREE HOUSE®

DINOSAURS BEFORE DARK

MARY POPE OSBORNE'S

MAGIC TREE HOUSE®

DINOSAURS BEFORE DARK

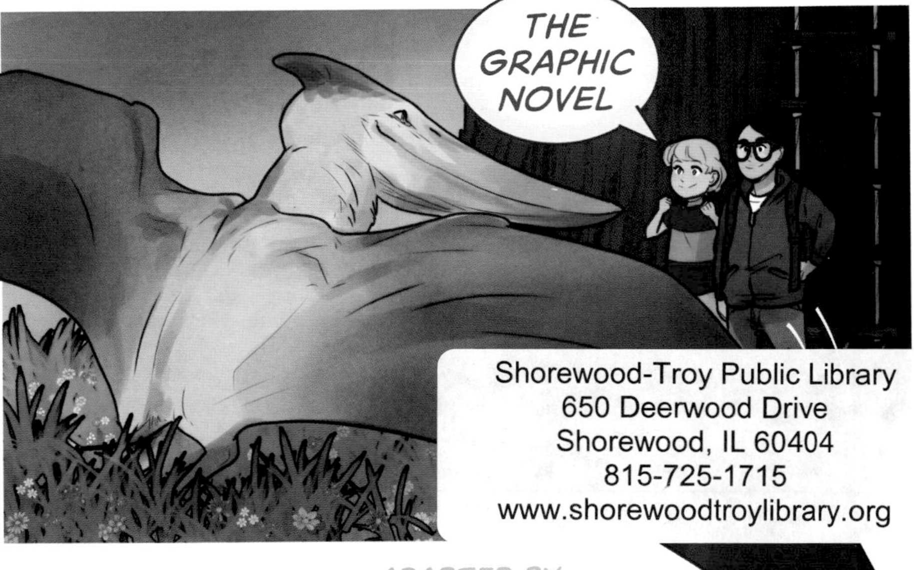
THE GRAPHIC NOVEL

ADAPTED BY

JENNY LAIRD

WITH ART BY

KELLY & NICHOLE MATTHEWS

A STEPPING STONE BOOK™
RANDOM HOUSE NEW YORK

Text copyright © 2021 by Mary Pope Osborne
Art copyright © 2021 by Kelly Matthews & Nichole Matthews
Text adapted by Jenny Laird

All rights reserved. Published in the United States by Random House Children's Books, a division
of Penguin Random House LLC, New York. Adapted from *Dinosaurs Before Dark*, published by
Random House Children's Books, a division of Penguin Random House LLC, New York, in 1992.

Random House and the colophon are registered trademarks and A Stepping Stone Book and the colophon
and RH Graphic with the book design are trademarks of Penguin Random House LLC. Magic Tree House
is a registered trademark of Mary Pope Osborne; used under license.

Visit us on the Web!
rhcbooks.com
MagicTreeHouse.com

Educators and librarians, for a variety of teaching tools, visit us at RHTeachersLibrarians.com

Library of Congress Cataloging-in-Publication Data
Names: Laird, Jenny, adapter. | Matthews, Kelly (comic book artist), illustrator. |
Matthews, Nichole, illustrator. | Osborne, Mary Pope. Dinosaurs before dark.
Title: Dinosaurs before dark / Jenny Laird; illustrated by Kelly and Nichole Matthews.
Description: New York: Random House Children's Books, [2021] | Series: Mary Pope Osborne's Magic tree house |
Summary: Retells, in graphic novel form, the tale of eight-year-old Jack and his younger sister, Annie, who find
a magic tree house which whisks them back to an ancient time zone where they see live dinosaurs.
Identifiers: LCCN 2020032698 (print) | LCCN 2020032699 (ebook) |
ISBN 978-0-593-17471-5 (trade paperback) | ISBN 978-0-593-17468-5 (hardcover) |
ISBN 978-0-593-17469-2 (library binding) | ISBN 978-0-593-17470-8 (ebook)
Subjects: LCSH: Graphic novels. | CYAC: Graphic novels. | Dinosaurs–Fiction. |
Time travel–Fiction. | Magic–Fiction. | Tree houses–Fiction.
Classification: LCC PZ7.7.L28 Din 2021 (print) | LCC PZ7.7.L28 (ebook) | DDC 741.5/973–dc23

The artists used Clip Studio Paint to create the illustrations for this book.
The text of this book is set in 13-point Cartoonist Hand Regular.

MANUFACTURED IN CHINA
10 9 8 7 6 5 4 3 2 1
First Graphic Novel Edition

For Mallory and Jenna,
two of Jack and Annie's best friends
—M.P.O.

For Quinn, who was born to fly
—J.L.

We dedicate this book to our mother,
a teacher, who taught us to love reading, drawing,
and learning; our brothers, for inspiring us to follow
in their footsteps; and our cats, for never letting
us forget what is truly important (feeding them).
—K.M. & N.M.

CHAPTER ONE
Into the Woods

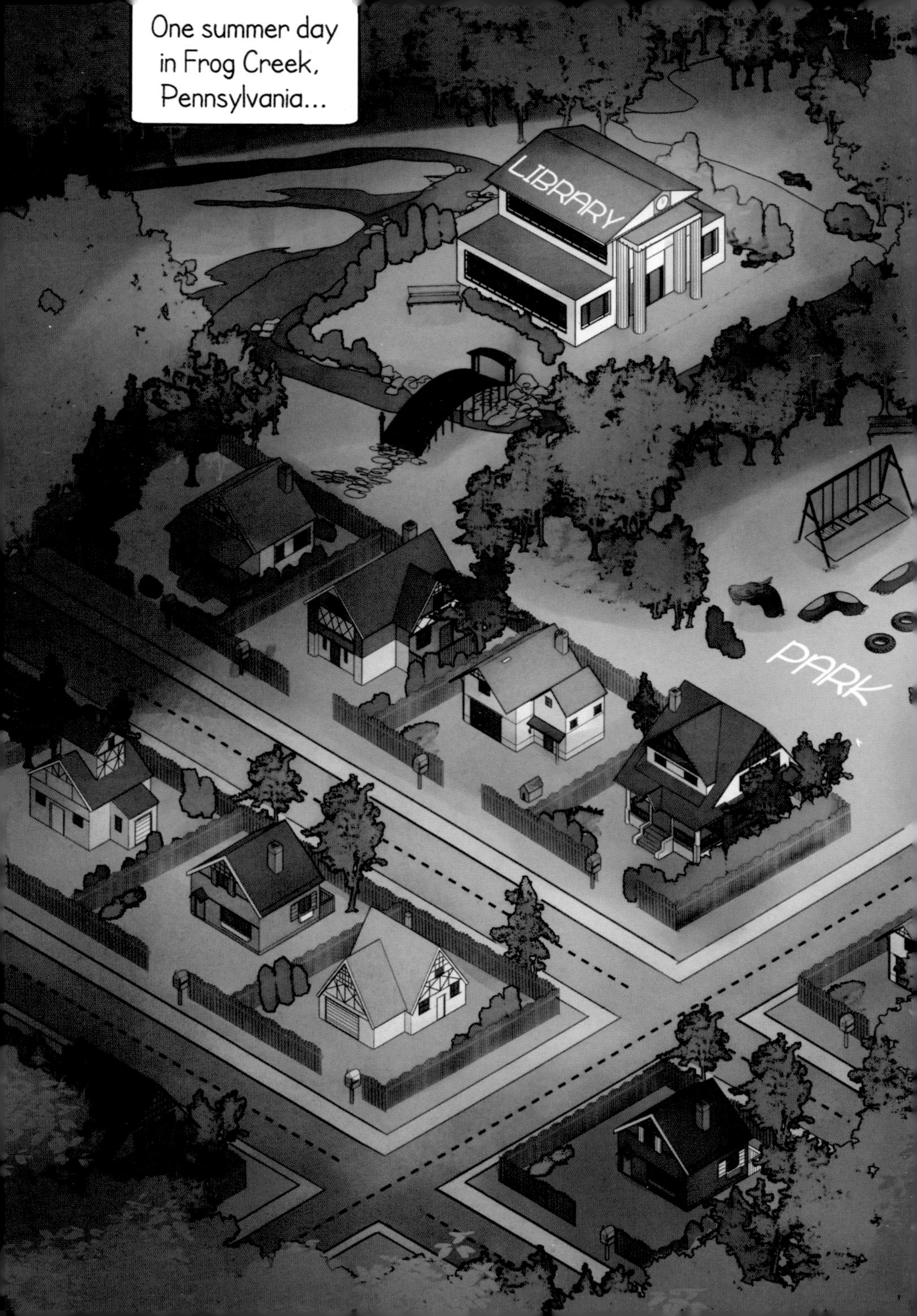
One summer day in Frog Creek, Pennsylvania...
LIBRARY
PARK

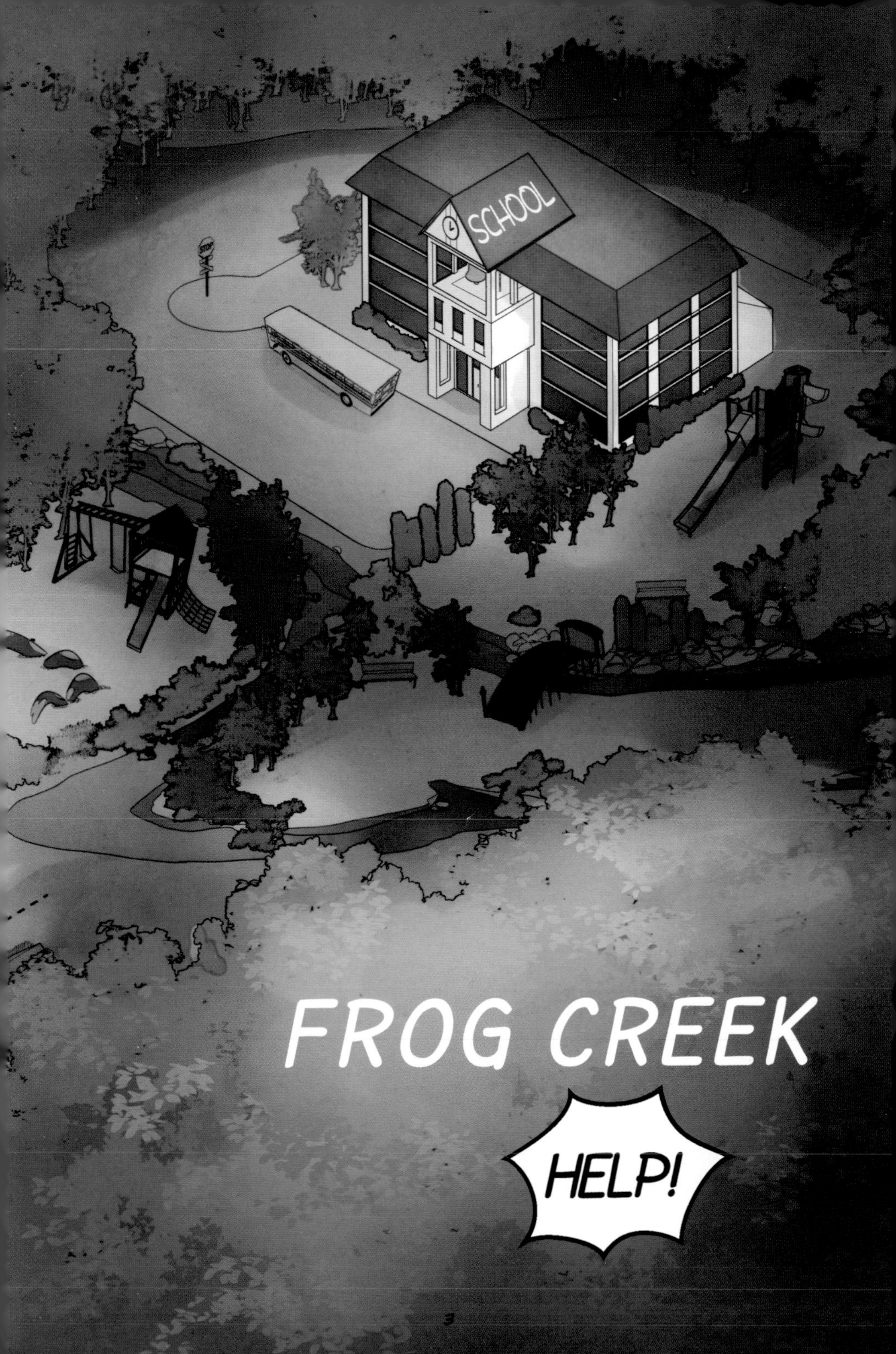
SCHOOL
STOP
FROG CREEK
HELP!

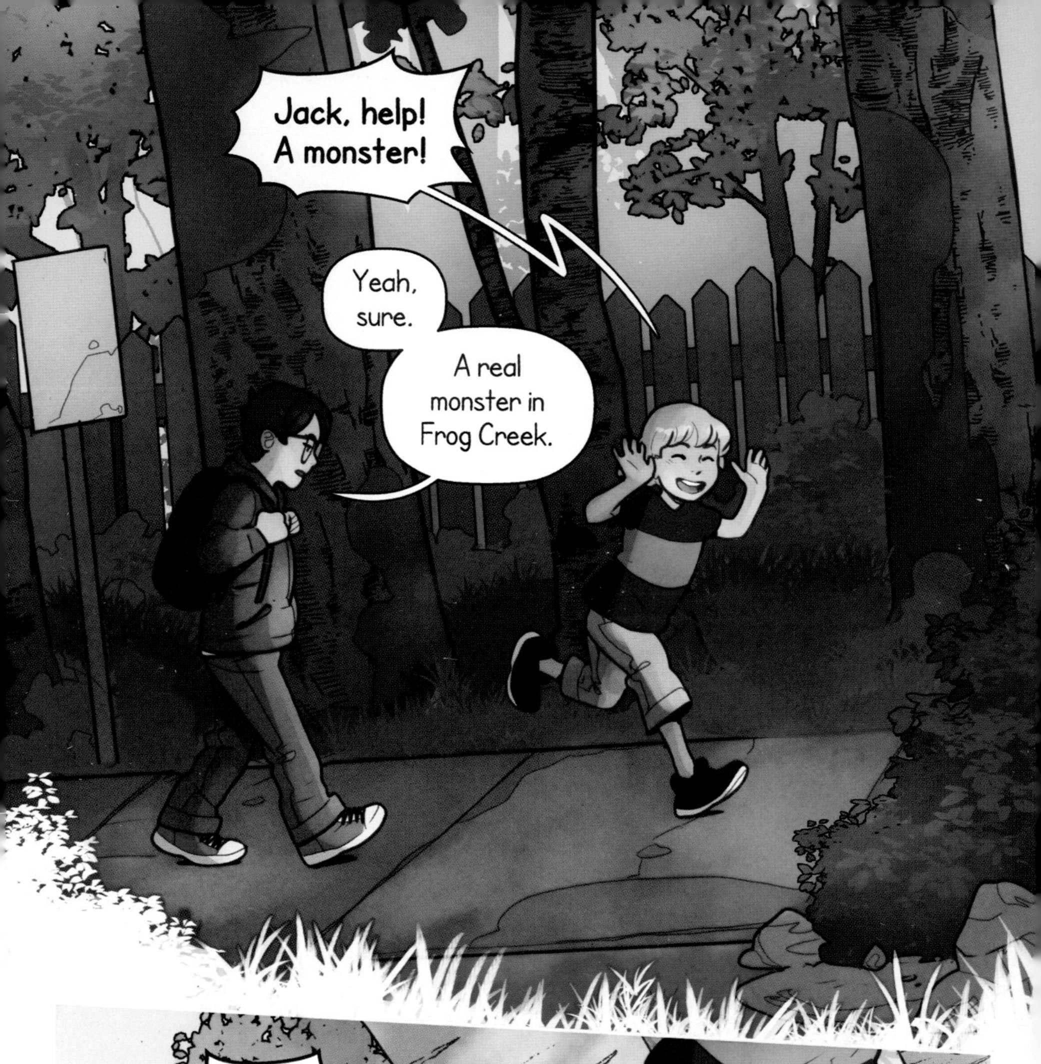
Jack, help! A monster!
Yeah, sure.
A real monster in Frog Creek.

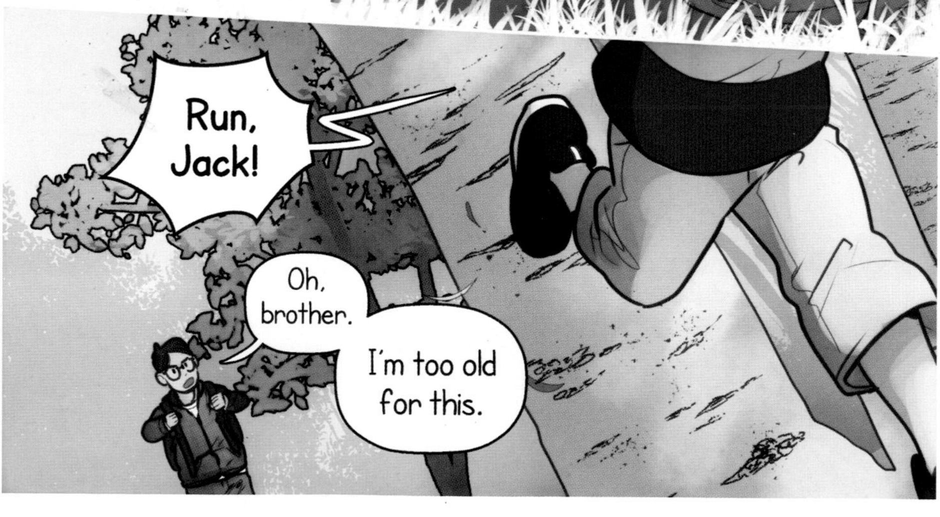
Run, Jack!
Oh, brother.
I'm too old for this.

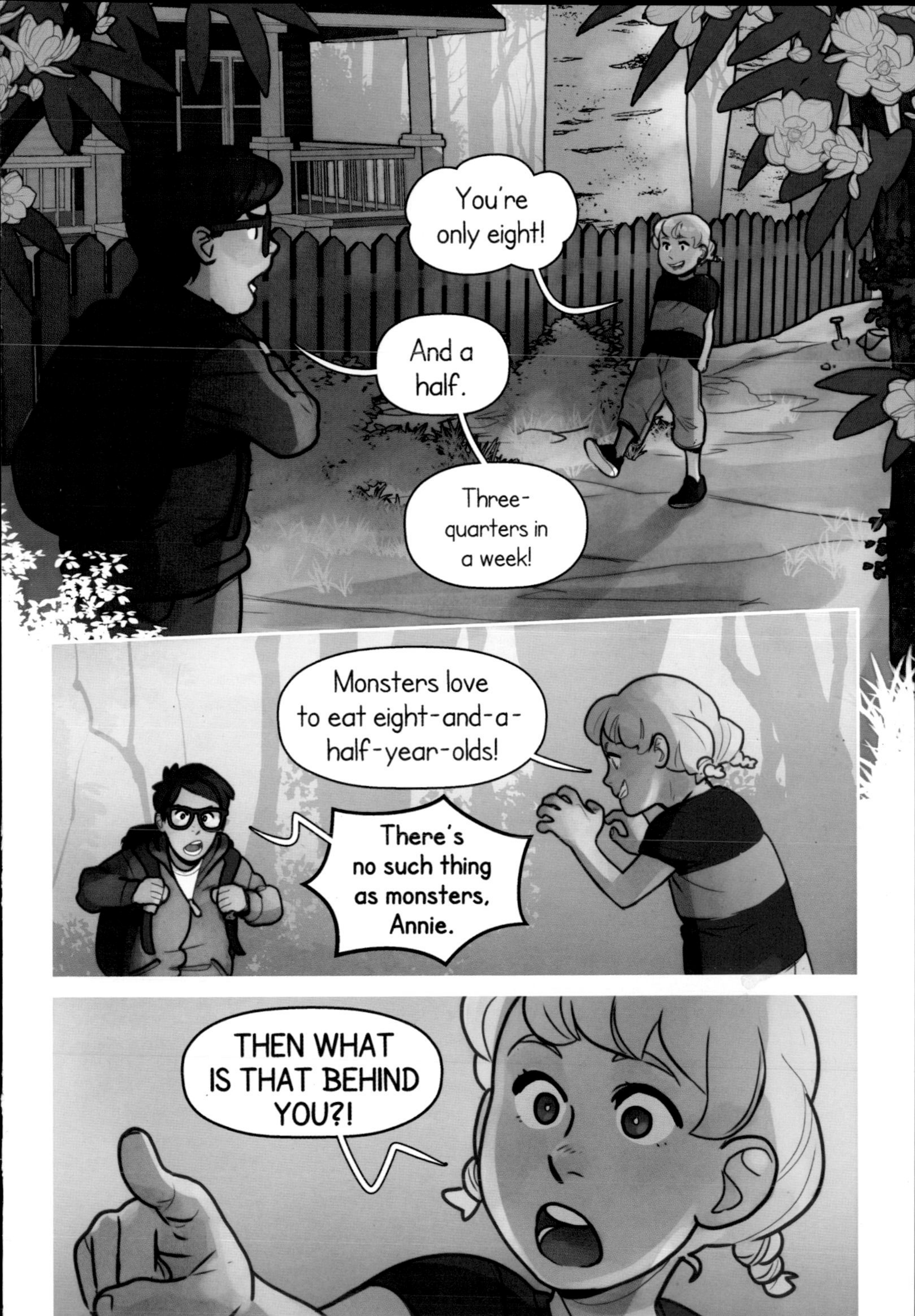
You're only eight!
And a half.
Three-quarters in a week!
Monsters love to eat eight-and-a-half-year-olds!
There's no such thing as monsters, Annie.
THEN WHAT IS THAT BEHIND YOU?!

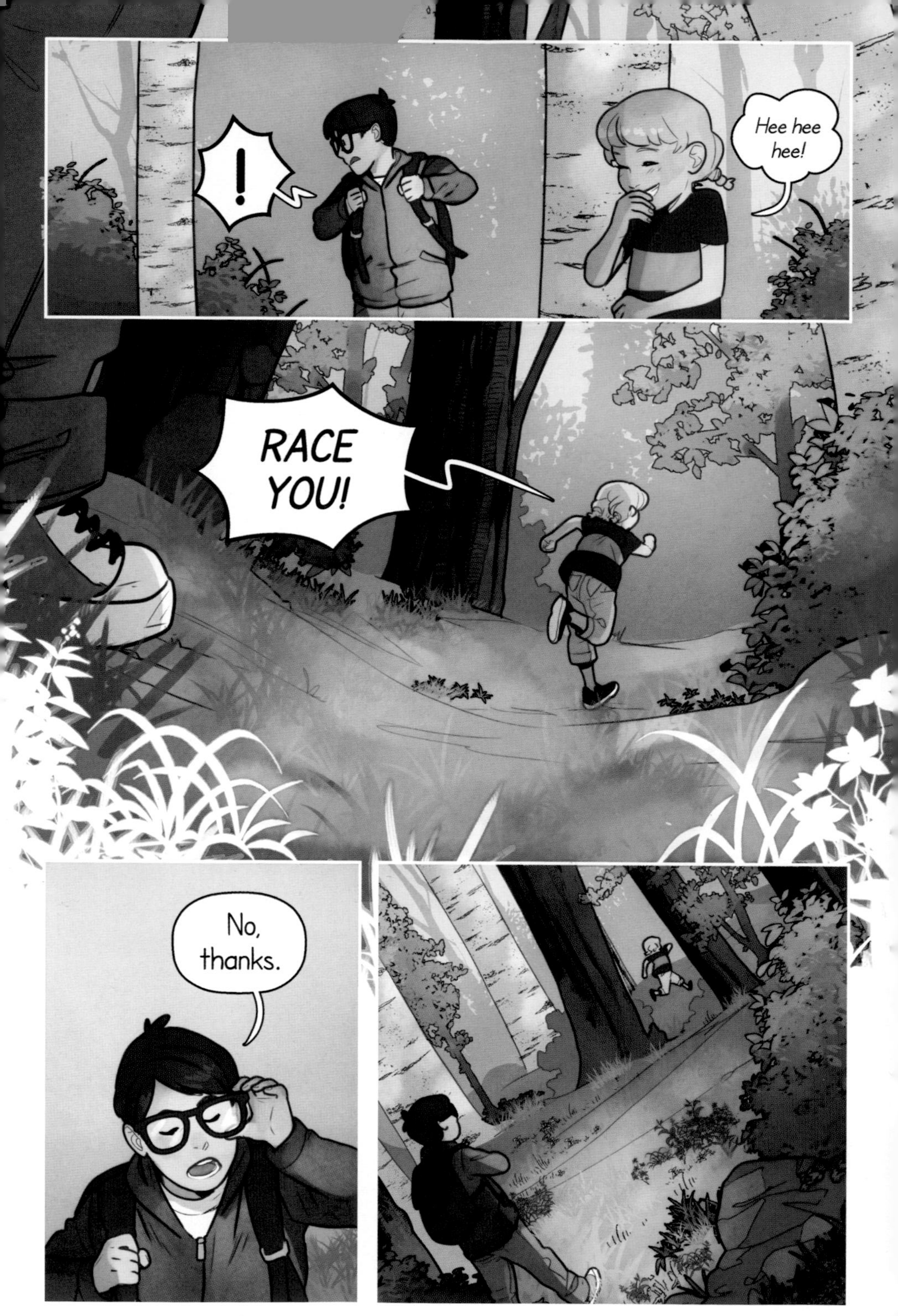
!
Hee hee hee!
RACE YOU!
No, thanks.

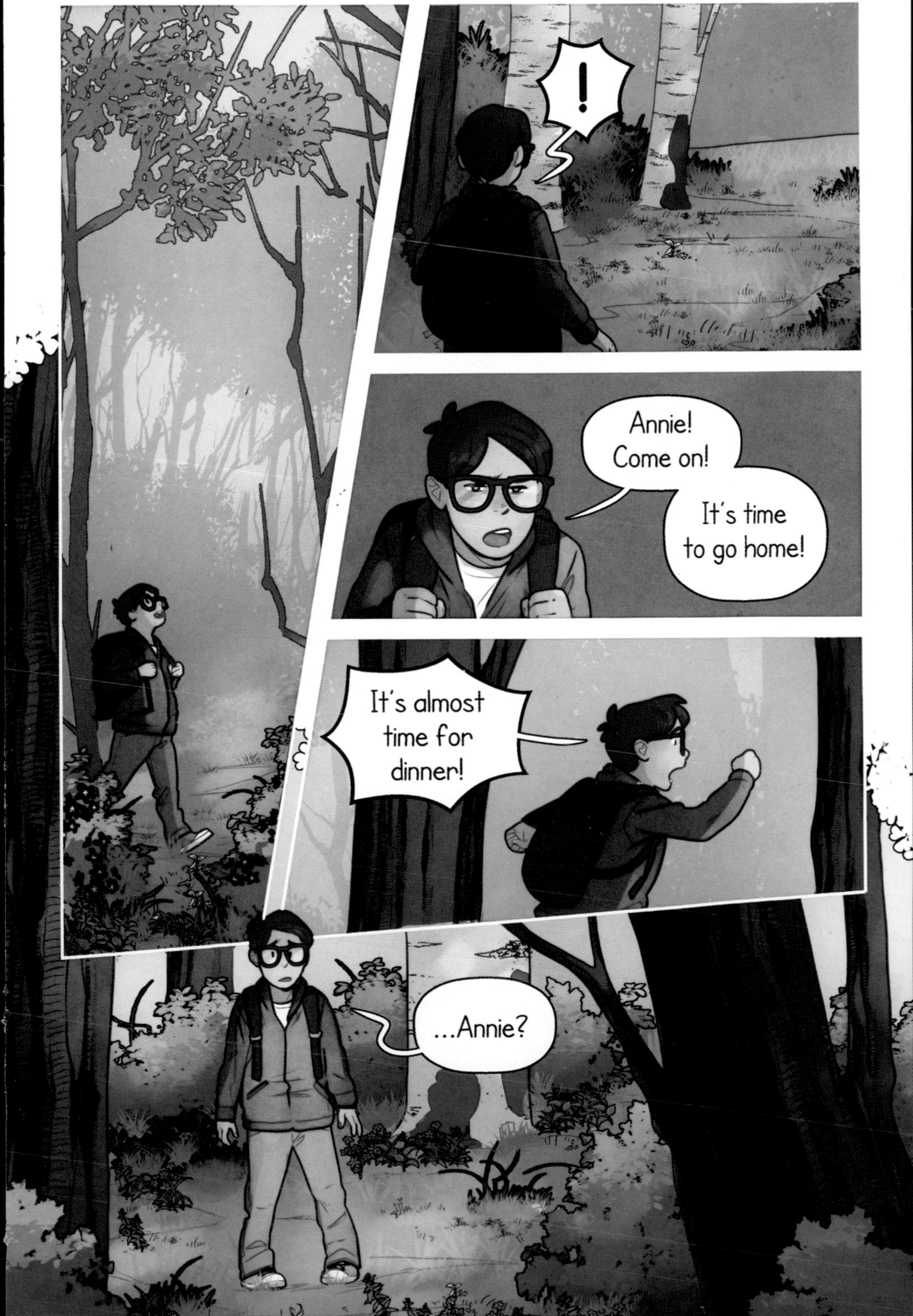
!
Annie! Come on!
It's time to go home!
It's almost time for dinner!
...Annie?

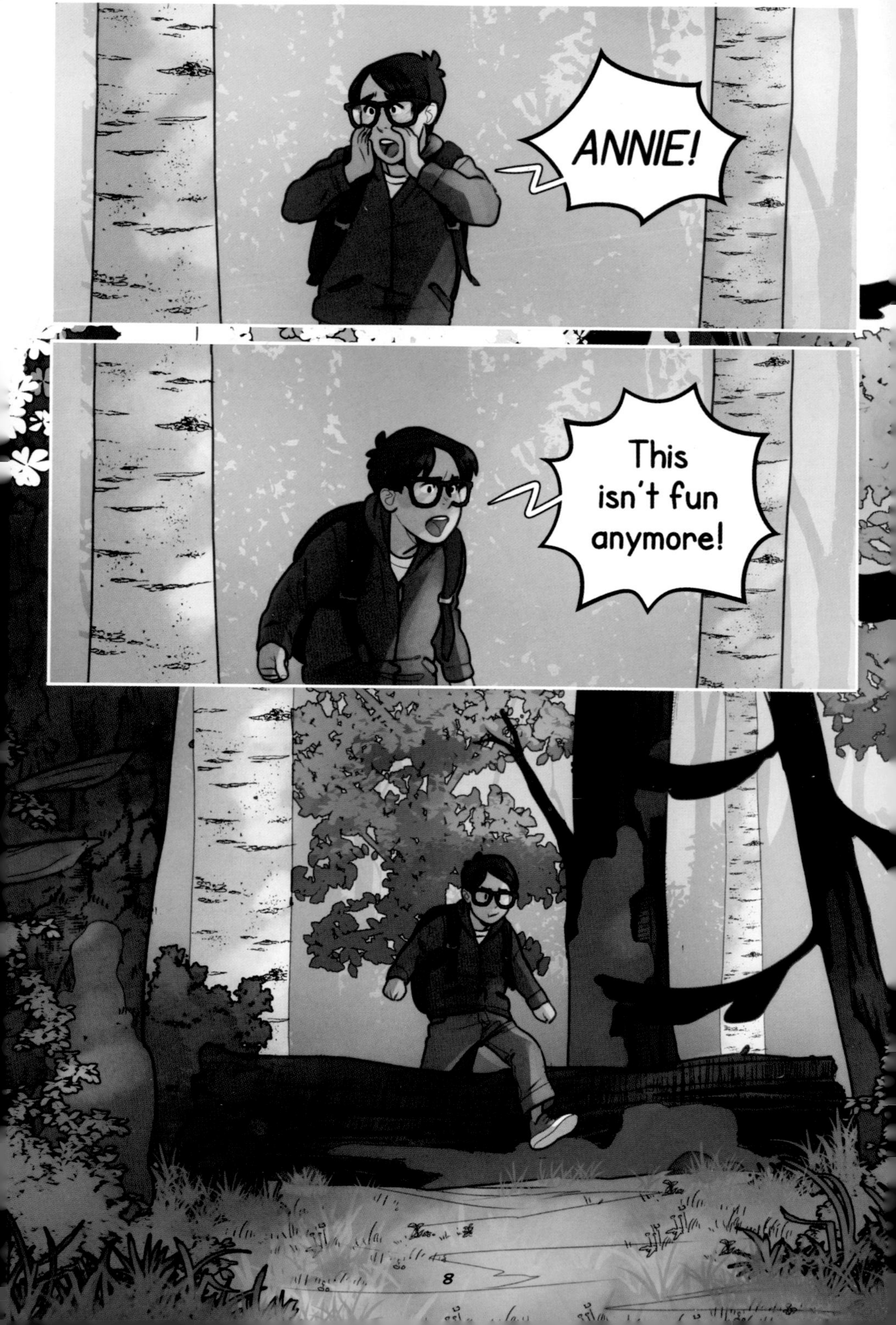
ANNIE!
This isn't fun anymore!

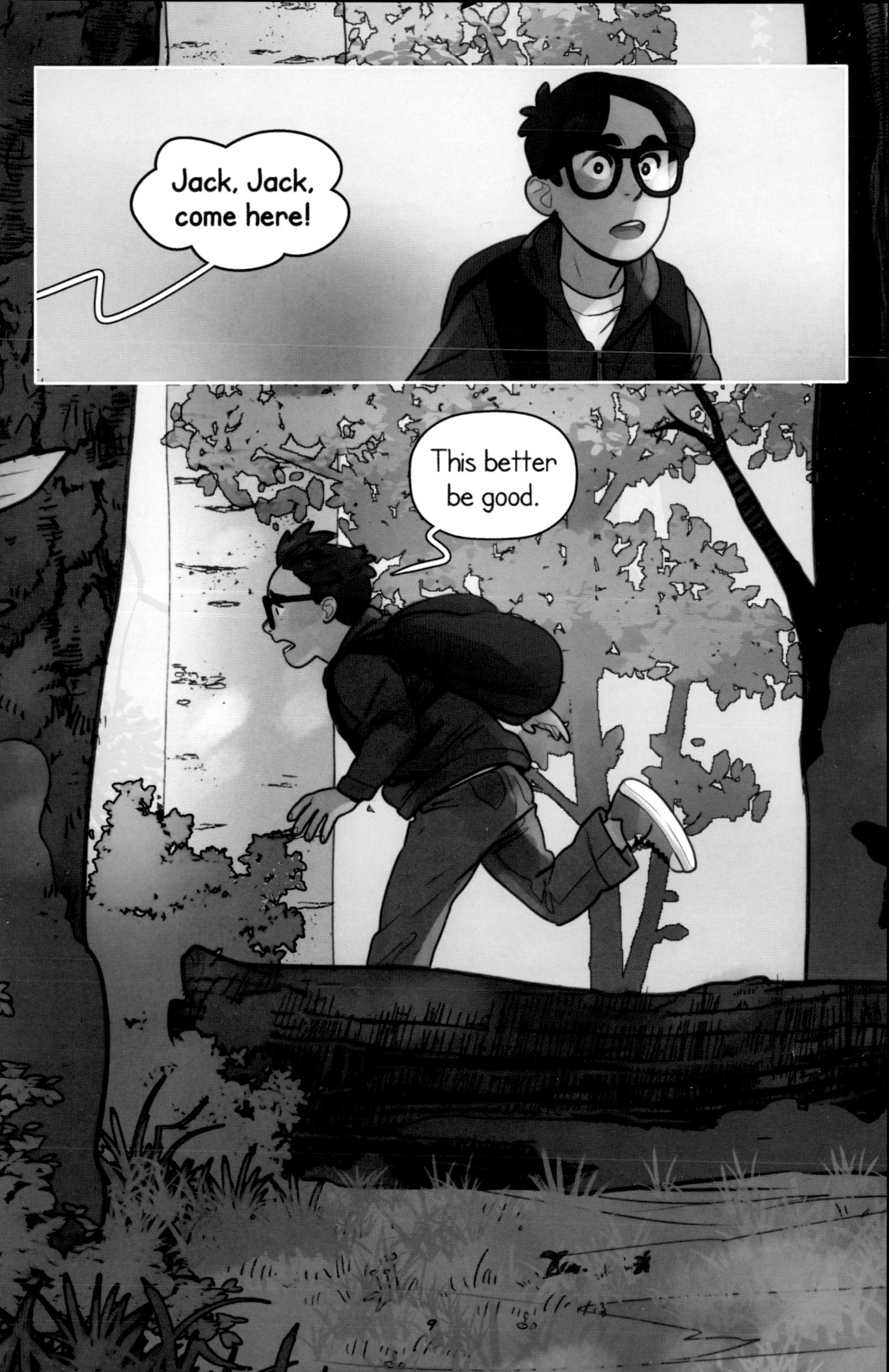
Jack, Jack, come here!
This better be good.

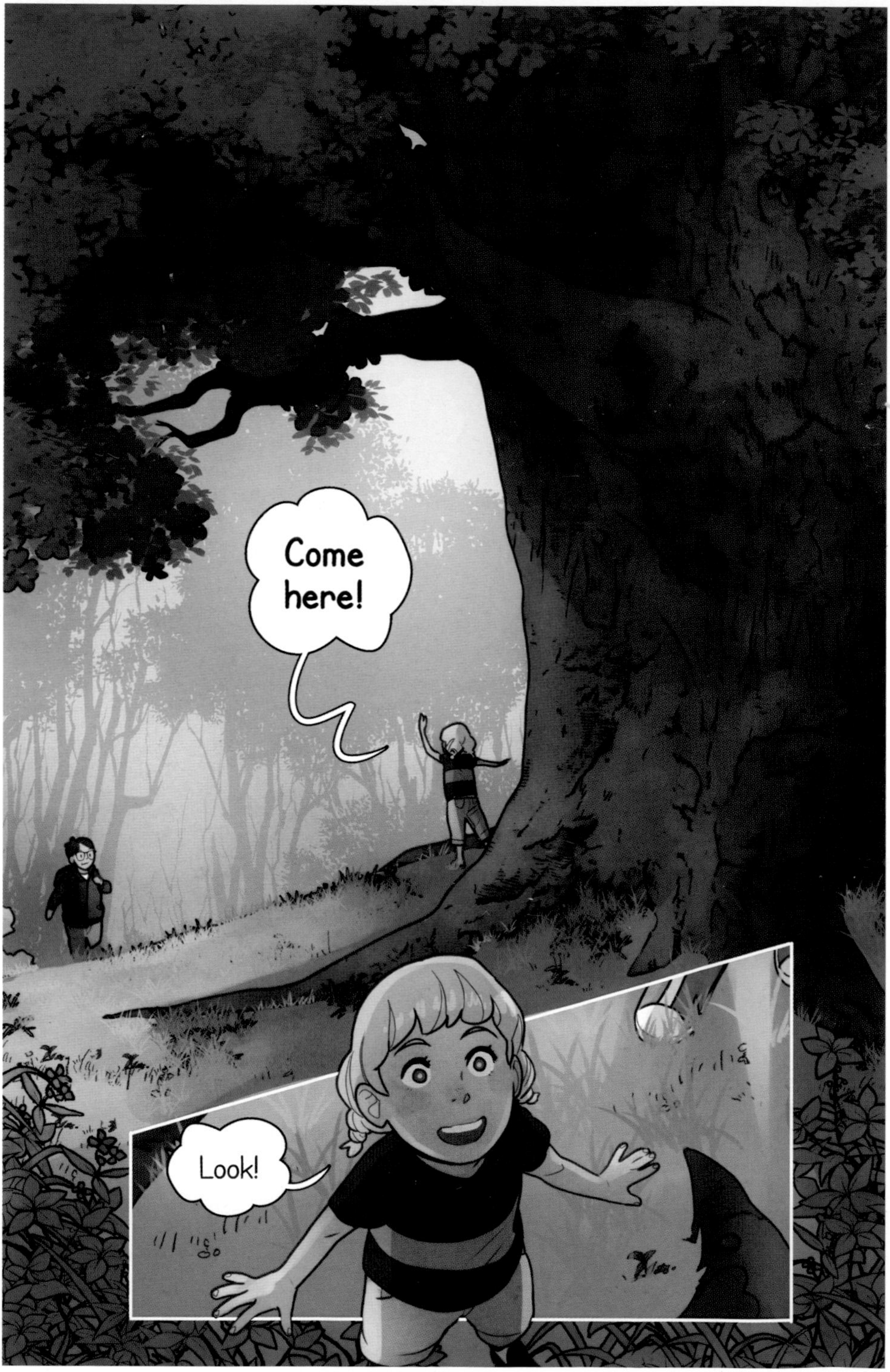
Come here!
Look!

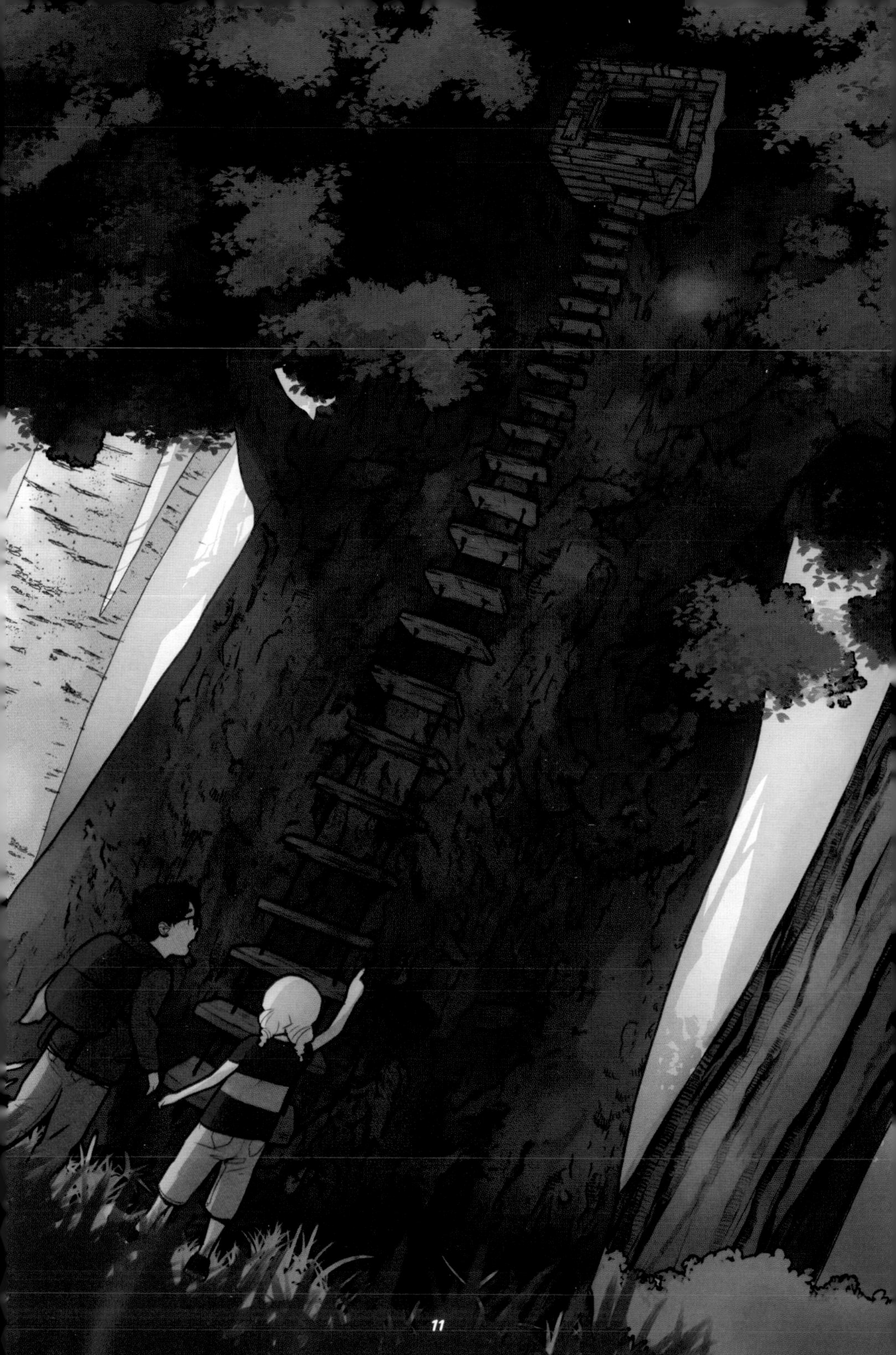

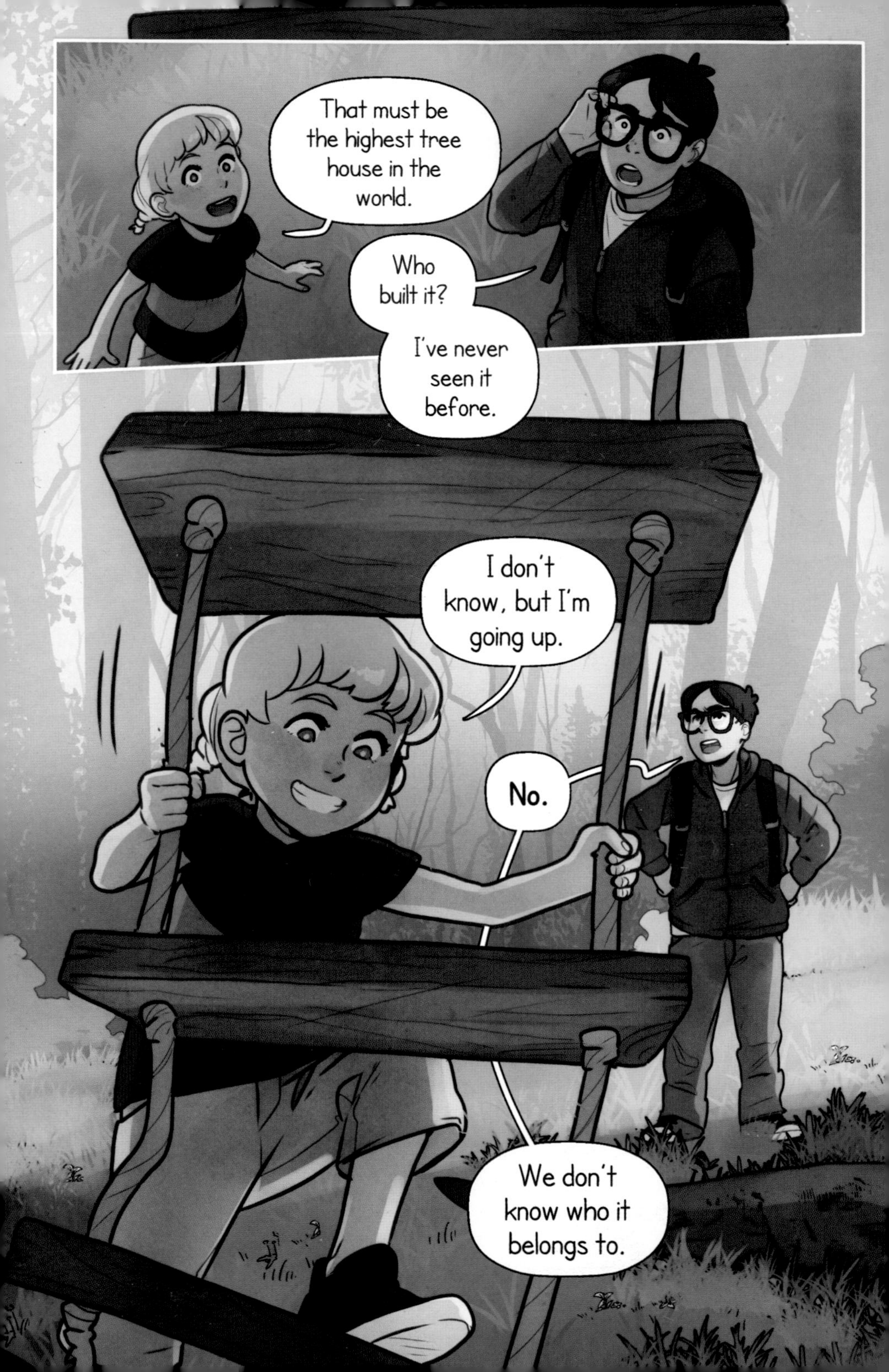
That must be the highest tree house in the world.
Who built it?
I've never seen it before.
I don't know, but I'm going up.
No.
We don't know who it belongs to.

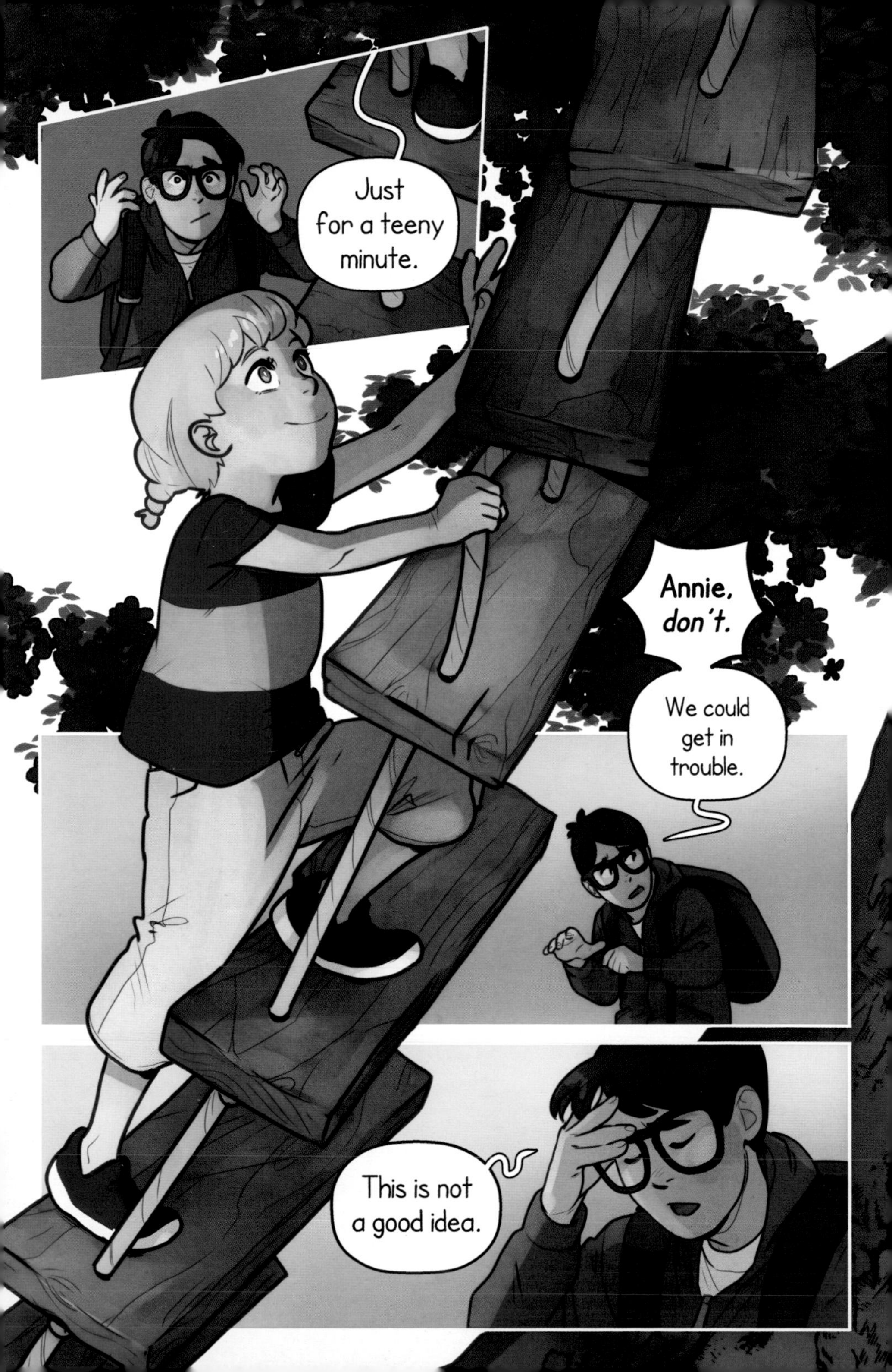
Just for a teeny minute.
Annie, *don't.*
We could get in trouble.
This is not a good idea.

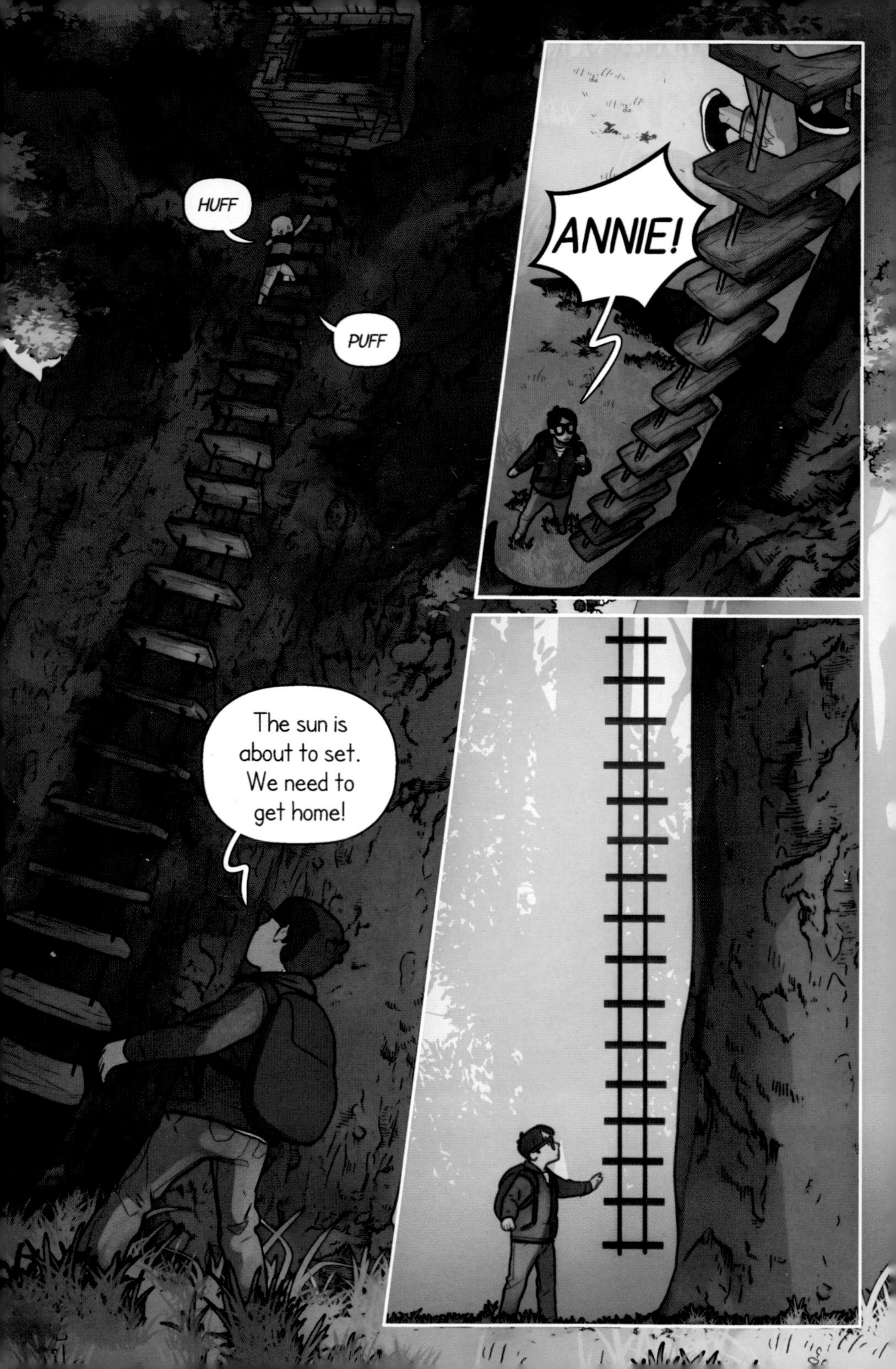
HUFF
PUFF
The sun is about to set. We need to get home!
ANNIE!

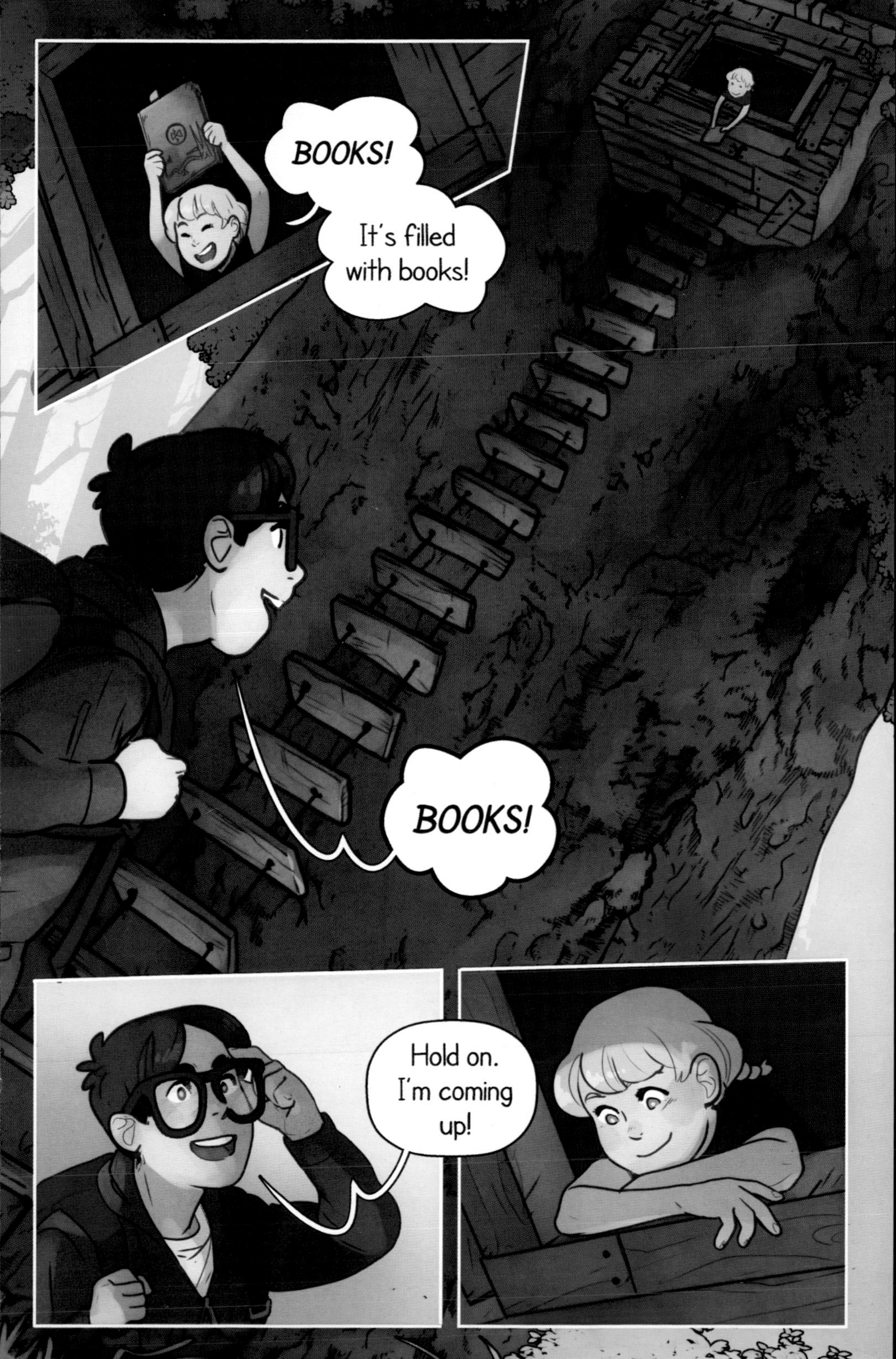
BOOKS!
It's filled with books!
BOOKS!
Hold on. I'm coming up!

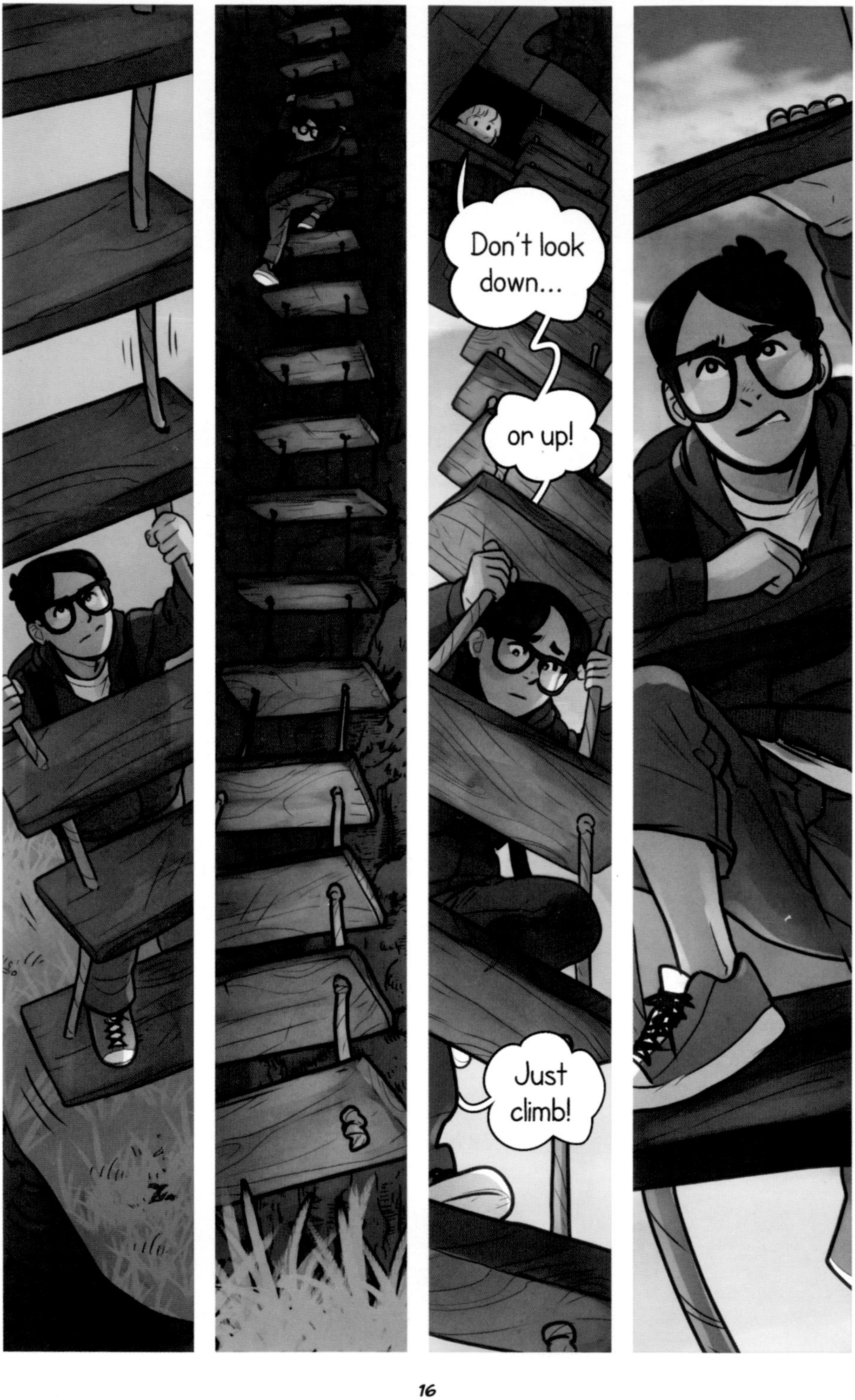

Don't look down...
or up!
Just climb!

CHAPTER TWO

The Wish

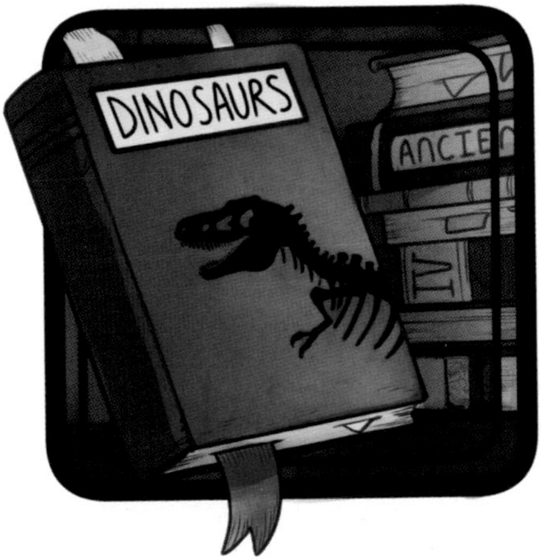
DINOSAURS
ANCIE
IV

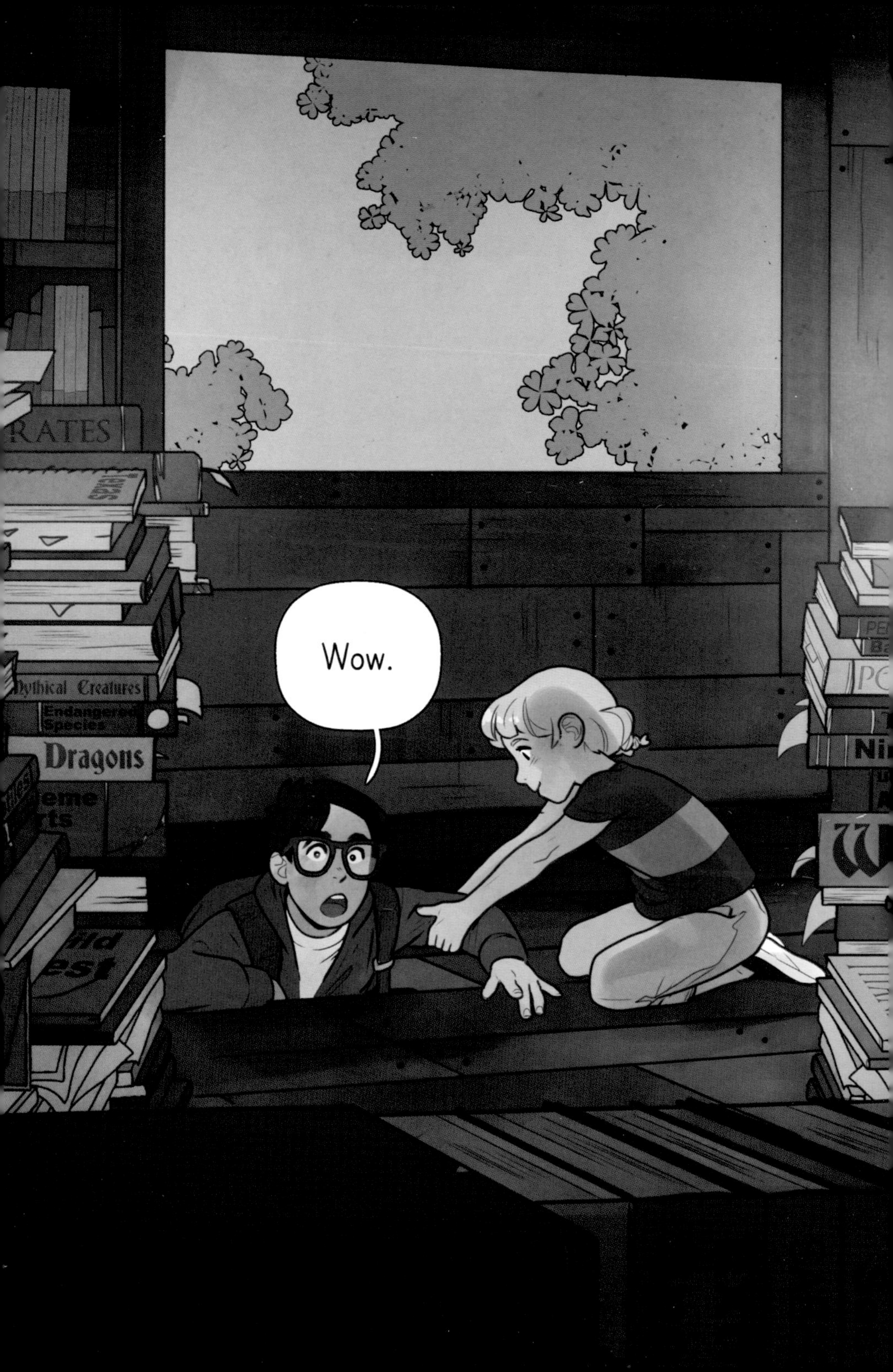
Wow.
Endangered Species
Dragons

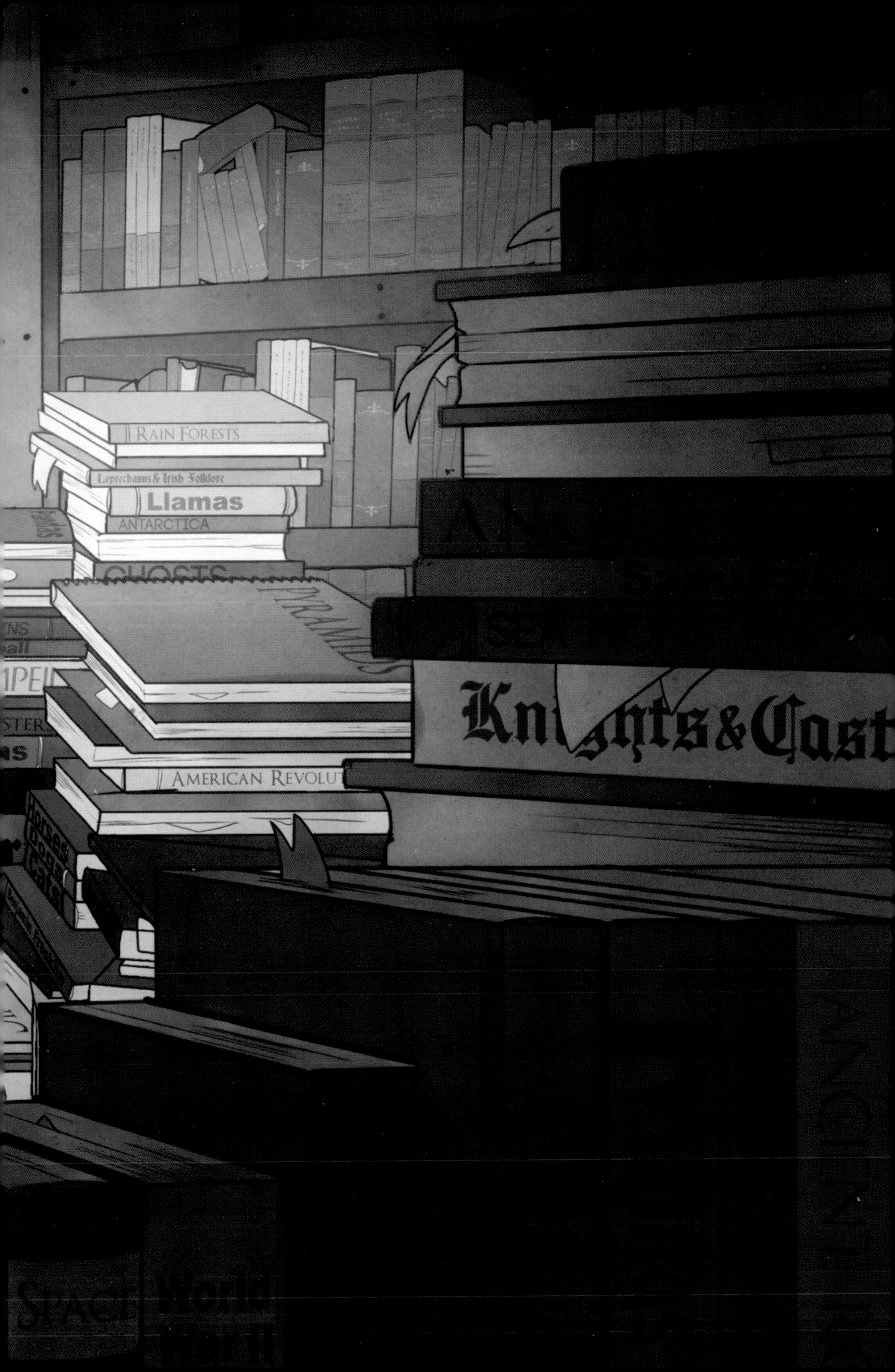
RAIN FORESTS
Leprechauns & Irish Folklore
Llamas
ANTARCTICA
PYRAMIDS
AMERICAN REVOLUT
Knights&Cast
Horses
Dogs
Cats
SPACE
World

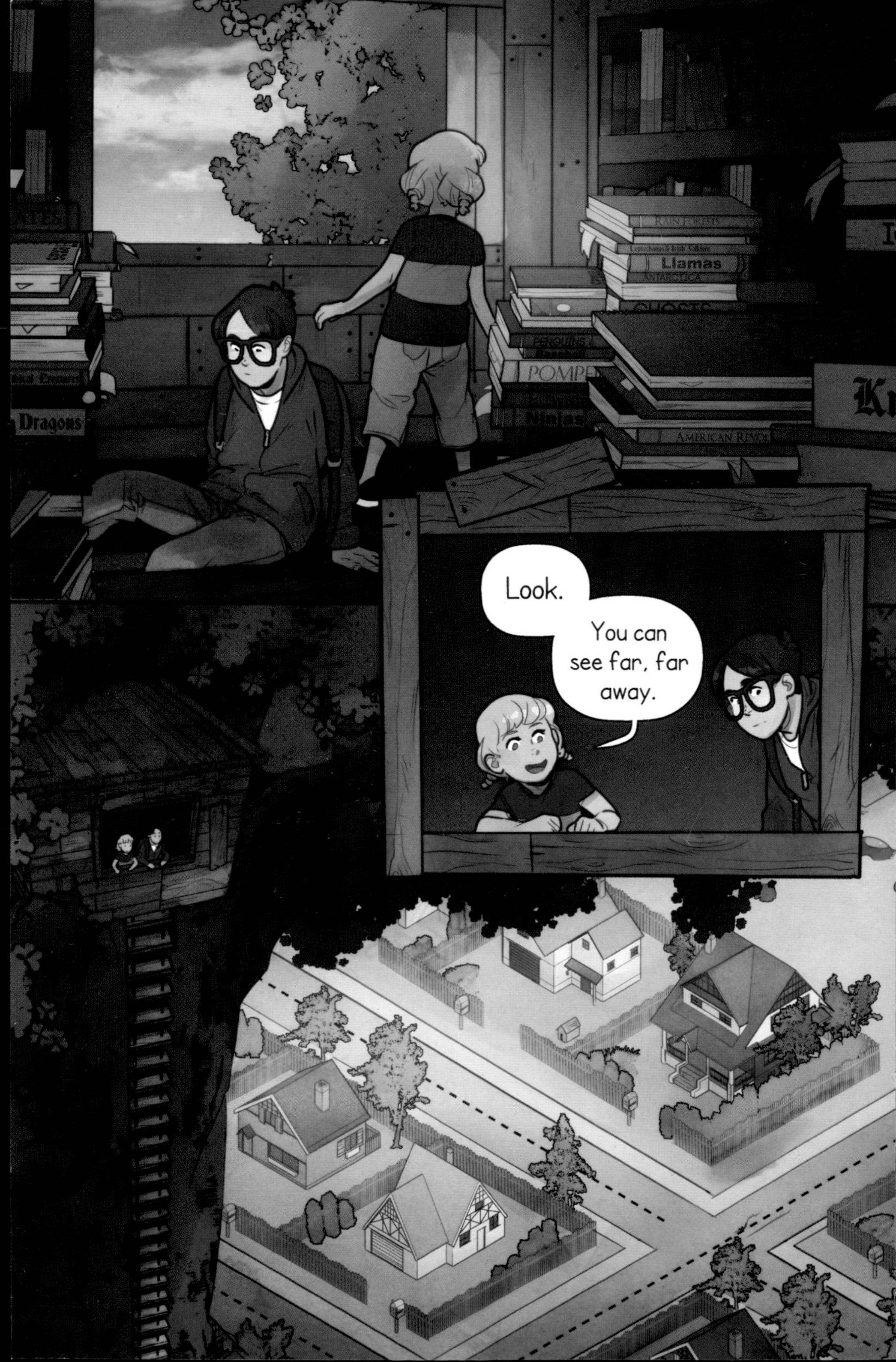
Rain Forests
Llamas
Antarctica
Penguins
Baseball
Ninjas
Dragons
Look.
You can see far, far away.

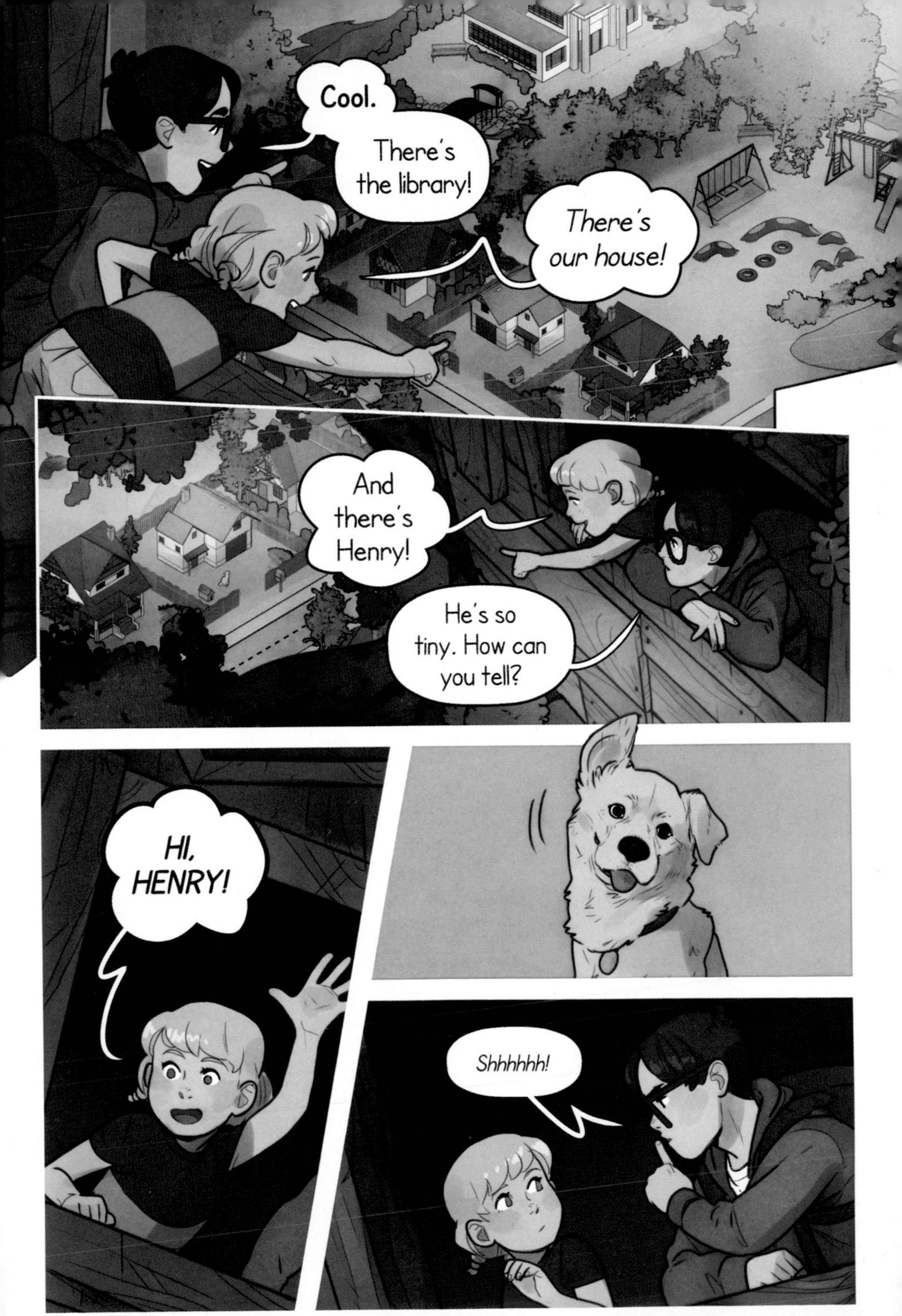
Cool.
There's the library!
There's our house!
And there's Henry!
He's so tiny. How can you tell?
HI, HENRY!
Shhhhhh!

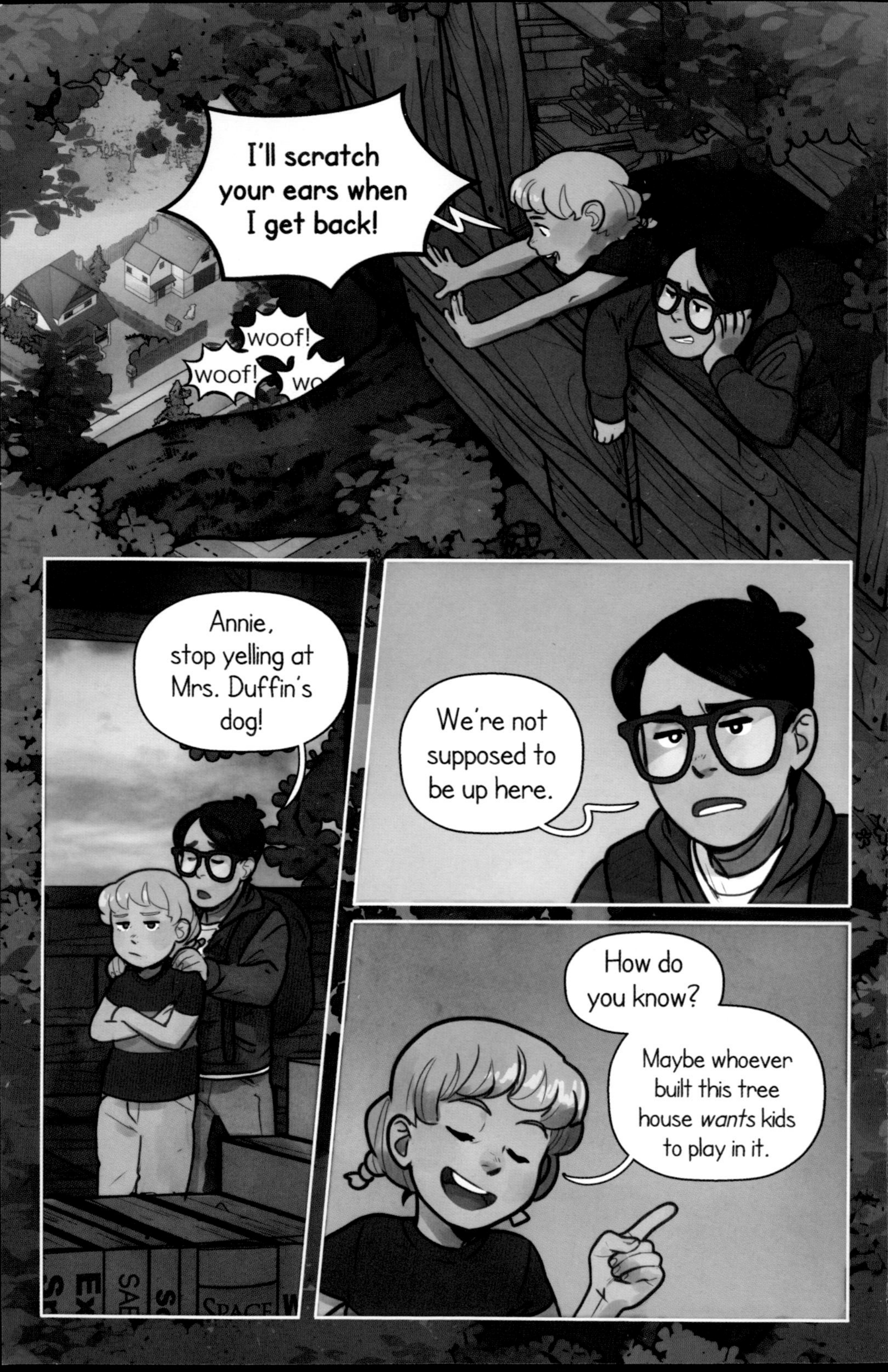
I'll scratch your ears when I get back!
woof!
woof!
Annie, stop yelling at Mrs. Duffin's dog!
We're not supposed to be up here.
How do you know?
Maybe whoever built this tree house *wants* kids to play in it.
SPACE

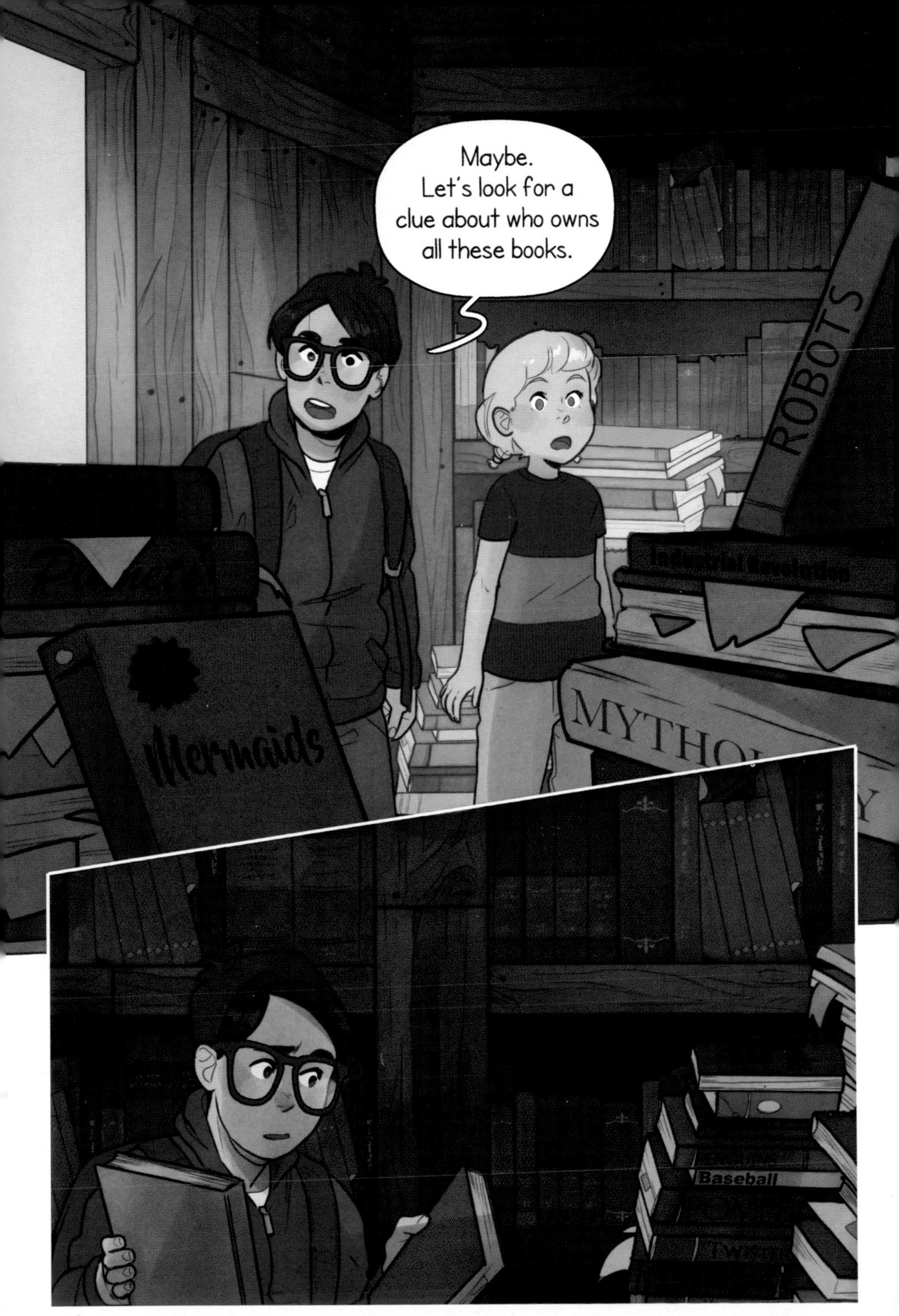
Maybe.
Let's look for a clue about who owns all these books.
ROBOTS
Industrial Revolution
Mermaids
Baseball

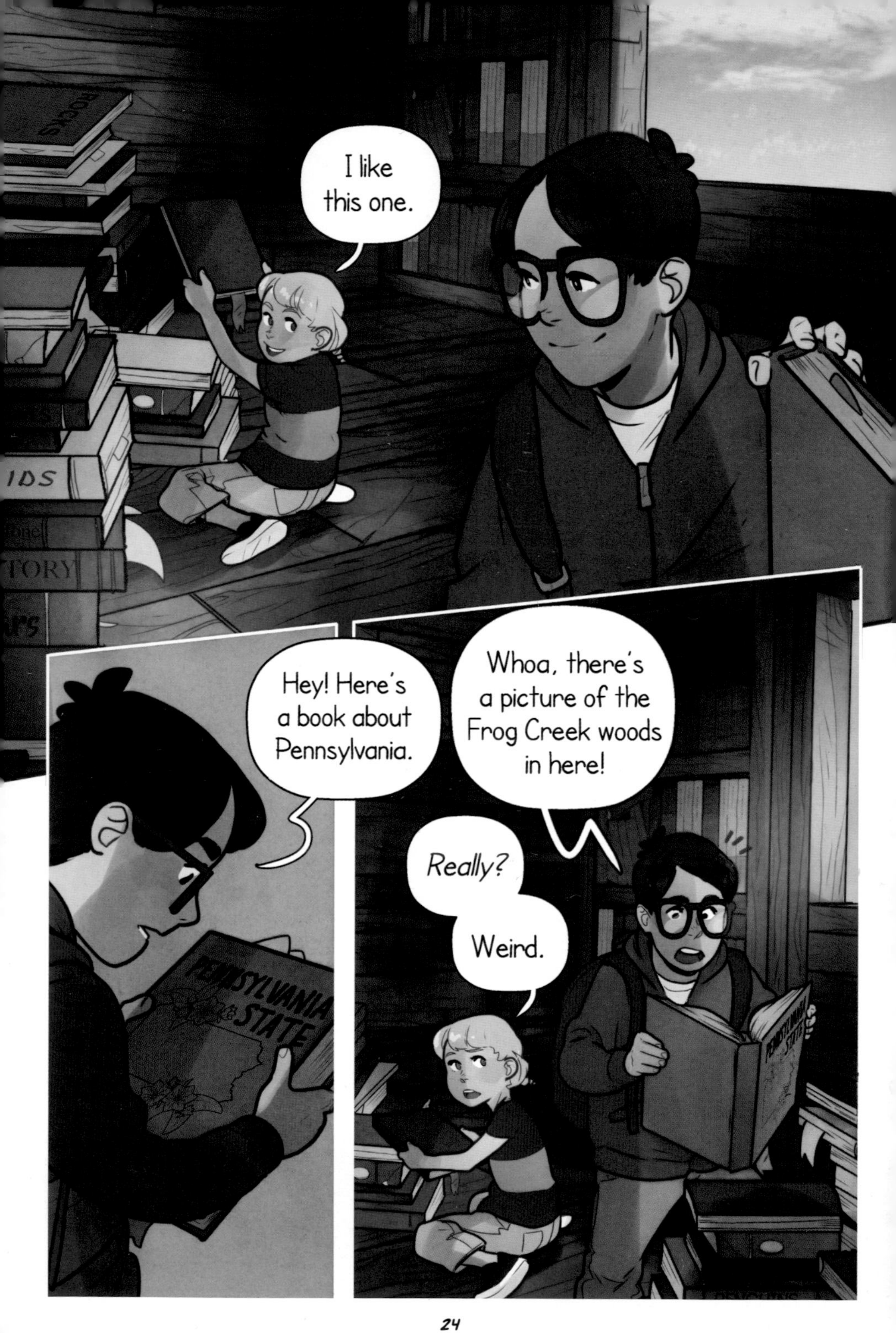

ROCKS
I like this one.
Hey! Here's a book about Pennsylvania.
PENNSYLVANIA STATE
Whoa, there's a picture of the Frog Creek woods in here!
Really?
Weird.

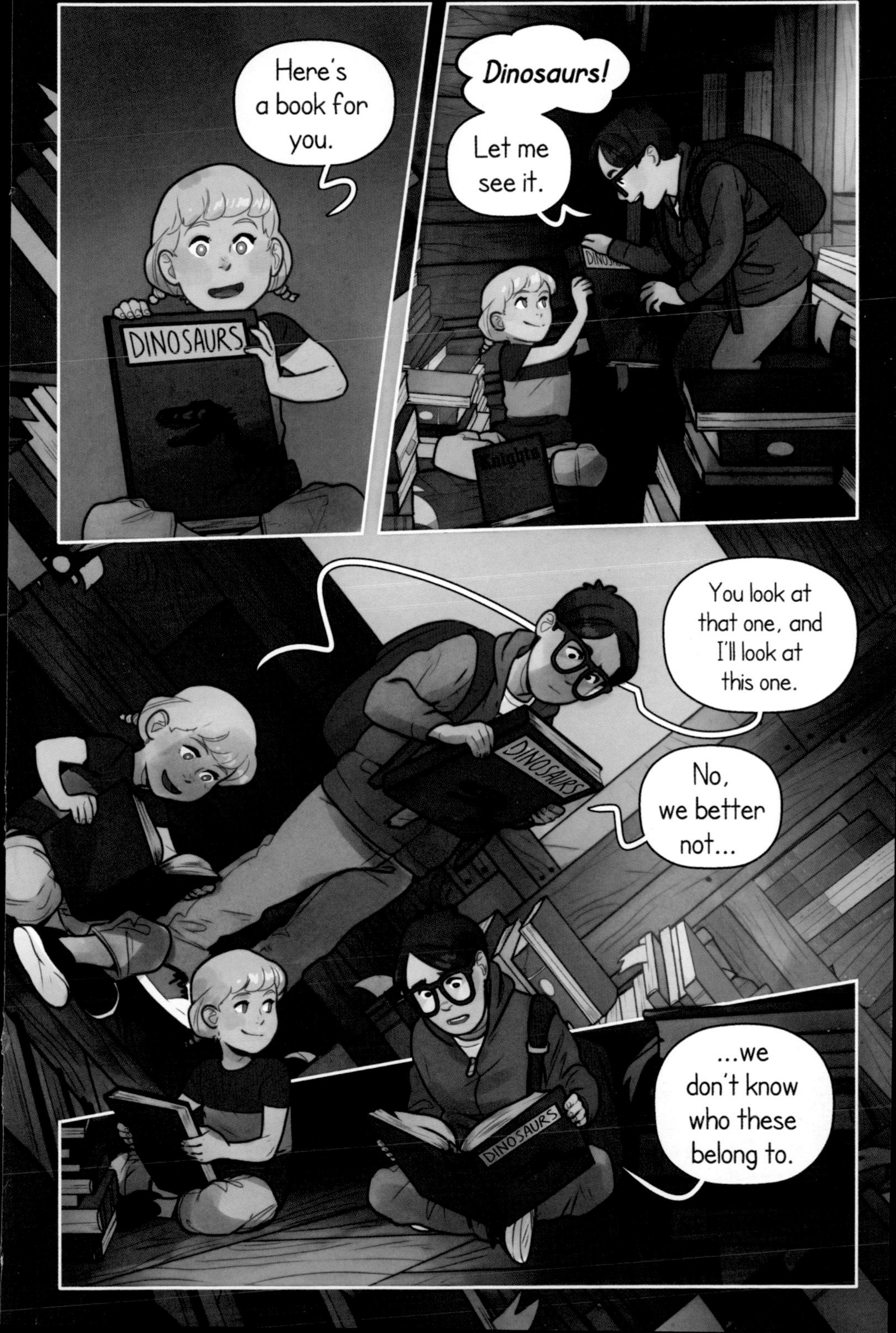
Here's a book for you.
DINOSAURS
Dinosaurs!
Let me see it.
Knights
You look at that one, and I'll look at this one.
DINOSAURS
No, we better not...
...we don't know who these belong to.
DINOSAURS

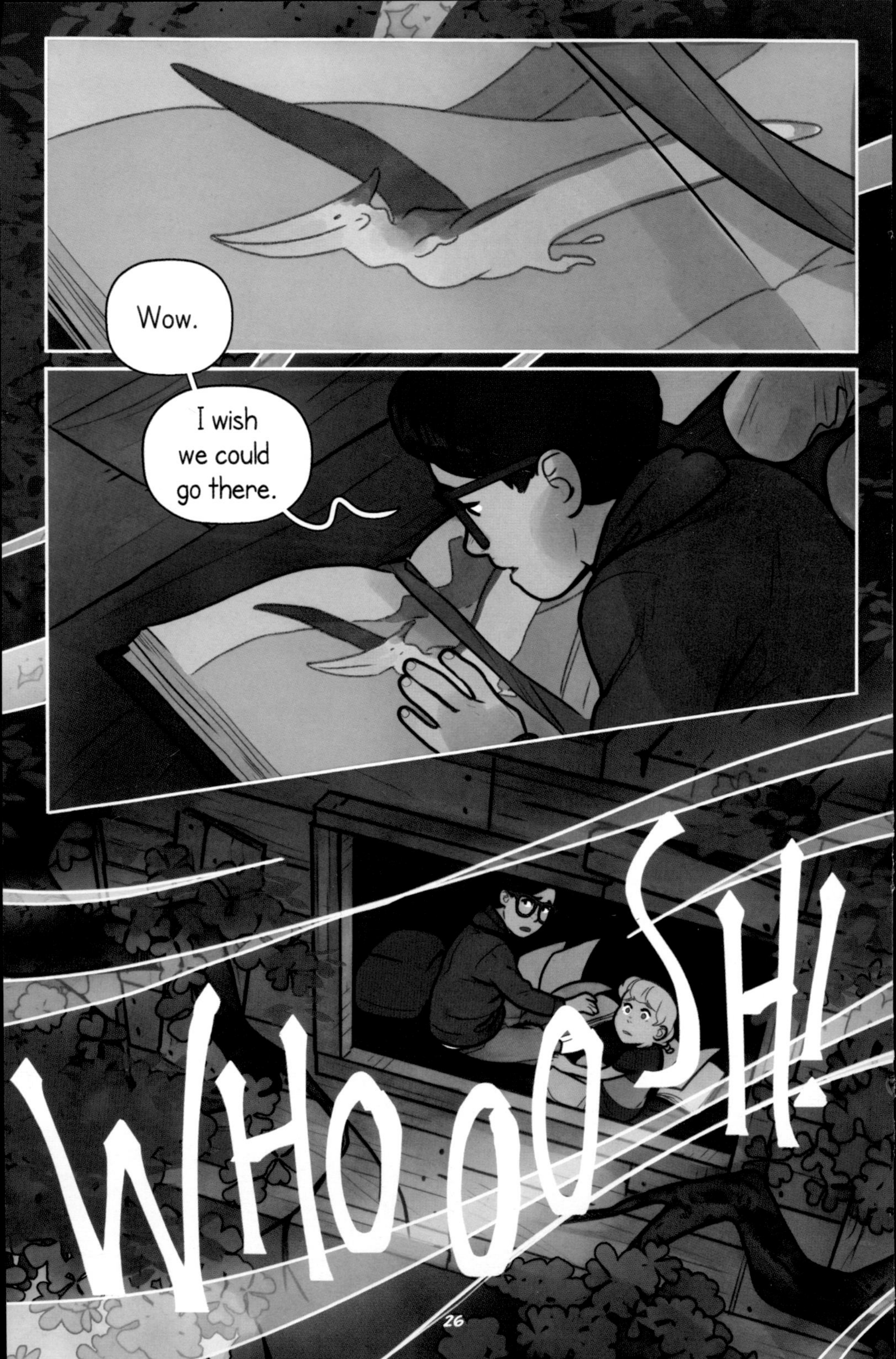
Wow.
I wish we could go there.
WHOOOSH!

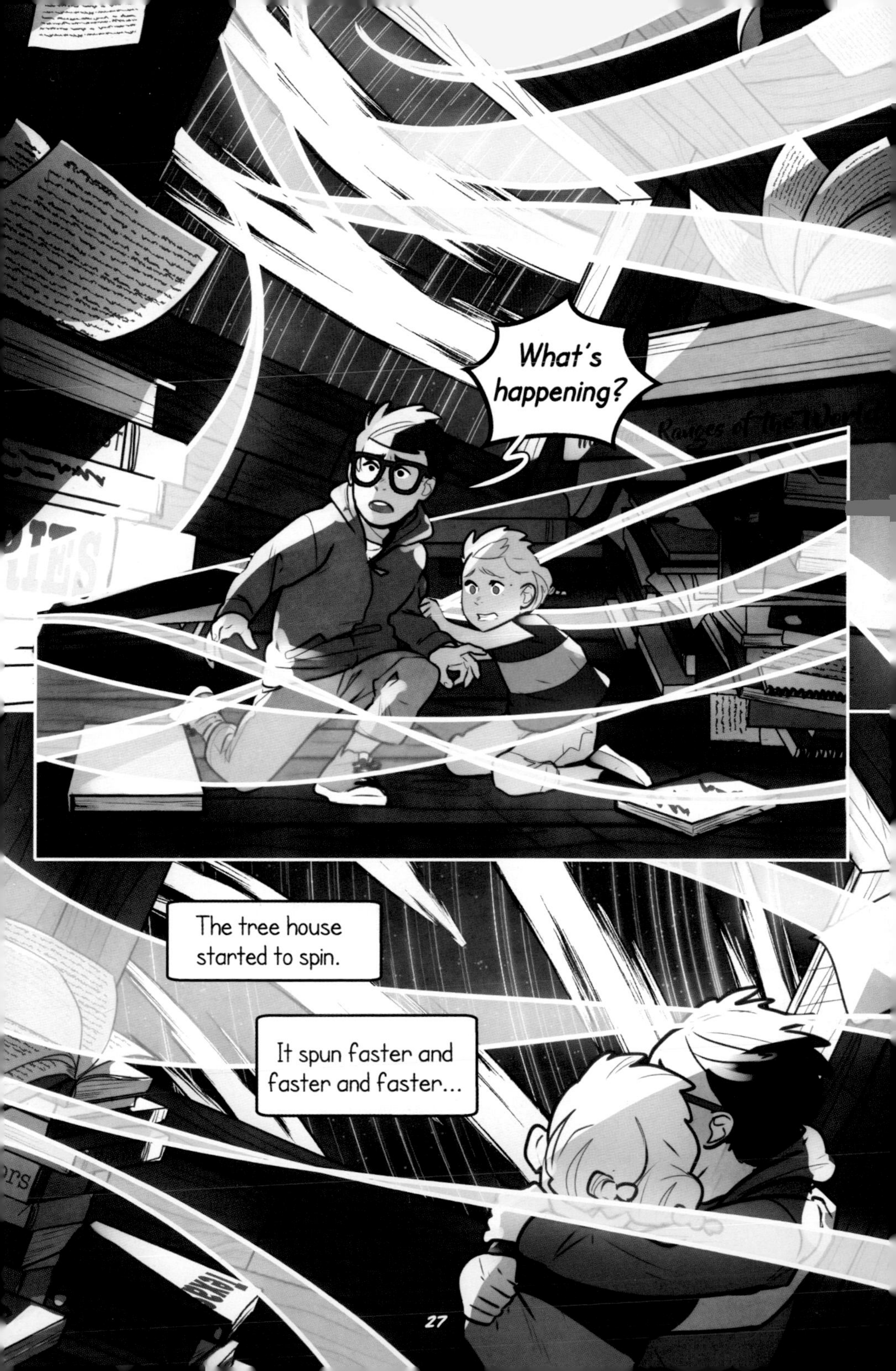
What's happening?
The tree house started to spin.
It spun faster and faster and faster...

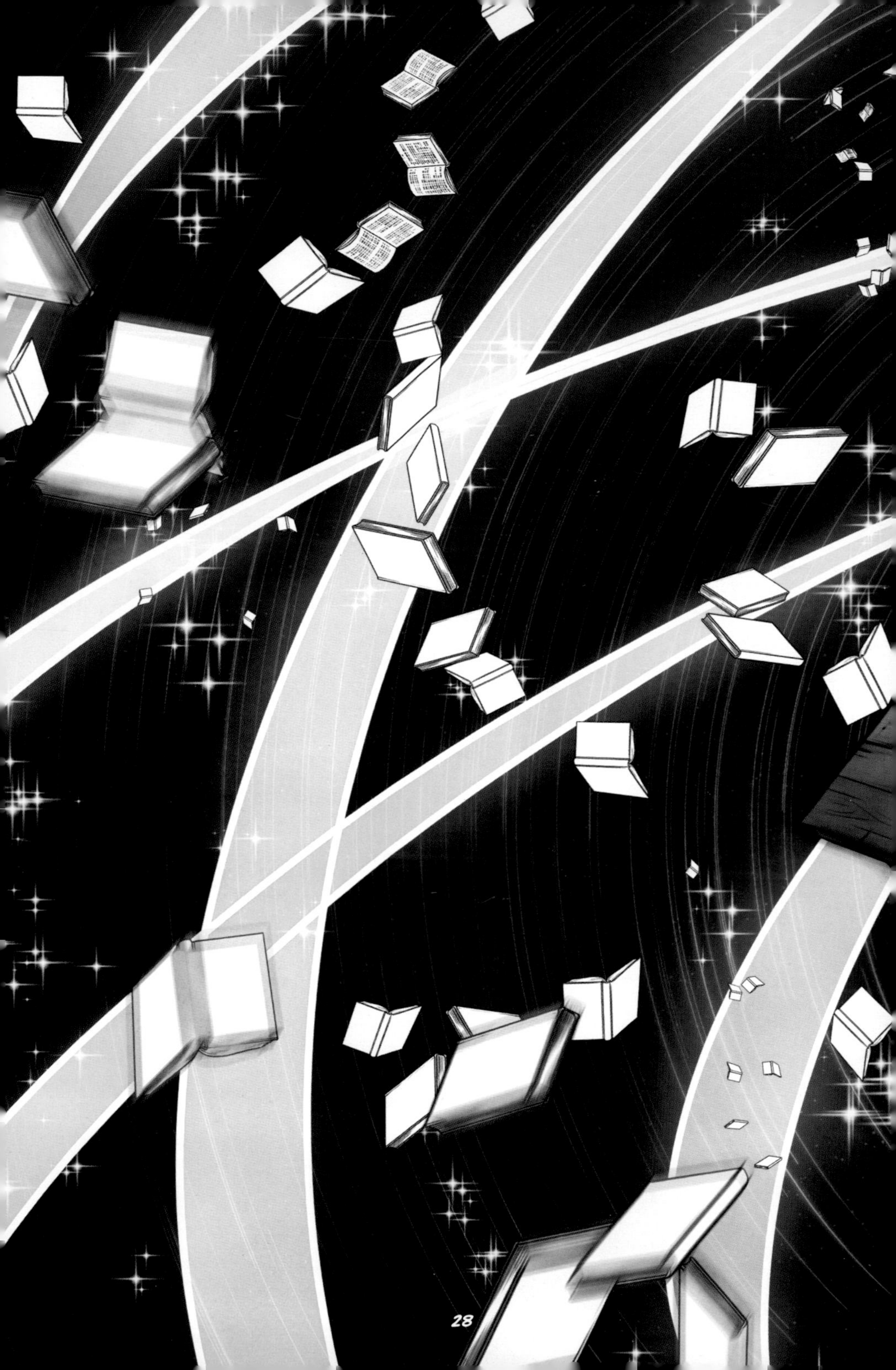

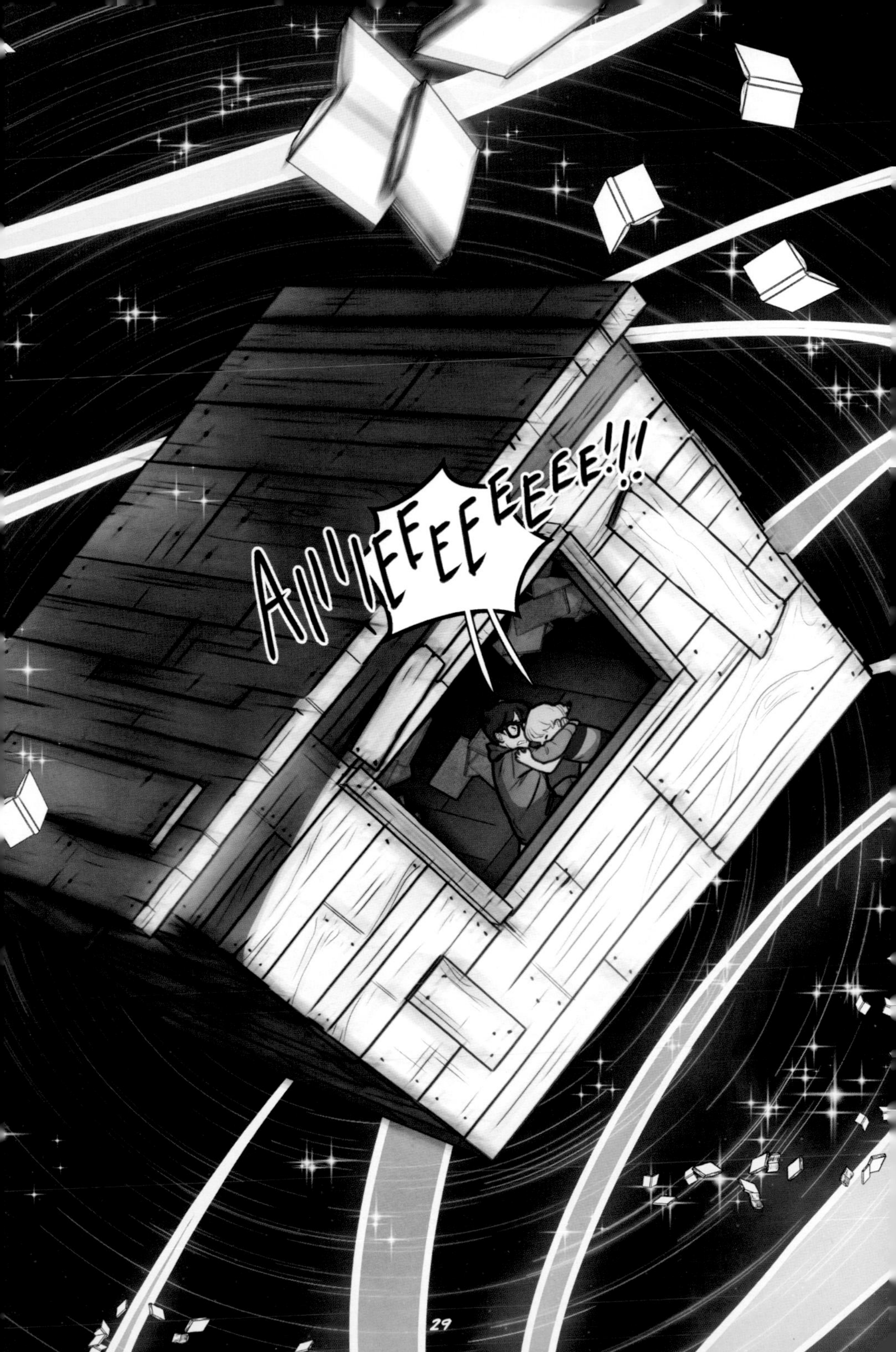
AIIIEEEEEEEEE!!!

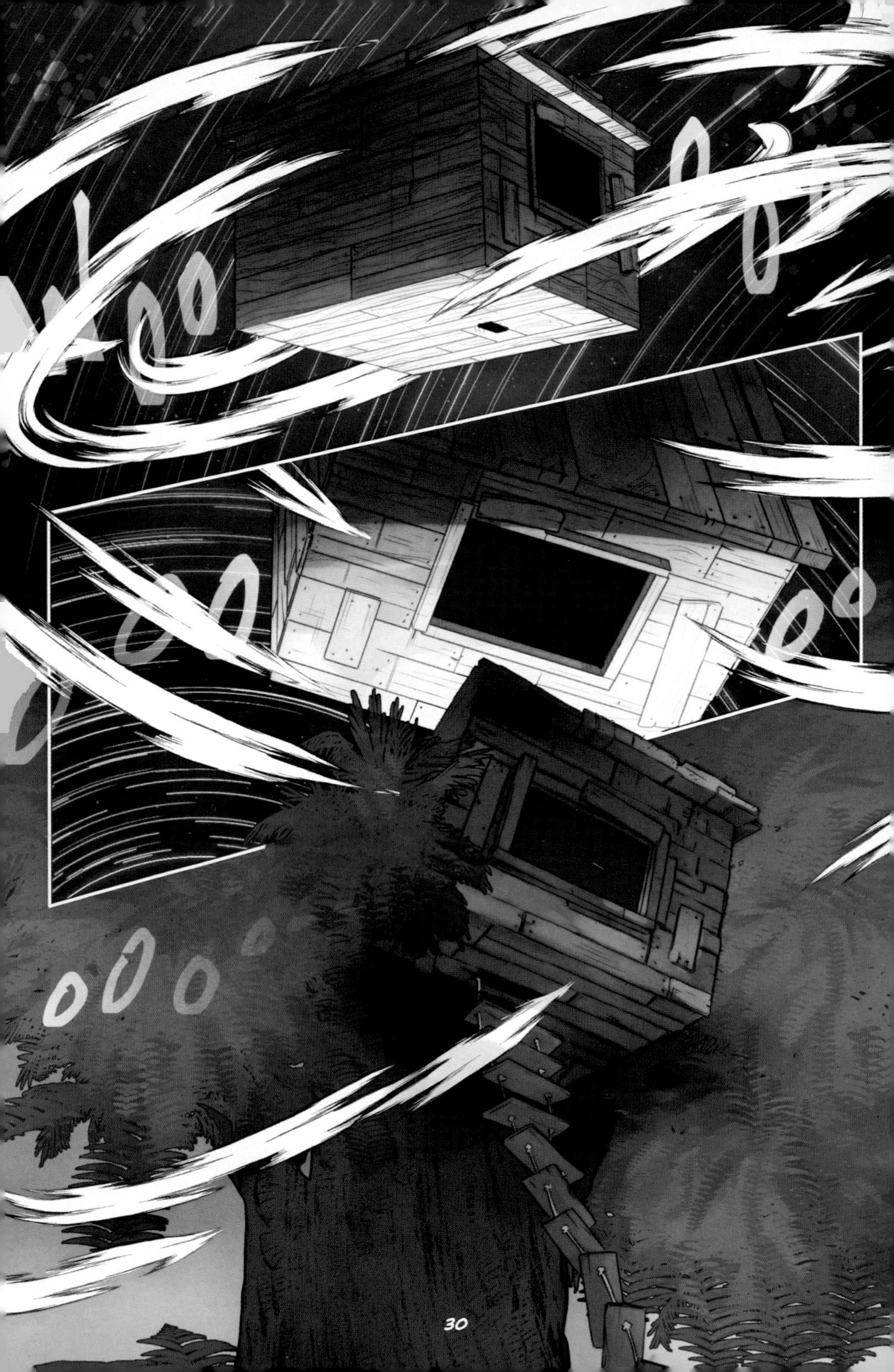

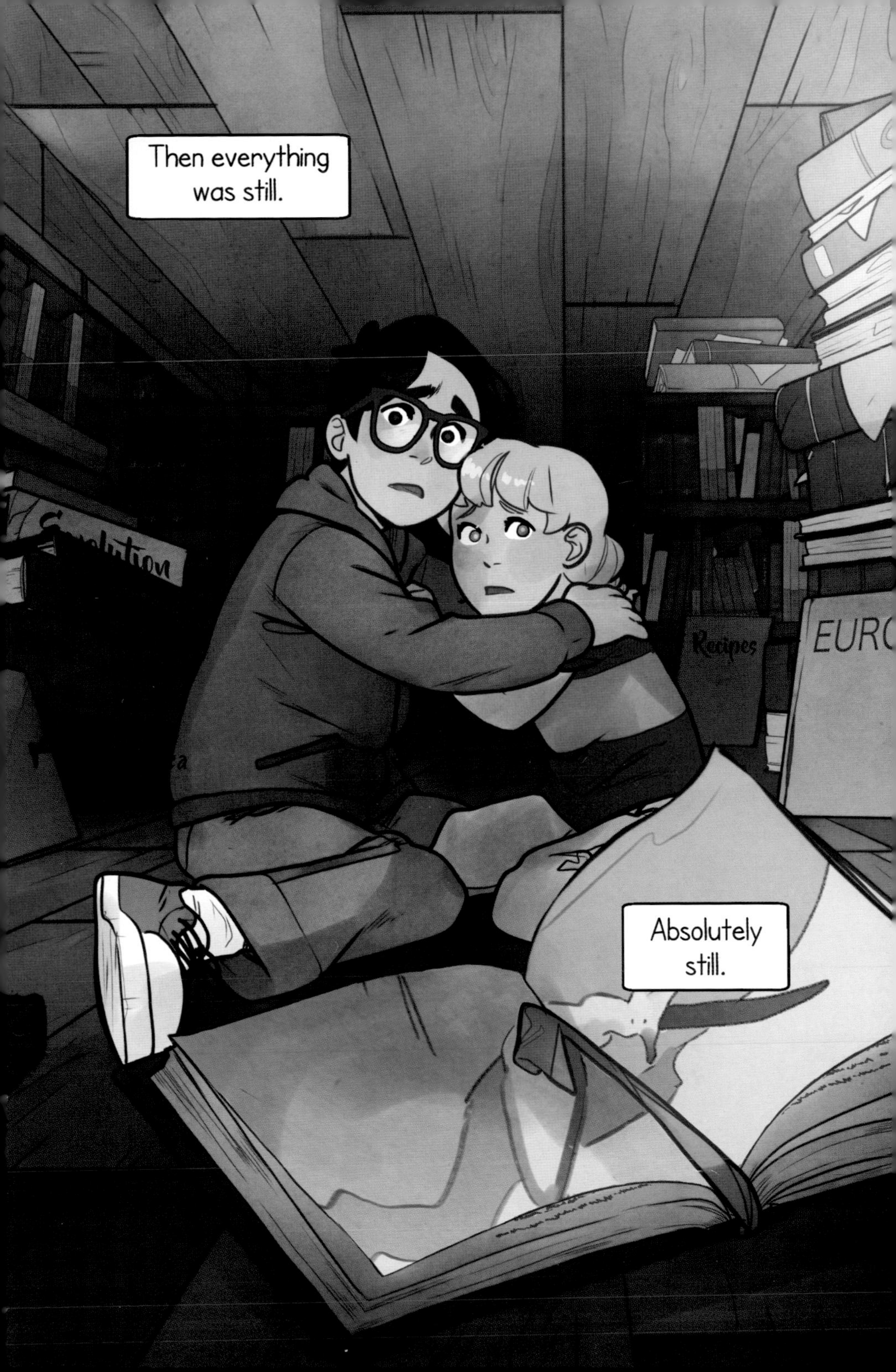
Then everything was still.
Recipes
Absolutely still.

CHAPTER THREE
Where Is Here?

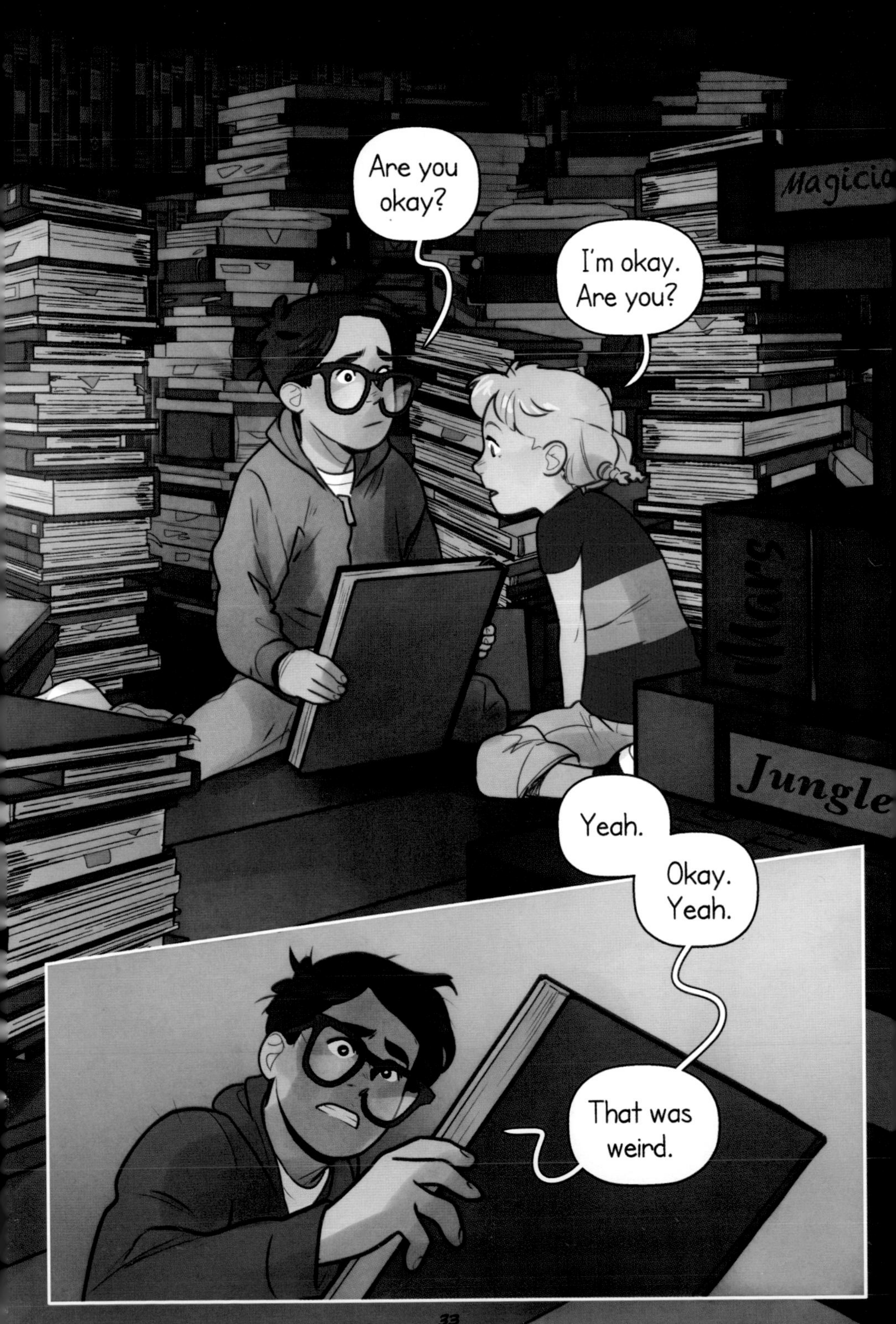
Are you okay?
I'm okay. Are you?
Jungle
Yeah.
Okay. Yeah.
That was weird.

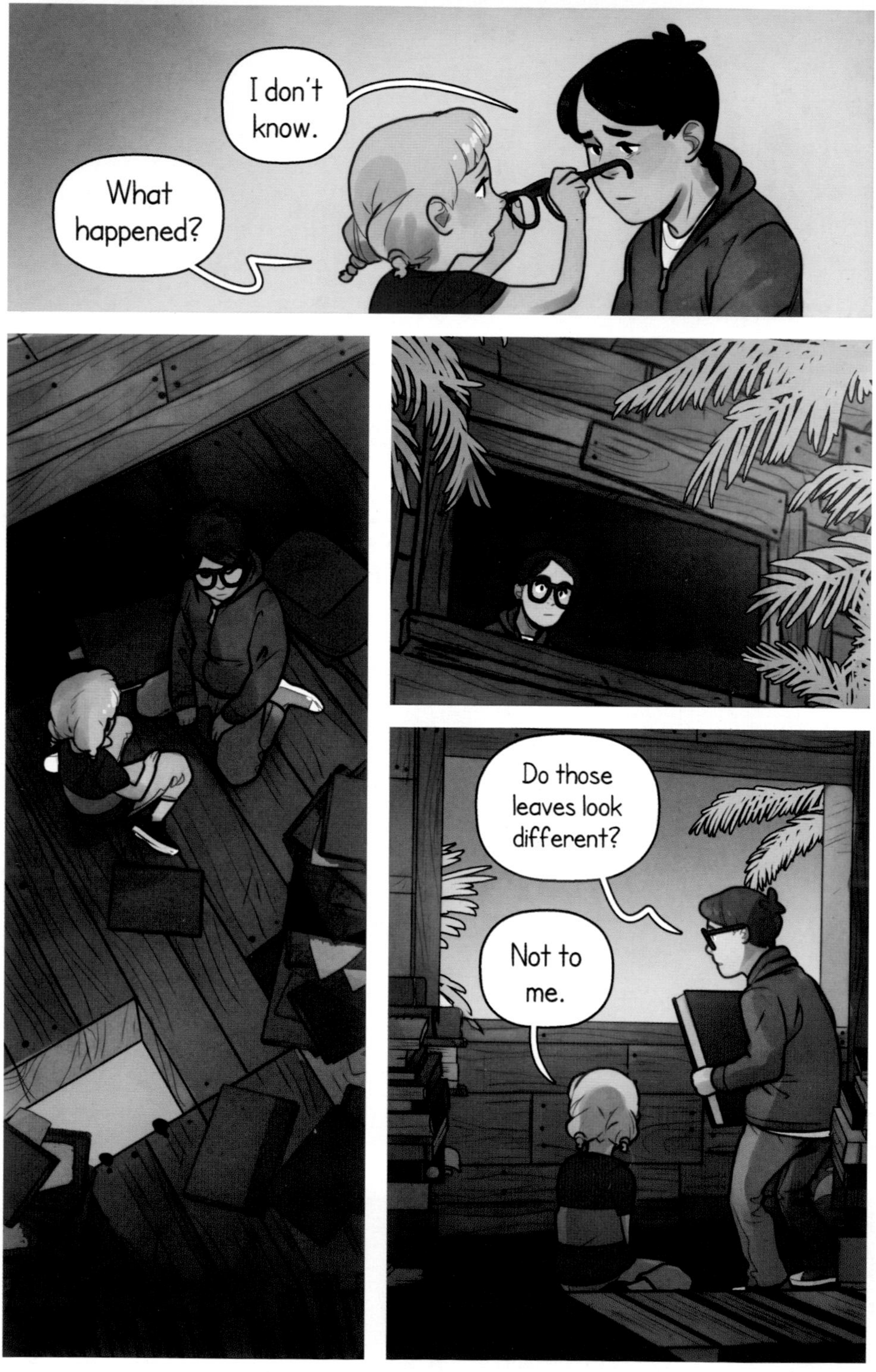
What happened?
I don't know.
Do those leaves look different?
Not to me.

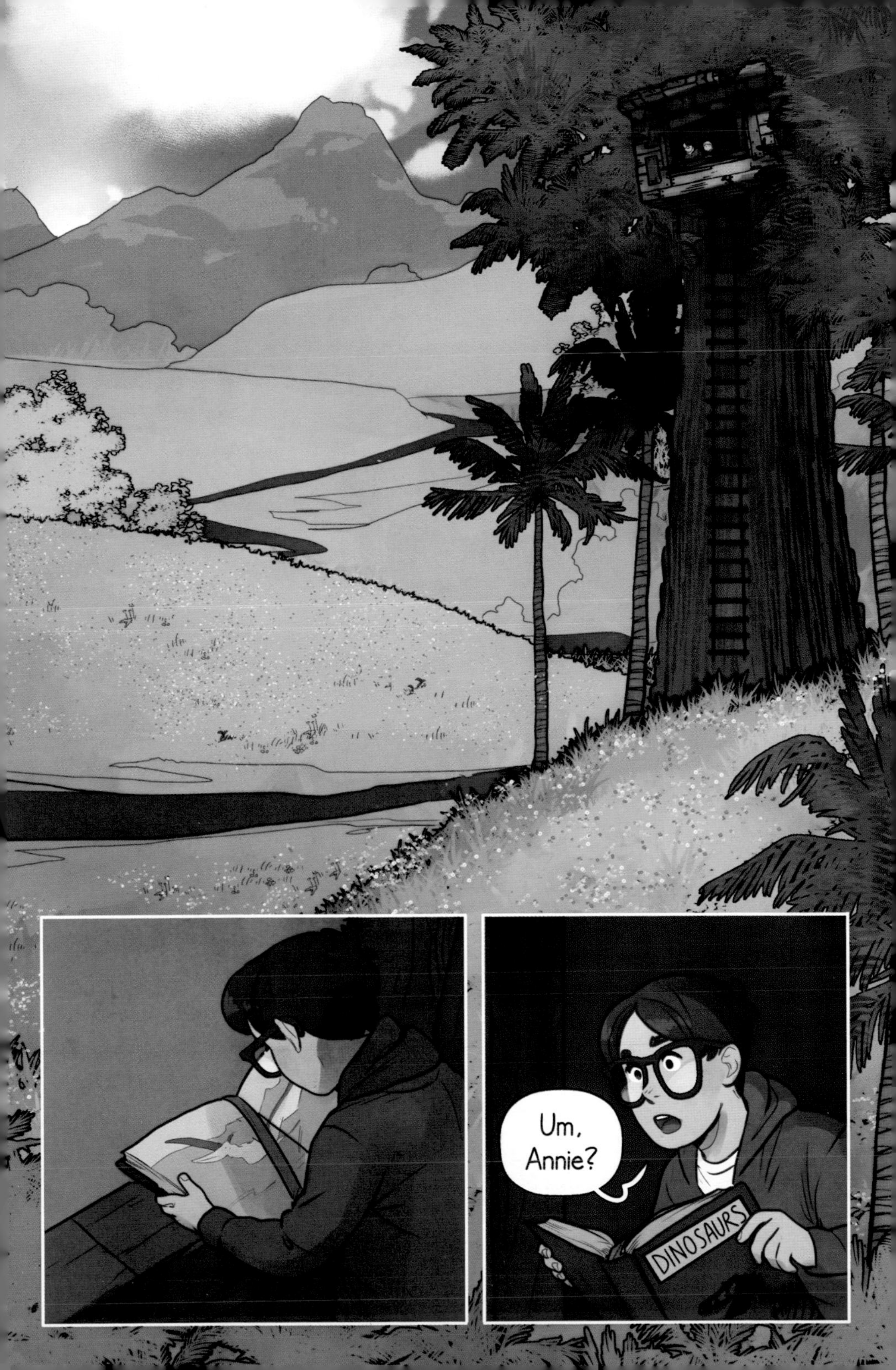
Um, Annie?
DINOSAURS

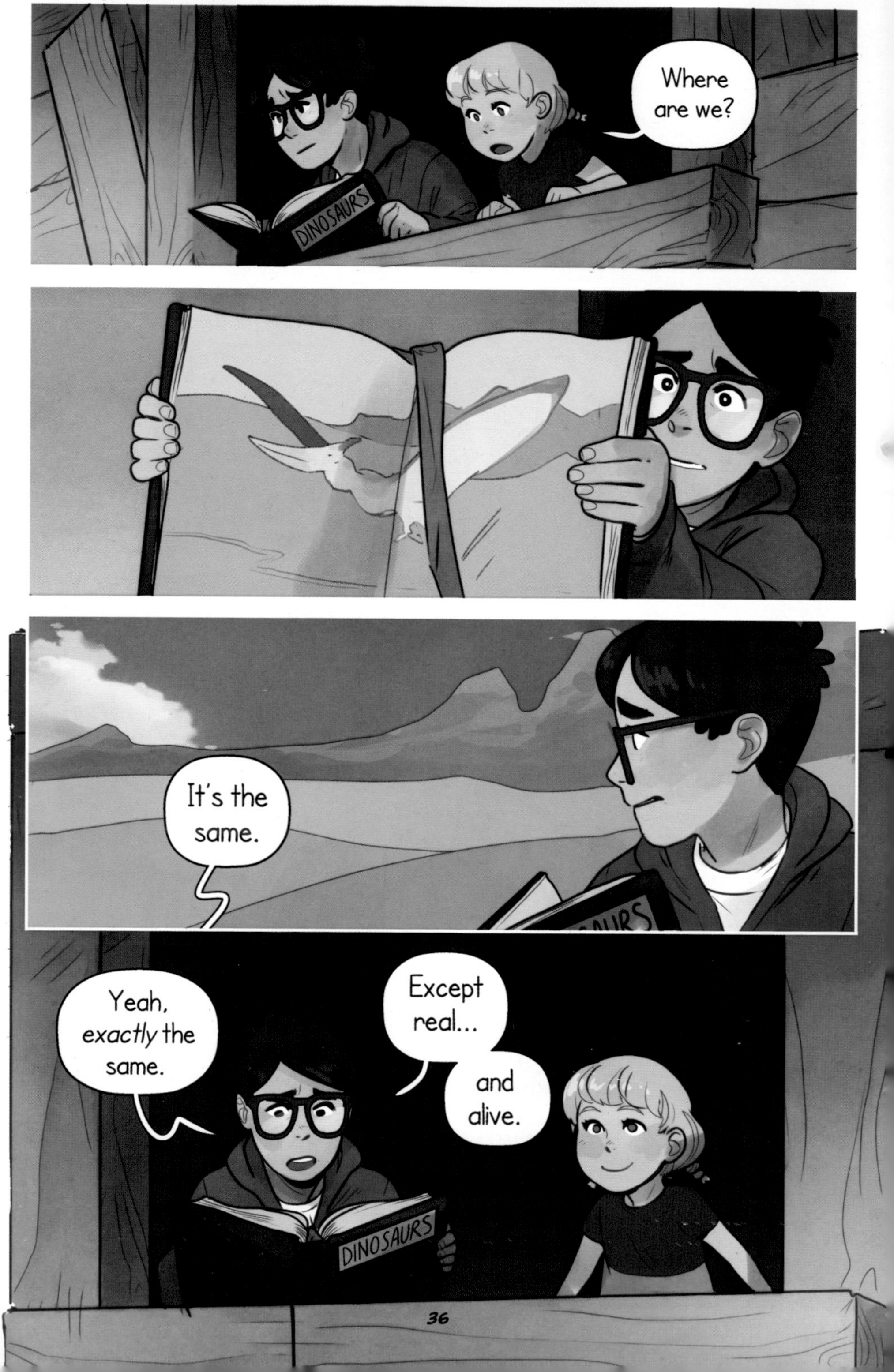
Where are we?
DINOSAURS
It's the same.
Yeah, *exactly* the same.
Except real...
and alive.
DINOSAURS

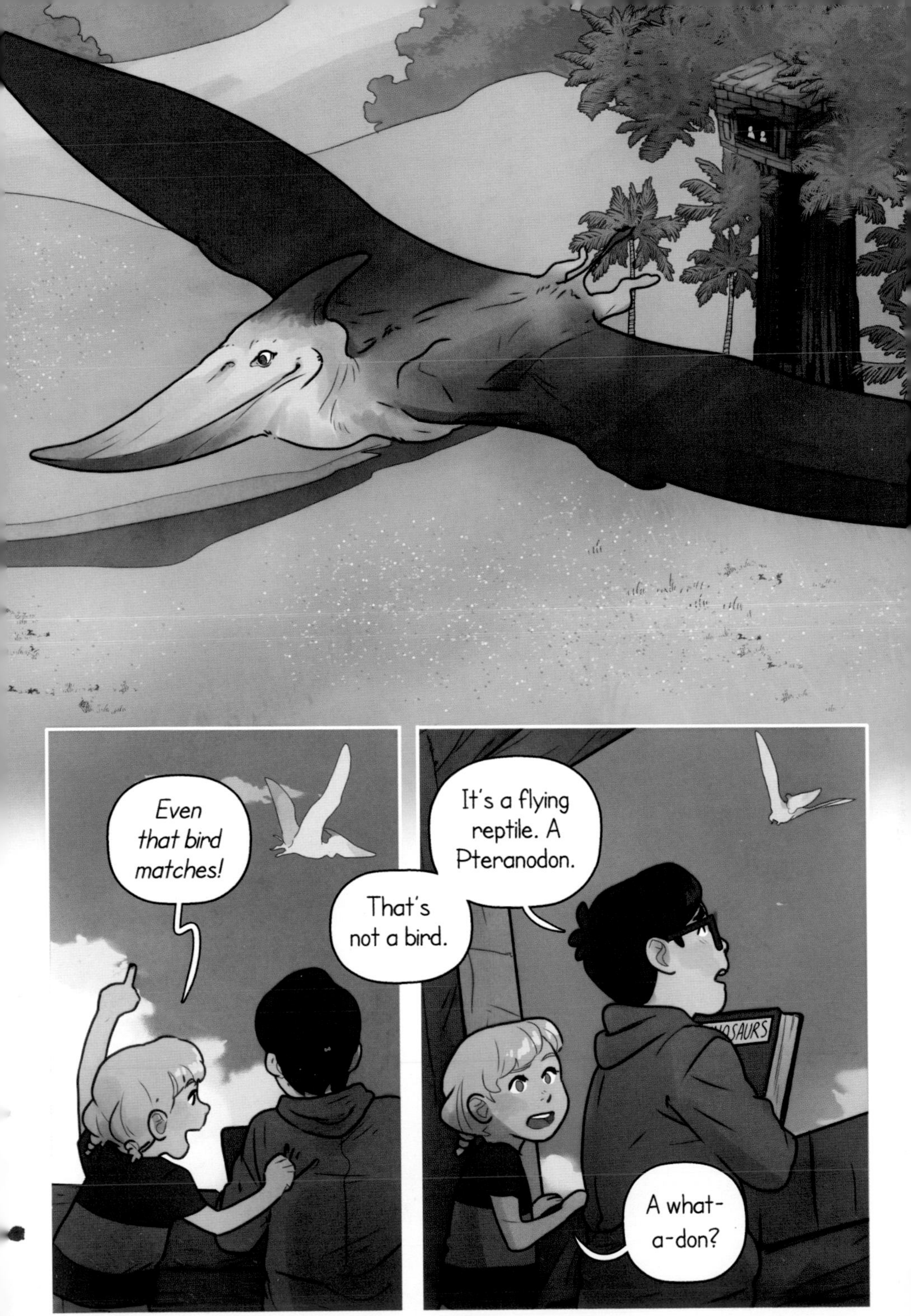
Even that bird matches!
It's a flying reptile. A Pteranodon.
That's not a bird.
DINOSAURS
A what-a-don?

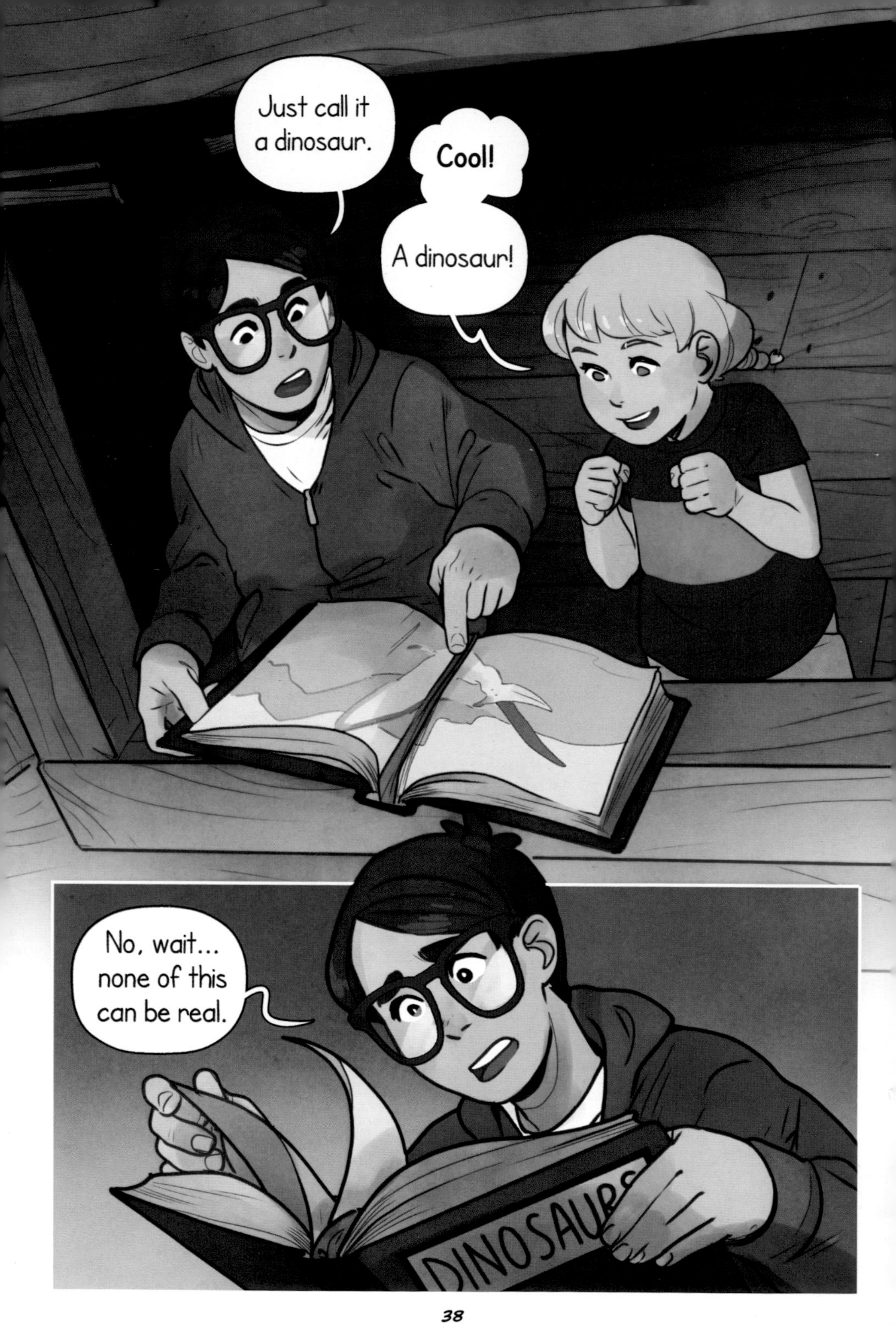
Just call it a dinosaur.
Cool!
A dinosaur!
No, wait... none of this can be real.
DINOSAURS

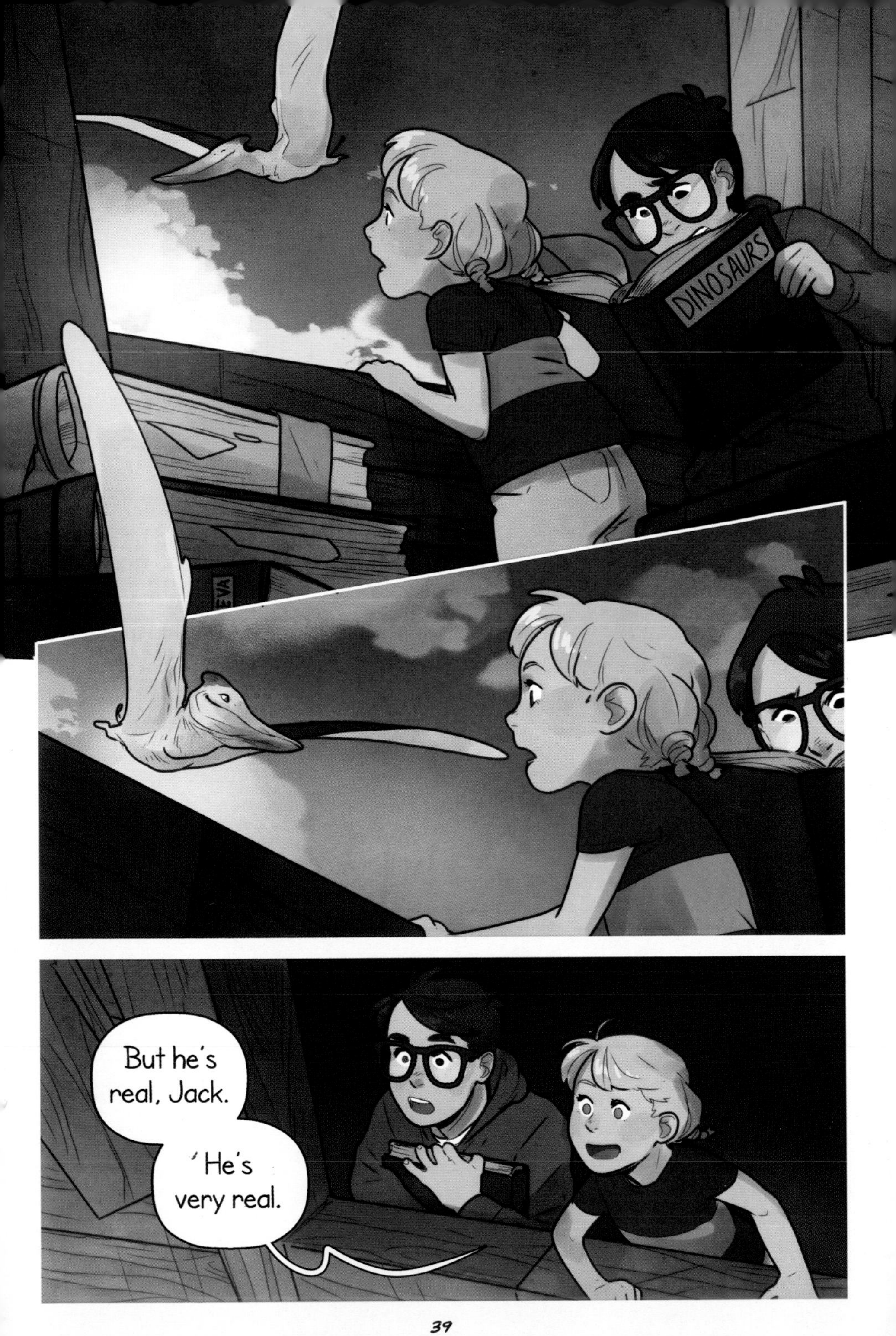
DINOSAURS
But he's real, Jack.
He's very real.

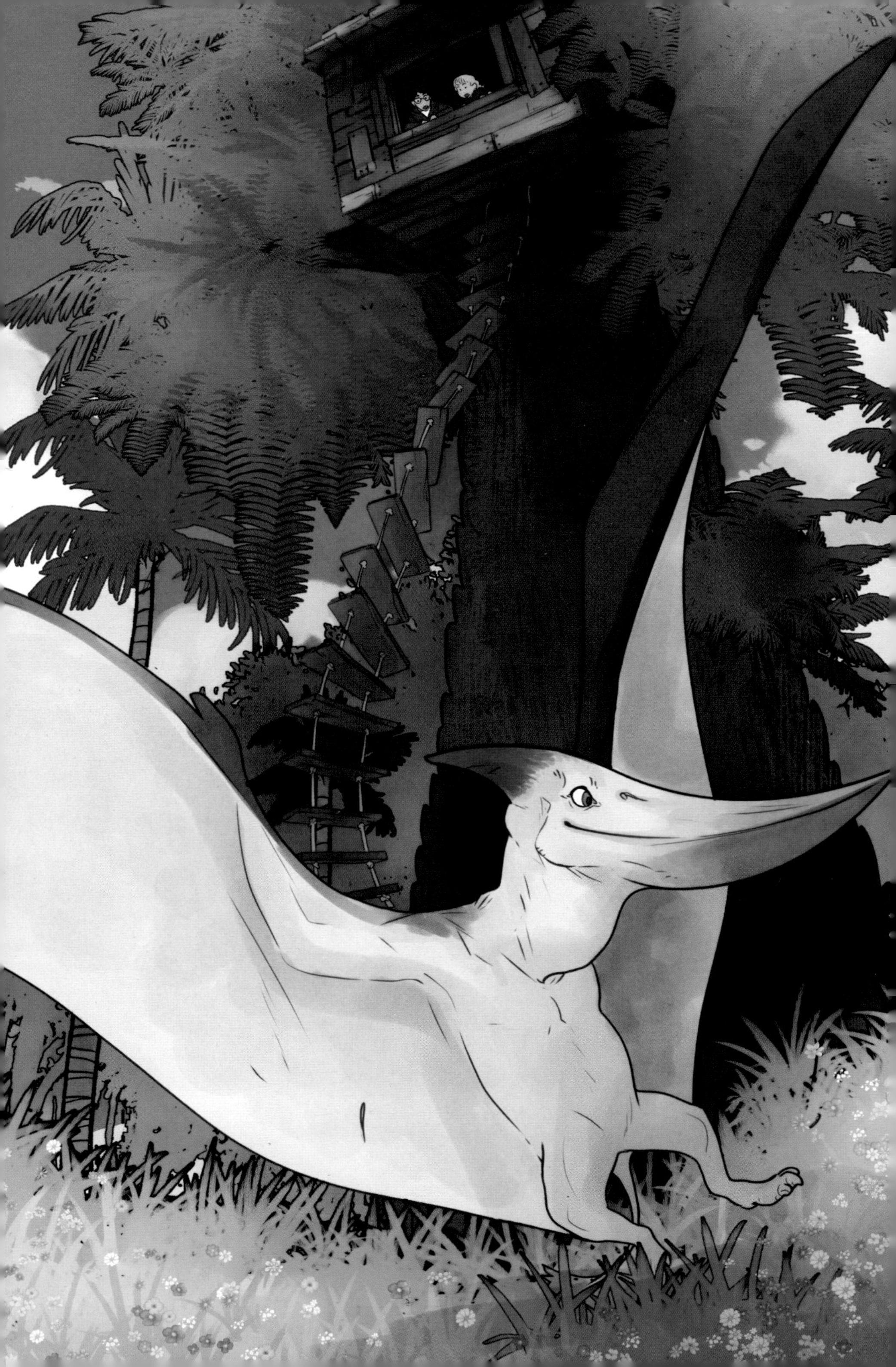

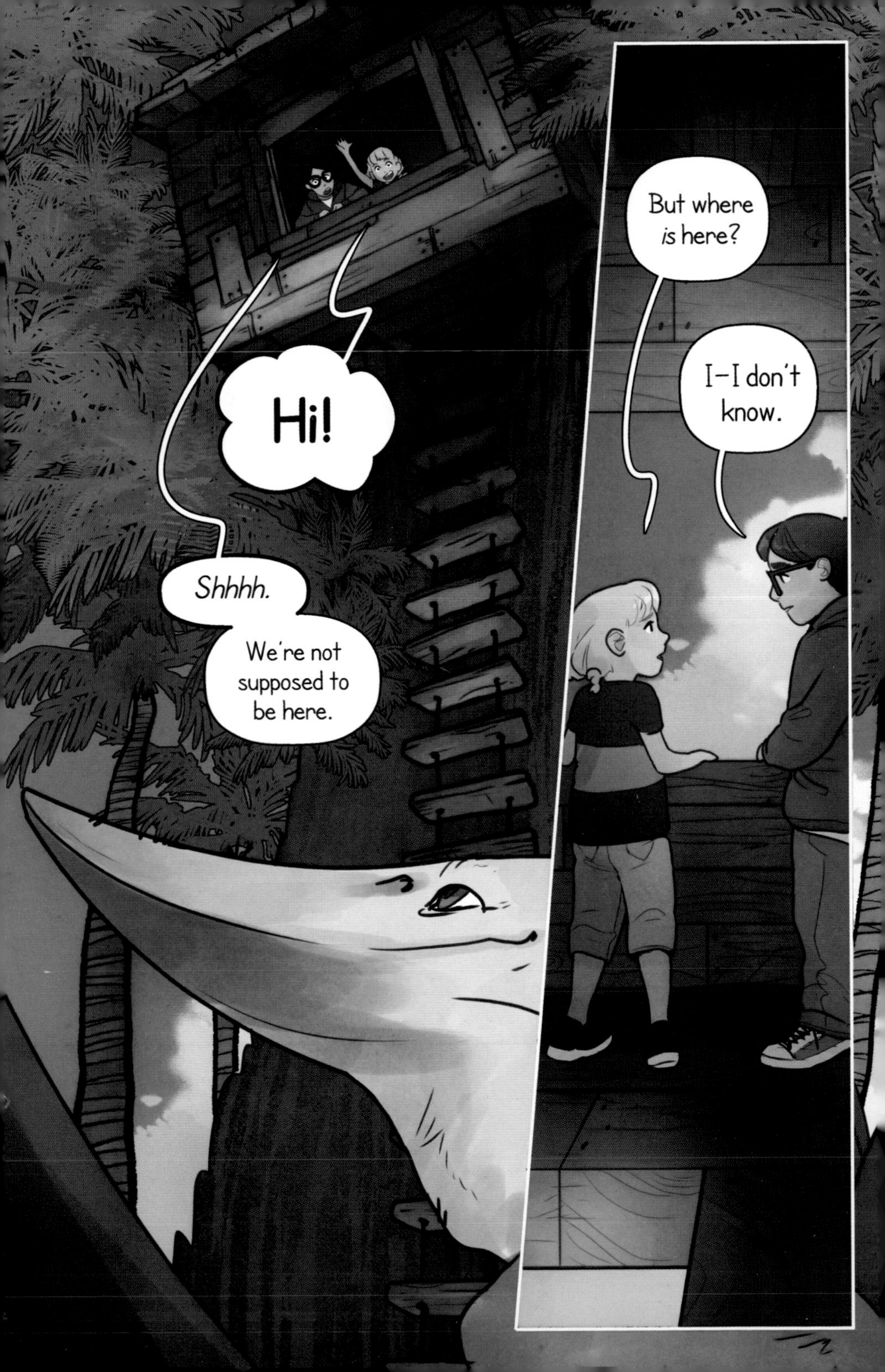
Hi!
Shhhh.
We're not supposed to be here.
But where is here?
I-I don't know.

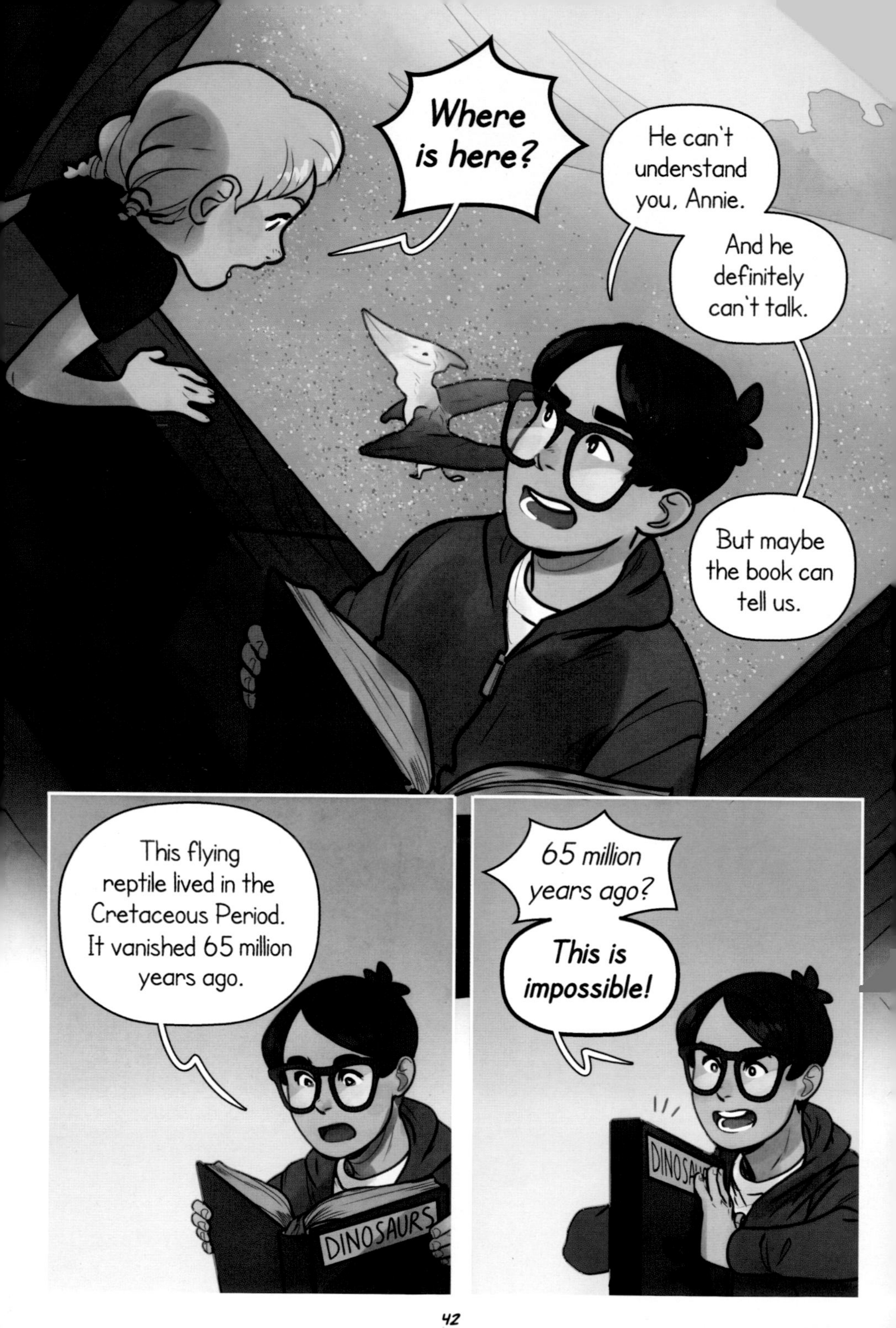
Where is here?
He can't understand you, Annie.
And he definitely can't talk.
But maybe the book can tell us.
This flying reptile lived in the Cretaceous Period. It vanished 65 million years ago.
DINOSAURS
65 million years ago?
This is impossible!
DINOSAURS

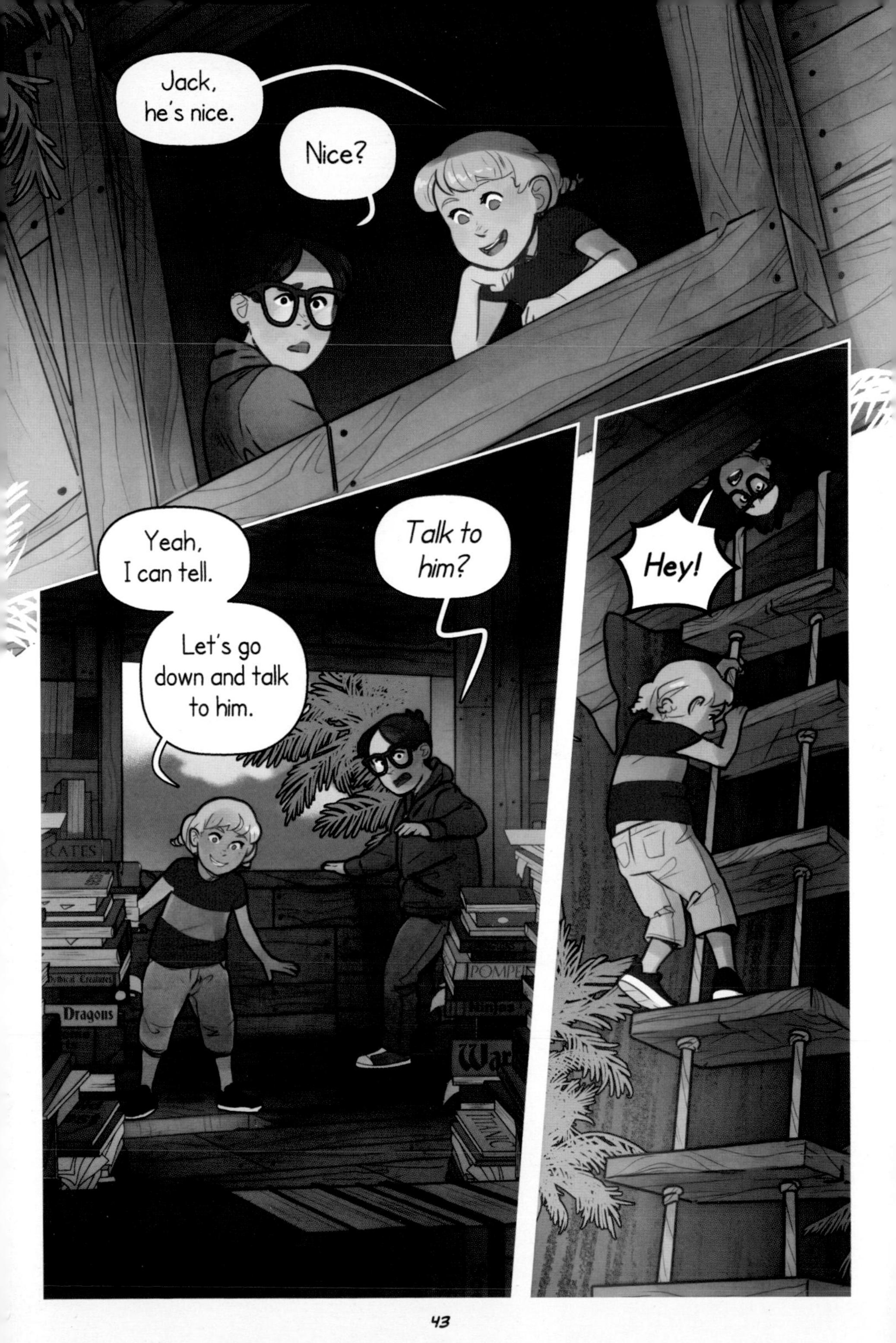
Jack, he's nice.
Nice?
Yeah, I can tell.
Let's go down and talk to him.
Talk to him?
Hey!
RATES
Mythical Creatures
Dragons
POMPEII
War

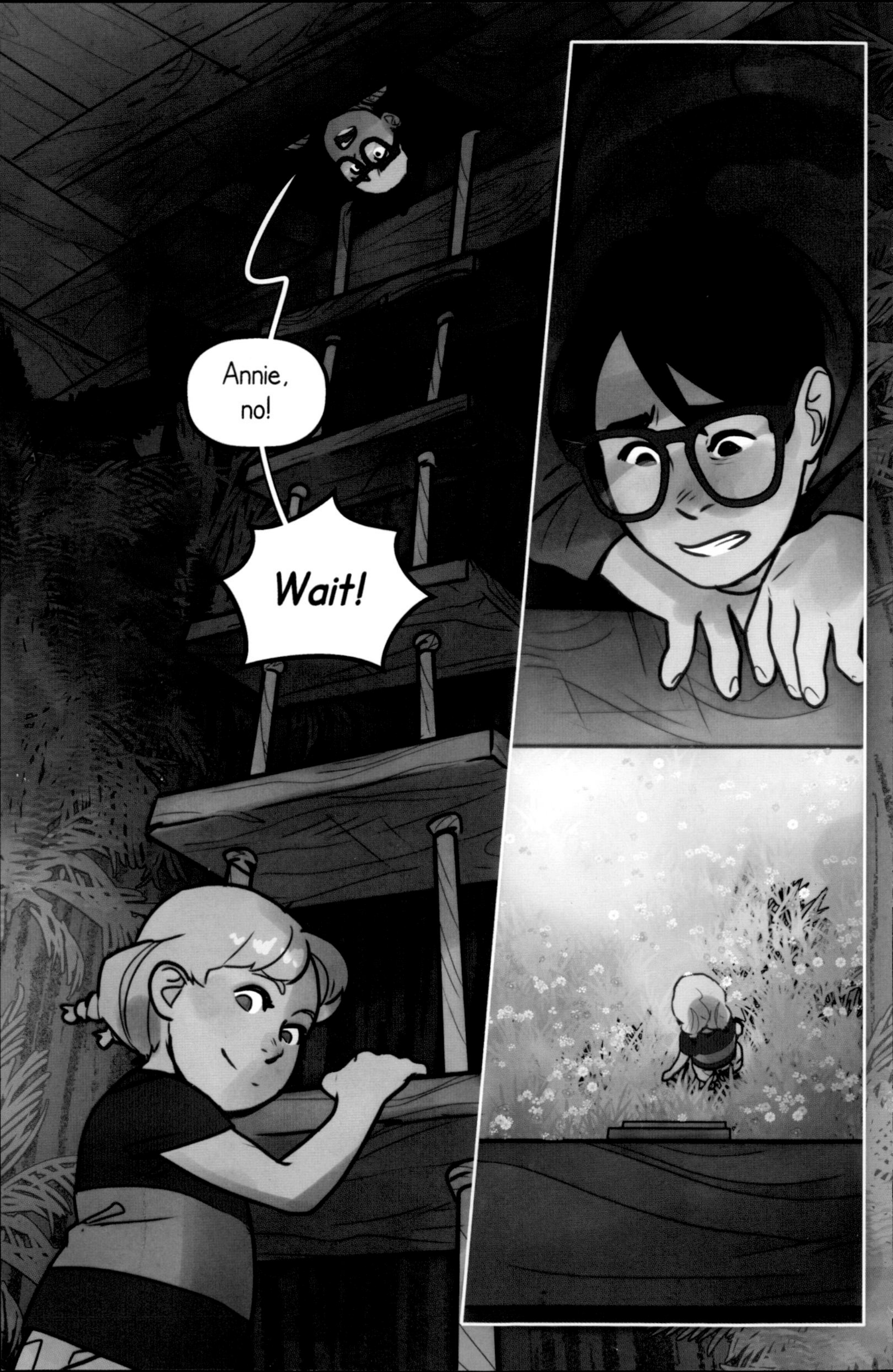
Annie, no!
Wait!

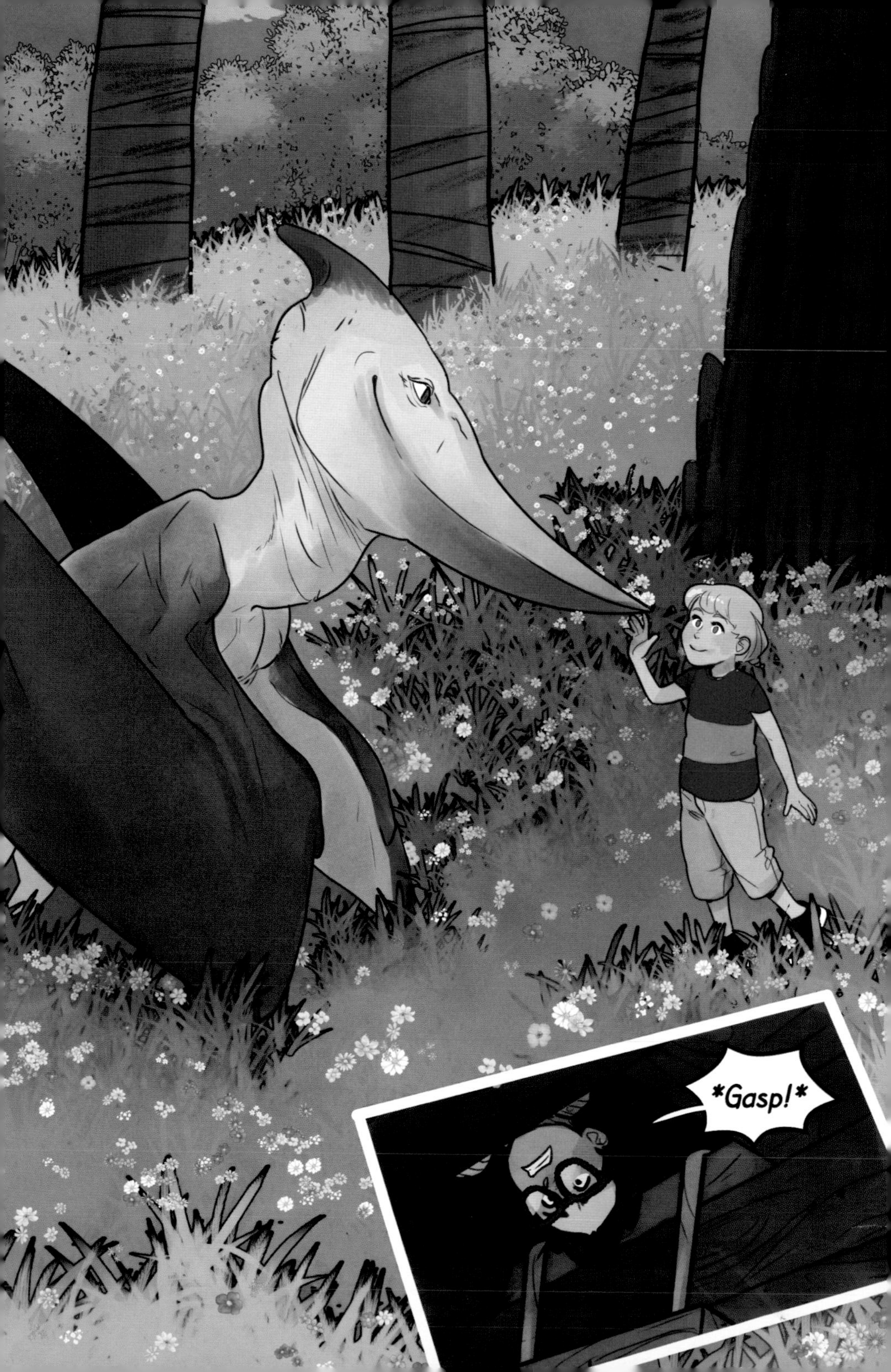
Gasp!

CHAPTER FOUR
Henry

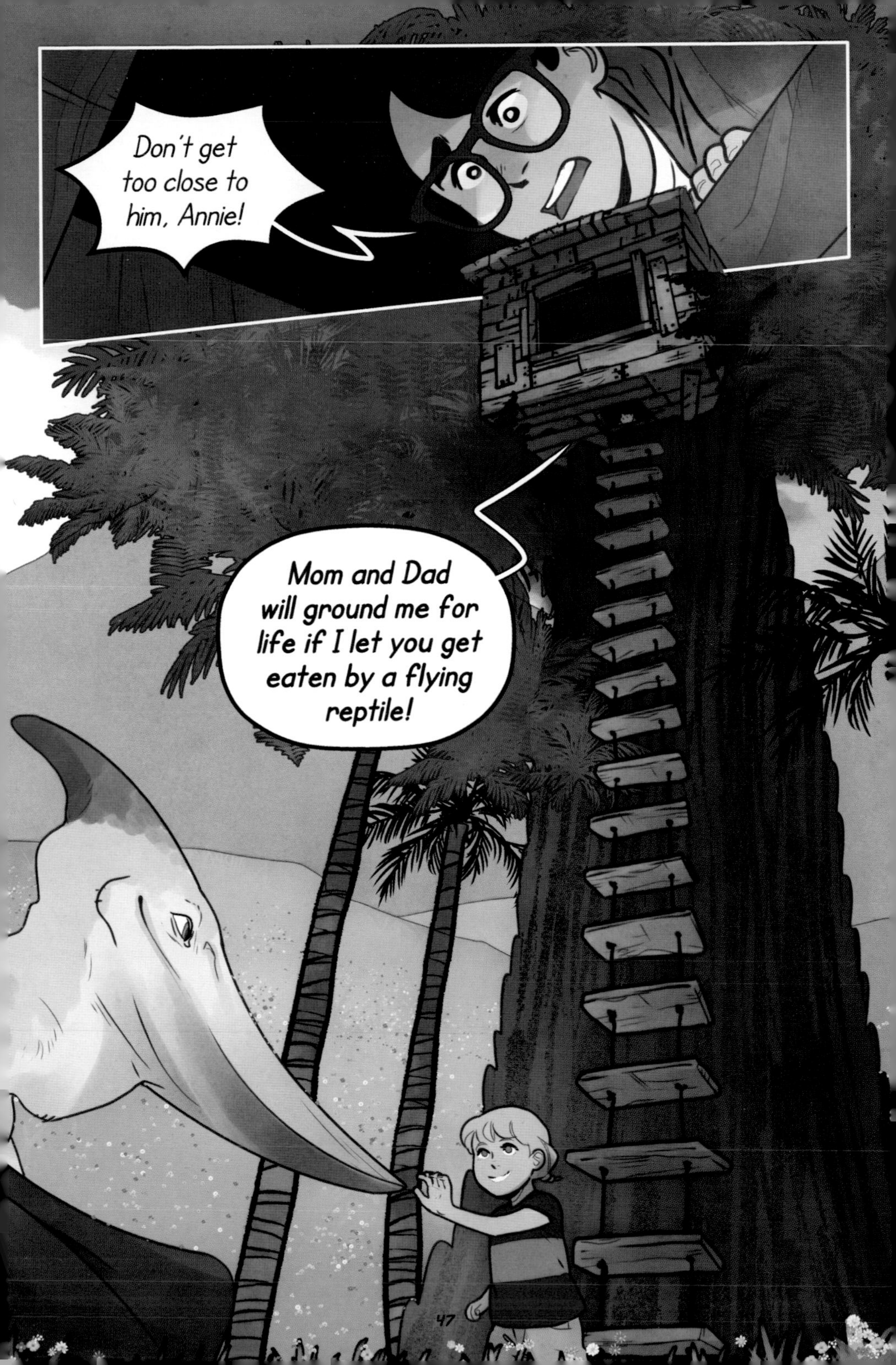
Don't get too close to him, Annie!
Mom and Dad will ground me for life if I let you get eaten by a flying reptile!

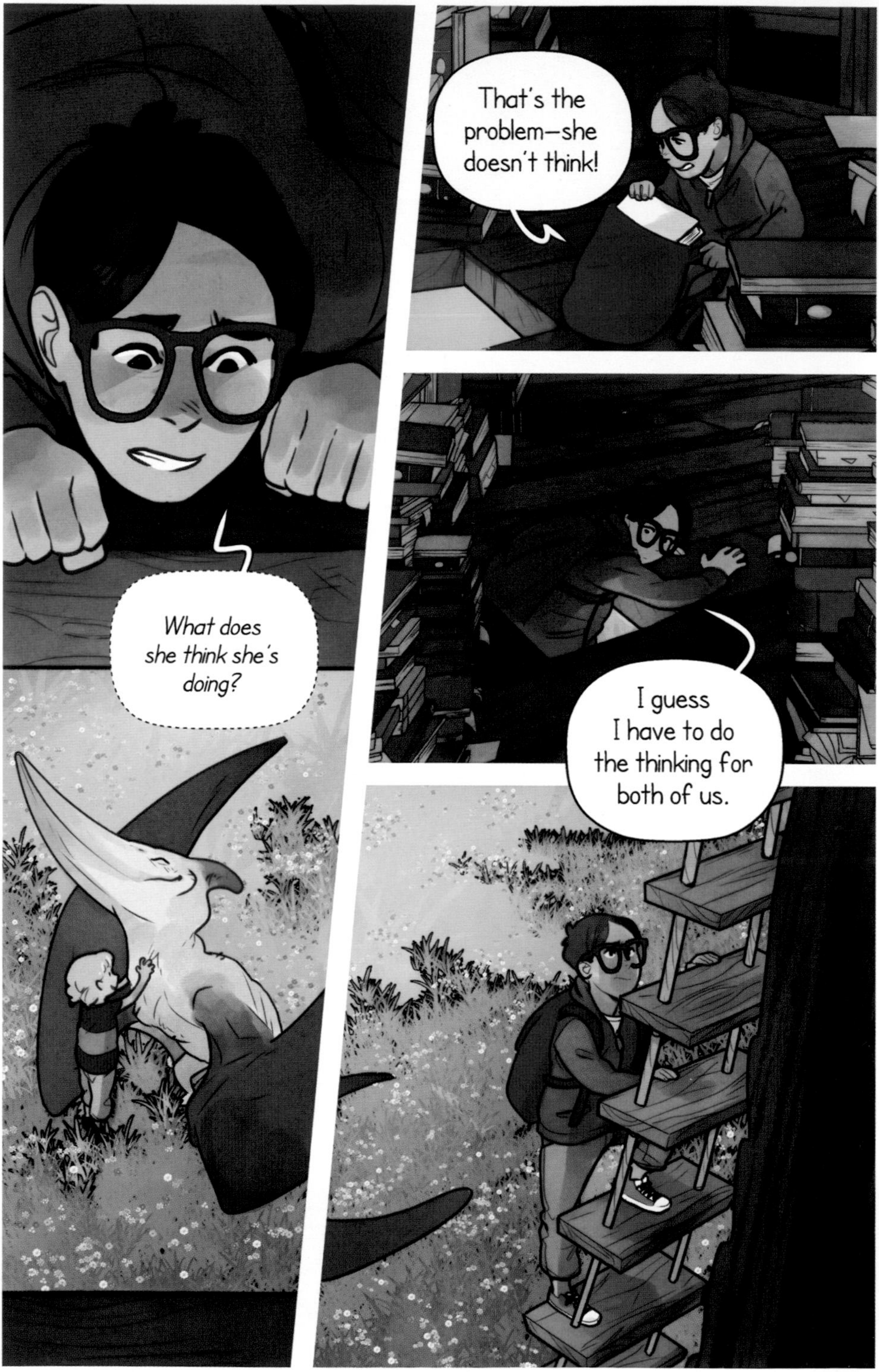
What does she think she's doing?
That's the problem—she doesn't think!
I guess I have to do the thinking for both of us.

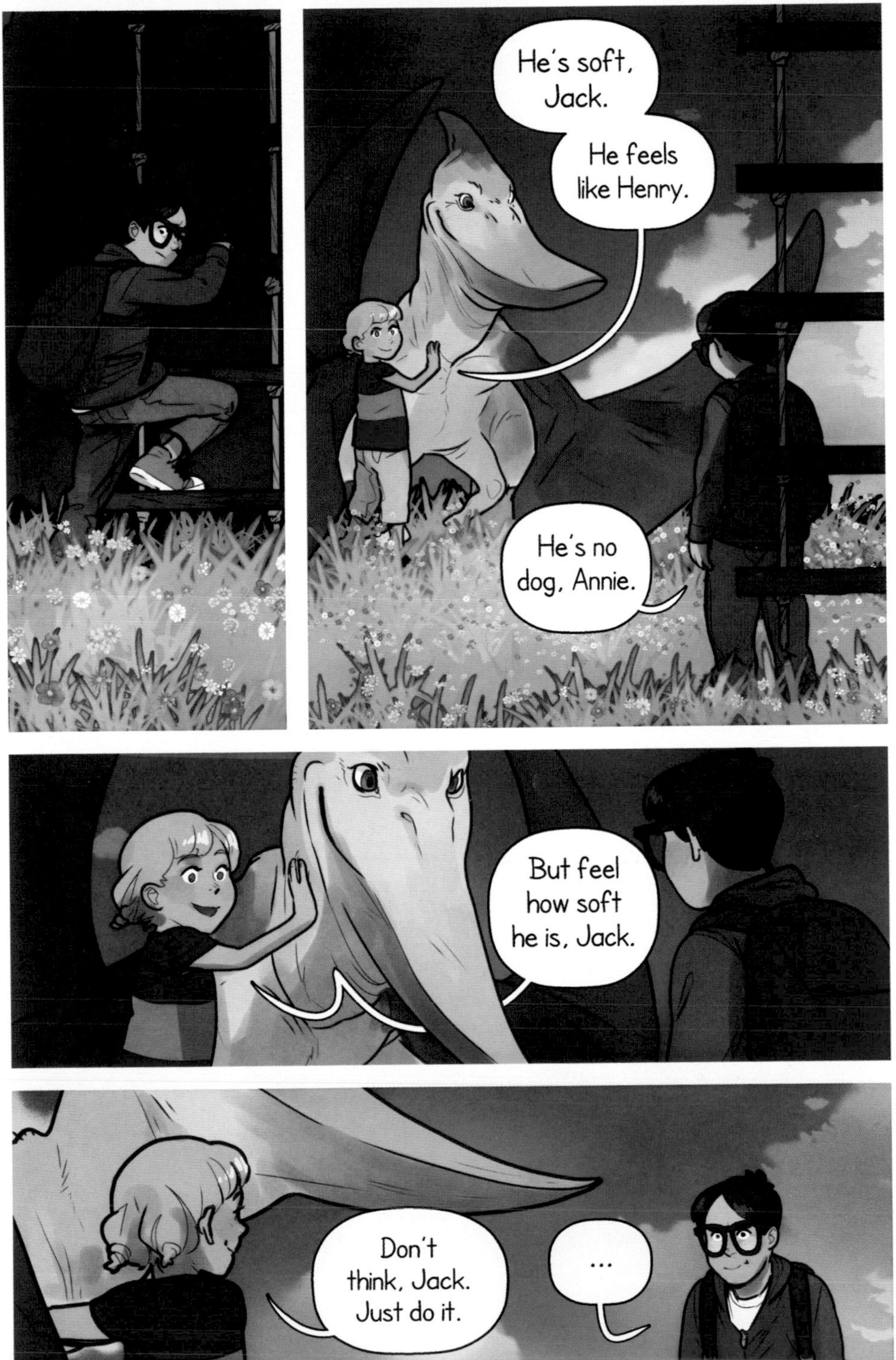
He's soft, Jack.
He feels like Henry.
He's no dog, Annie.
But feel how soft he is, Jack.
Don't think, Jack. Just do it.
...

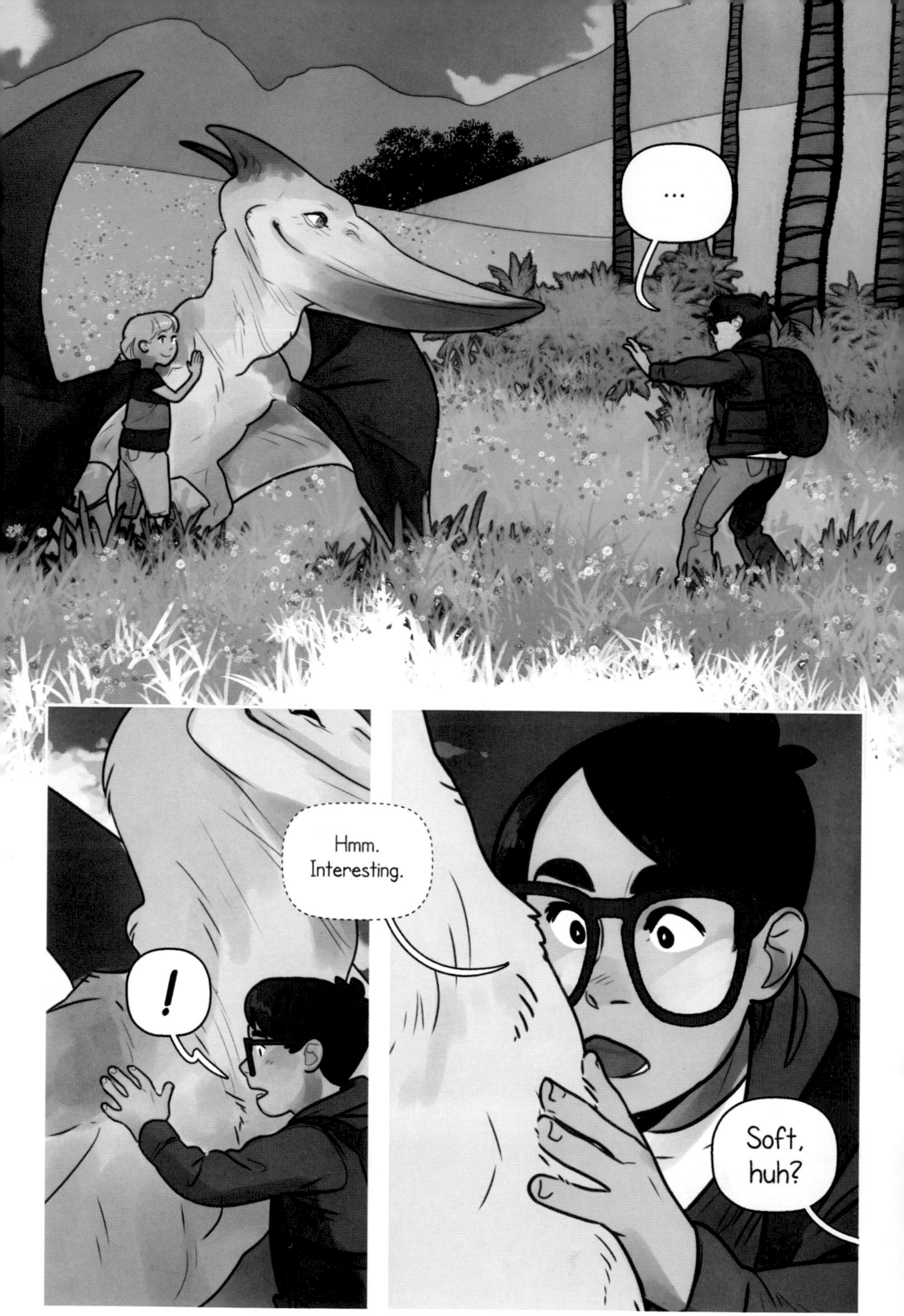
...
Hmm. Interesting.
!
Soft, huh?

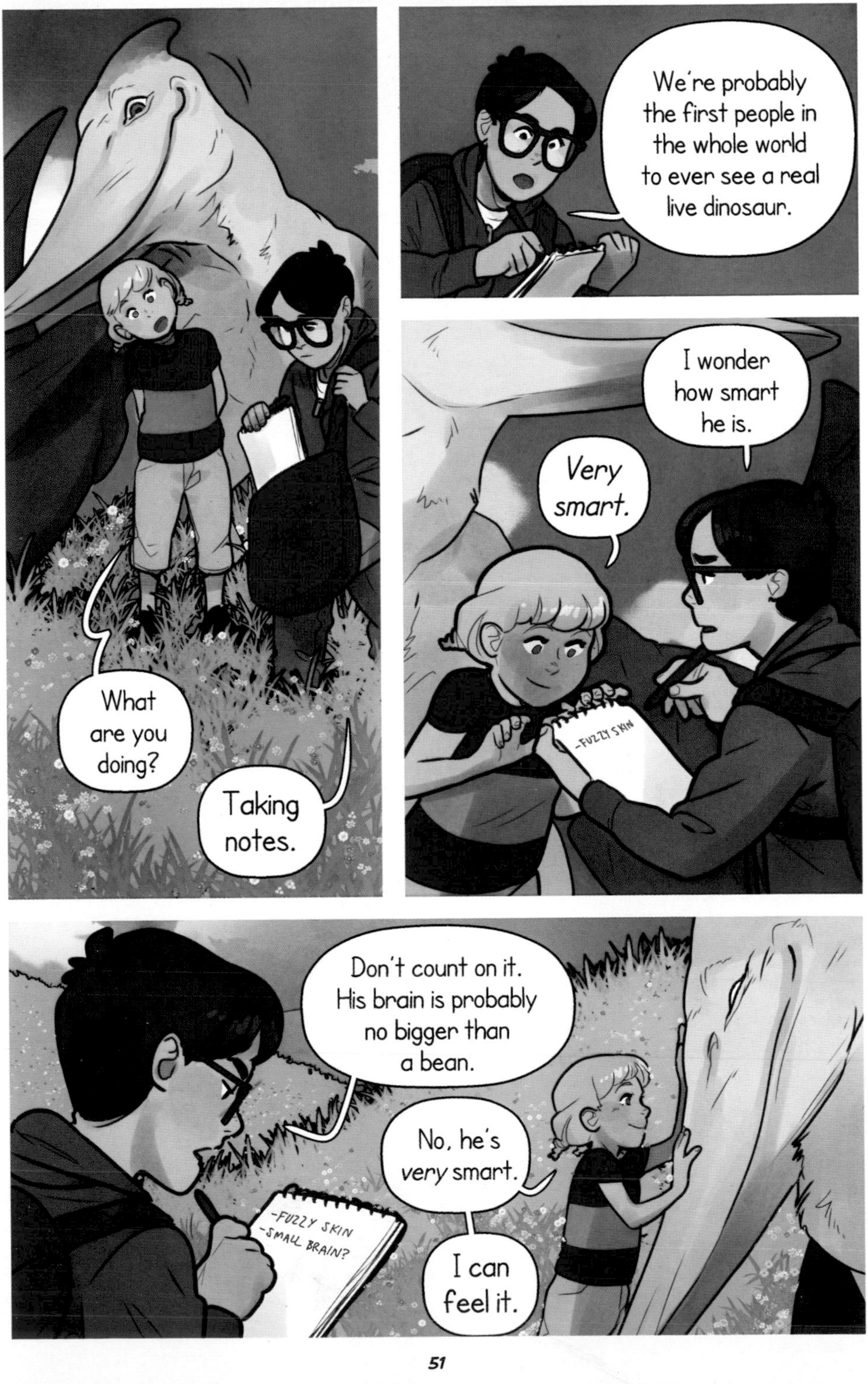
What are you doing?
Taking notes.
We're probably the first people in the whole world to ever see a real live dinosaur.
I wonder how smart he is.
Very smart.
-FUZZY SKIN
Don't count on it. His brain is probably no bigger than a bean.
-FUZZY SKIN
-SMALL BRAIN?
No, he's very smart.
I can feel it.

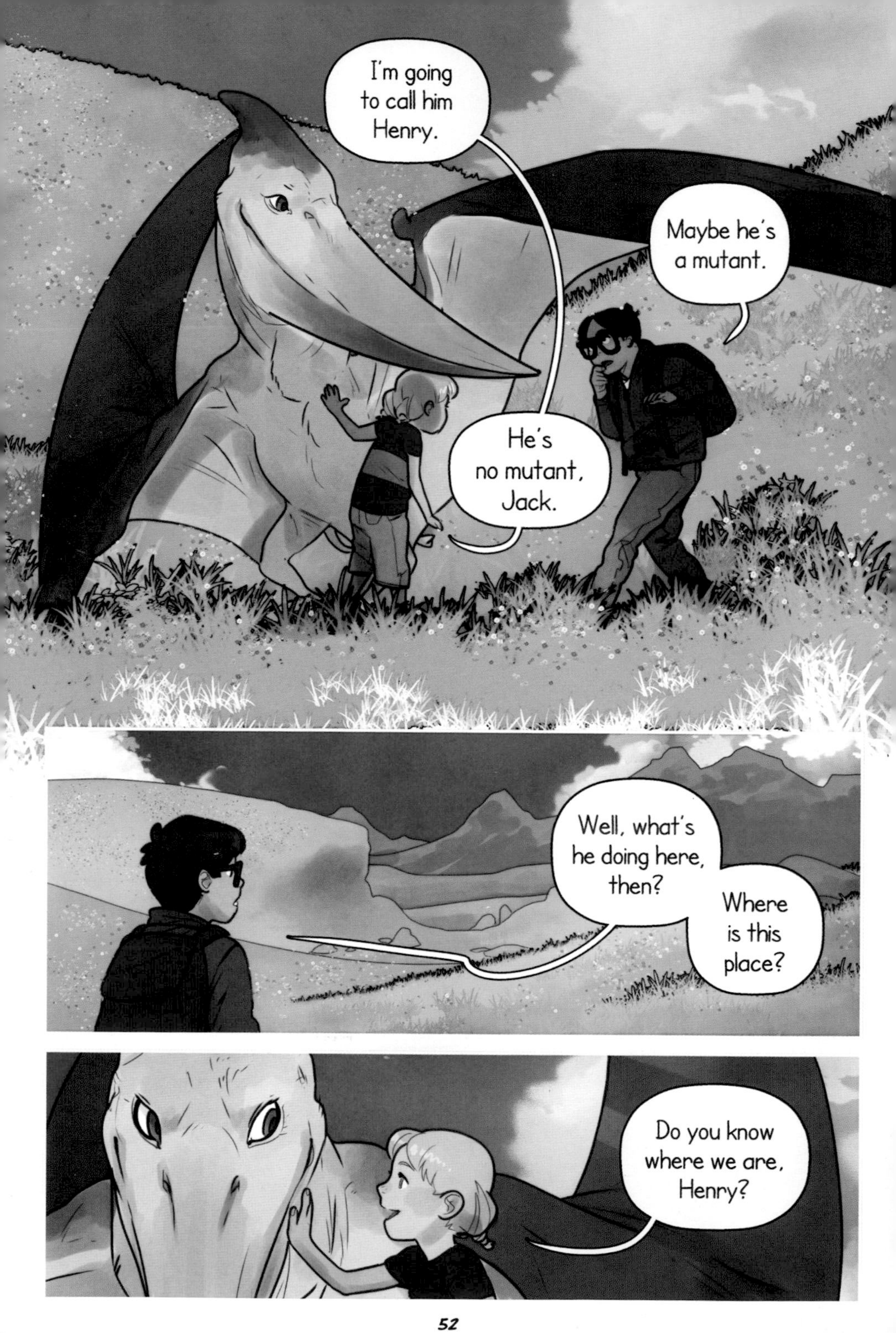
I'm going to call him Henry.
Maybe he's a mutant.
He's no mutant, Jack.
Well, what's he doing here, then?
Where is this place?
Do you know where we are, Henry?

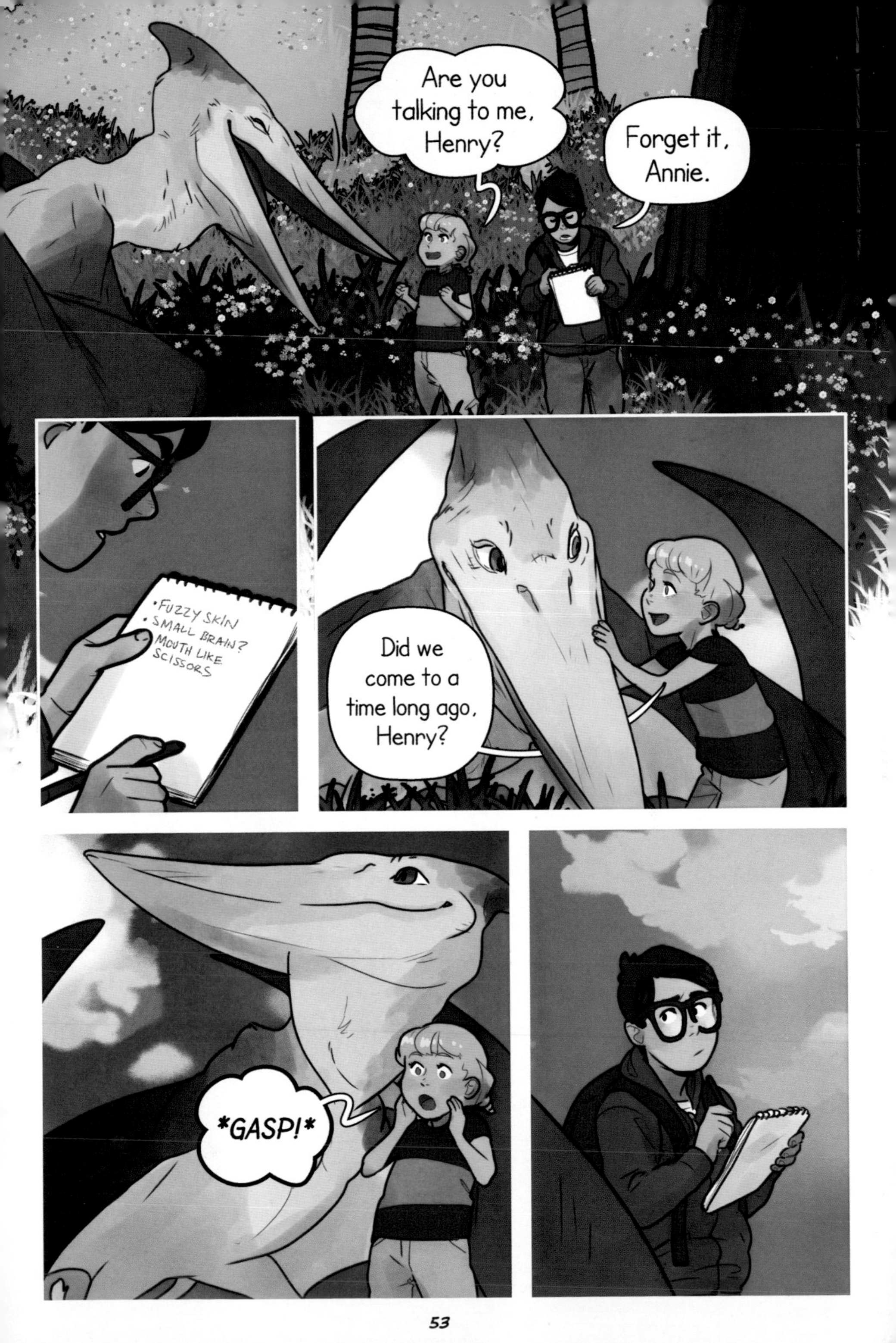
Are you talking to me, Henry?
Forget it, Annie.
•FUZZY SKIN
•SMALL BRAIN?
•MOUTH LIKE SCISSORS
Did we come to a time long ago, Henry?
GASP!

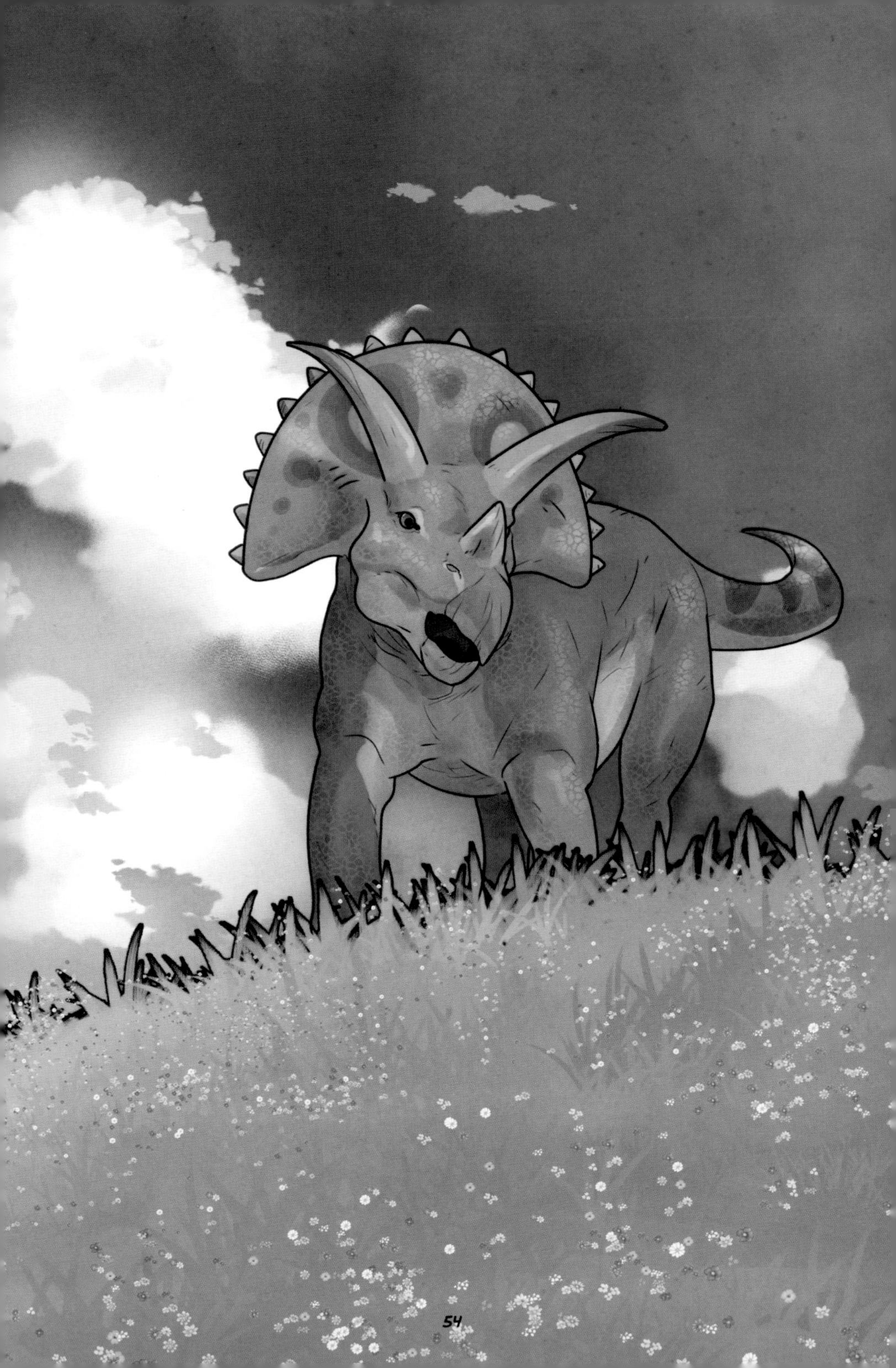

CHAPTER FIVE

Gold in the Grass

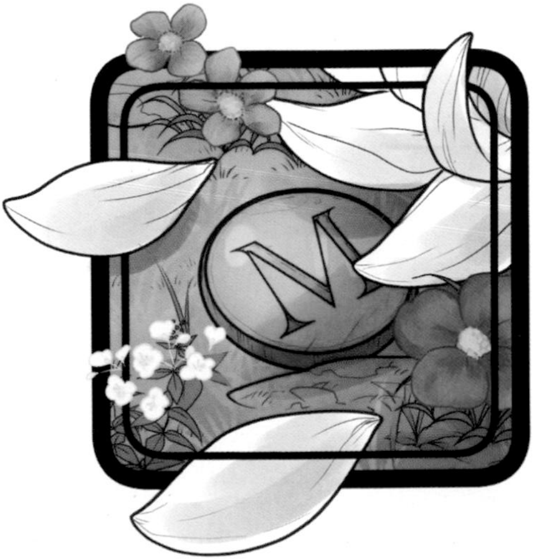
M

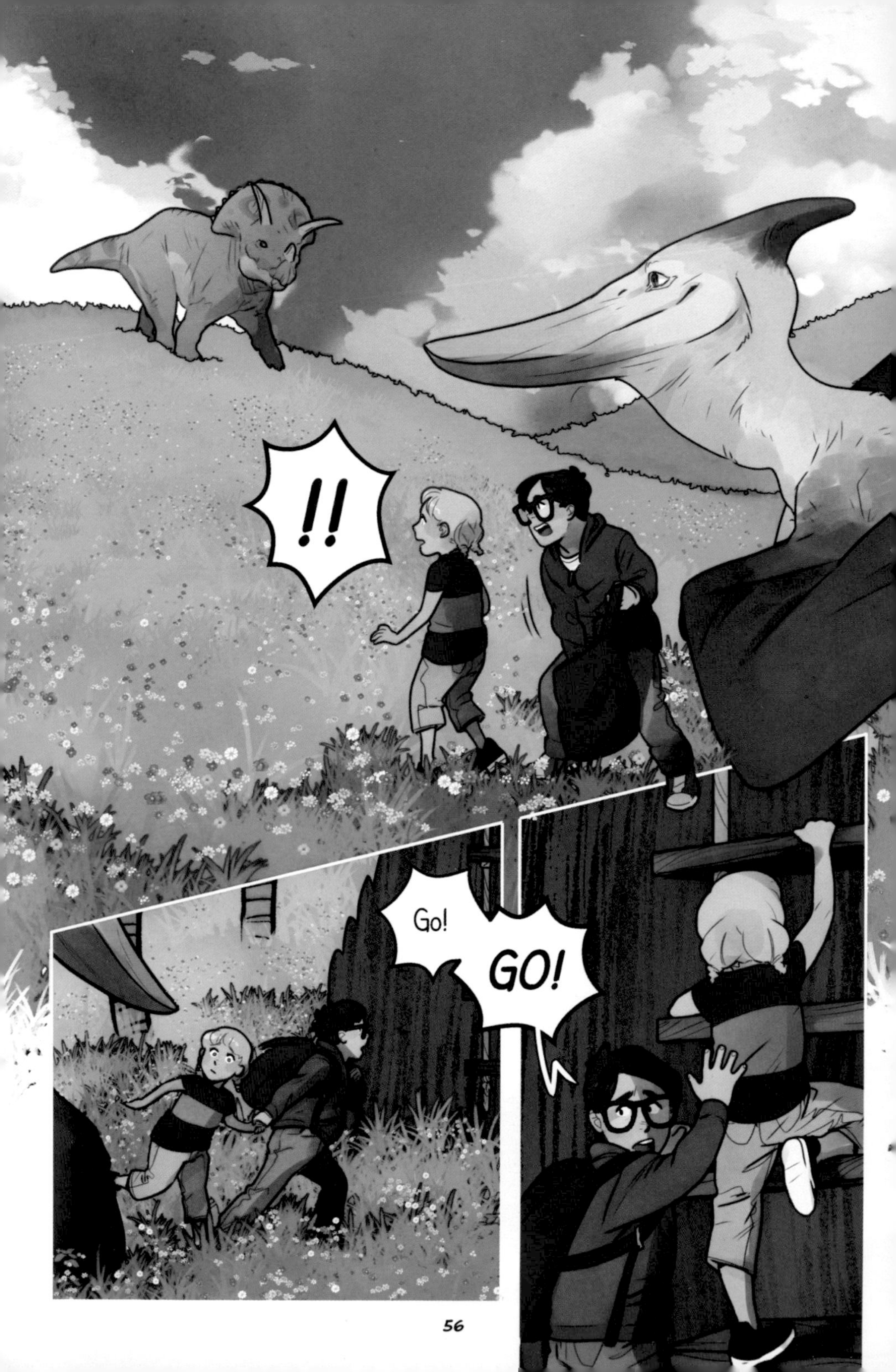
!!
Go!
GO!

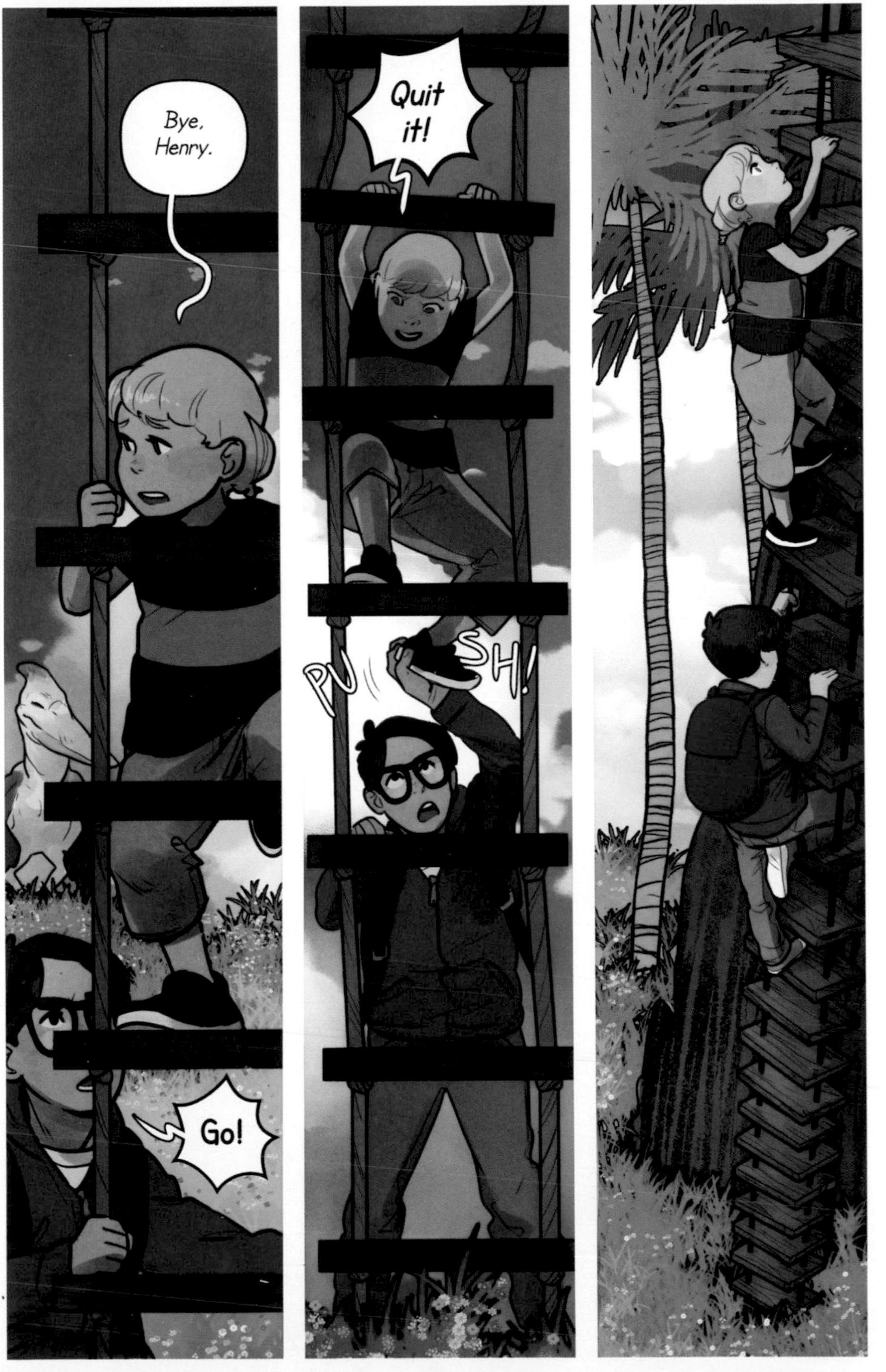
Bye, Henry.
Go!
Quit it!
PUSH!

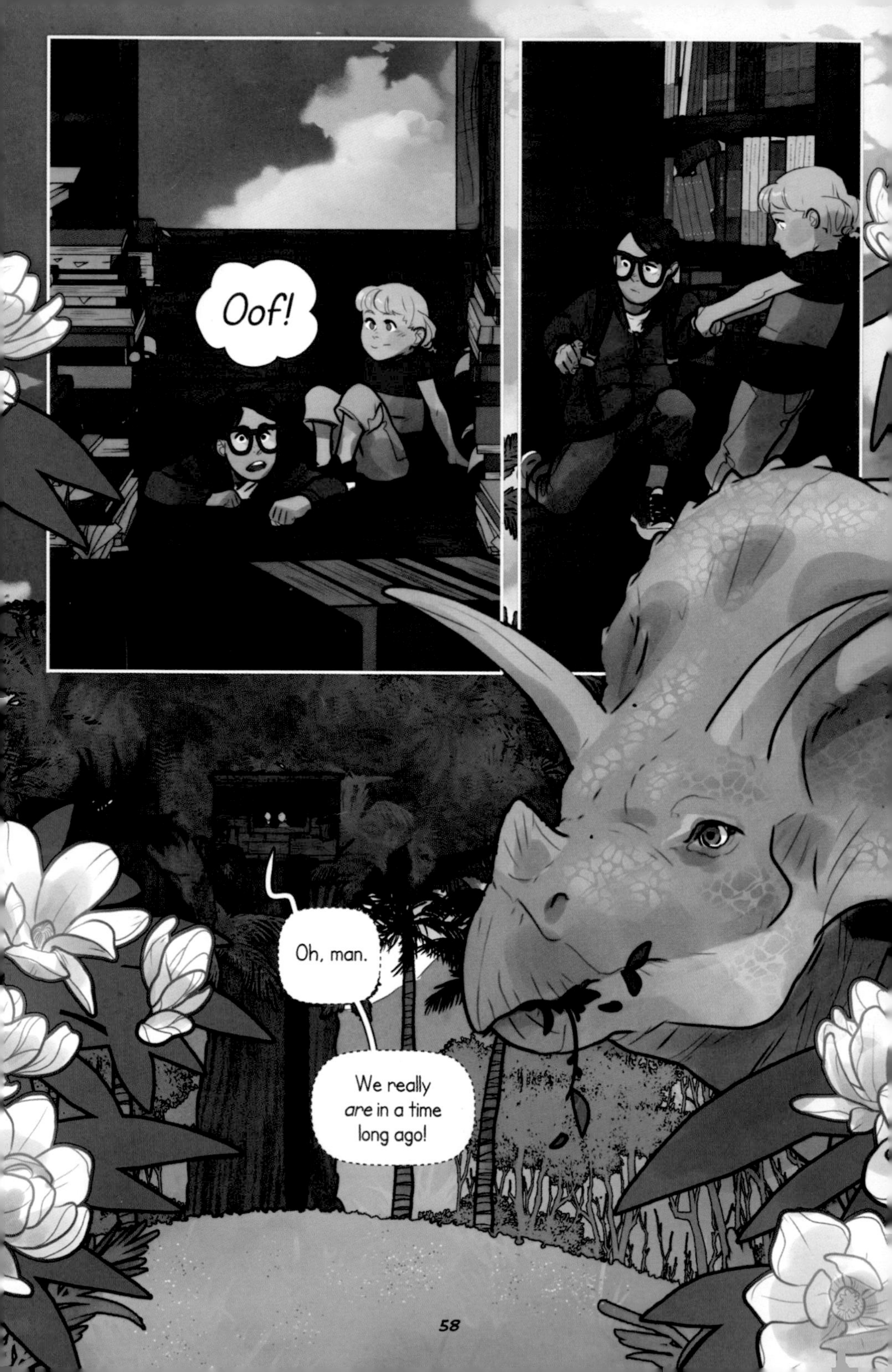
Oof!
Oh, man.
We really *are* in a time long ago!

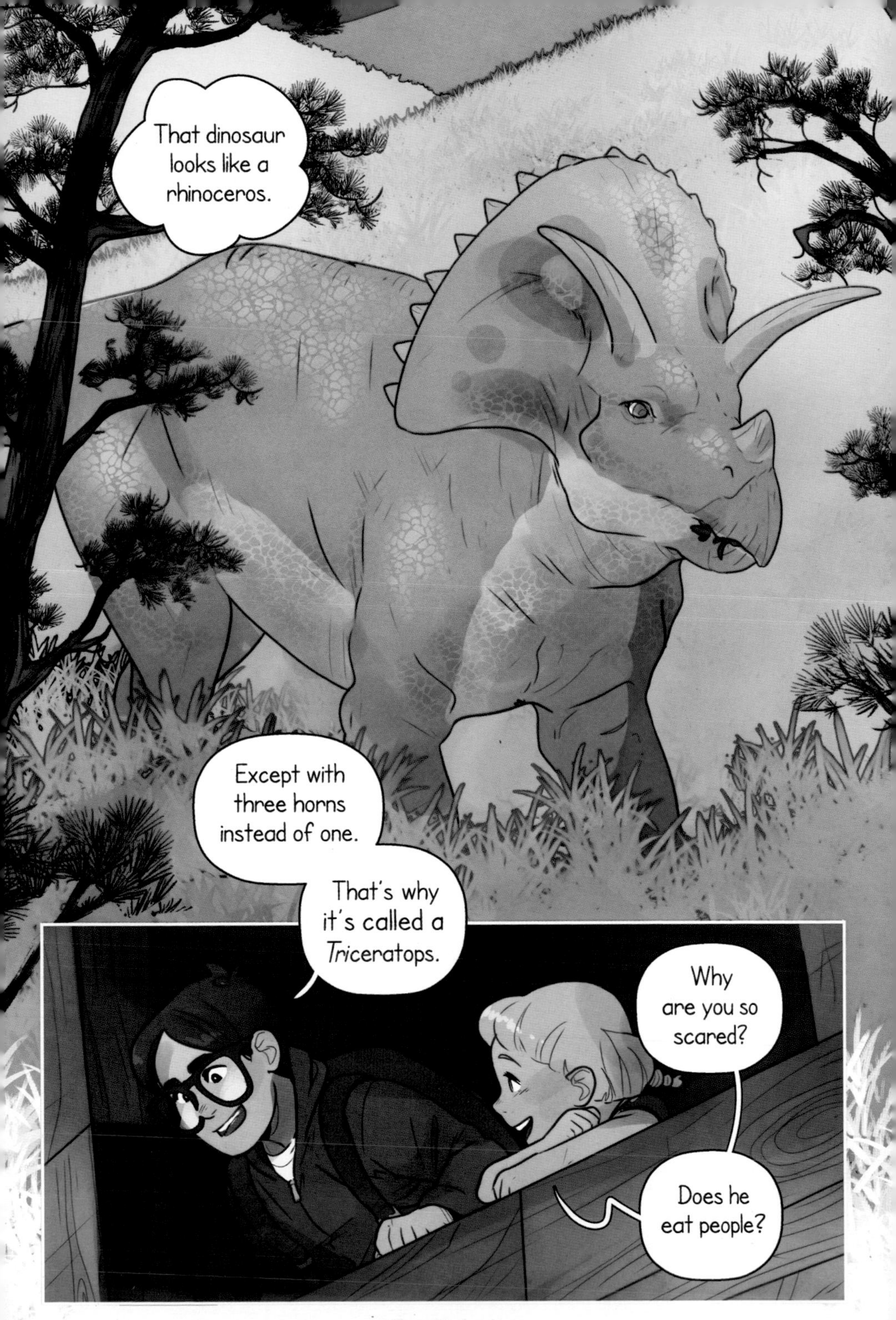
That dinosaur looks like a rhinoceros.
Except with three horns instead of one.
That's why it's called a *Tri*ceratops.
Why are you so scared?
Does he eat people?

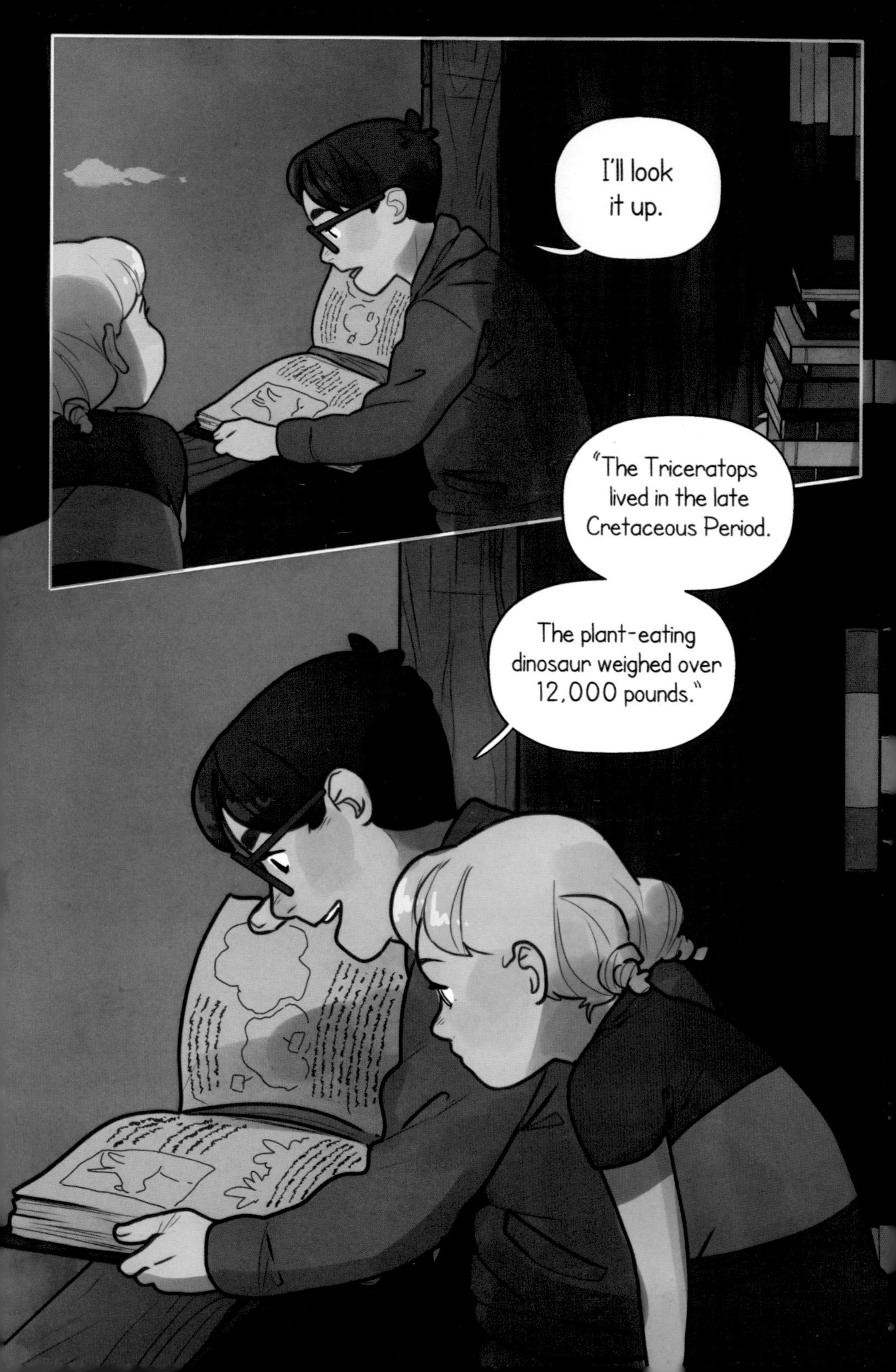
I'll look it up.
"The Triceratops lived in the late Cretaceous Period.
The plant-eating dinosaur weighed over 12,000 pounds."

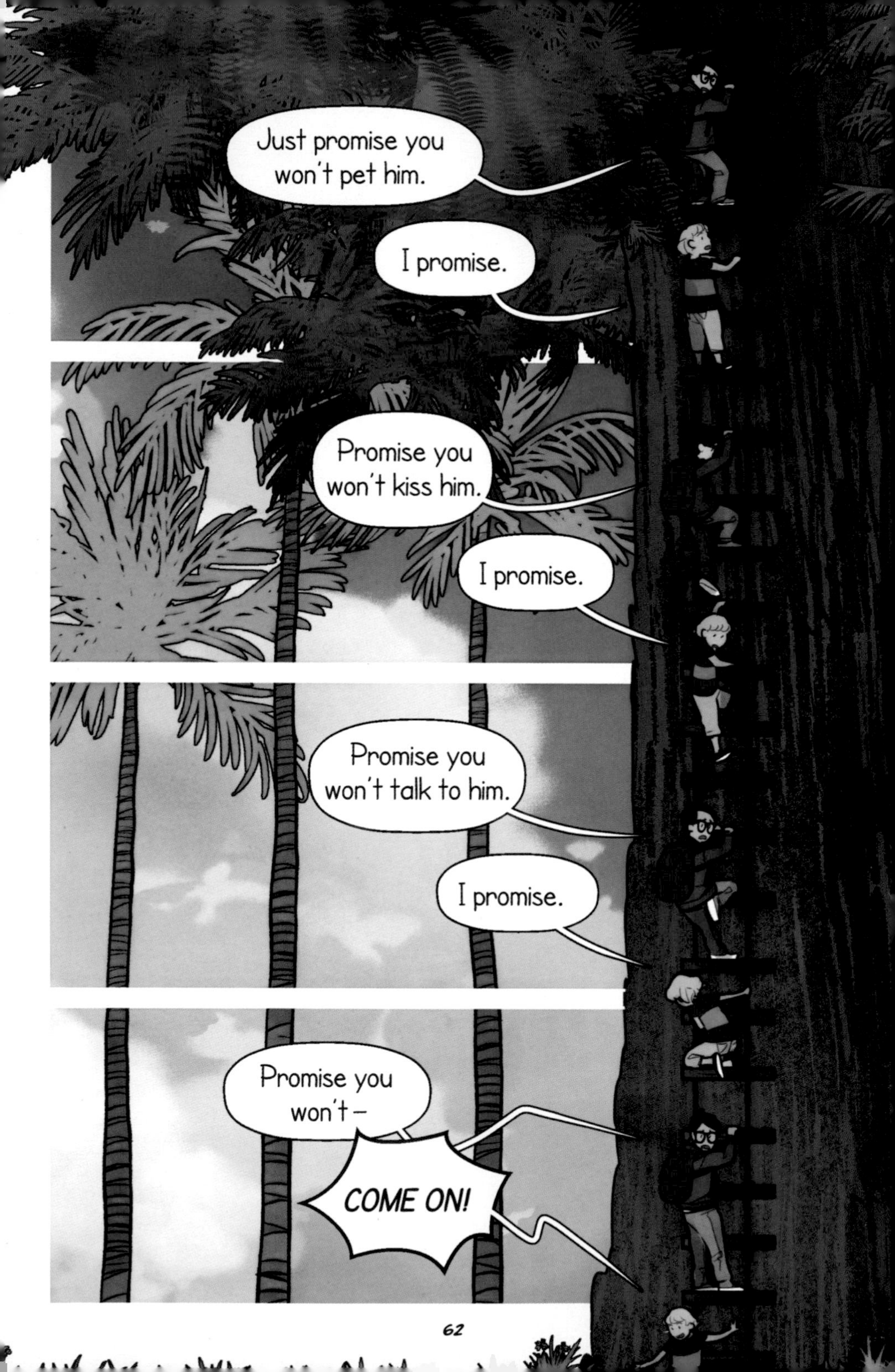
Just promise you won't pet him.
I promise.
Promise you won't kiss him.
I promise.
Promise you won't talk to him.
I promise.
Promise you won't–
COME ON!

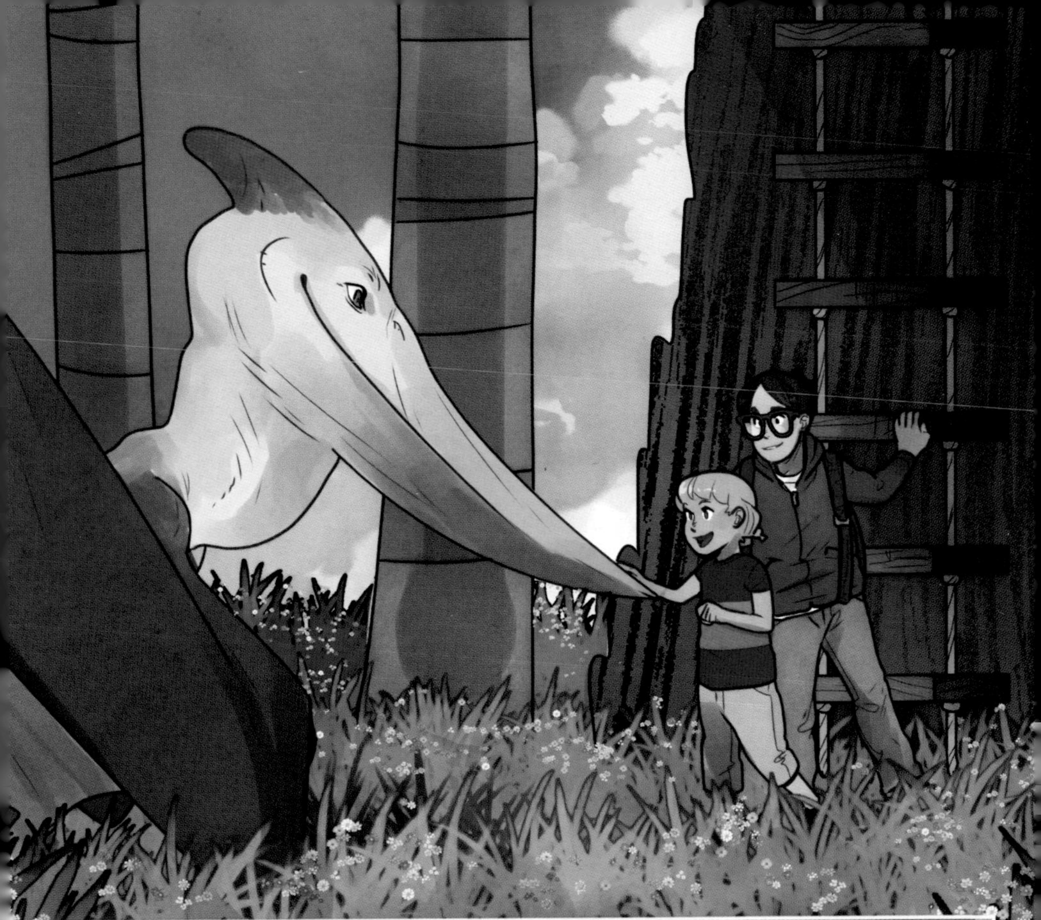

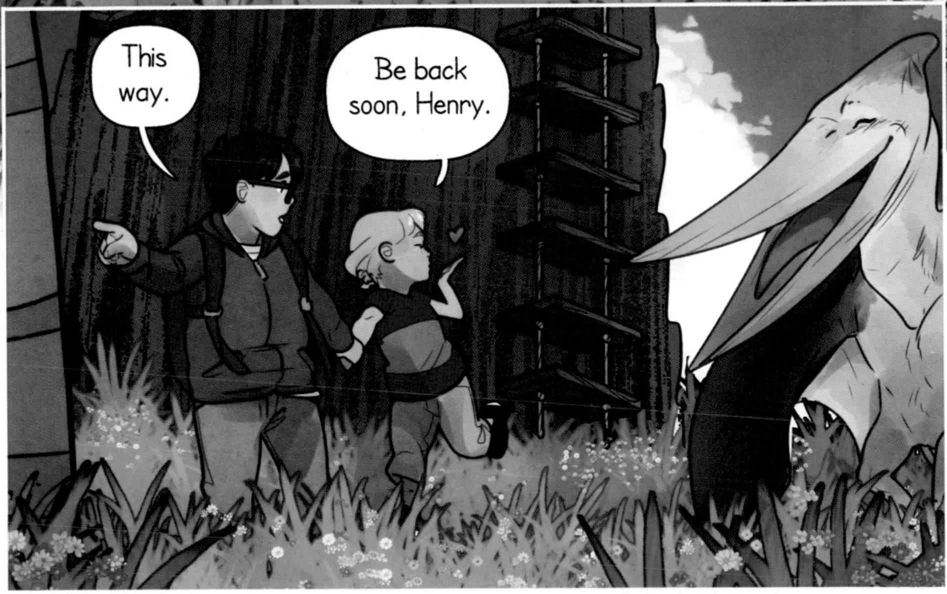
This way.
Be back soon, Henry.

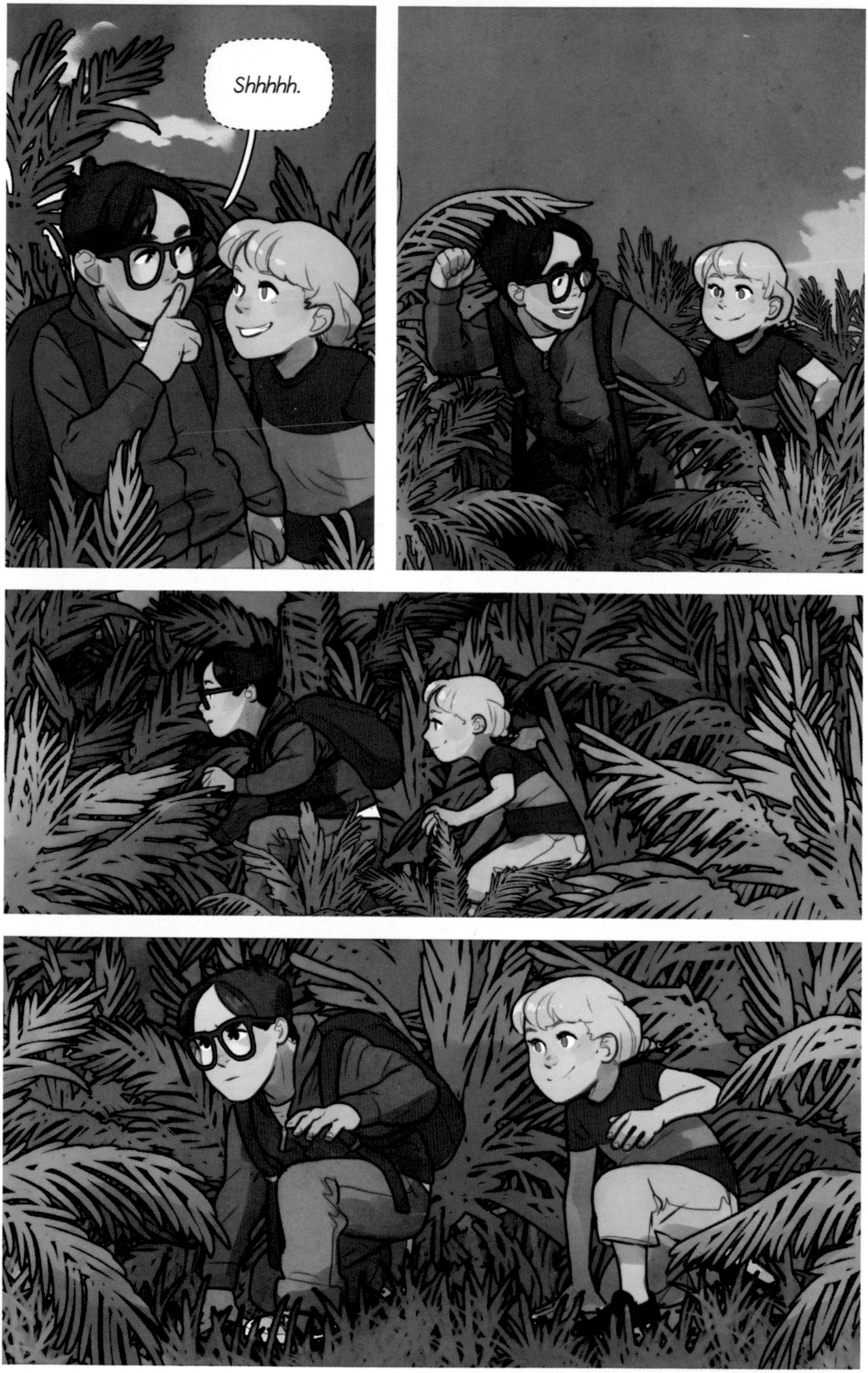
Shhhhh.

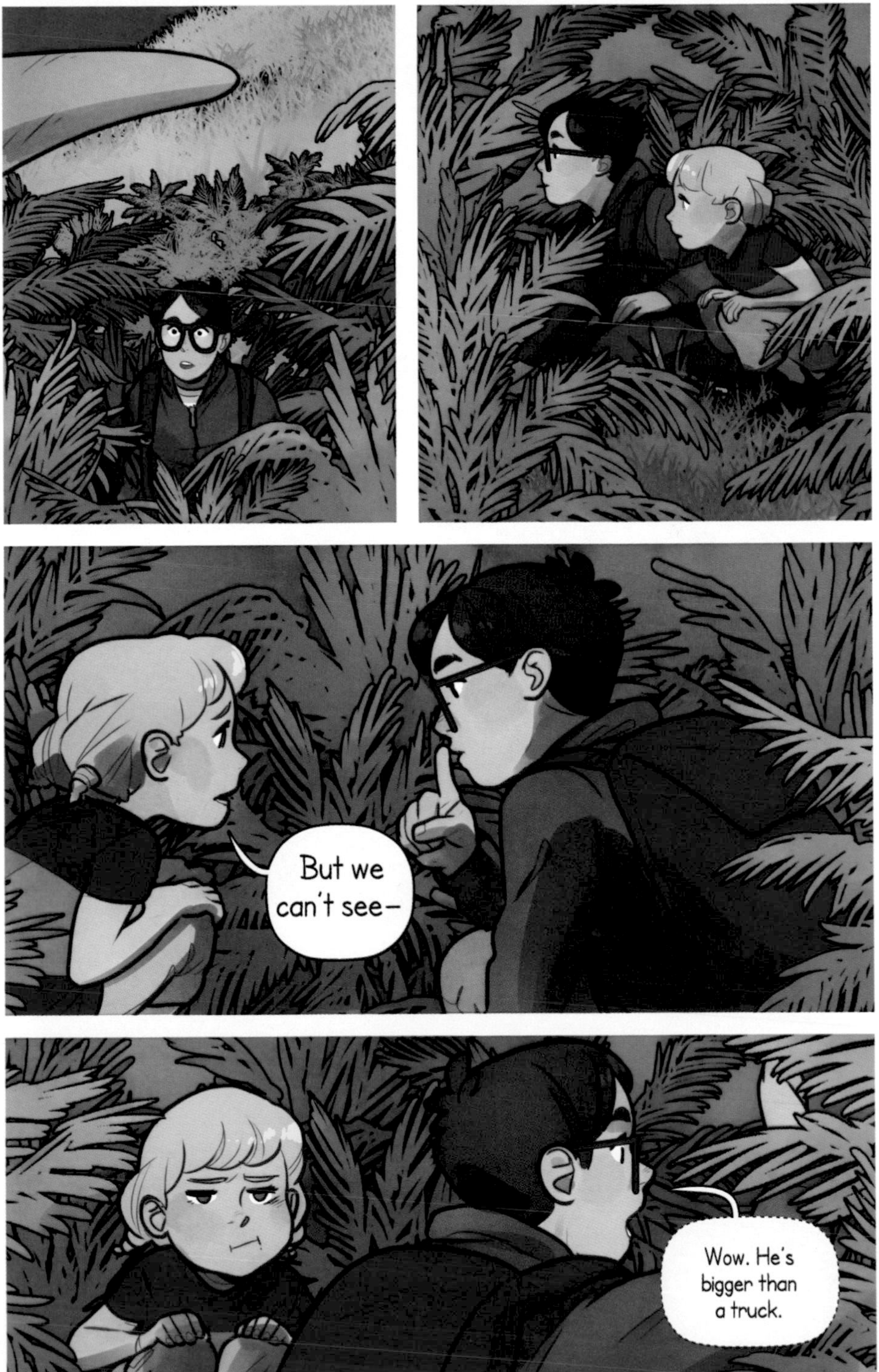
But we can't see—
Wow. He's bigger than a truck.

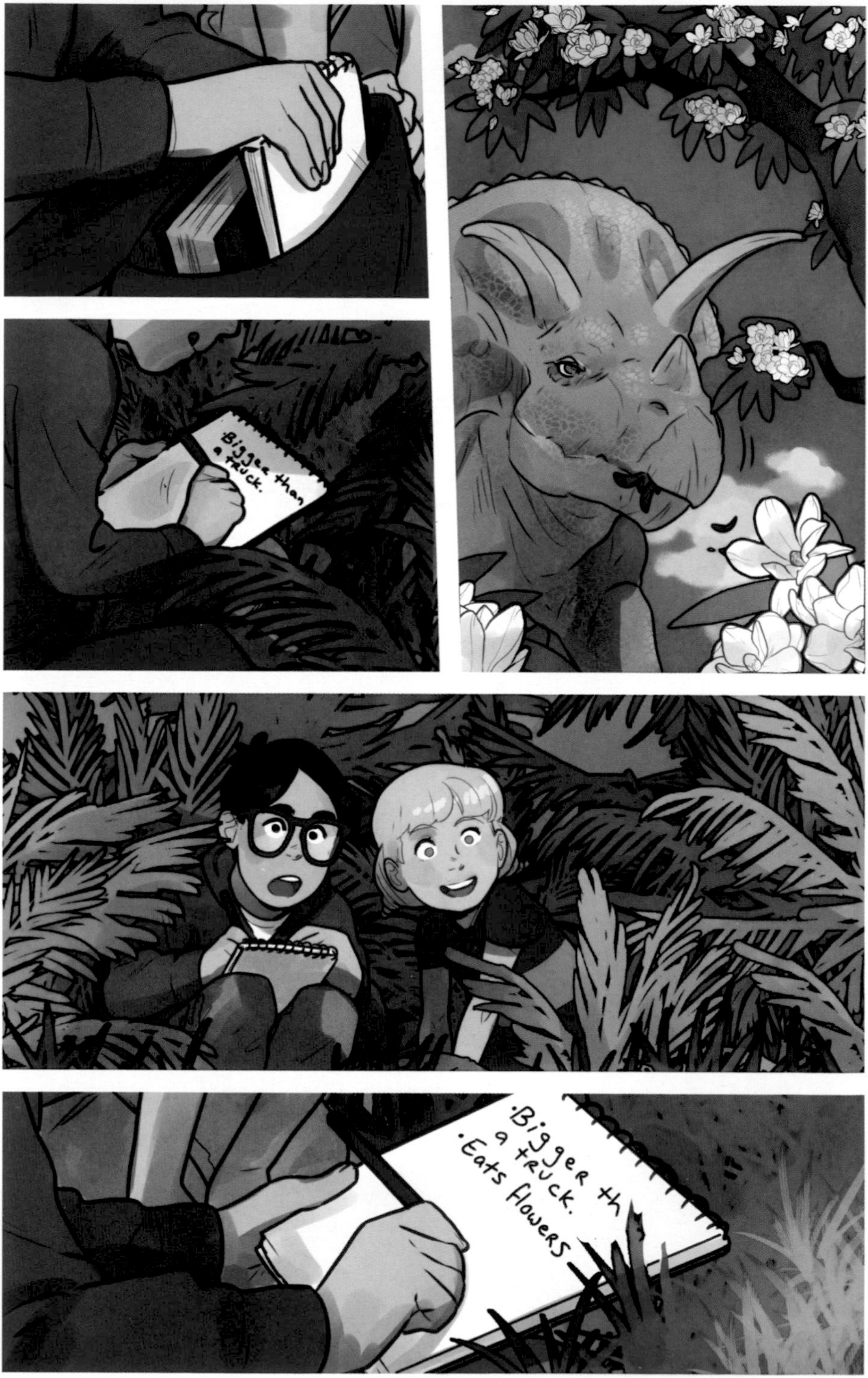
·Bigger than
a truck.
·Bigger th
a truck.
·Eats flowers

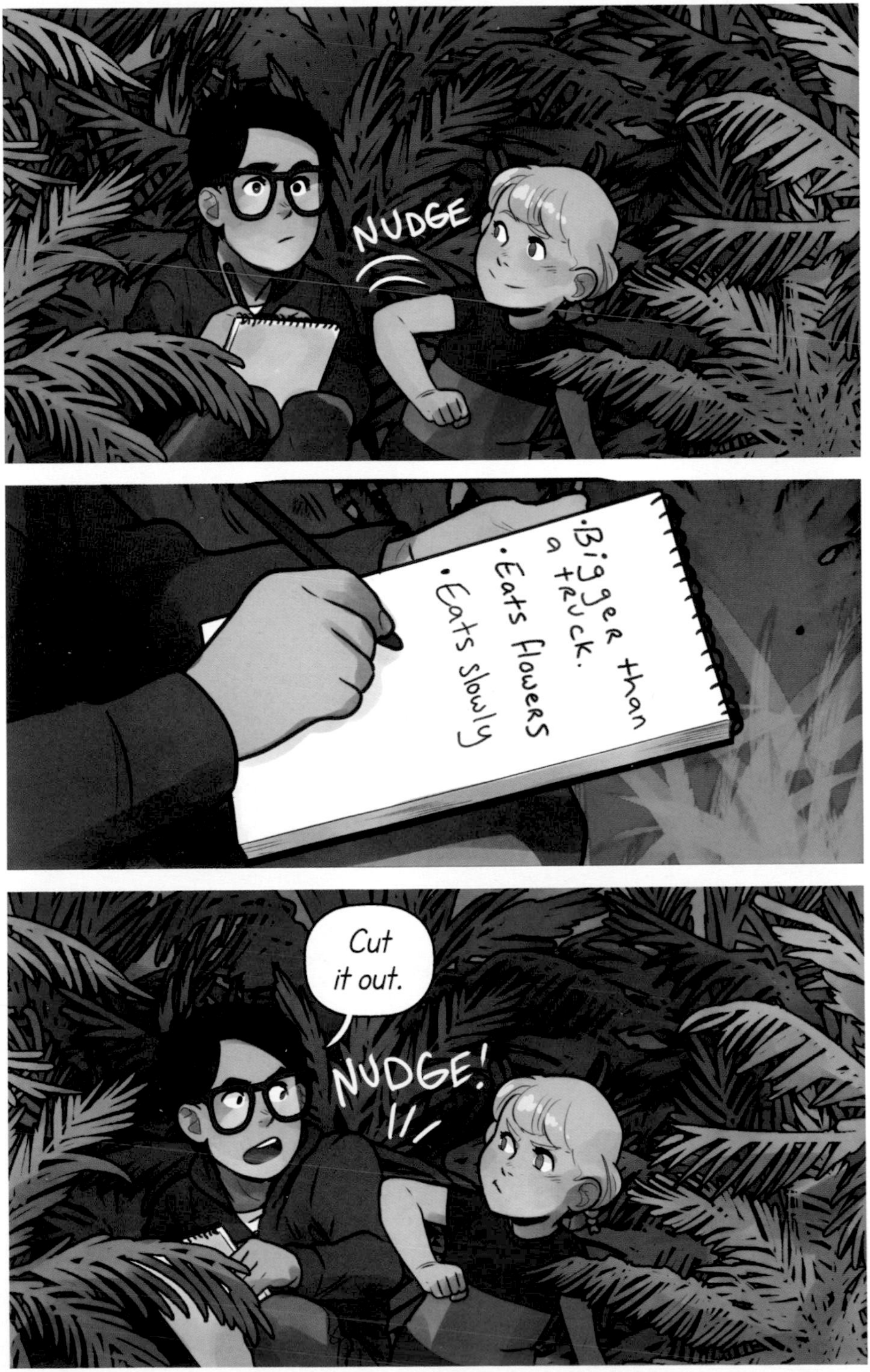
NUDGE
•Bigger than a truck.
•Eats flowers
•Eats slowly
Cut it out.
NUDGE!

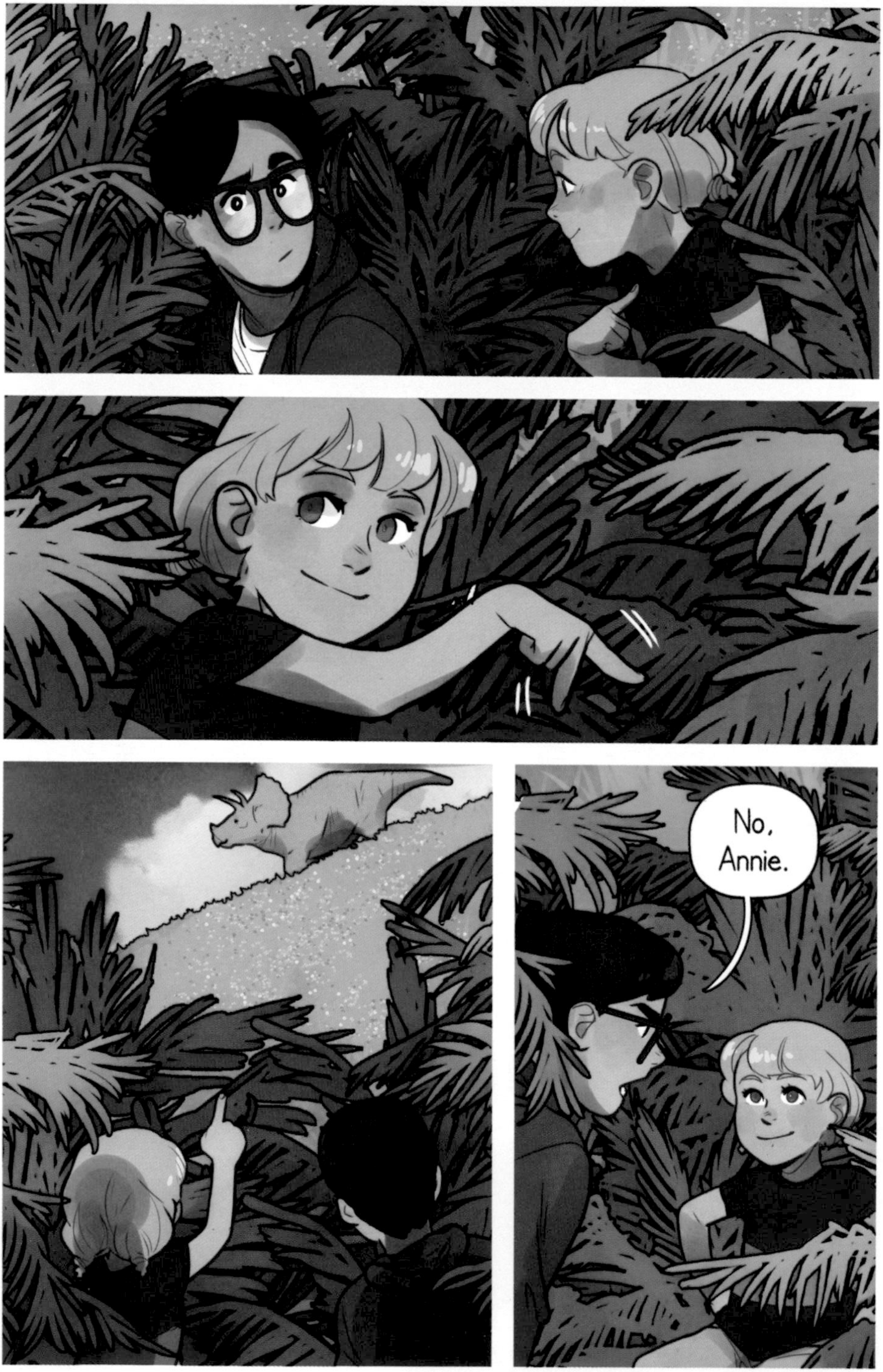
No, Annie.

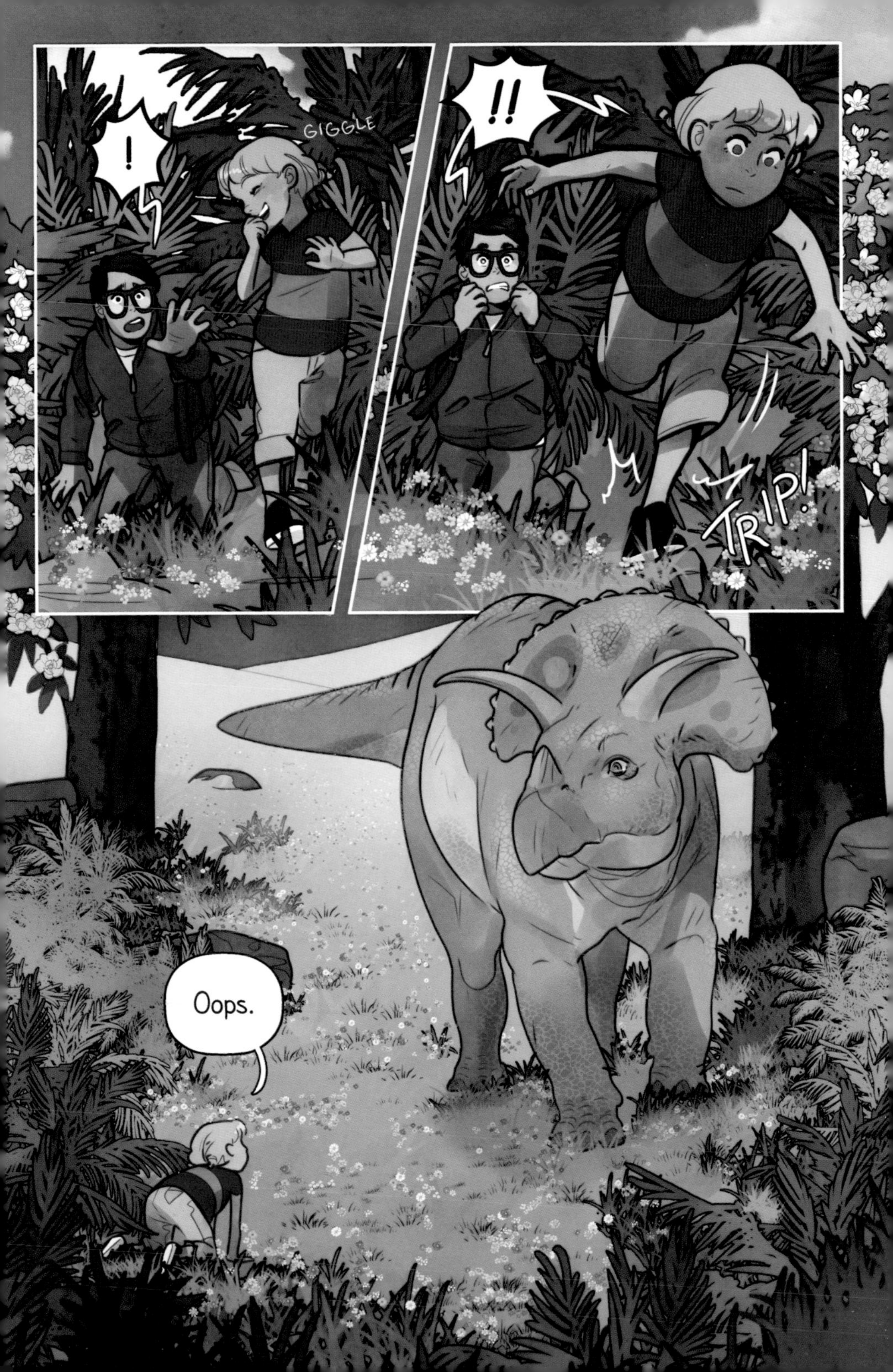

!
GIGGLE
!!
TRIP!
Oops.

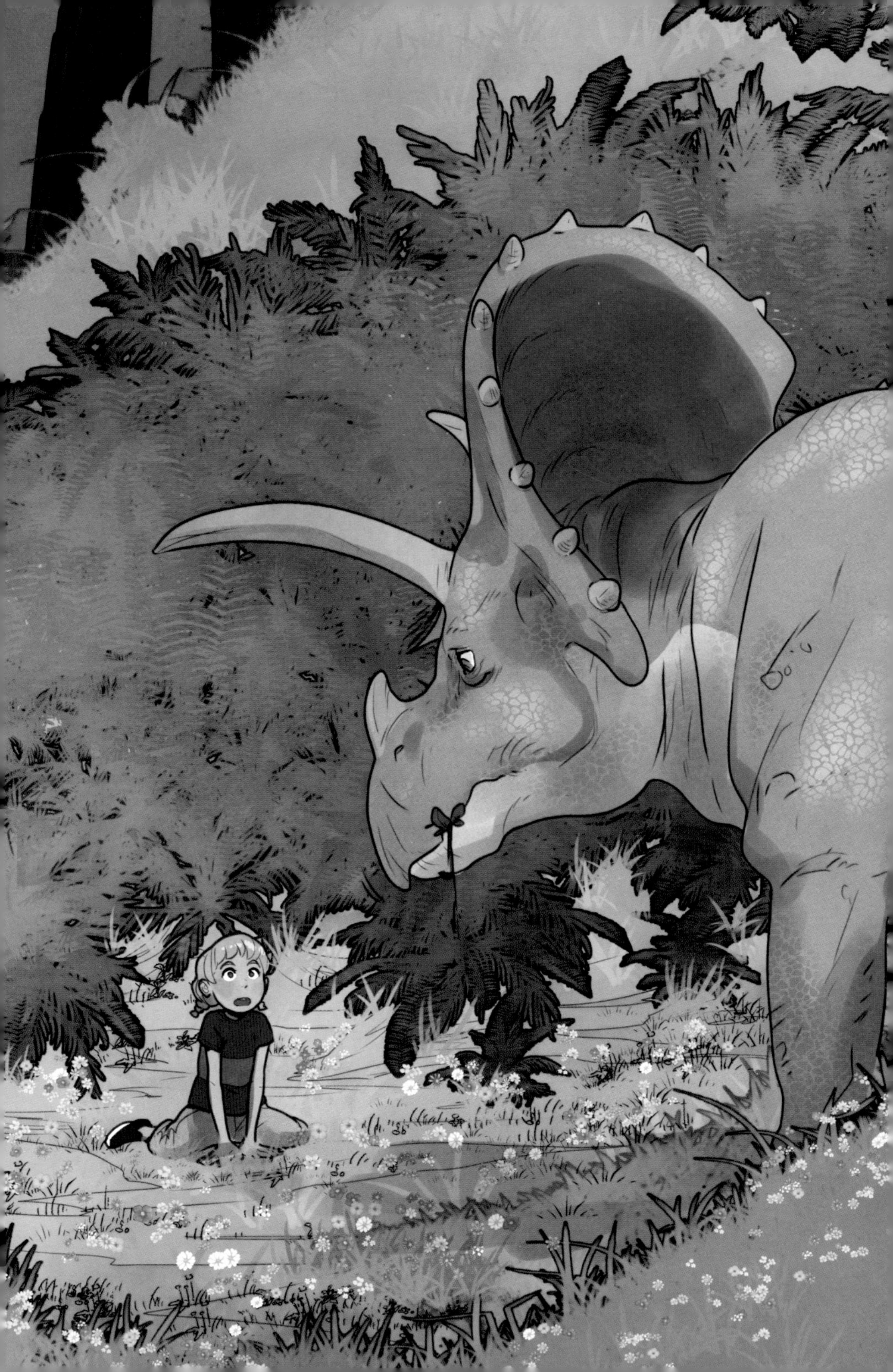

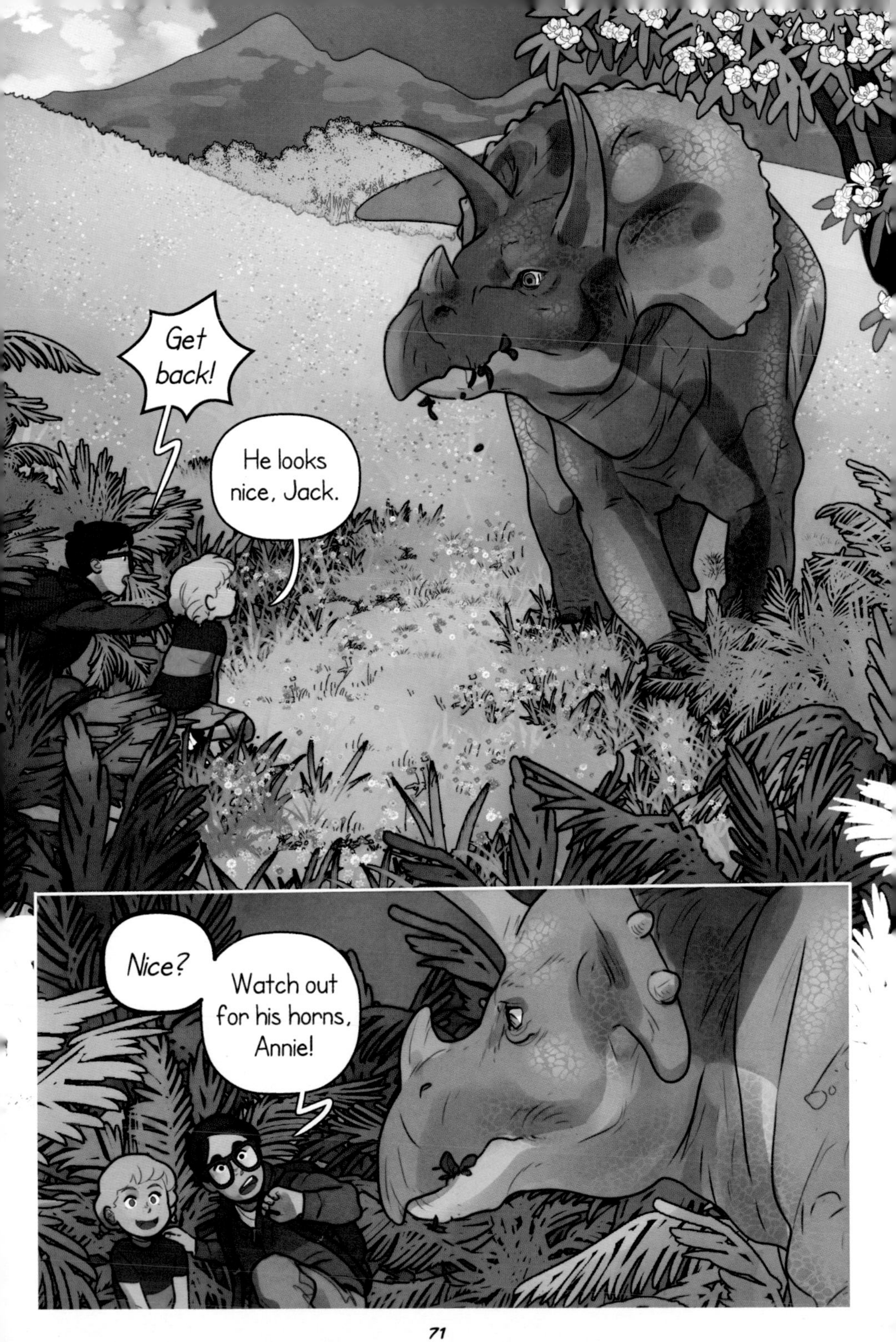
Get back!
He looks nice, Jack.
Nice?
Watch out for his horns, Annie!

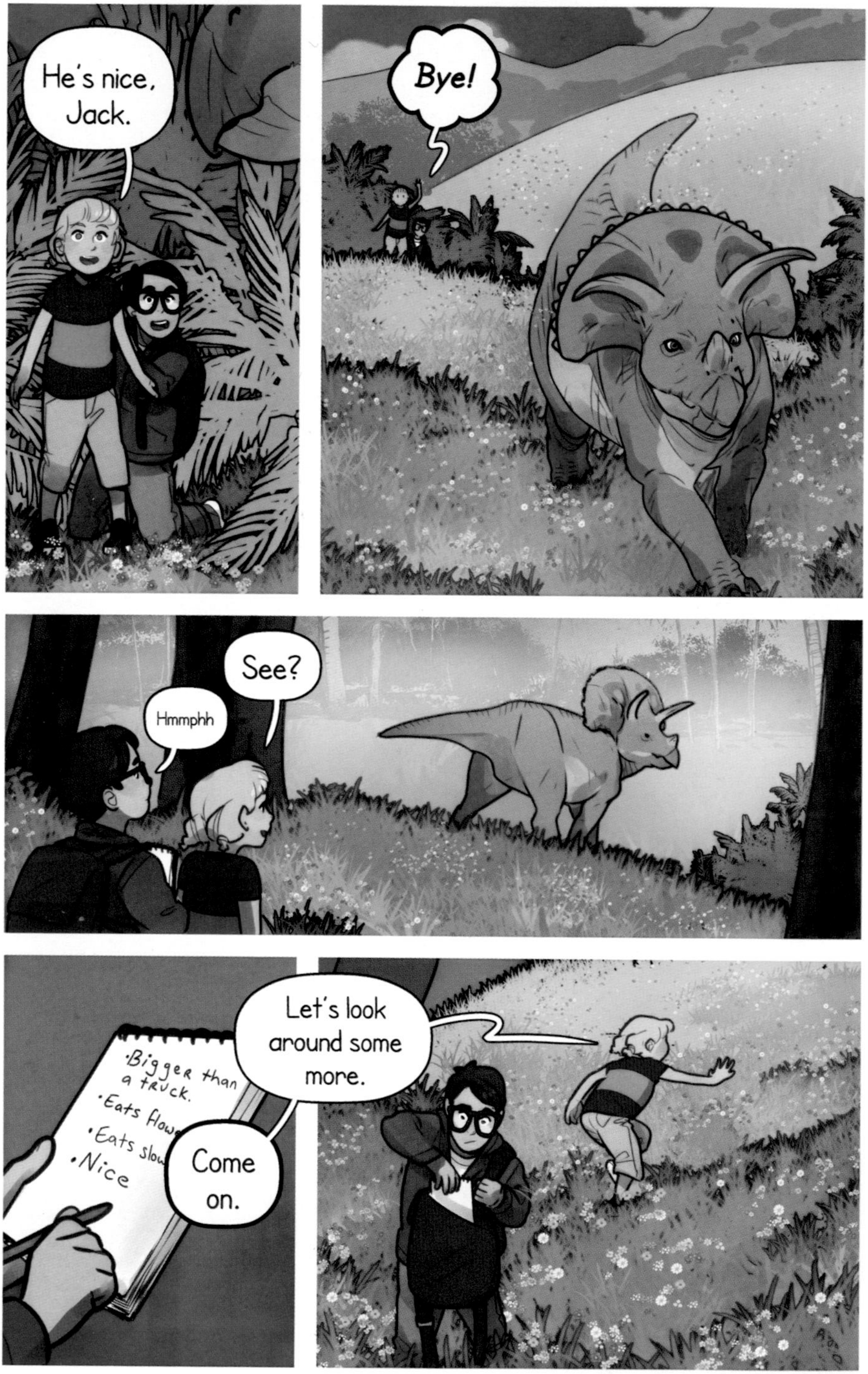
He's nice, Jack.
Bye!
See?
Hmmphh
•Bigger than a truck.
•Eats flow
•Eats slow
•Nice
Let's look around some more.
Come on.

CHAPTER SIX
Dinosaur Valley

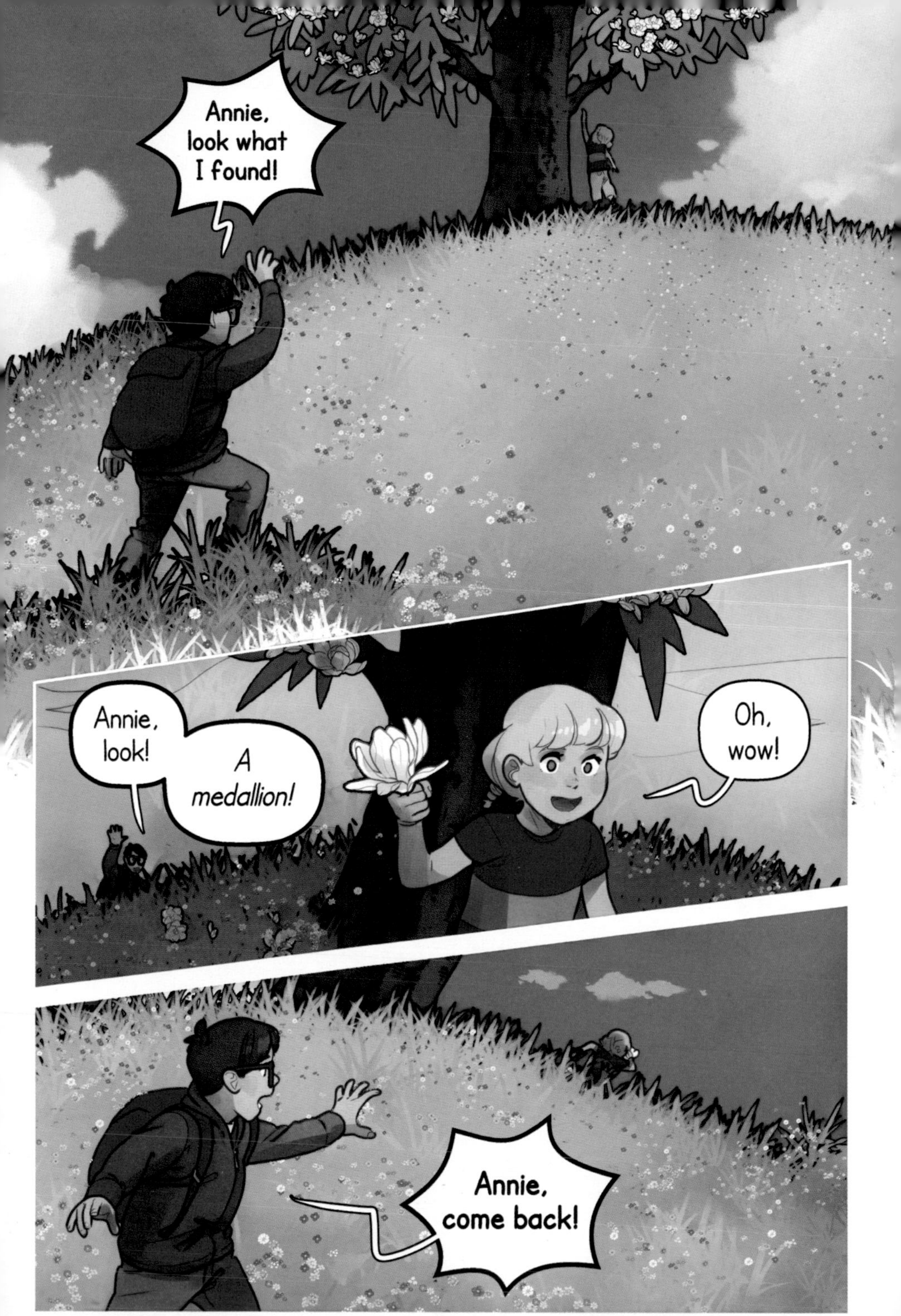
Annie, look what I found!
Annie, look!
A medallion!
Oh, wow!
Annie, come back!

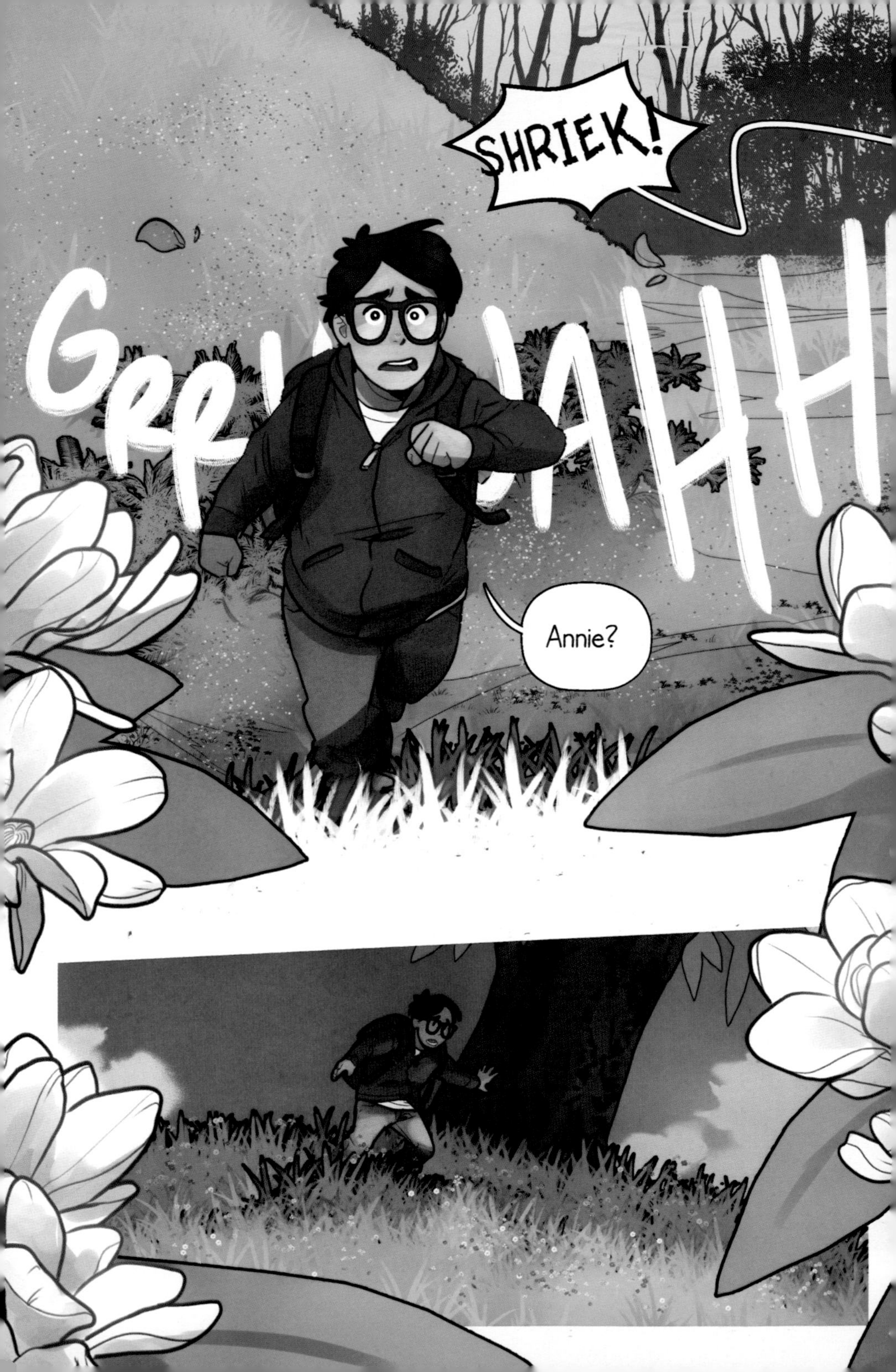
SHRIEK!
Annie?

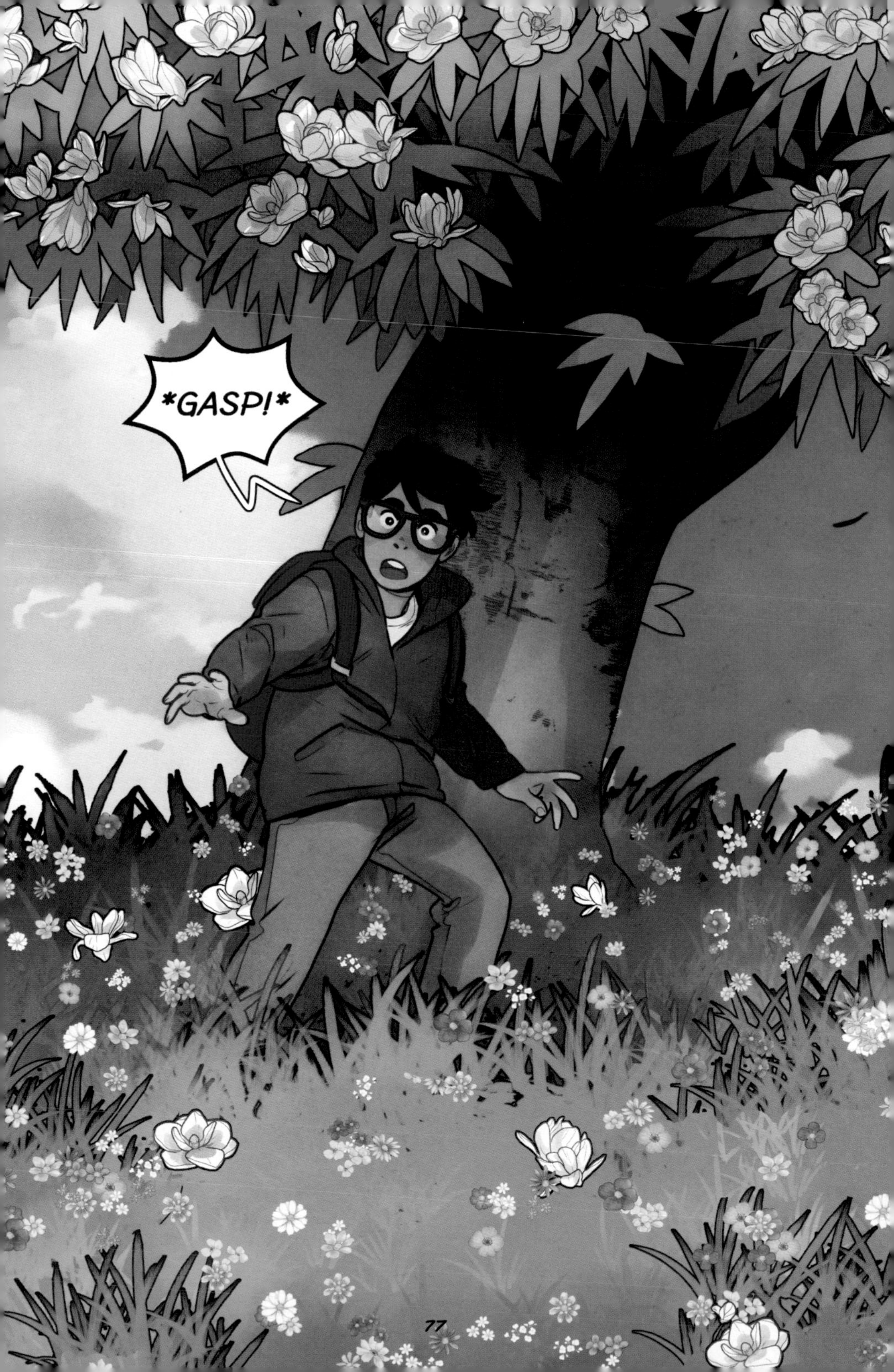
GASP!

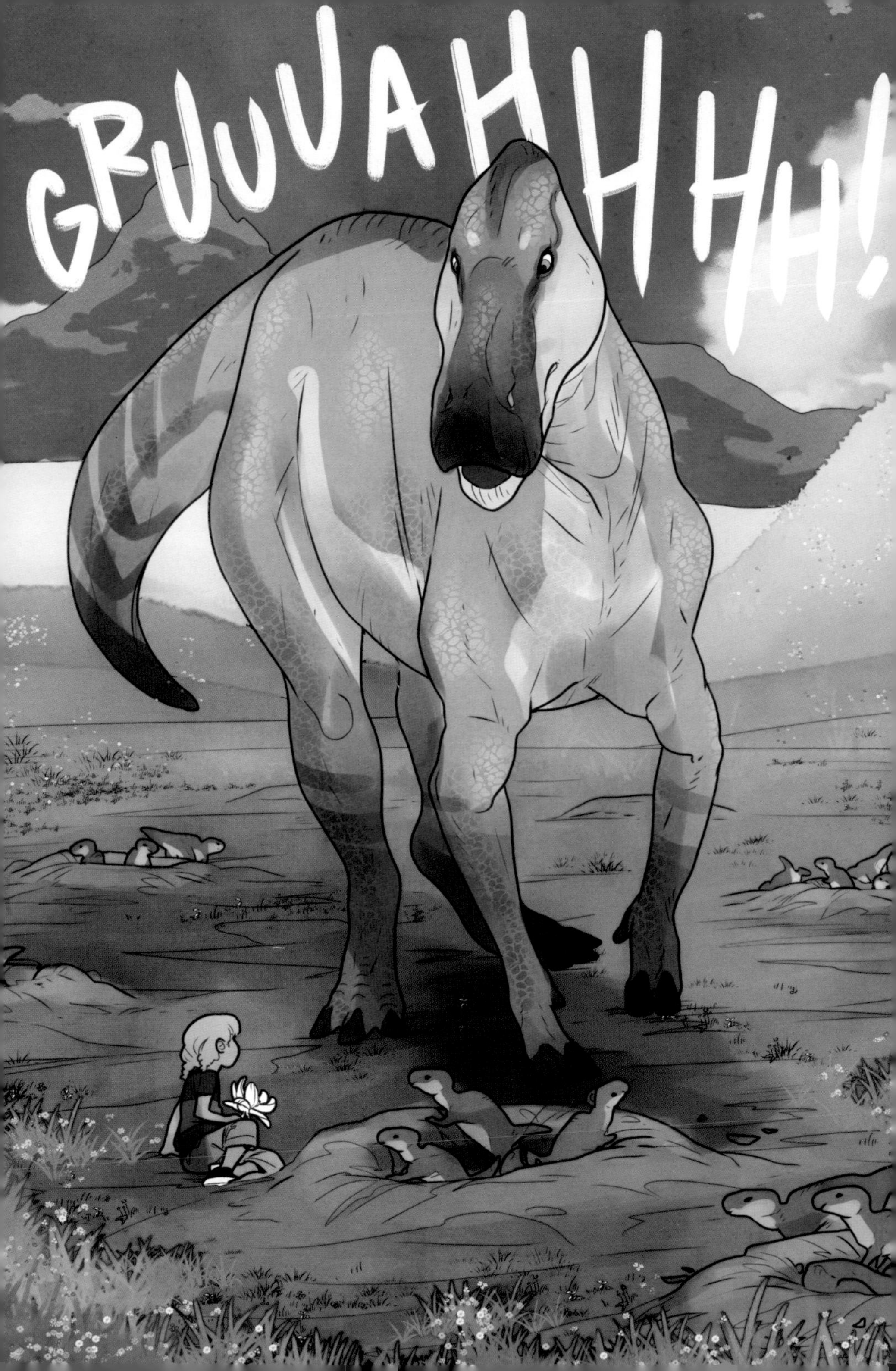
GRUUUAHHHHH!

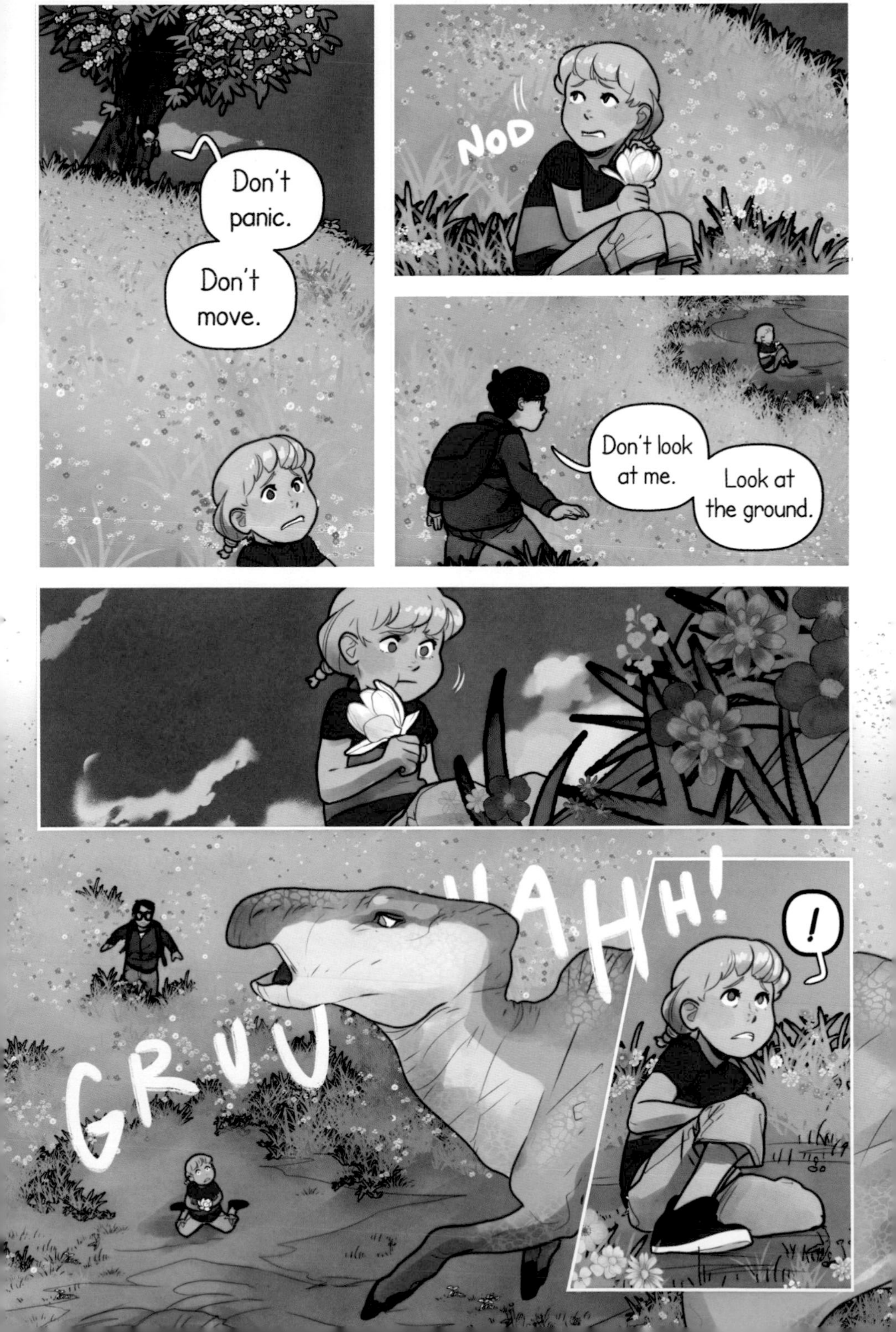
Don't panic.
Don't move.
NOD
Don't look at me.
Look at the ground.
GRUUUAHH!
!

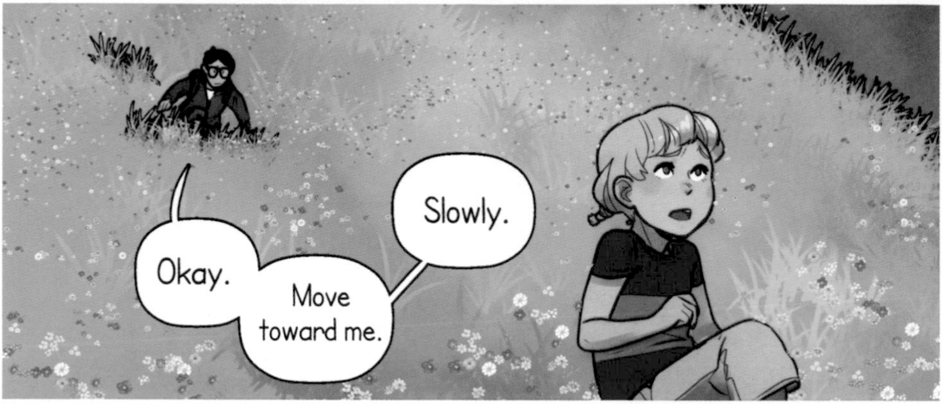
Okay.
Move toward me.
Slowly.

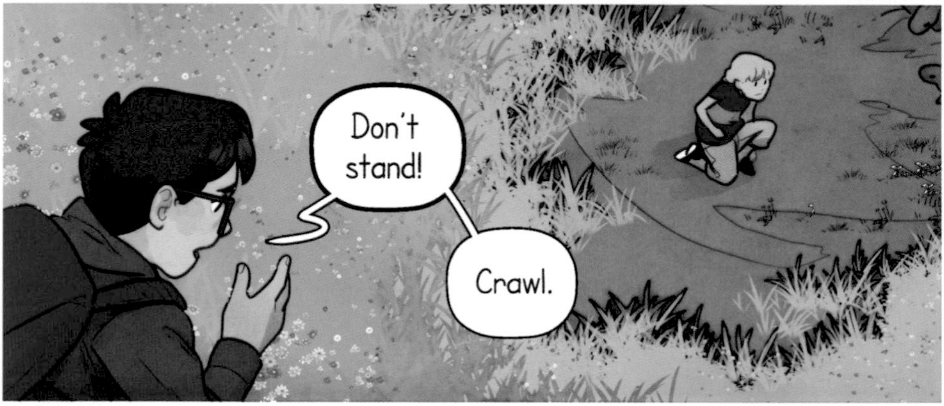
Don't stand!
Crawl.

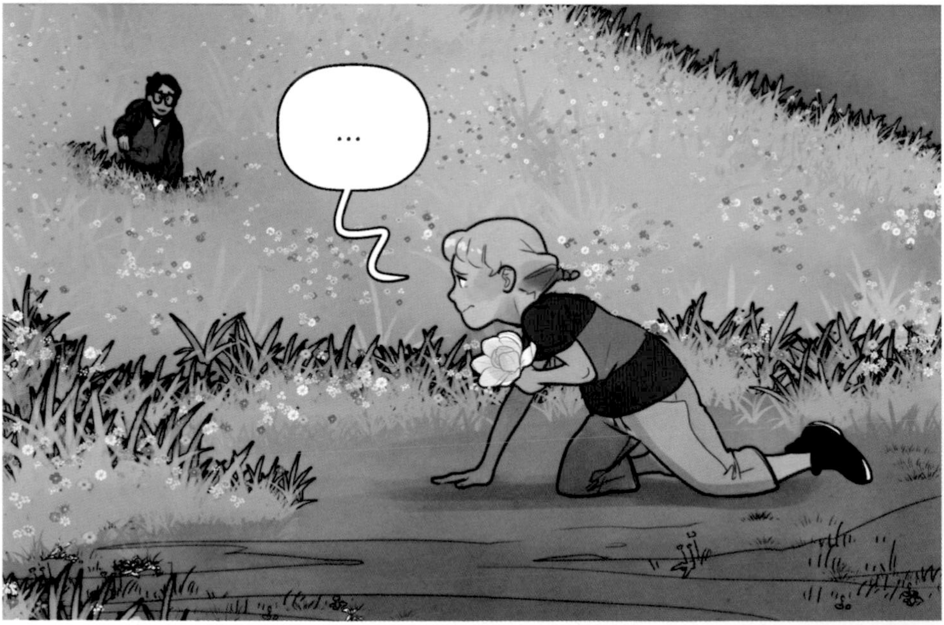
...

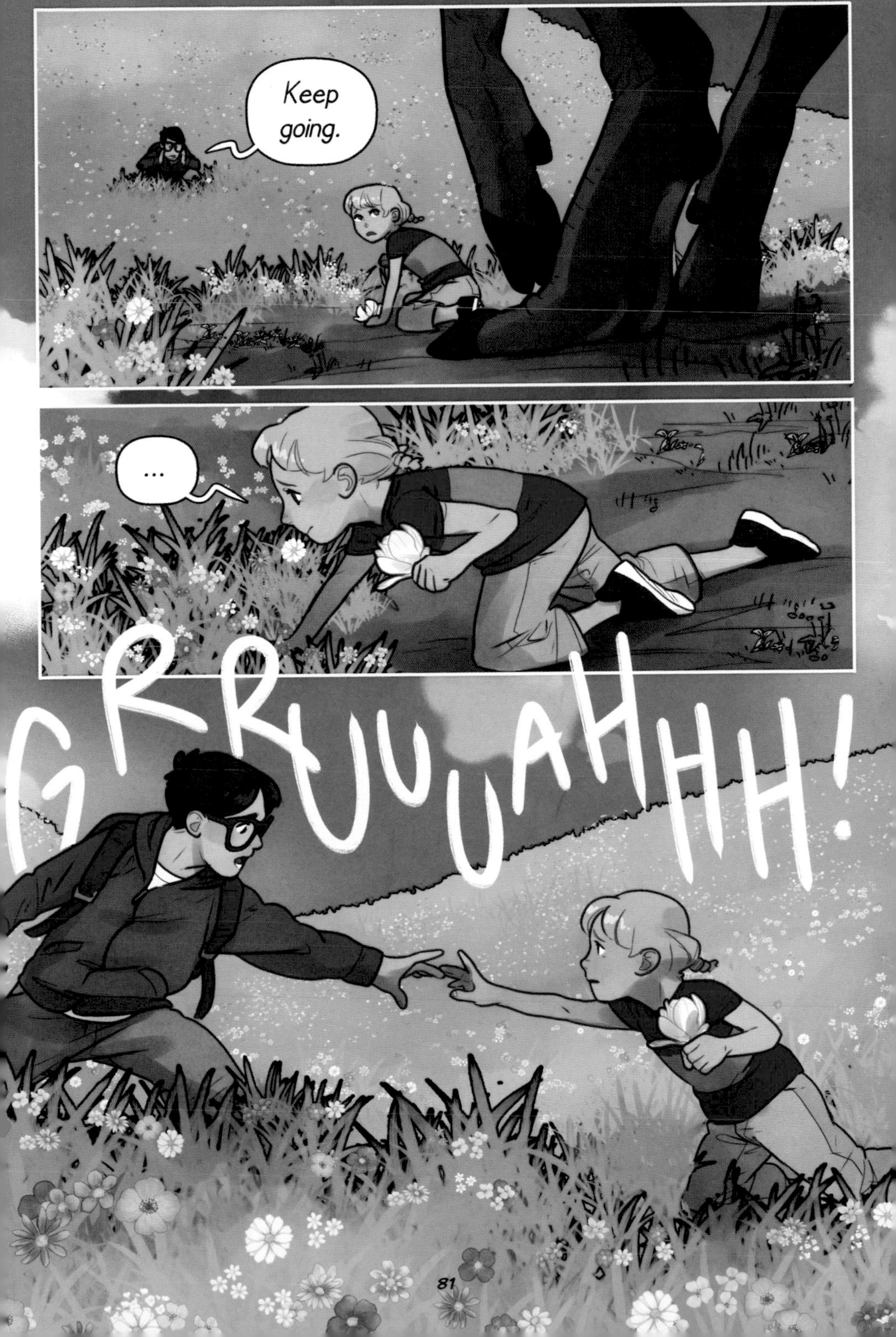
Keep going.
...
GRRUUUAHHHH!

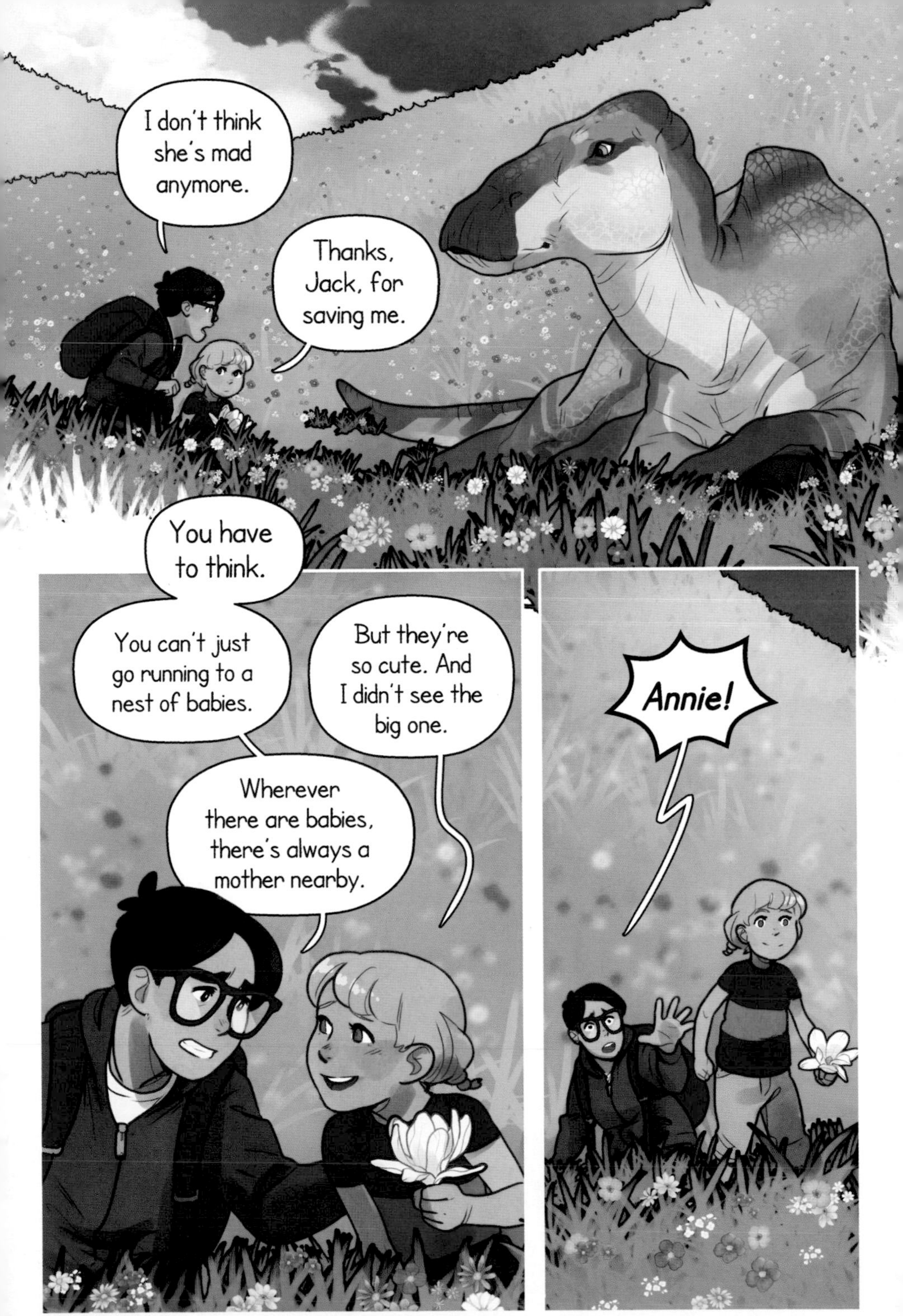
I don't think she's mad anymore.
Thanks, Jack, for saving me.
You have to think.
You can't just go running to a nest of babies.
But they're so cute. And I didn't see the big one.
Wherever there are babies, there's always a mother nearby.
Annie!

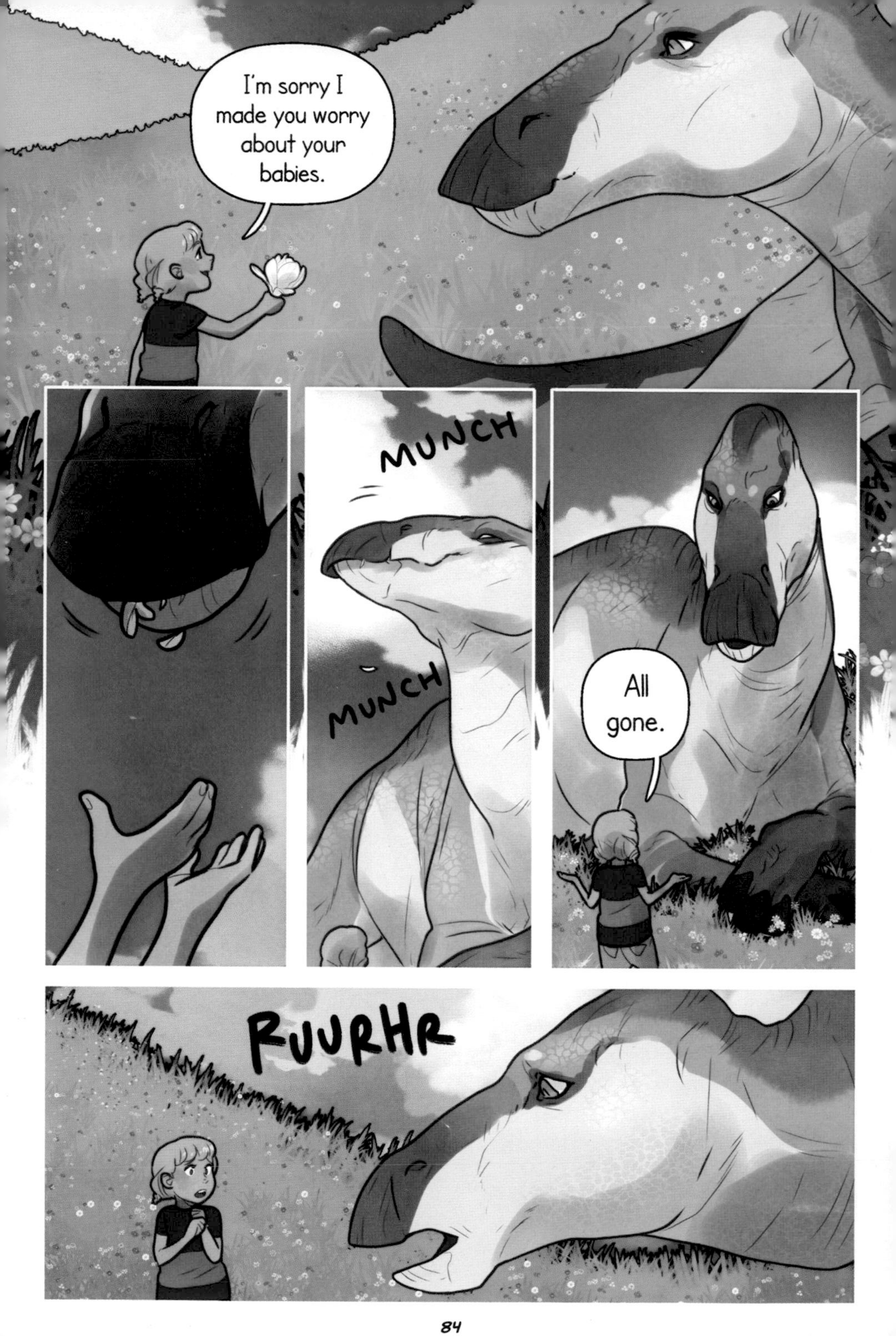
I'm sorry I made you worry about your babies.
MUNCH
MUNCH
All gone.
RUURHR

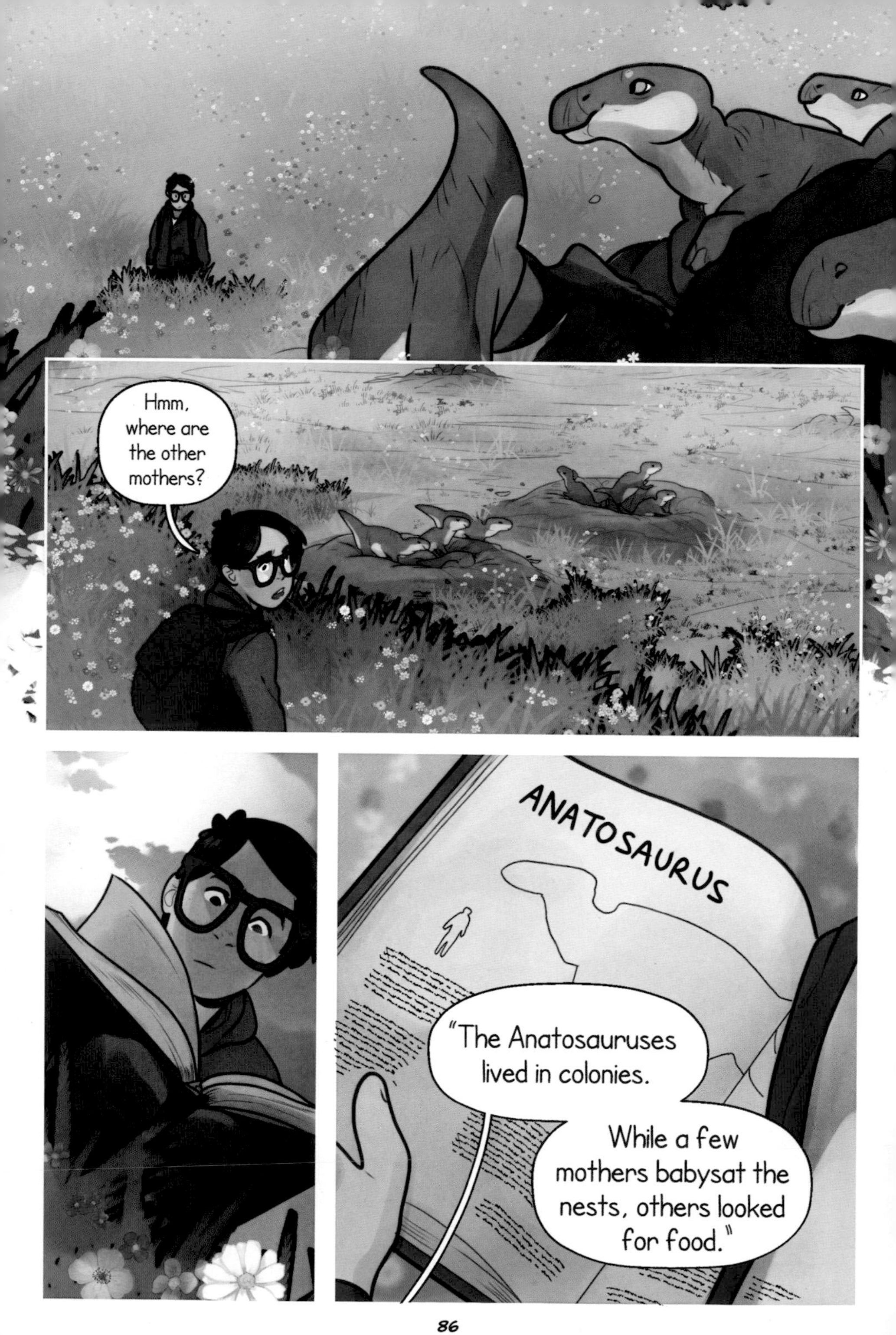
Hmm, where are the other mothers?
ANATOSAURUS
"The Anatosauruses lived in colonies.
While a few mothers babysat the nests, others looked for food."

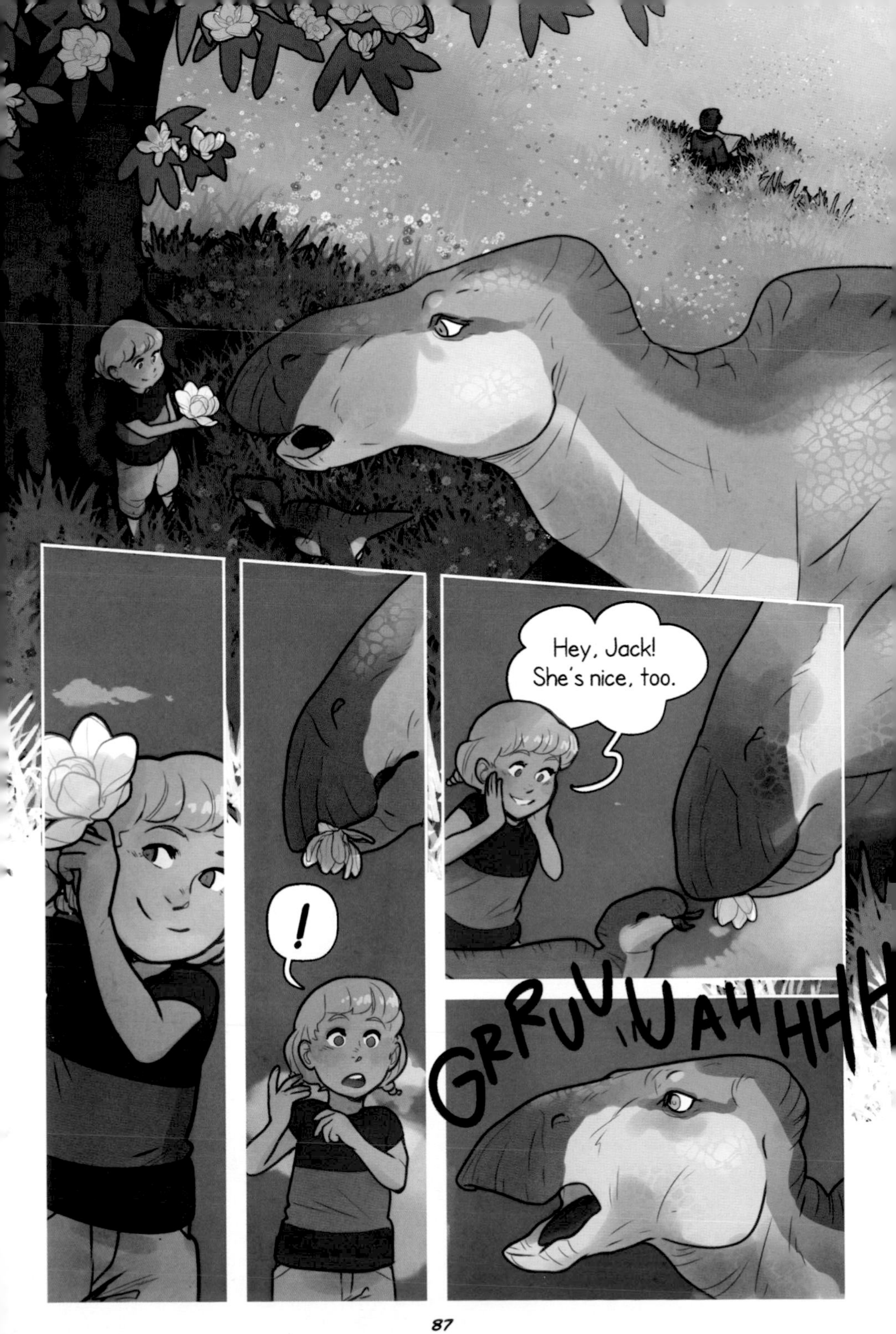
Hey, Jack!
She's nice, too.
!
GRRUUUNAHHHH

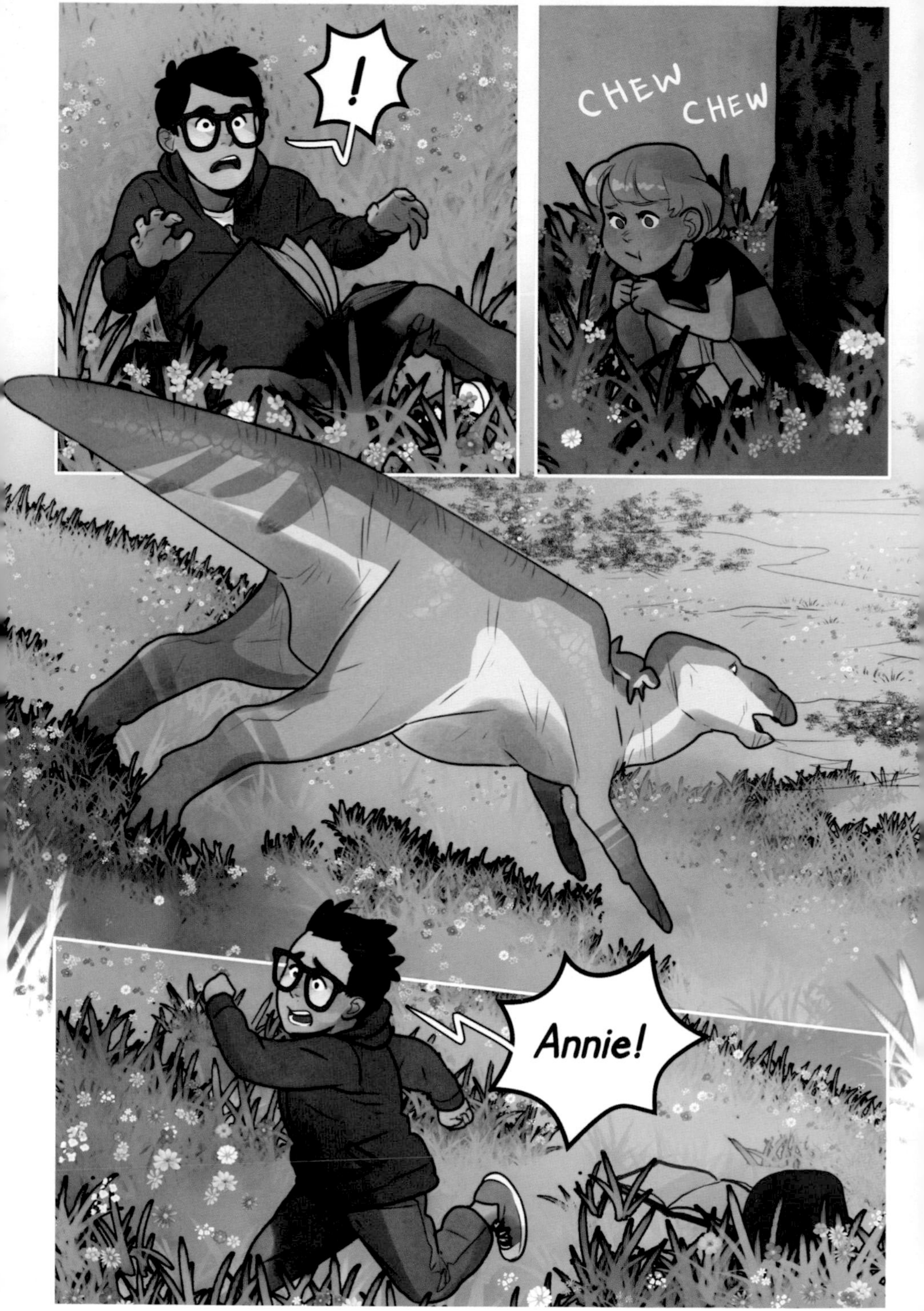
!
CHEW CHEW
Annie!

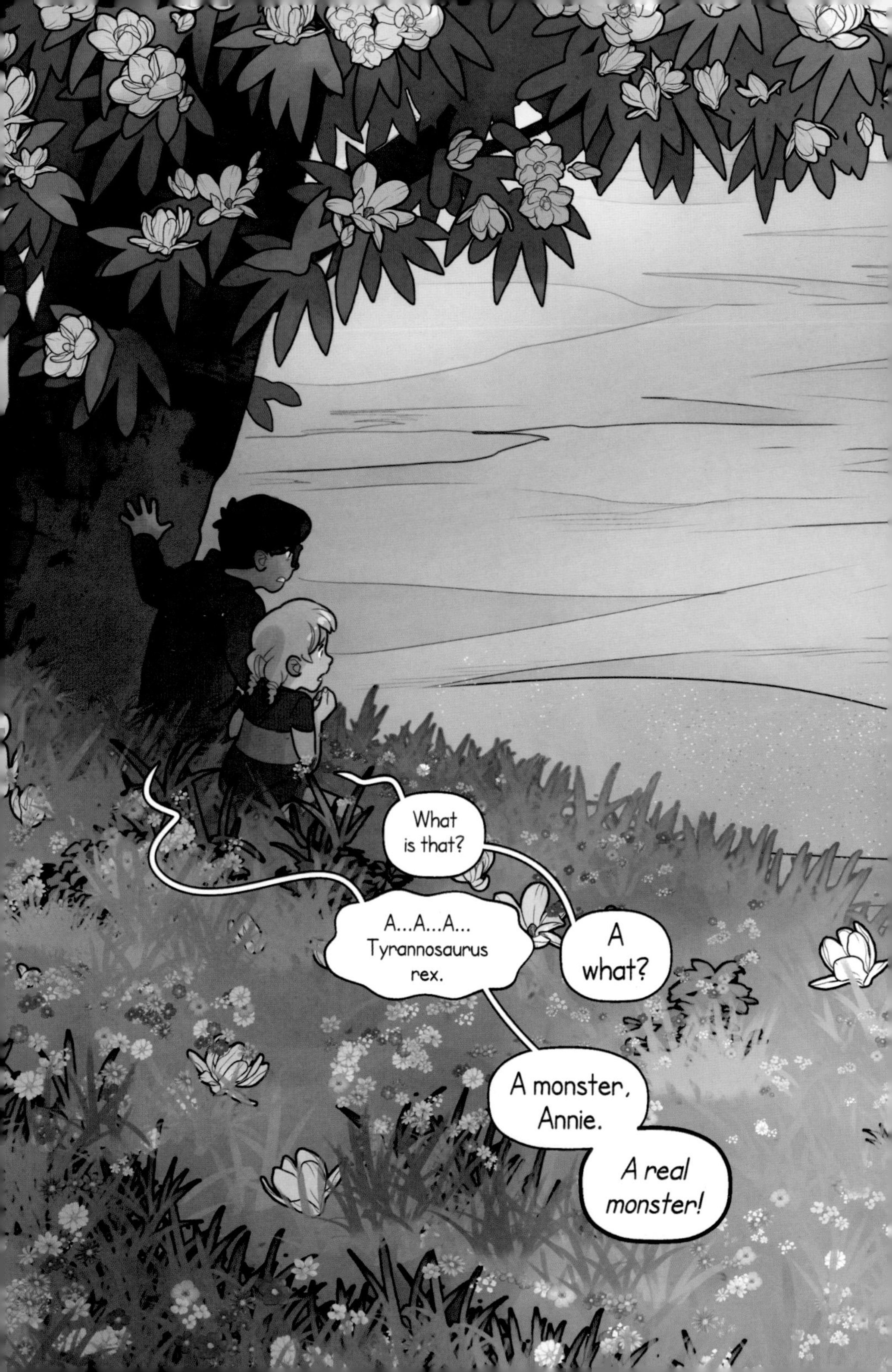

What is that?
A...A...A... Tyrannosaurus rex.
A what?
A monster, Annie.
A real monster!

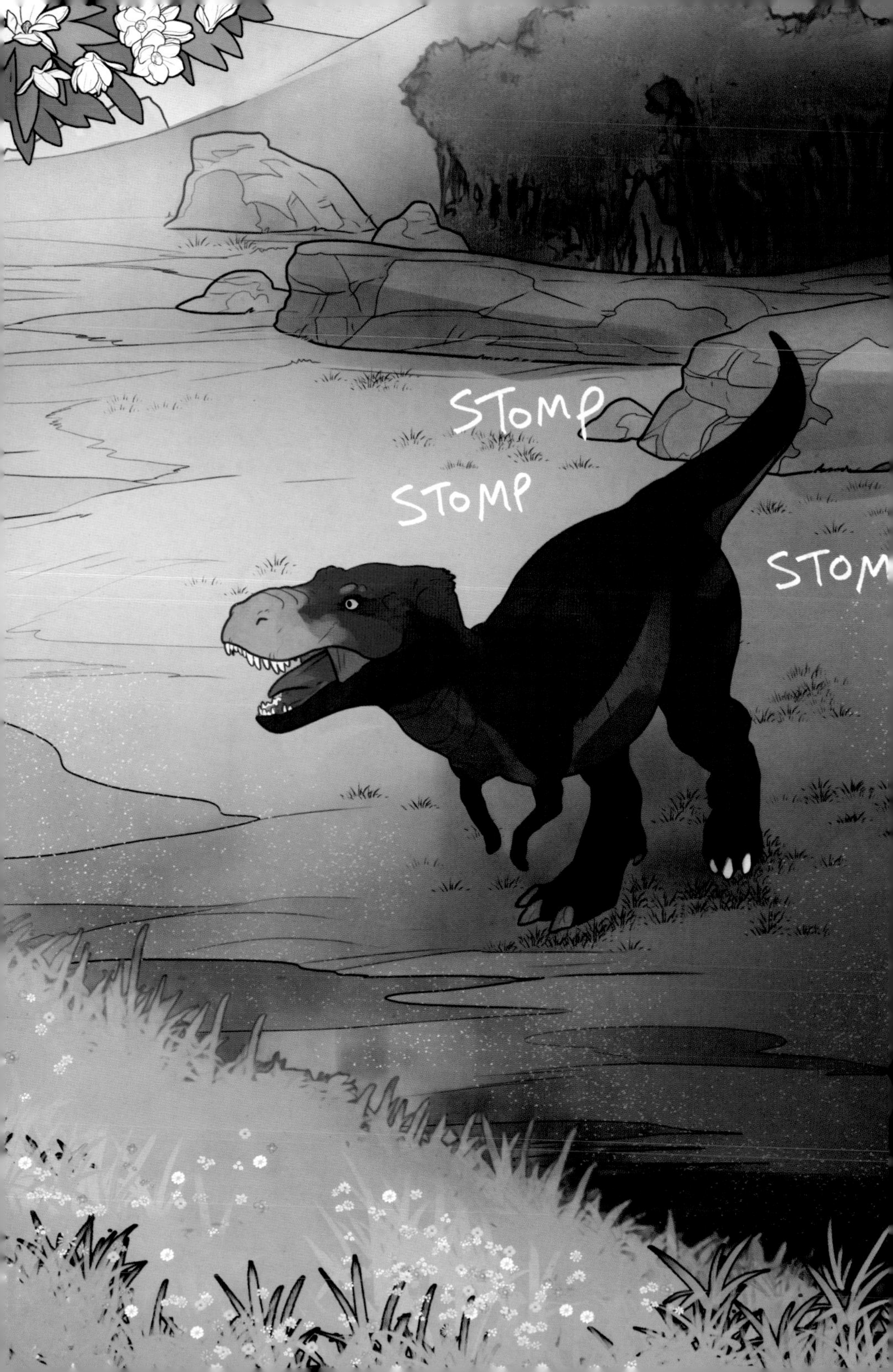
STOMP
STOMP
STOM

CHAPTER SEVEN
Ready, Set, Go!

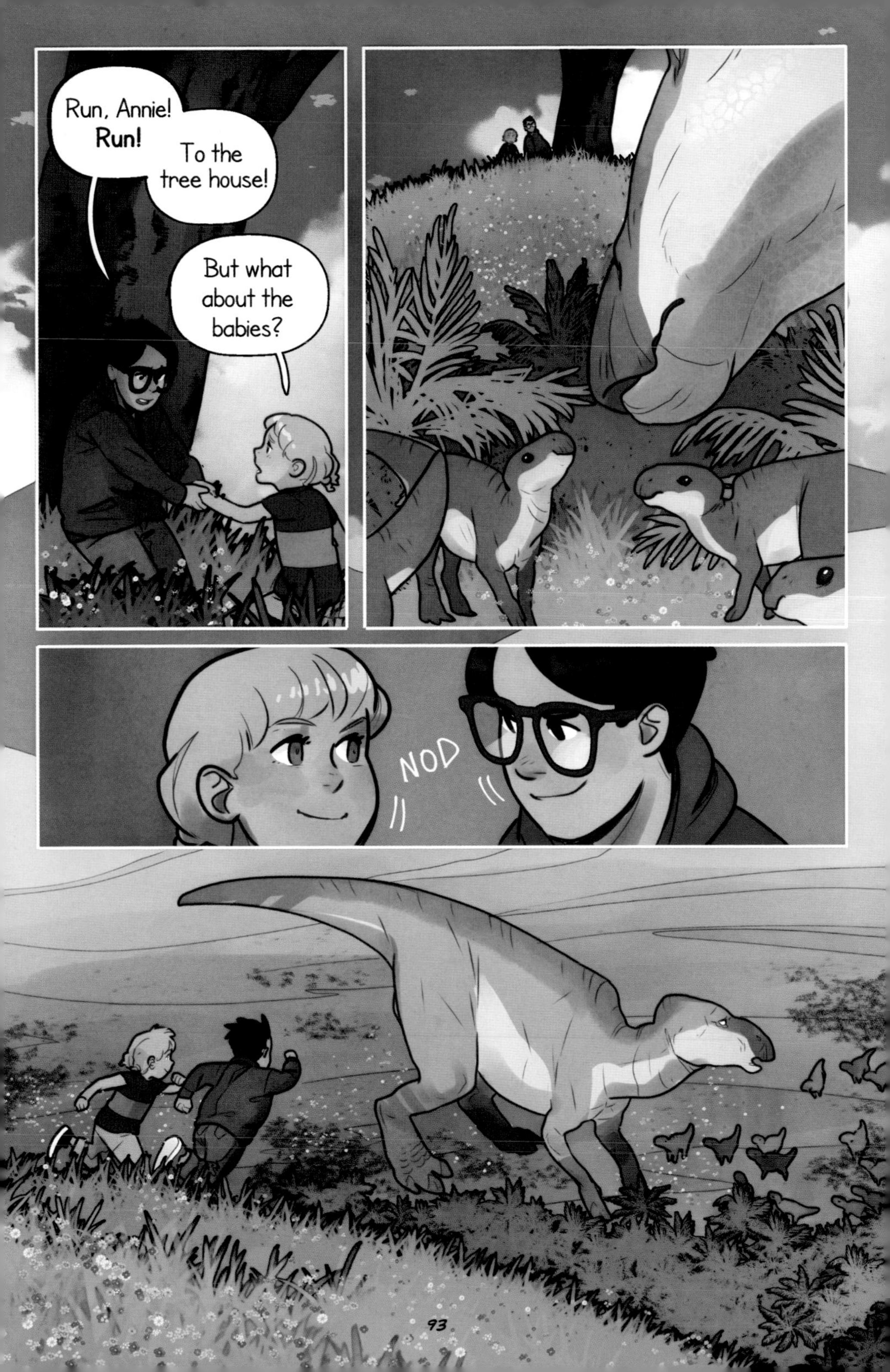
Run, Annie! Run!
To the tree house!
But what about the babies?
NOD

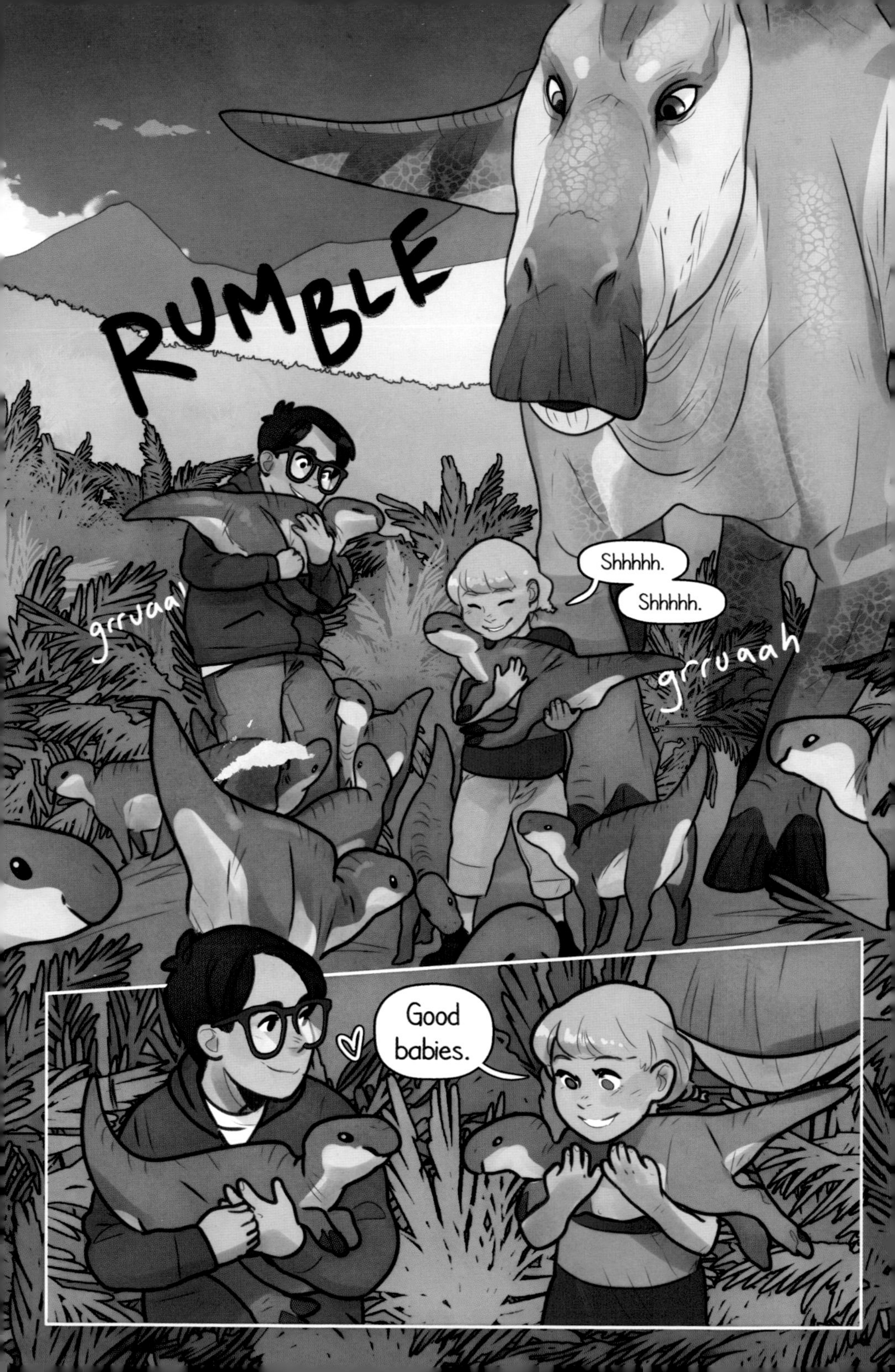
RUMBLE
grruaa
Shhhhh.
Shhhhh.
grruaah
Good babies.

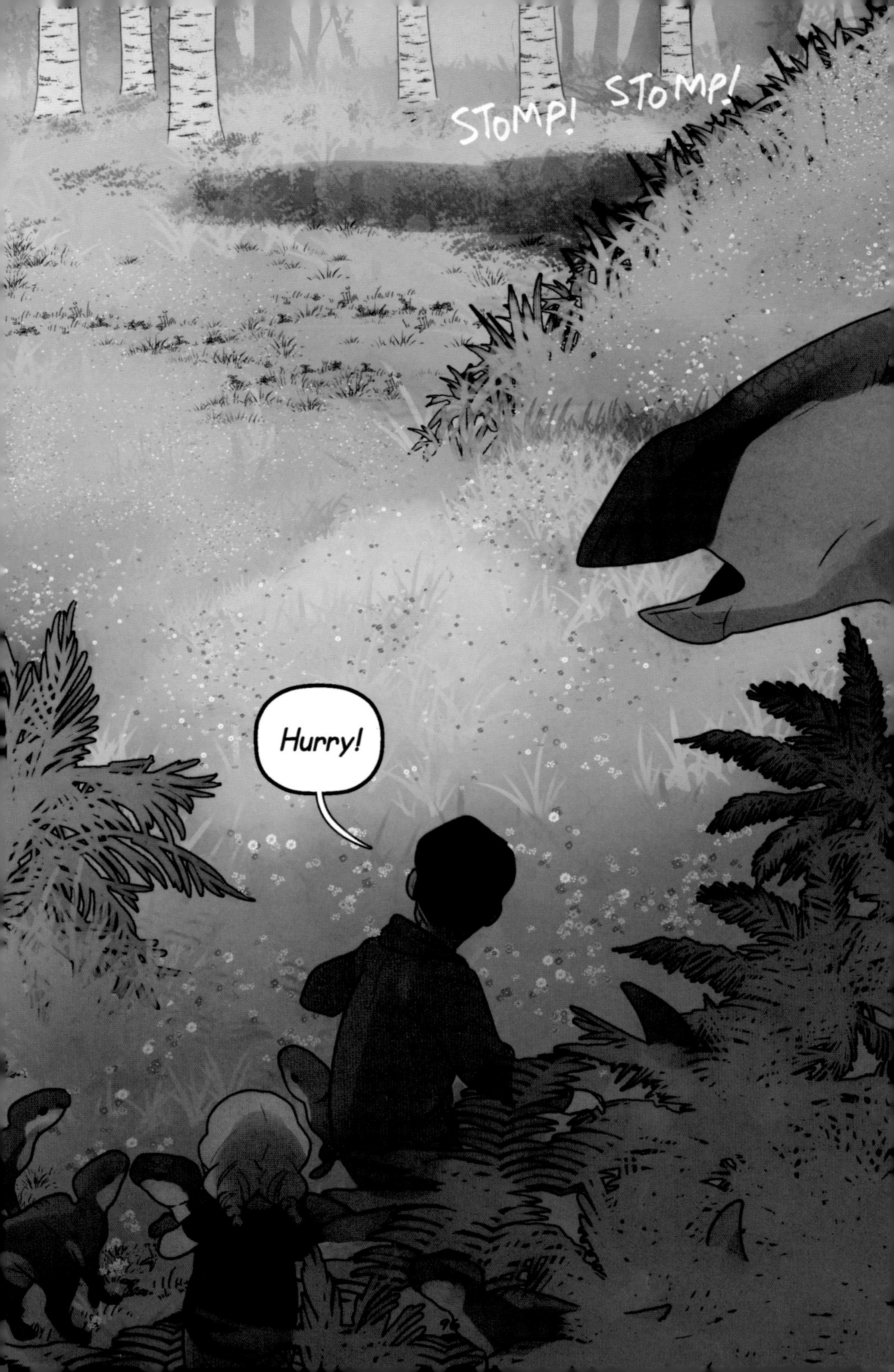
STOMP! STOMP!
Hurry!

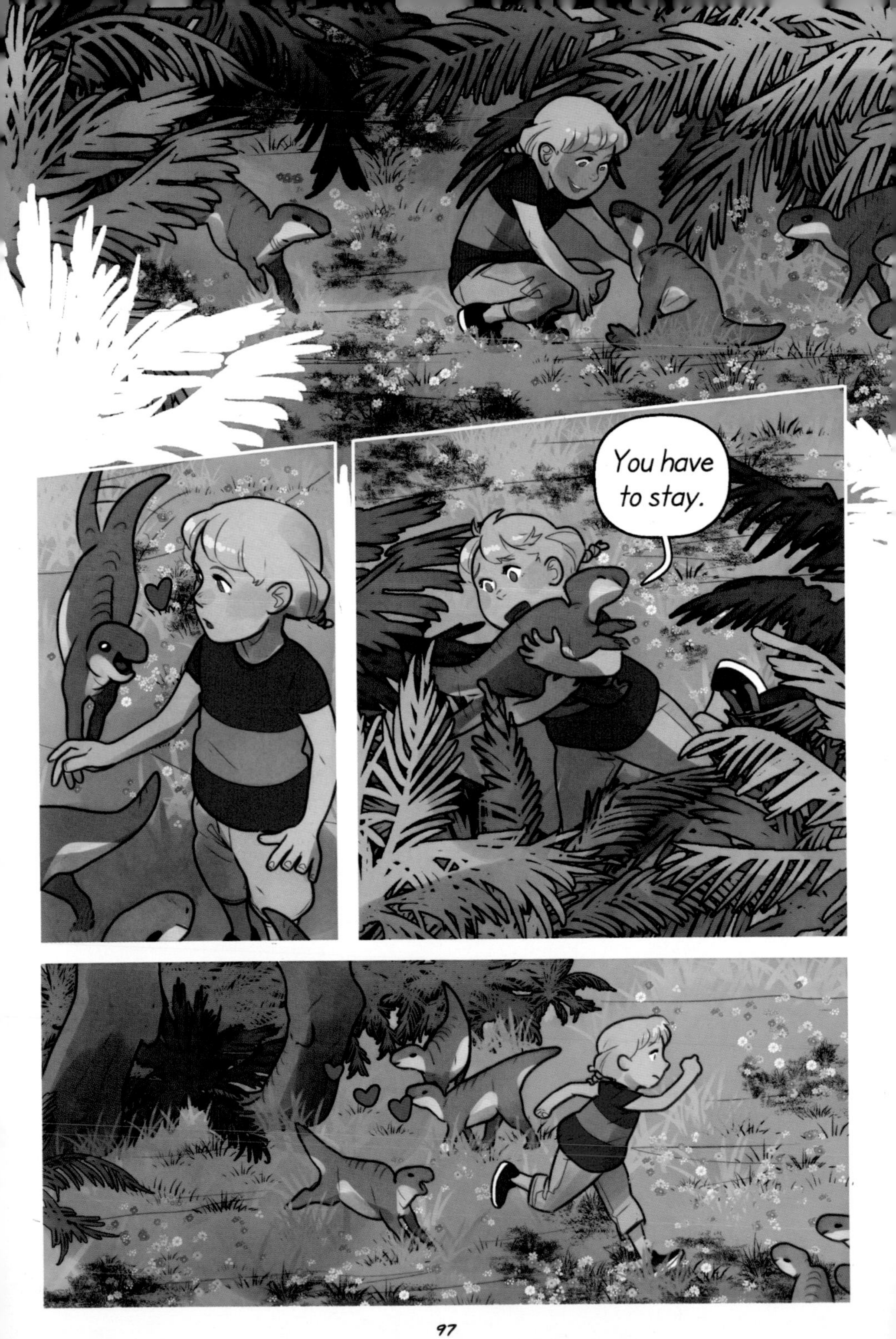
You have to stay.

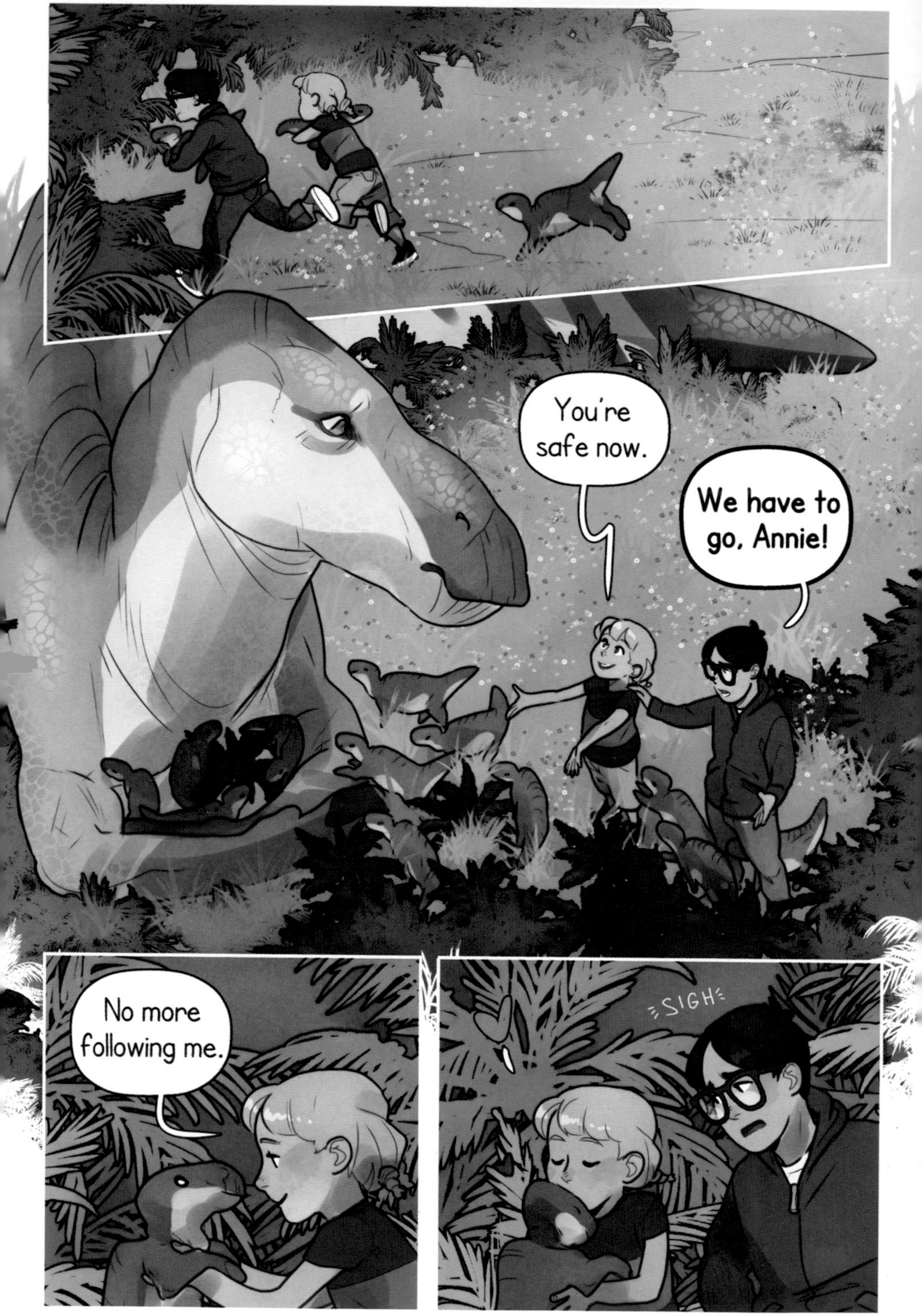
You're safe now.
We have to go, Annie!
No more following me.
SIGH

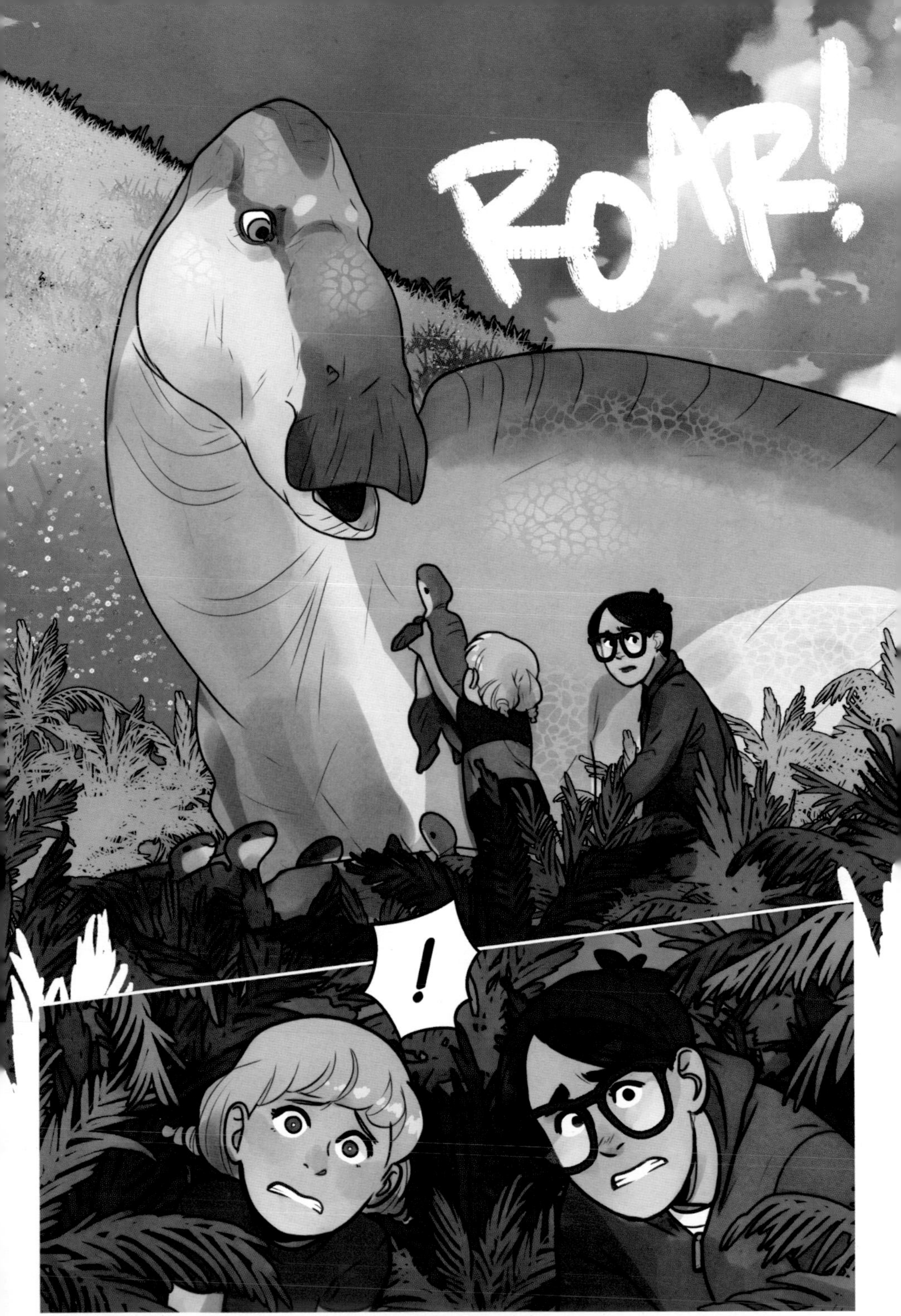
ROAR!
!

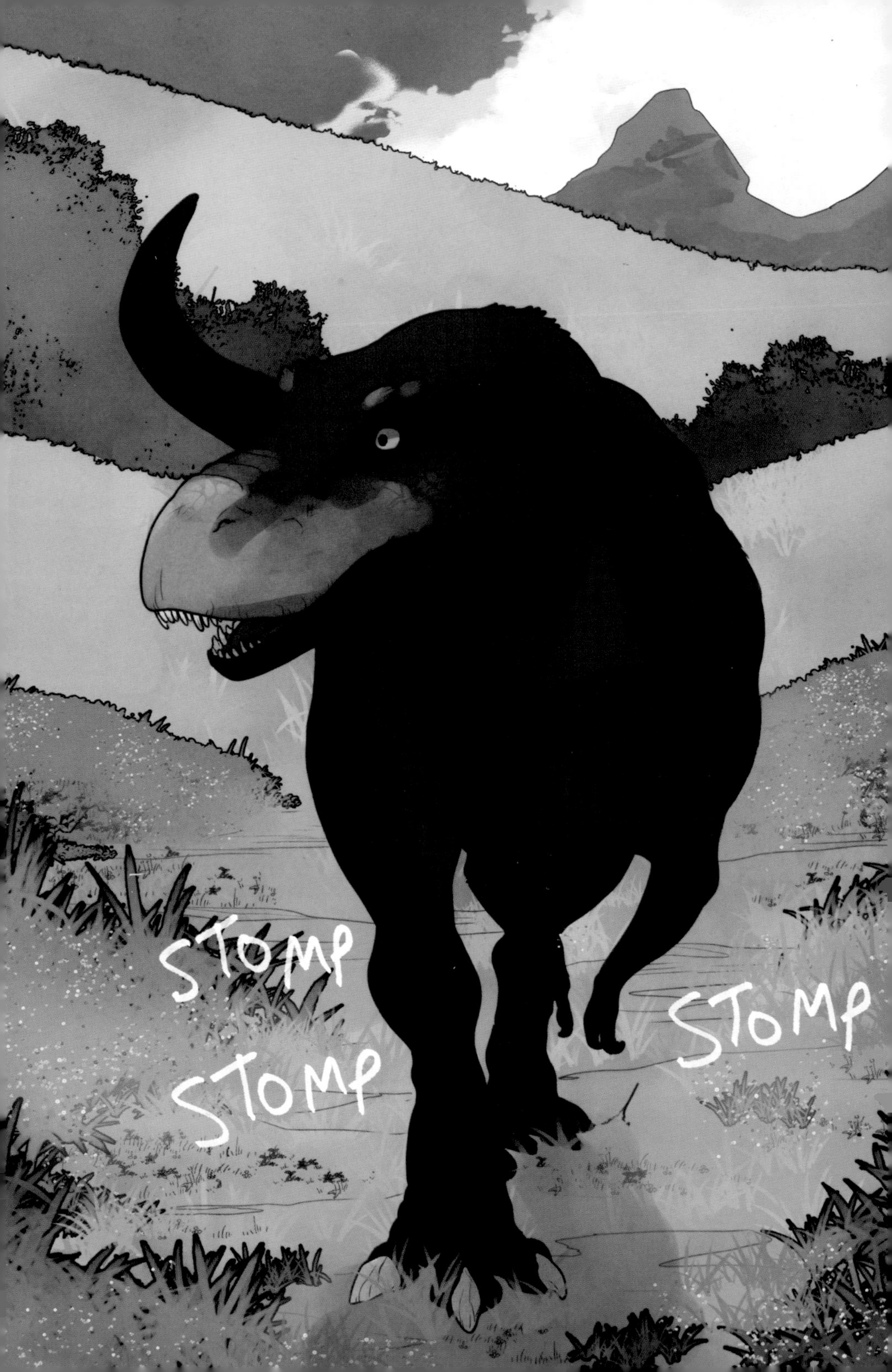
STOMP
STOMP
STOMP

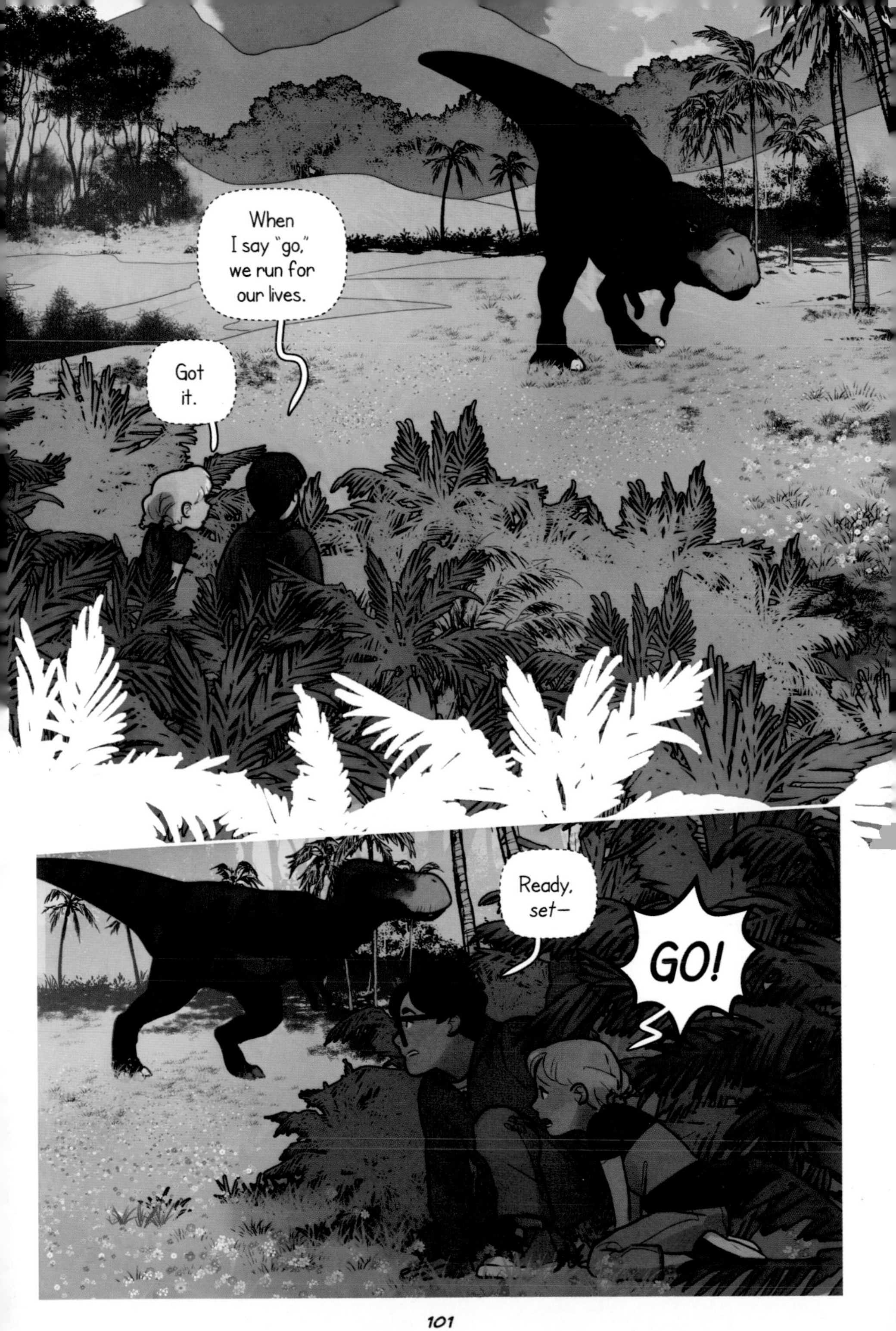
When I say "go," we run for our lives.
Got it.
Ready, set—
GO!

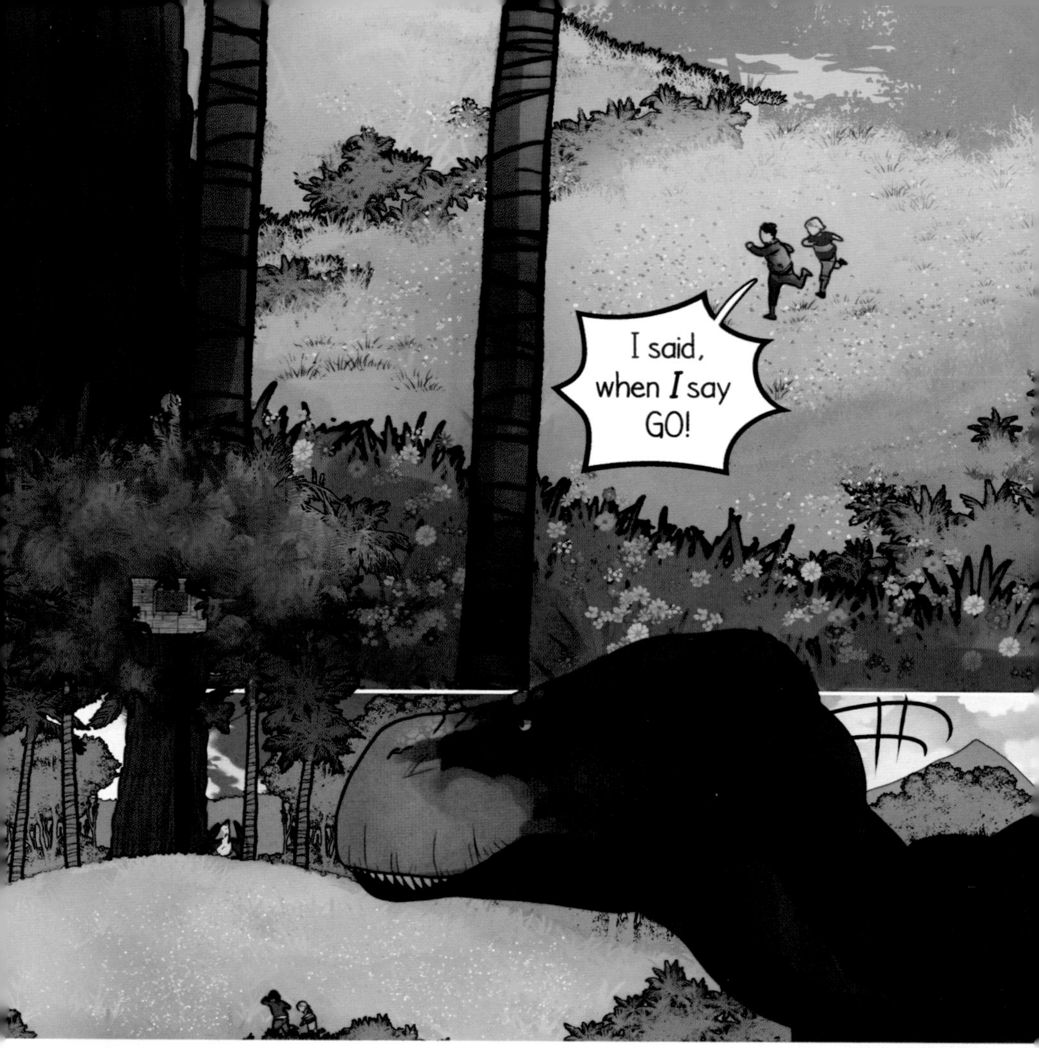
I said, when *I* say GO!

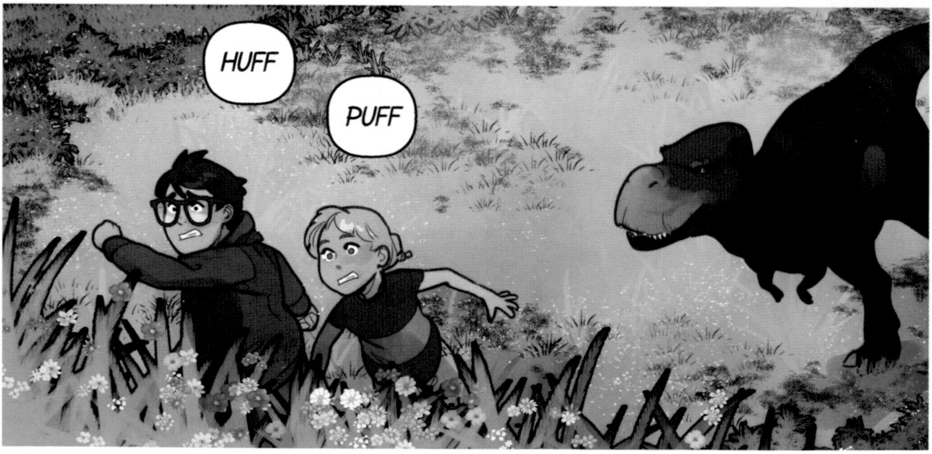
HUFF
PUFF

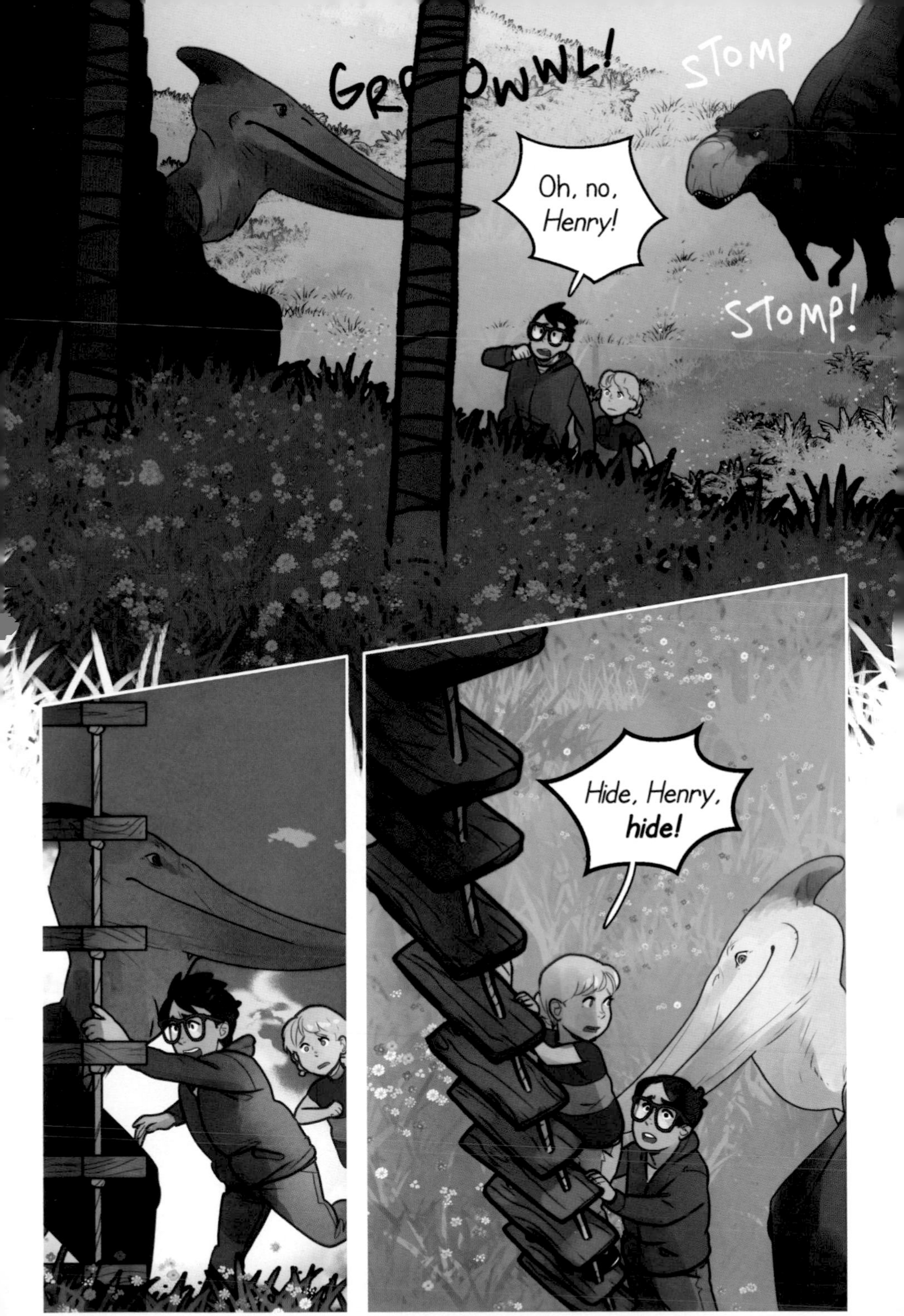
GRR OWWL!
STOMP
Oh, no, Henry!
STOMP!
Hide, Henry, **hide!**

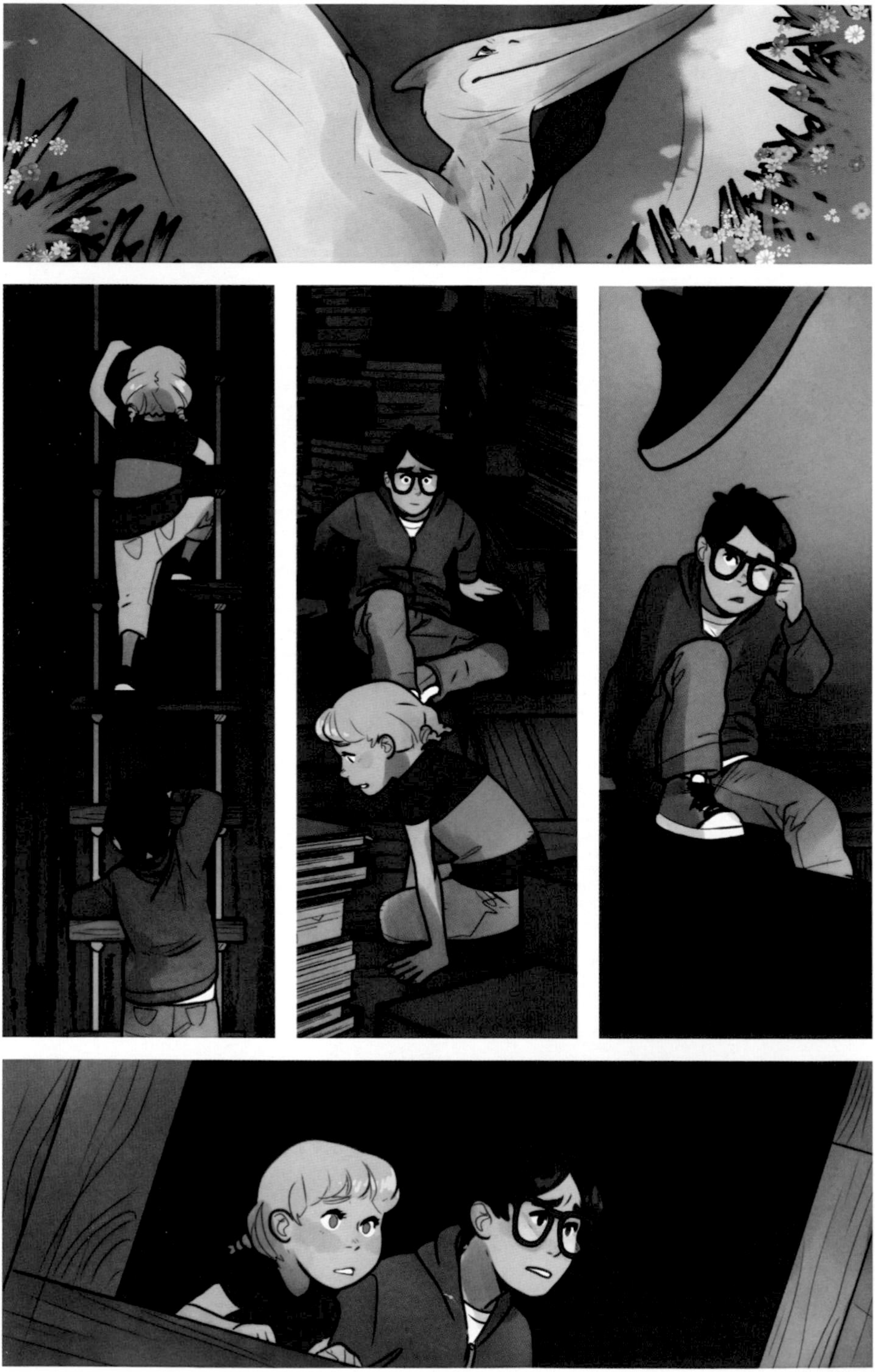

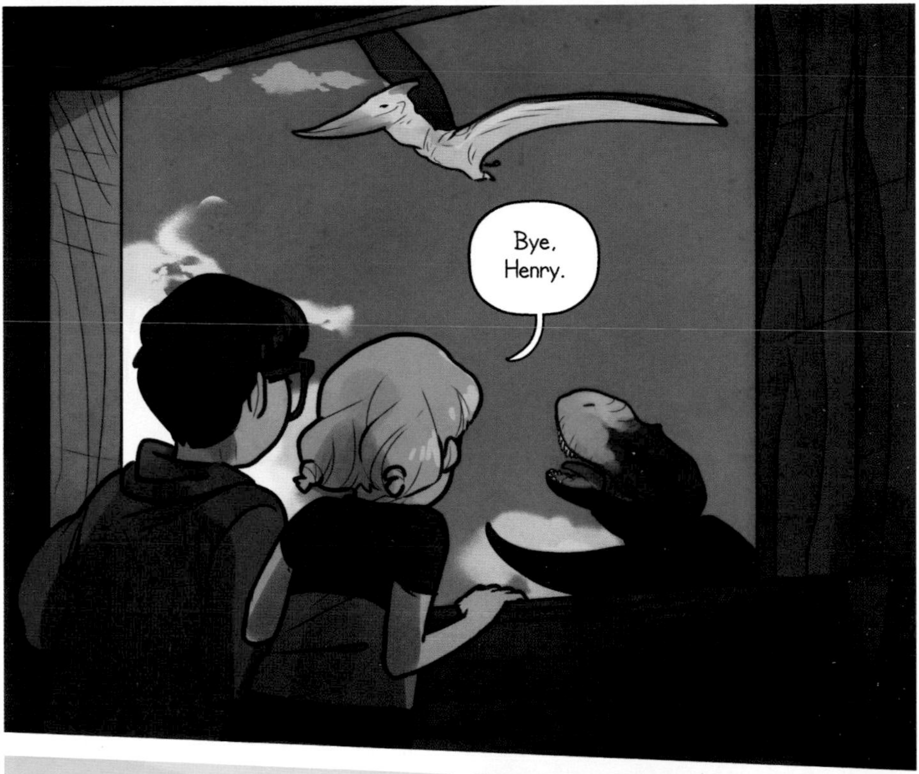
Bye,
Henry.

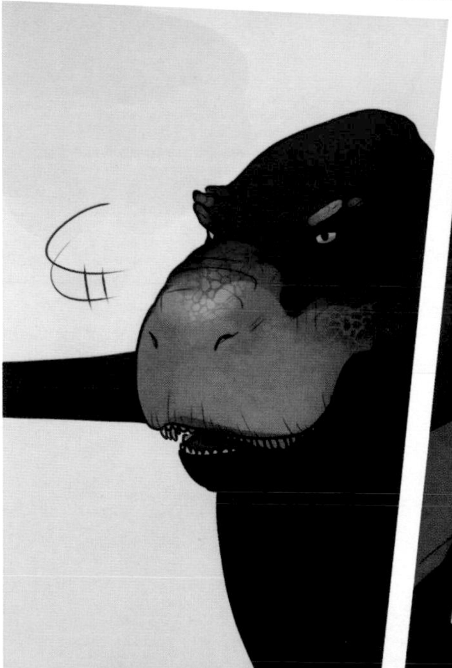

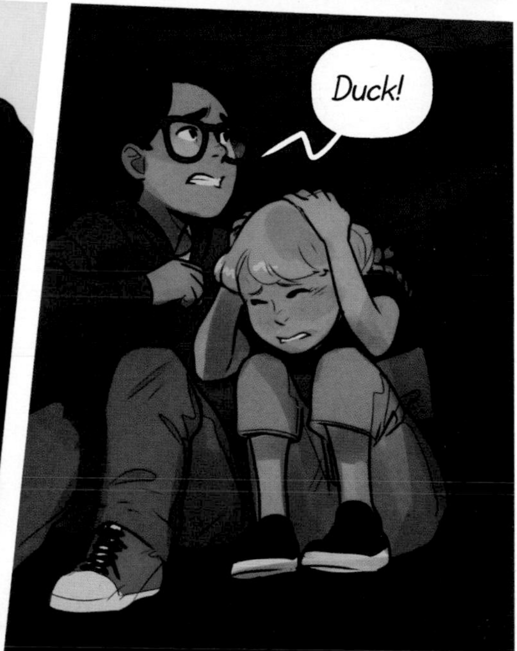
Duck!

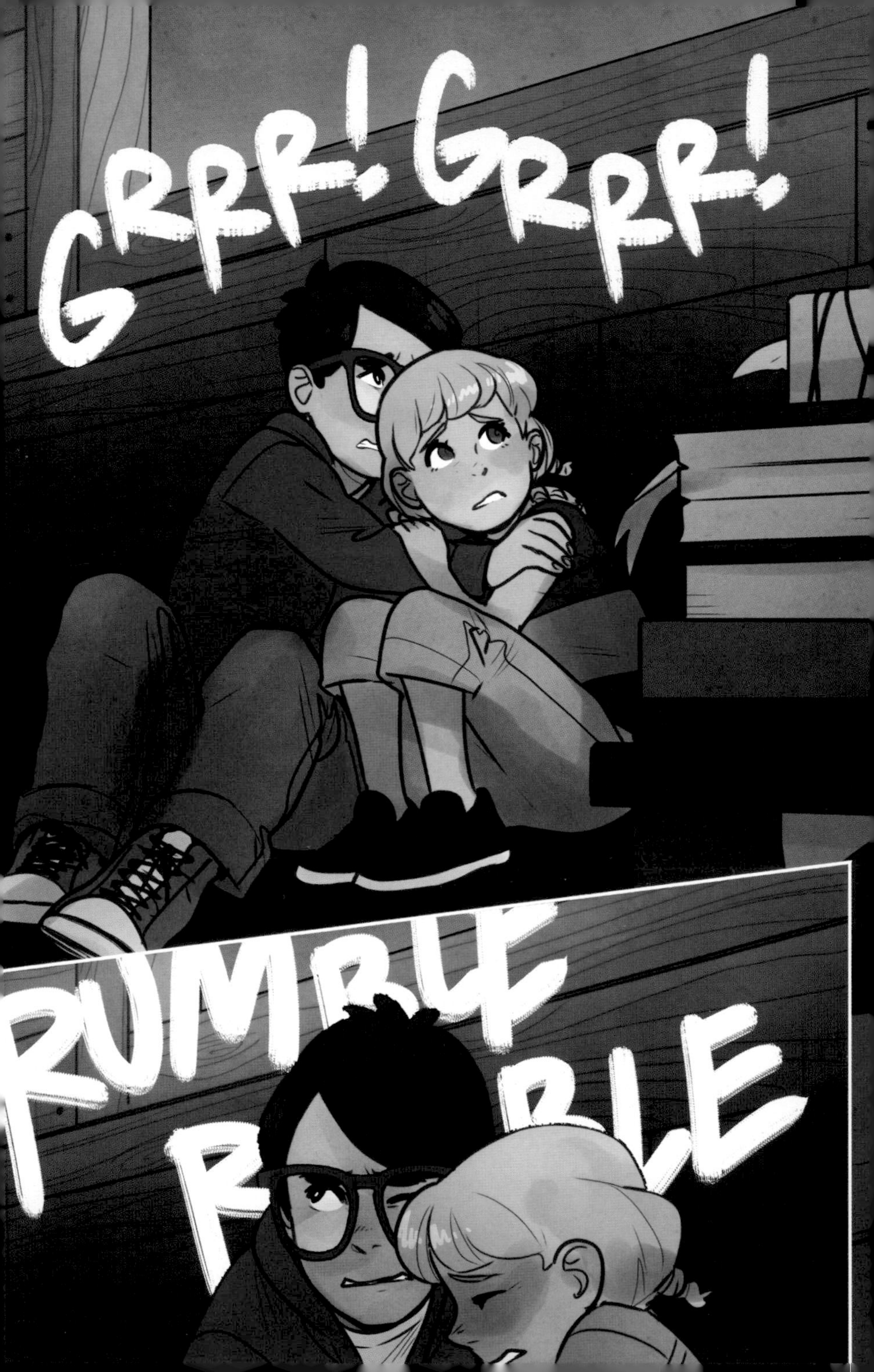
GRRR! GRRR!
RUMBLE RUMBLE

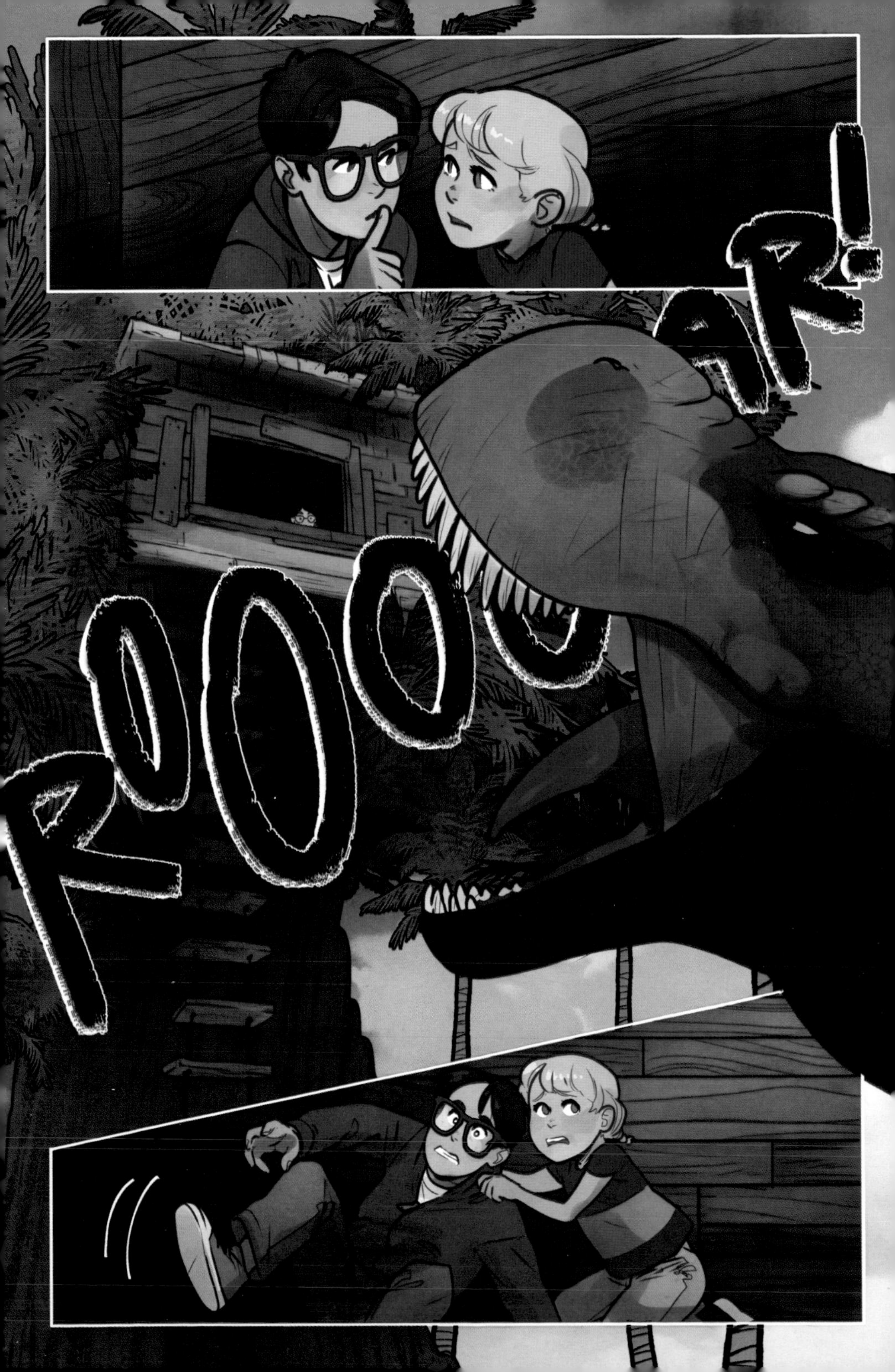
ROOOOAR!

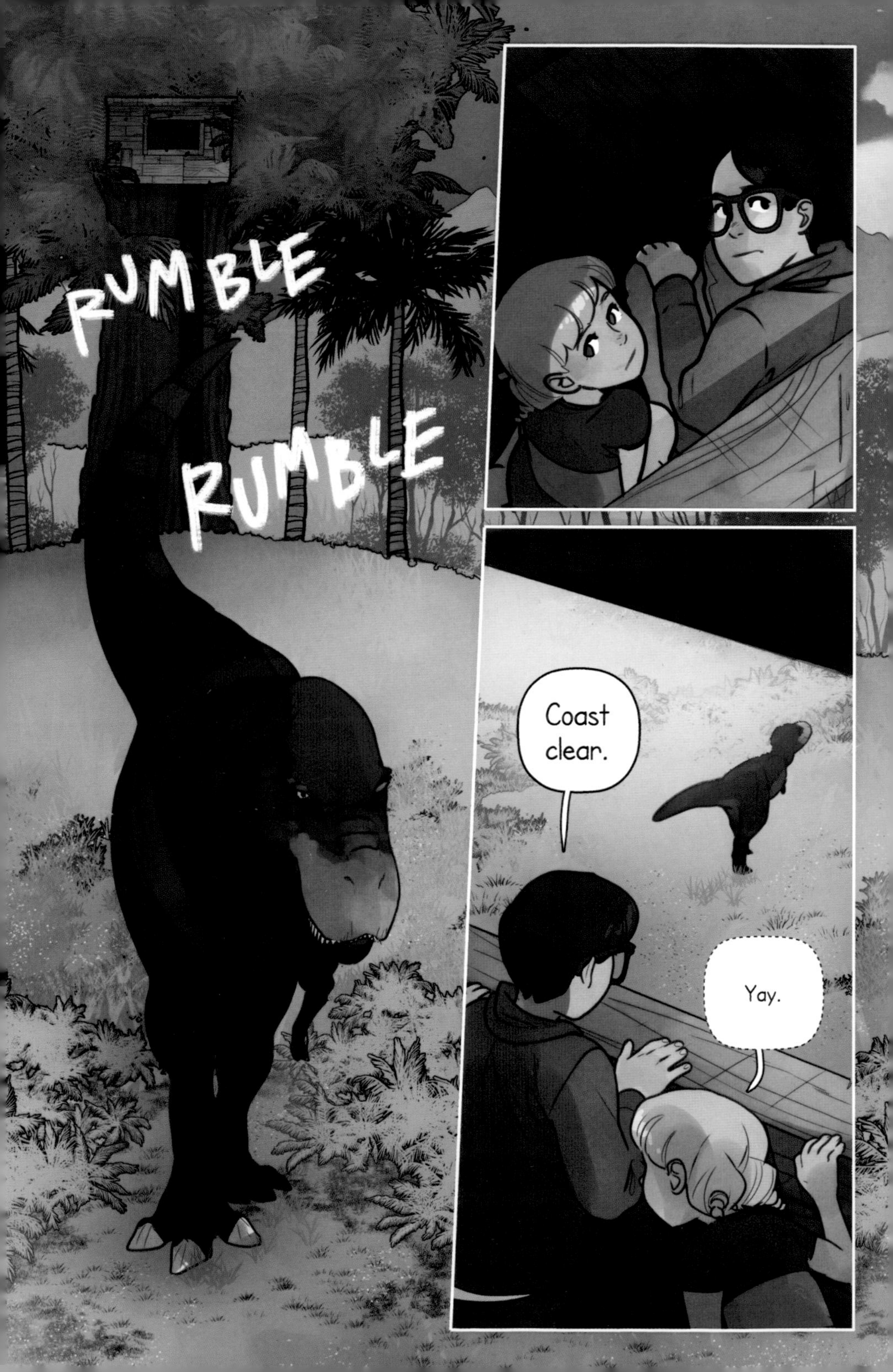
RUMBLE
RUMBLE
Coast clear.
Yay.

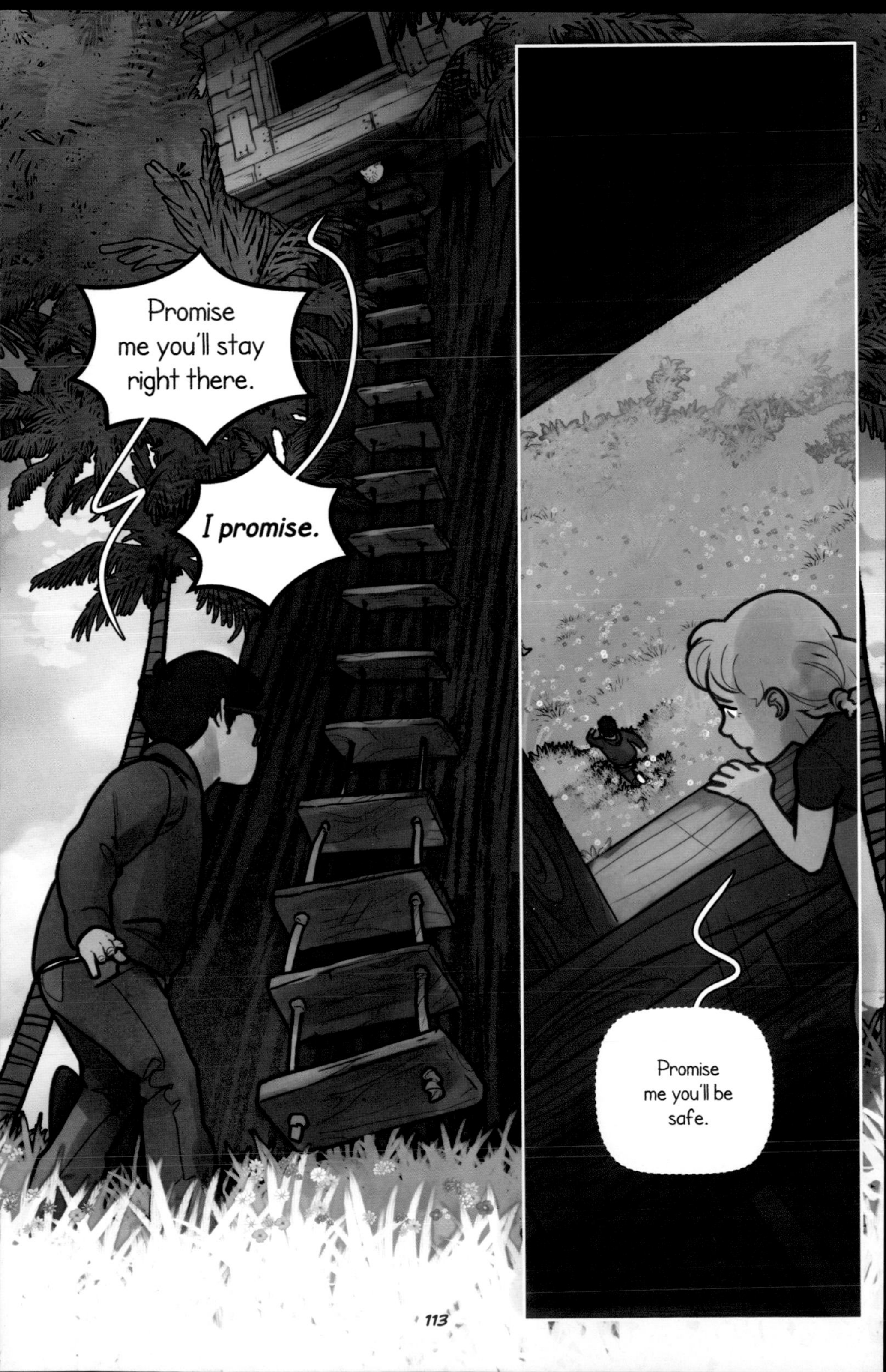
Promise me you'll stay right there.
I promise.
Promise me you'll be safe.

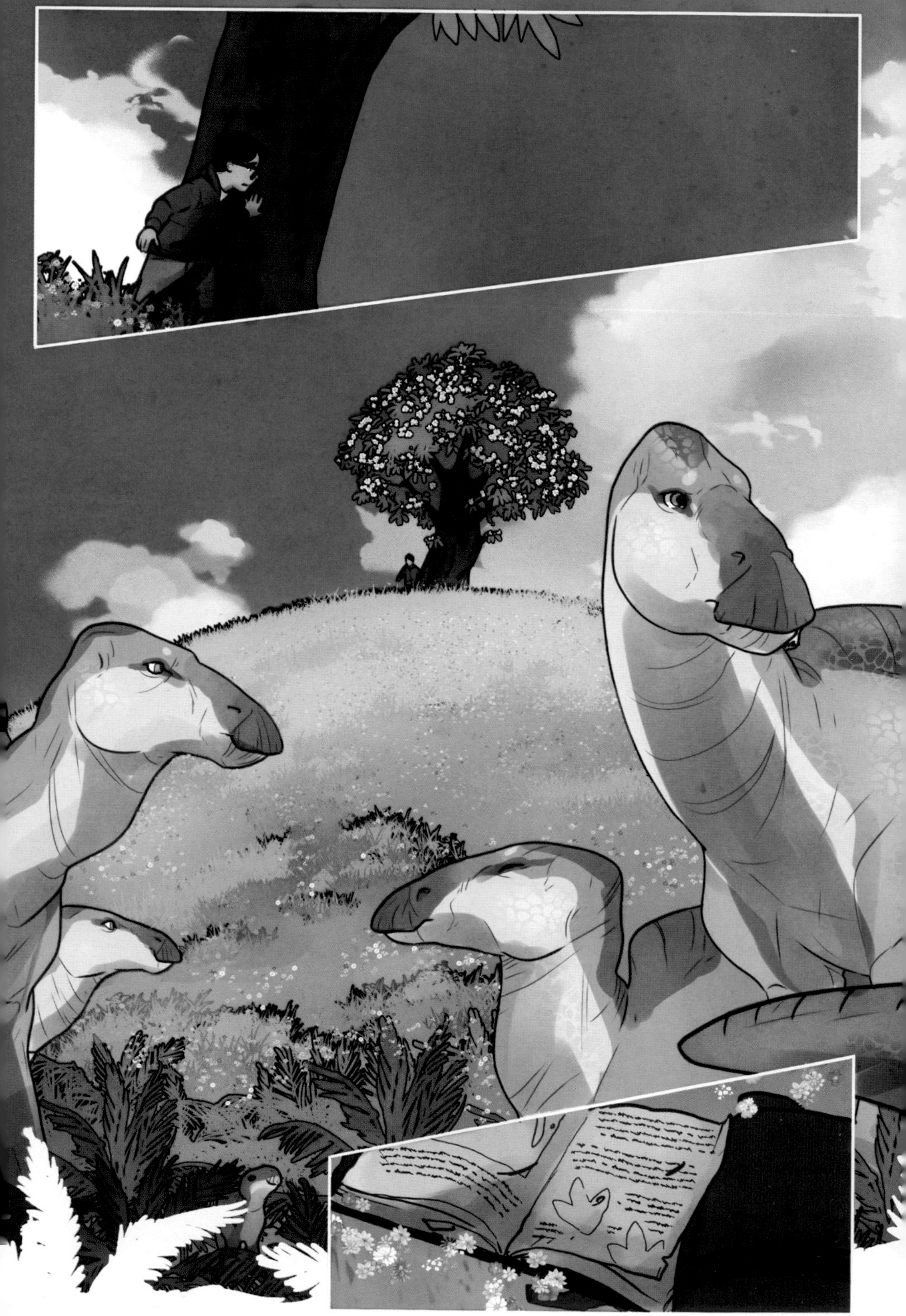

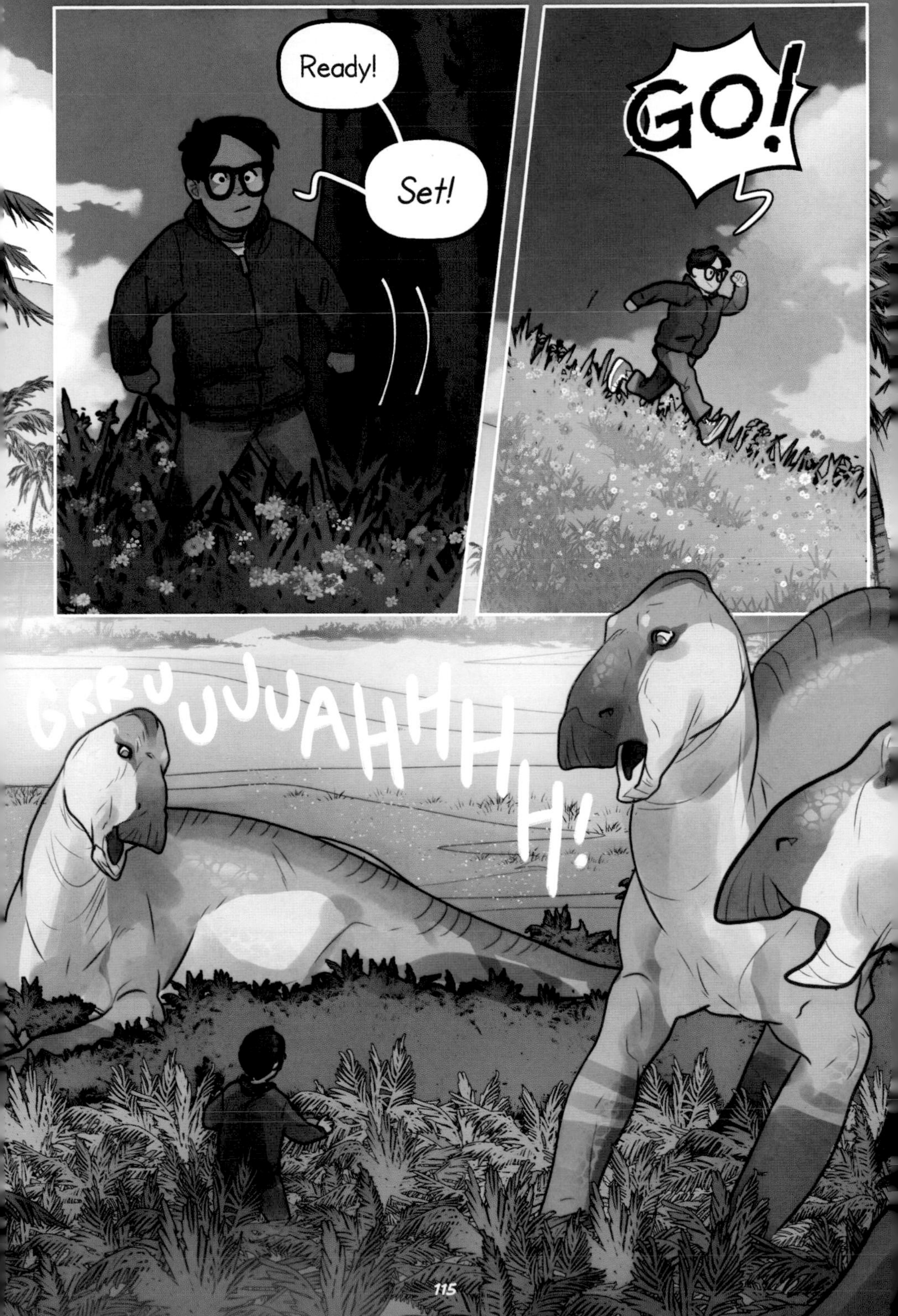
Ready!
Set!
GO!
GRRUUUUAHHHHH!

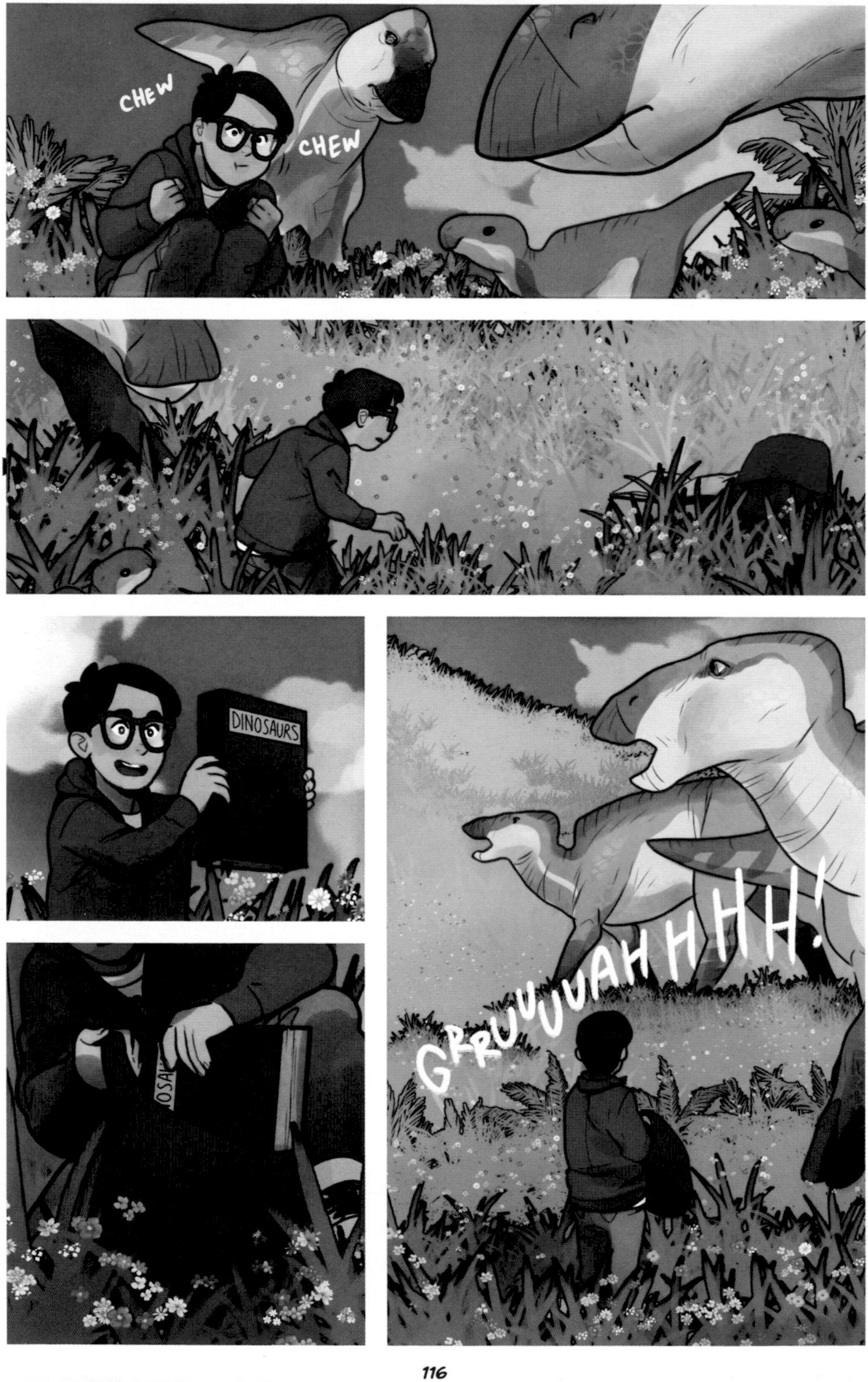
CHEW
CHEW
DINOSAURS
OSAU
GRRUUUUAHHHHH!

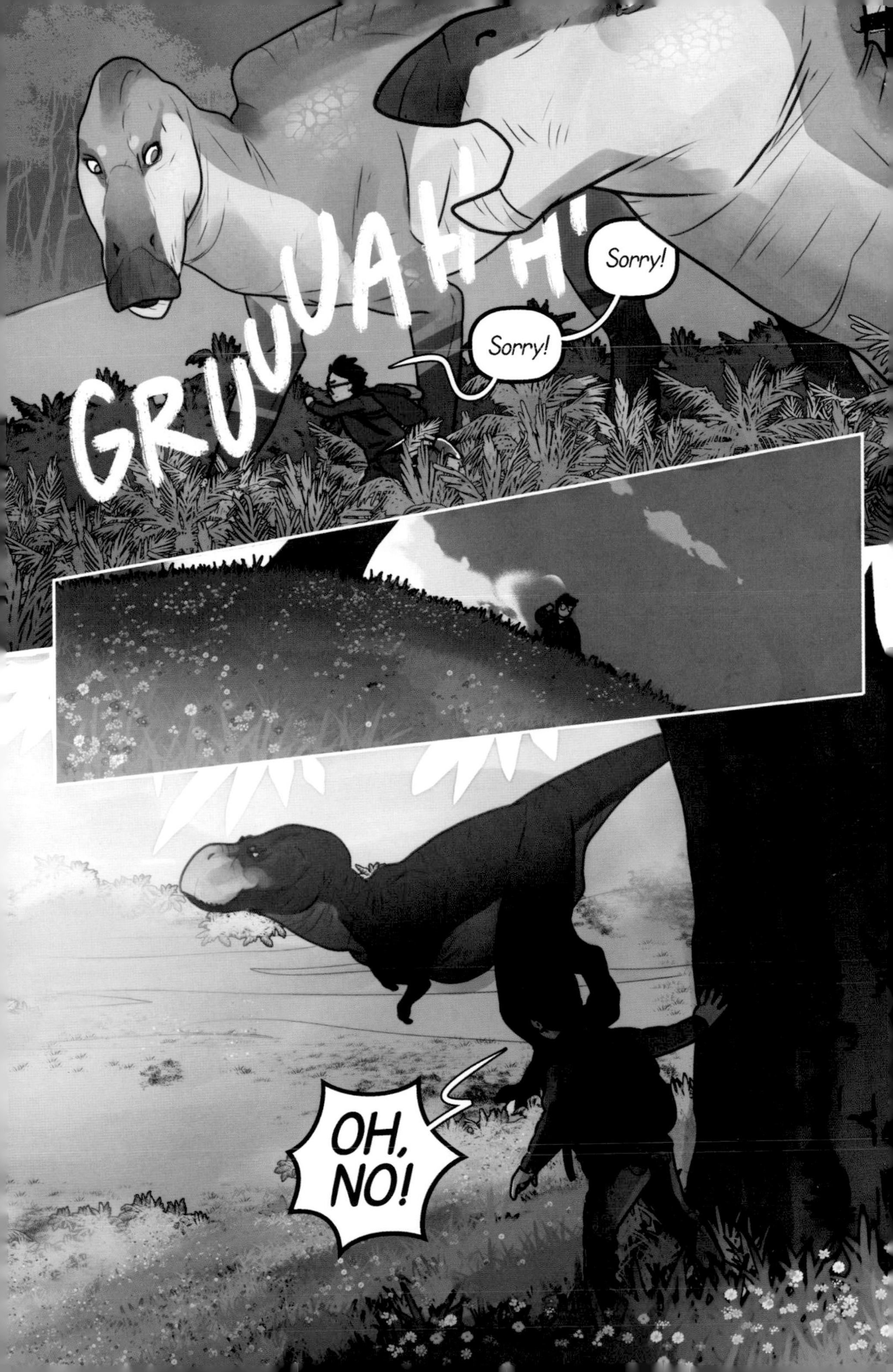
GRUUUAHH!
Sorry!
Sorry!
OH, NO!

CHAPTER EIGHT
A Giant Shadow

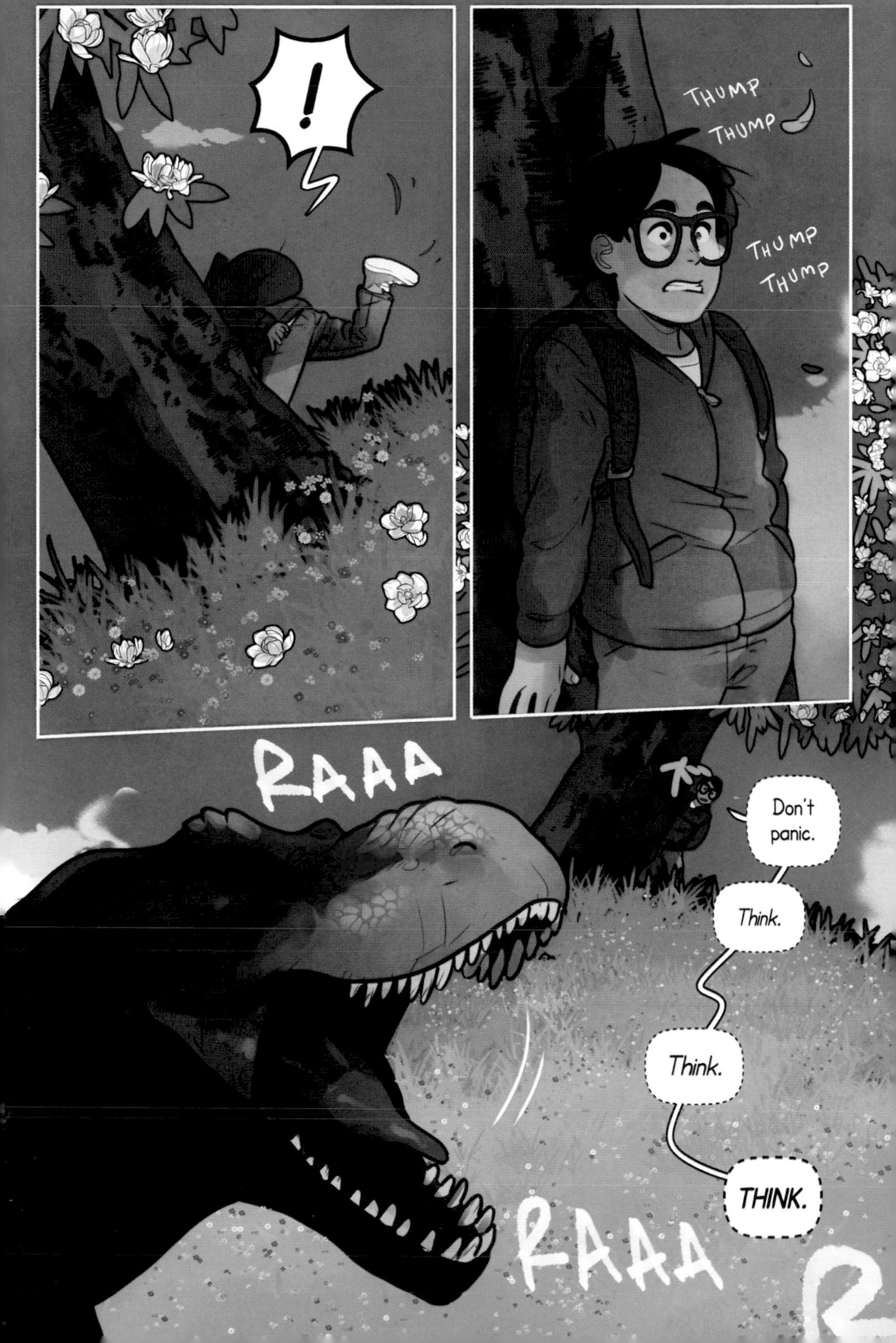
!
THUMP
THUMP
THUMP
THUMP
RAAA
Don't panic.
Think.
Think.
THINK.
RAAA

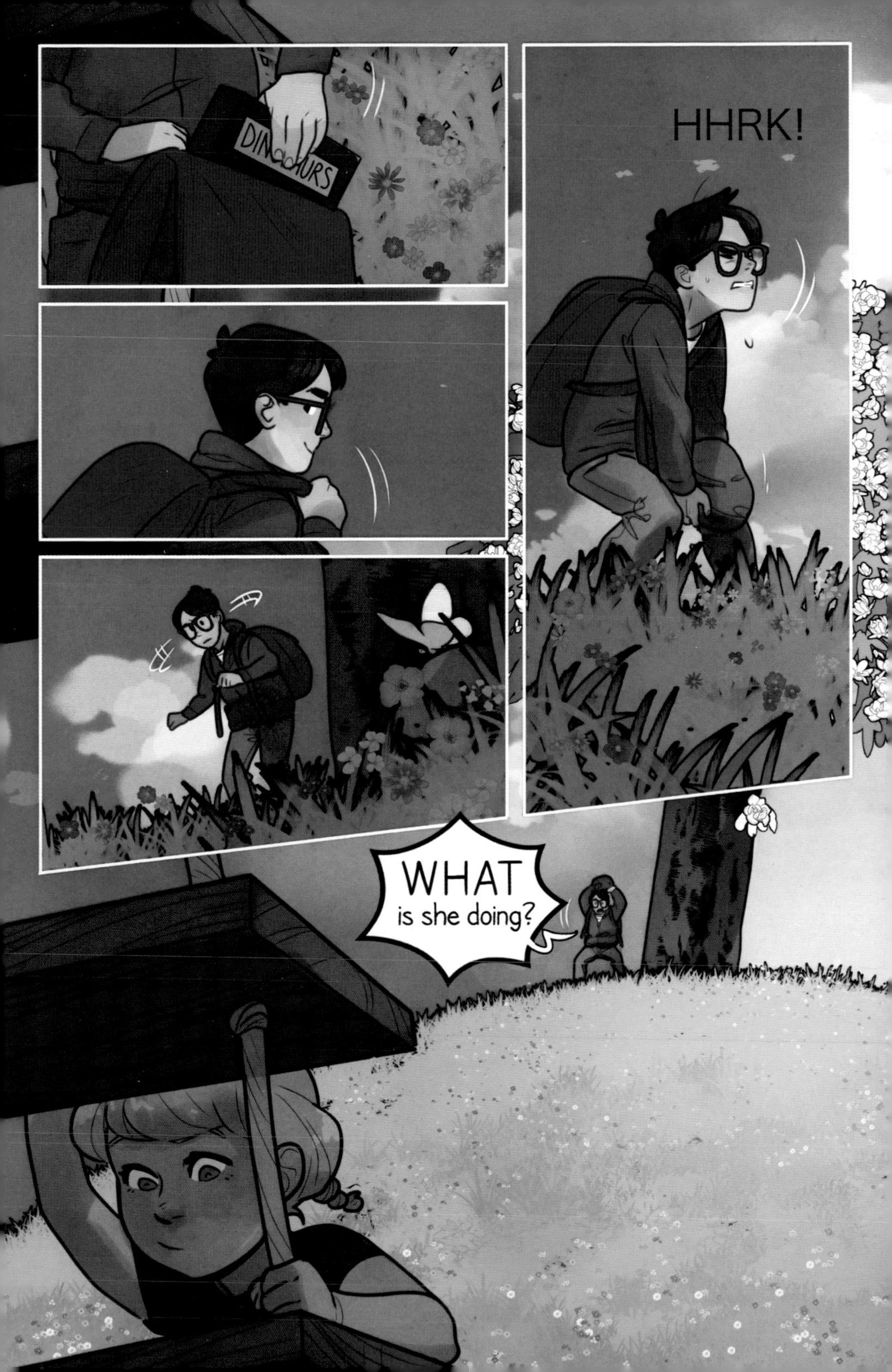
DINOSAURS
HHRK!
WHAT is she doing?

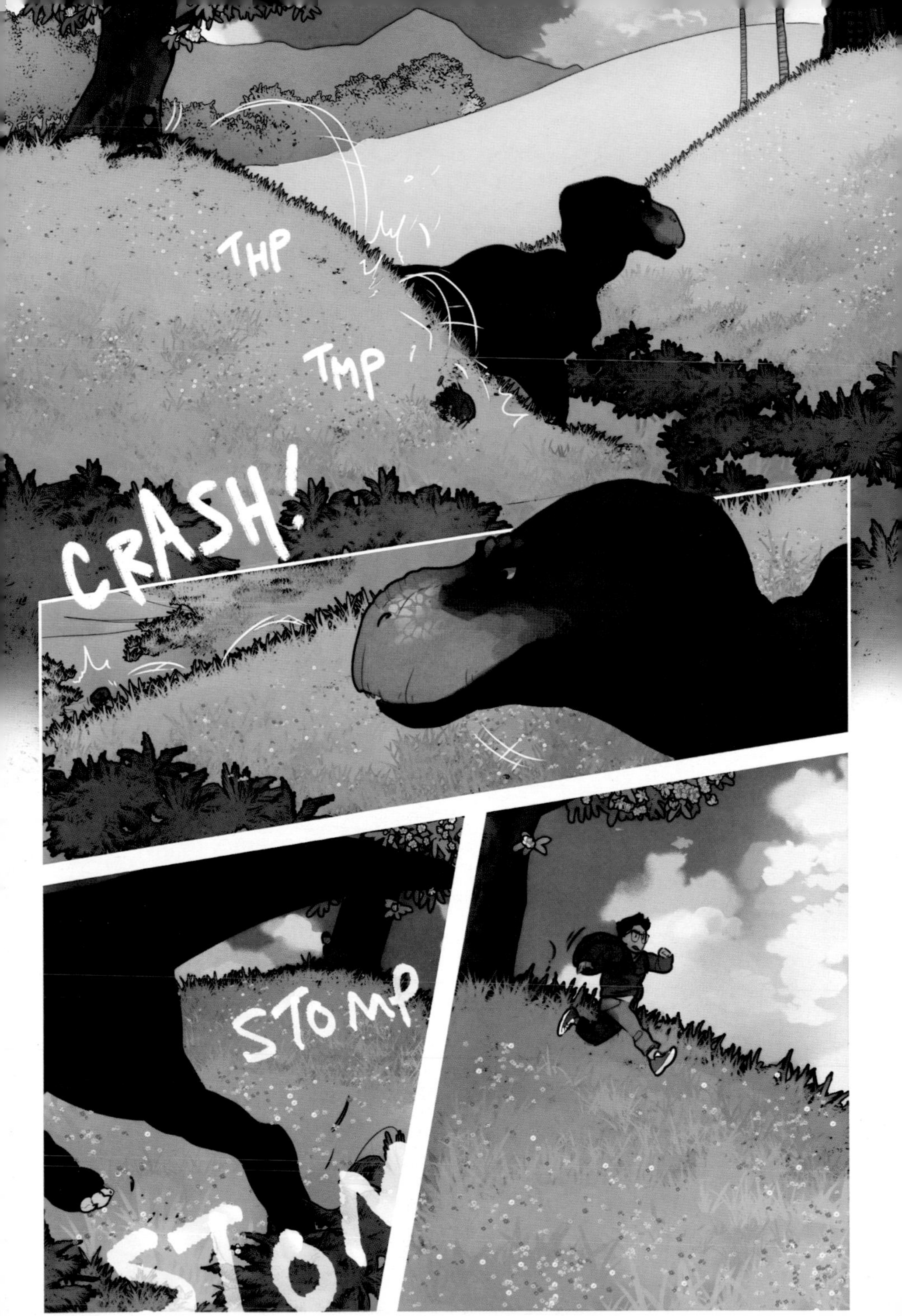
THP
TMP
CRASH!
STOMP
STOM

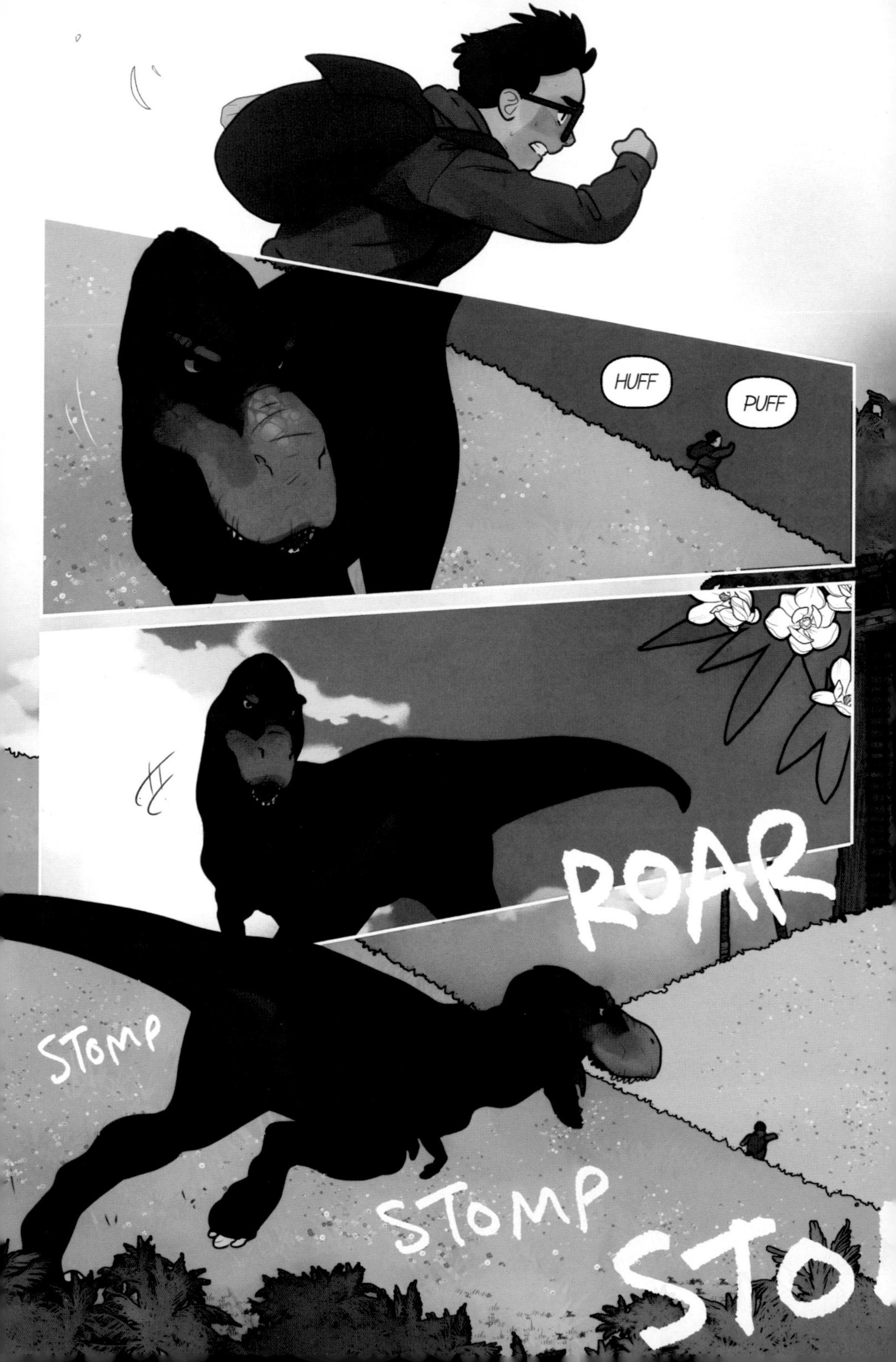
HUFF
PUFF
ROAR
STOMP
STOMP

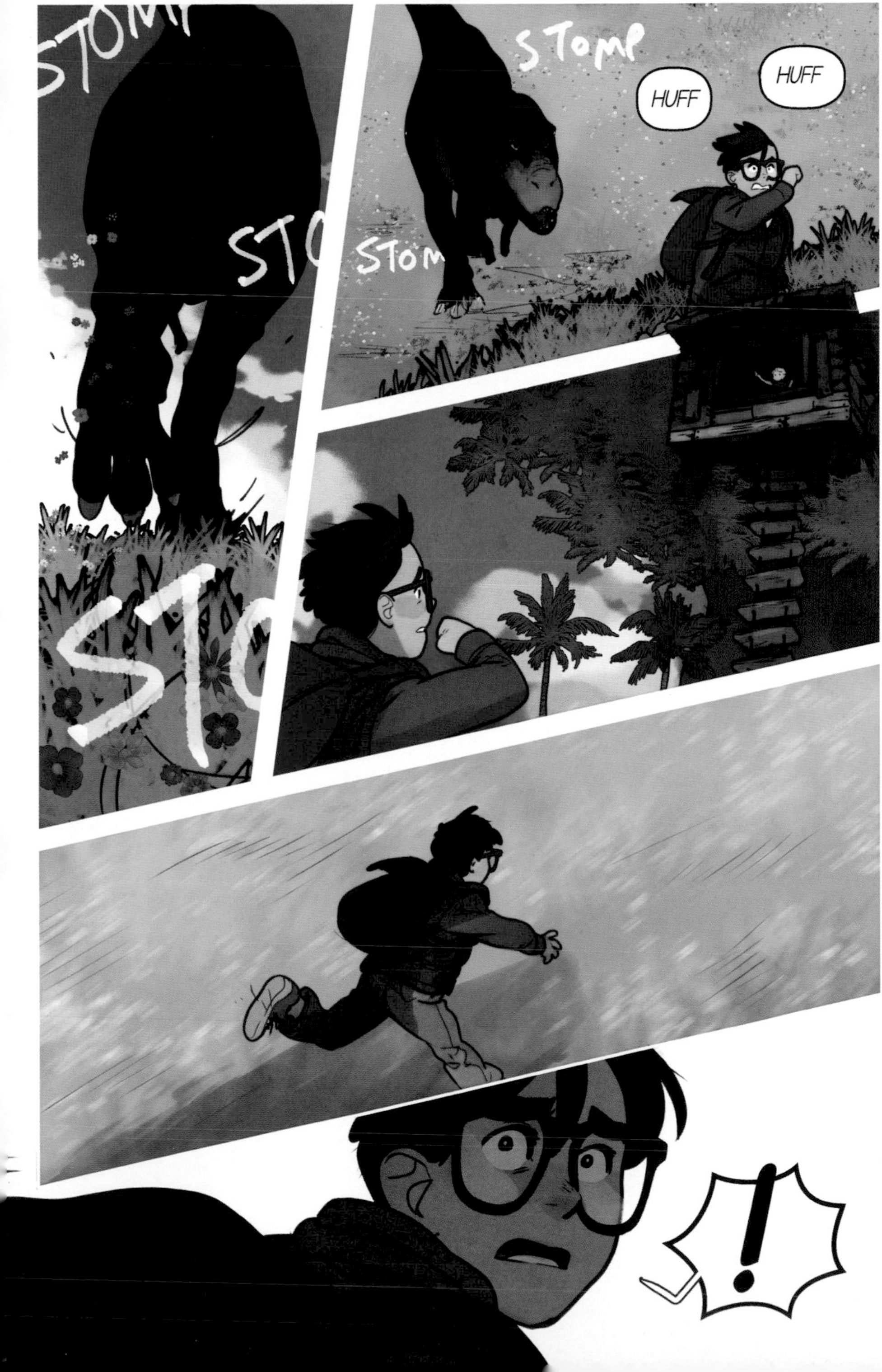
STOMP
STO
STO
STOM
STOMP
HUFF
HUFF
!

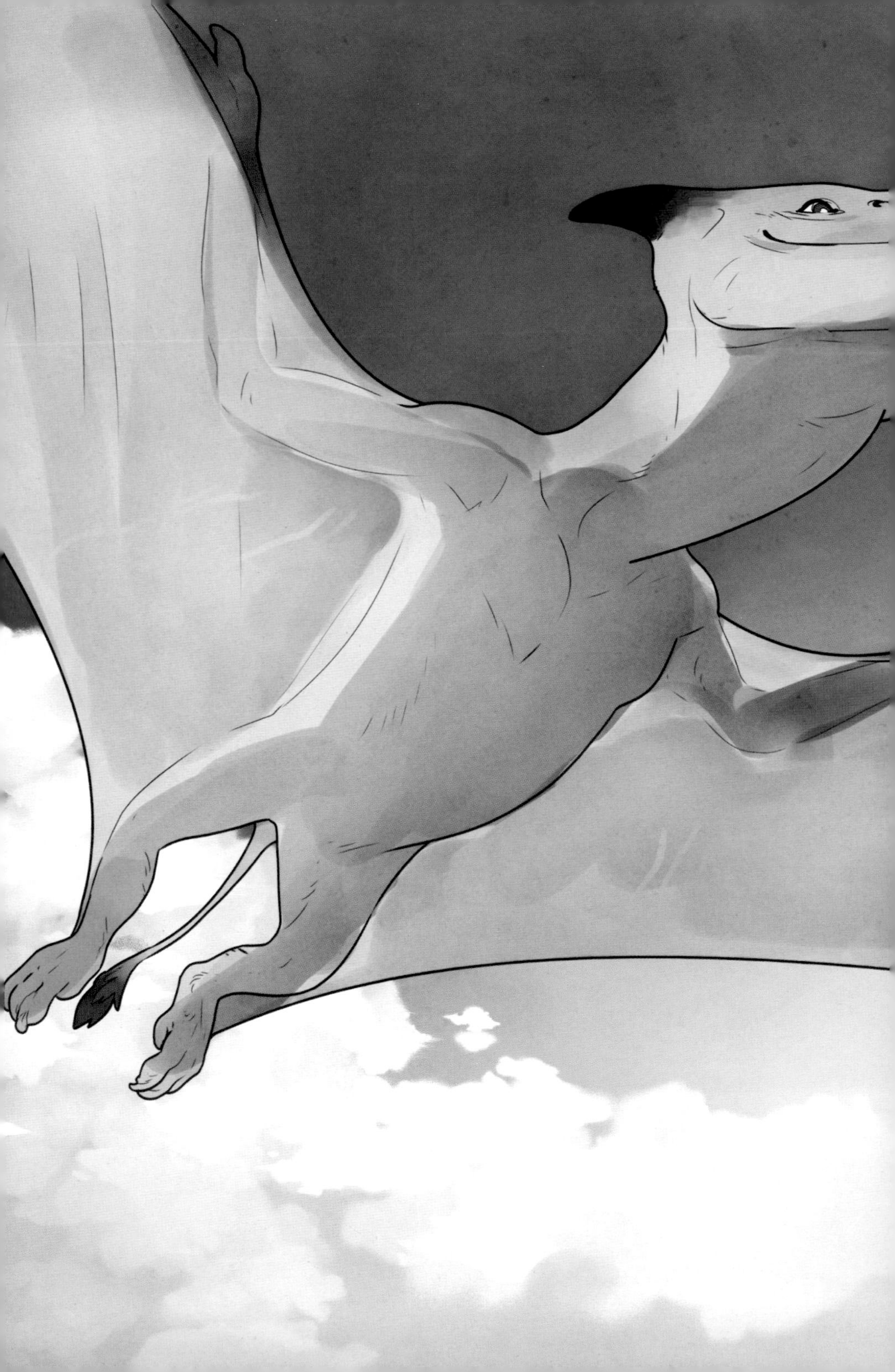

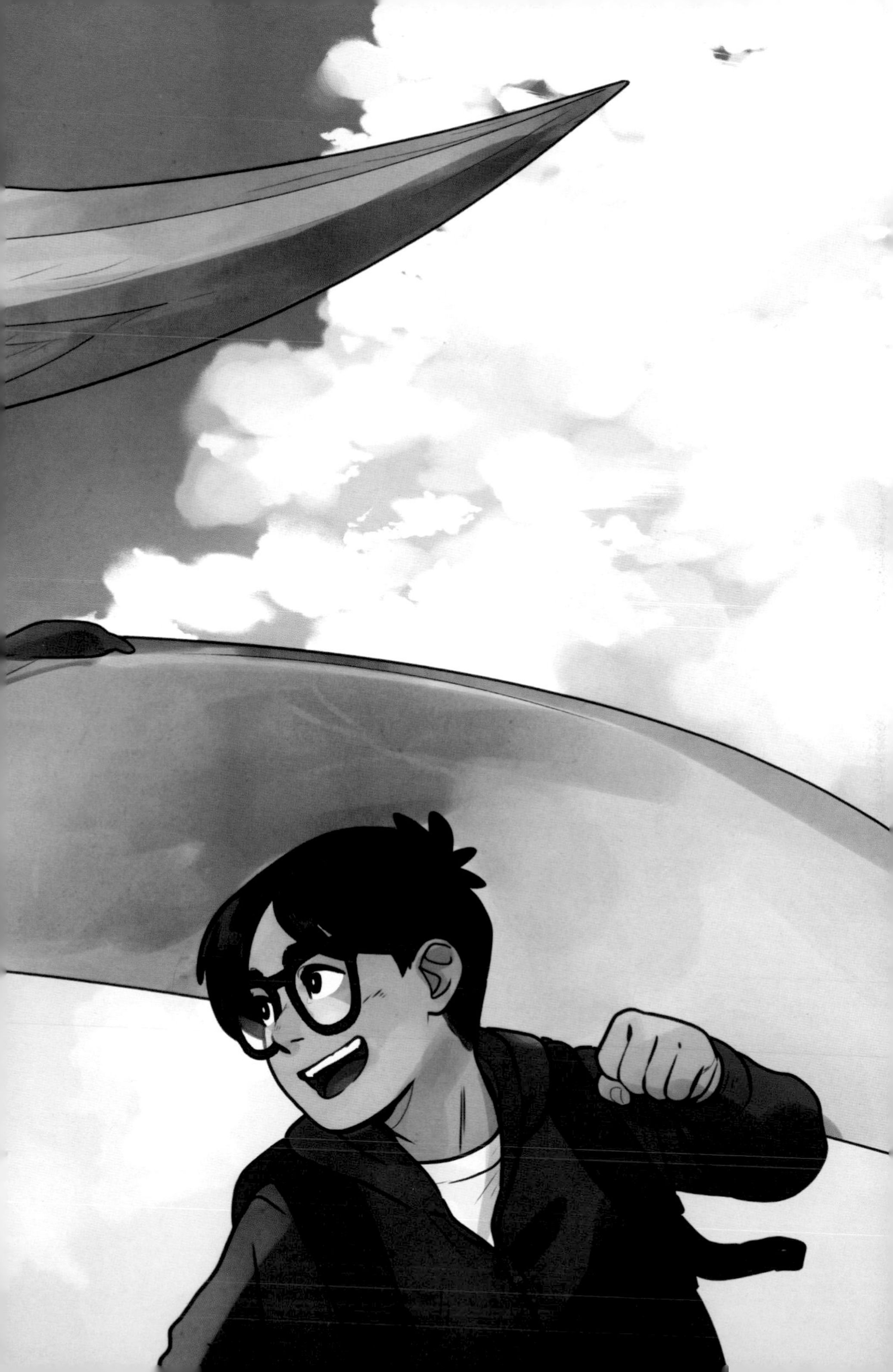

CHAPTER NINE

The Amazing Ride

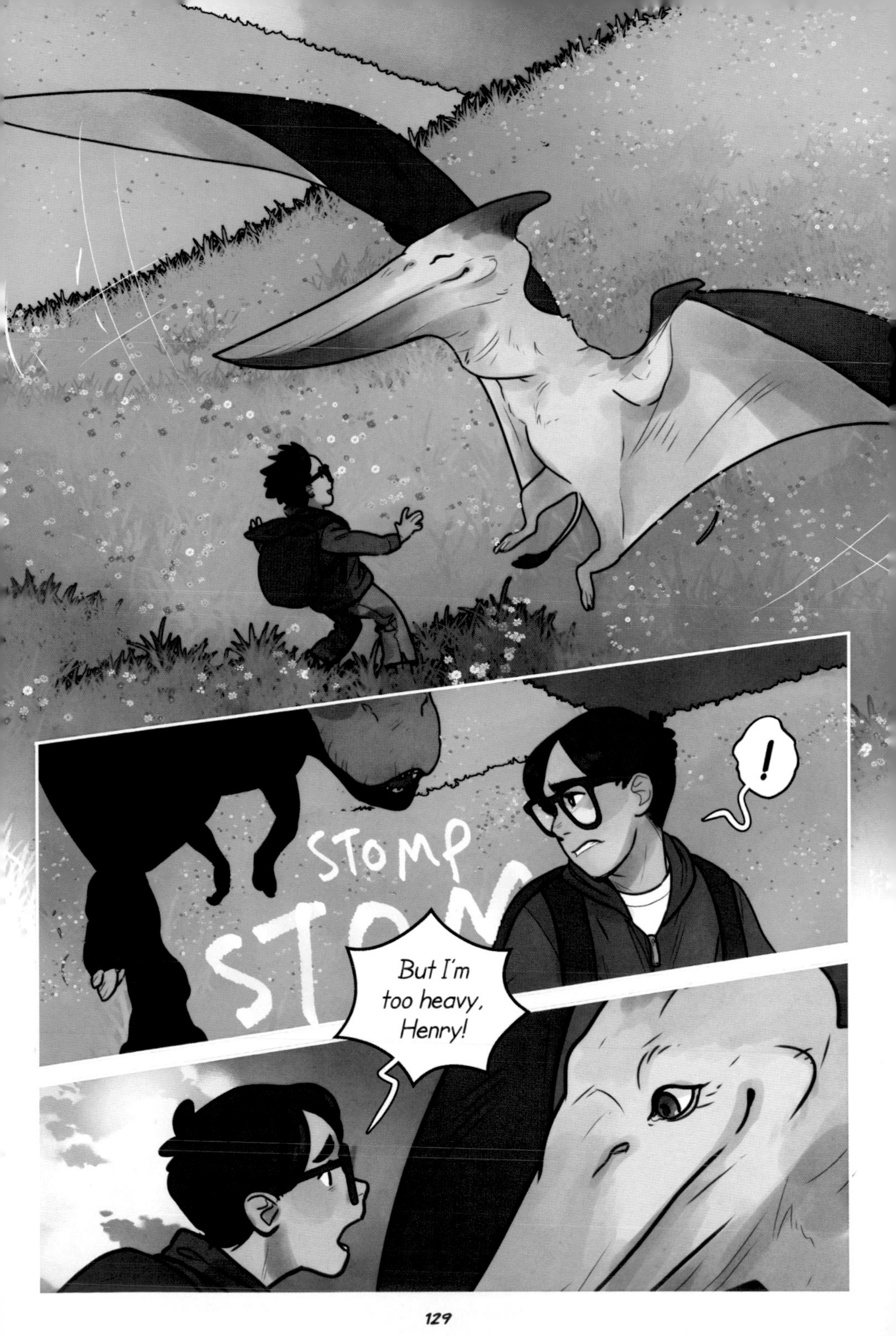

!
STOMP
STOMP
But I'm too heavy, Henry!

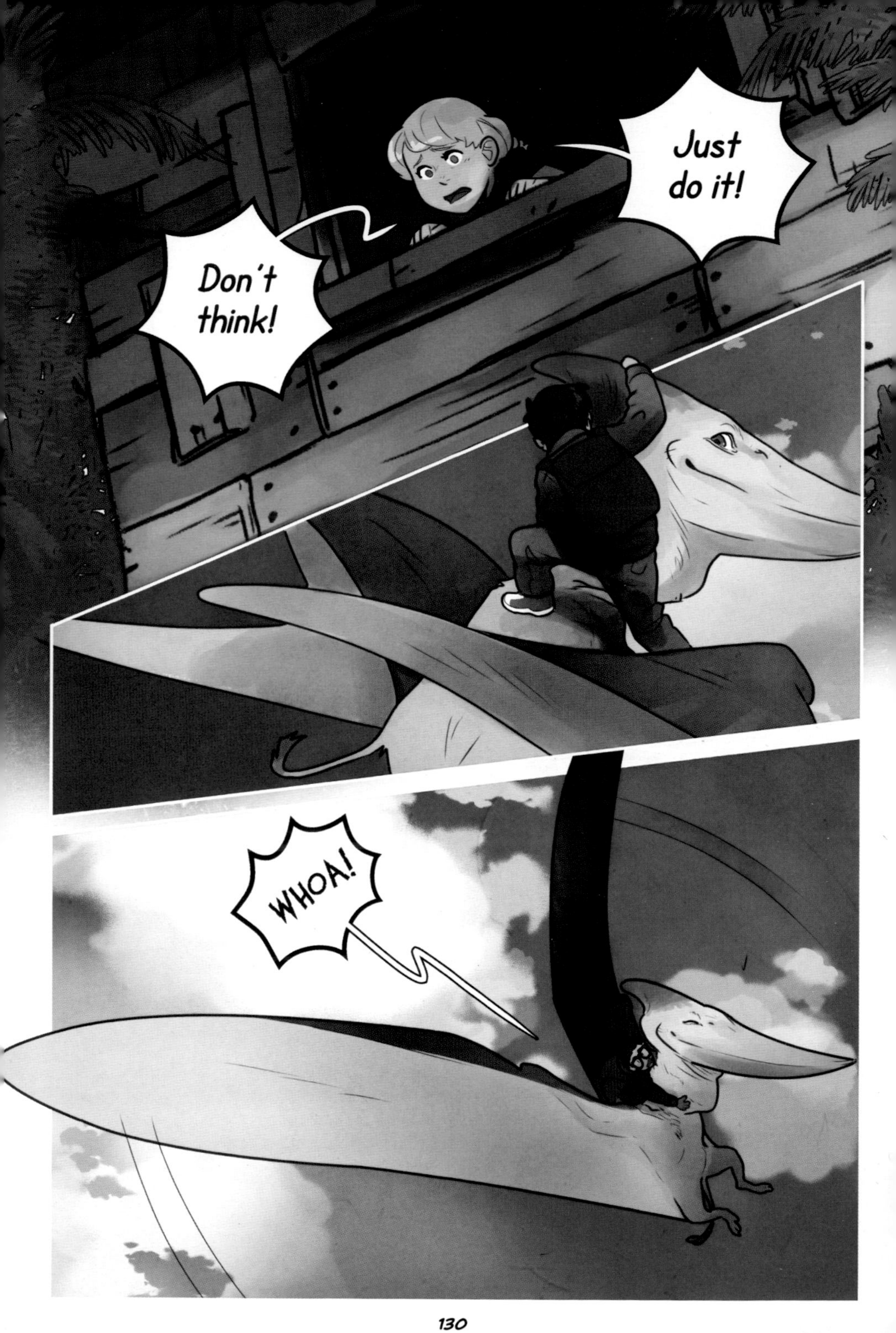
Just do it!
Don't think!
WHOA!

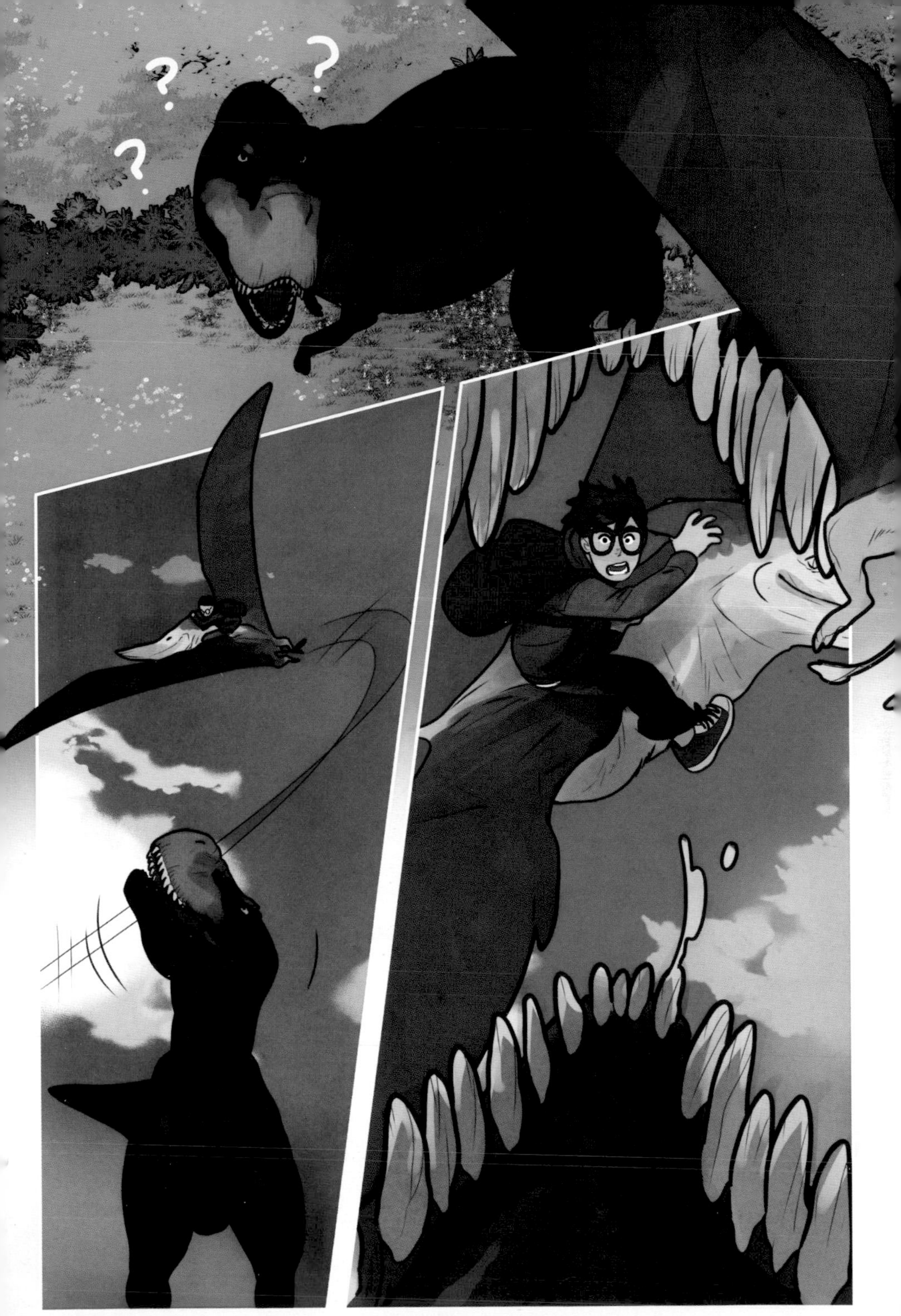
?
?
?

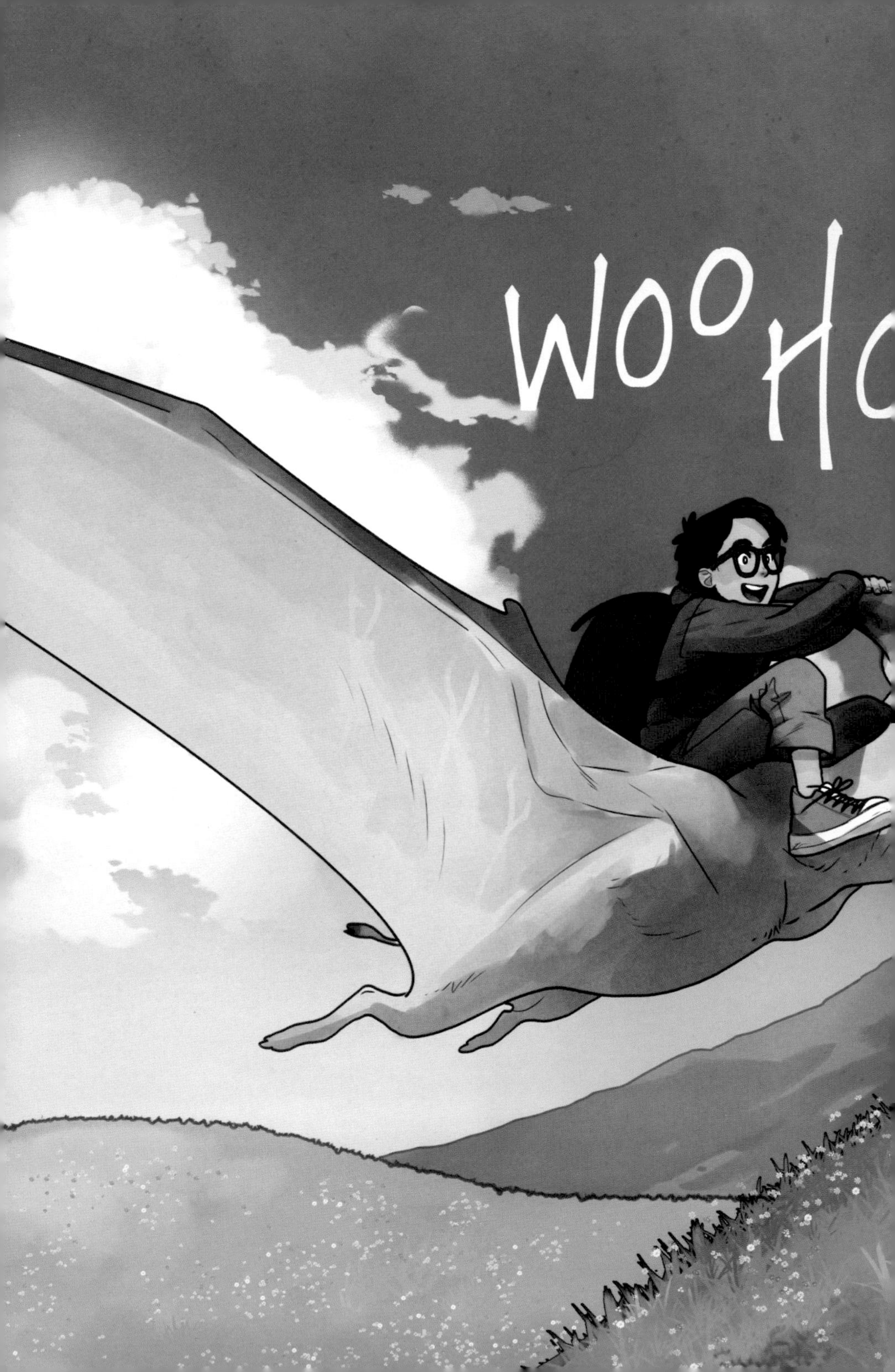
WOOHO

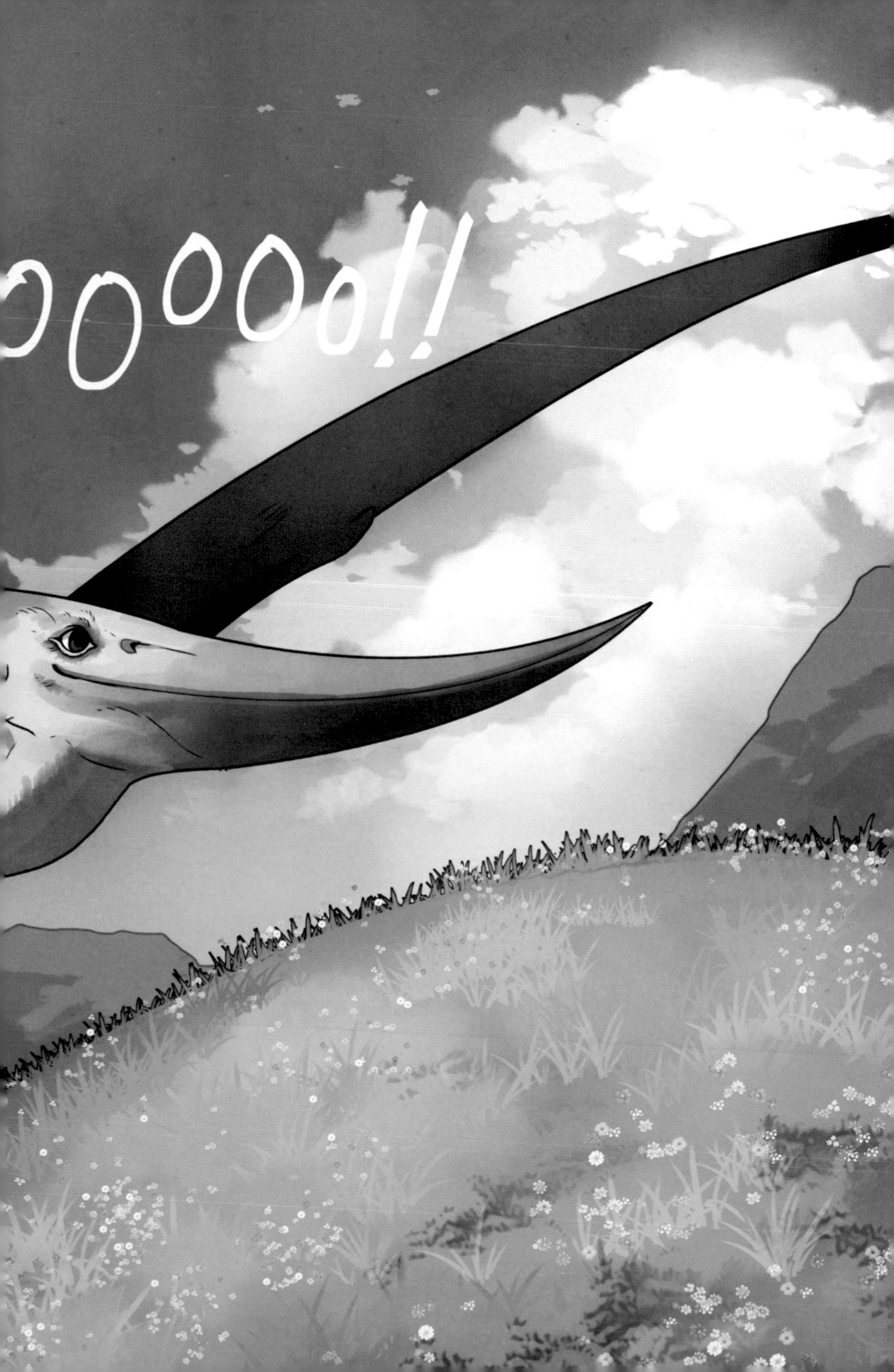
OOOOOo!!

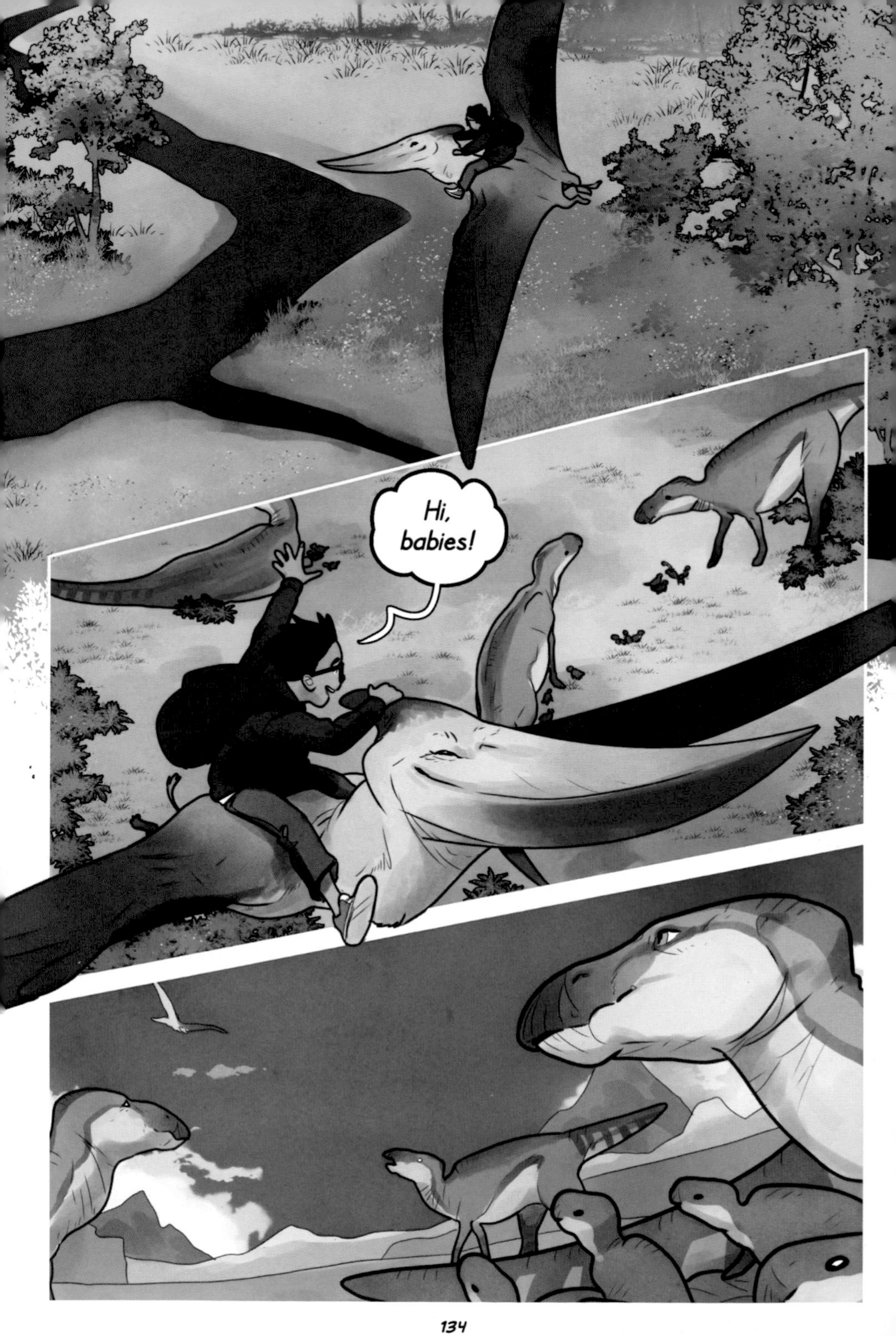
Hi, babies!

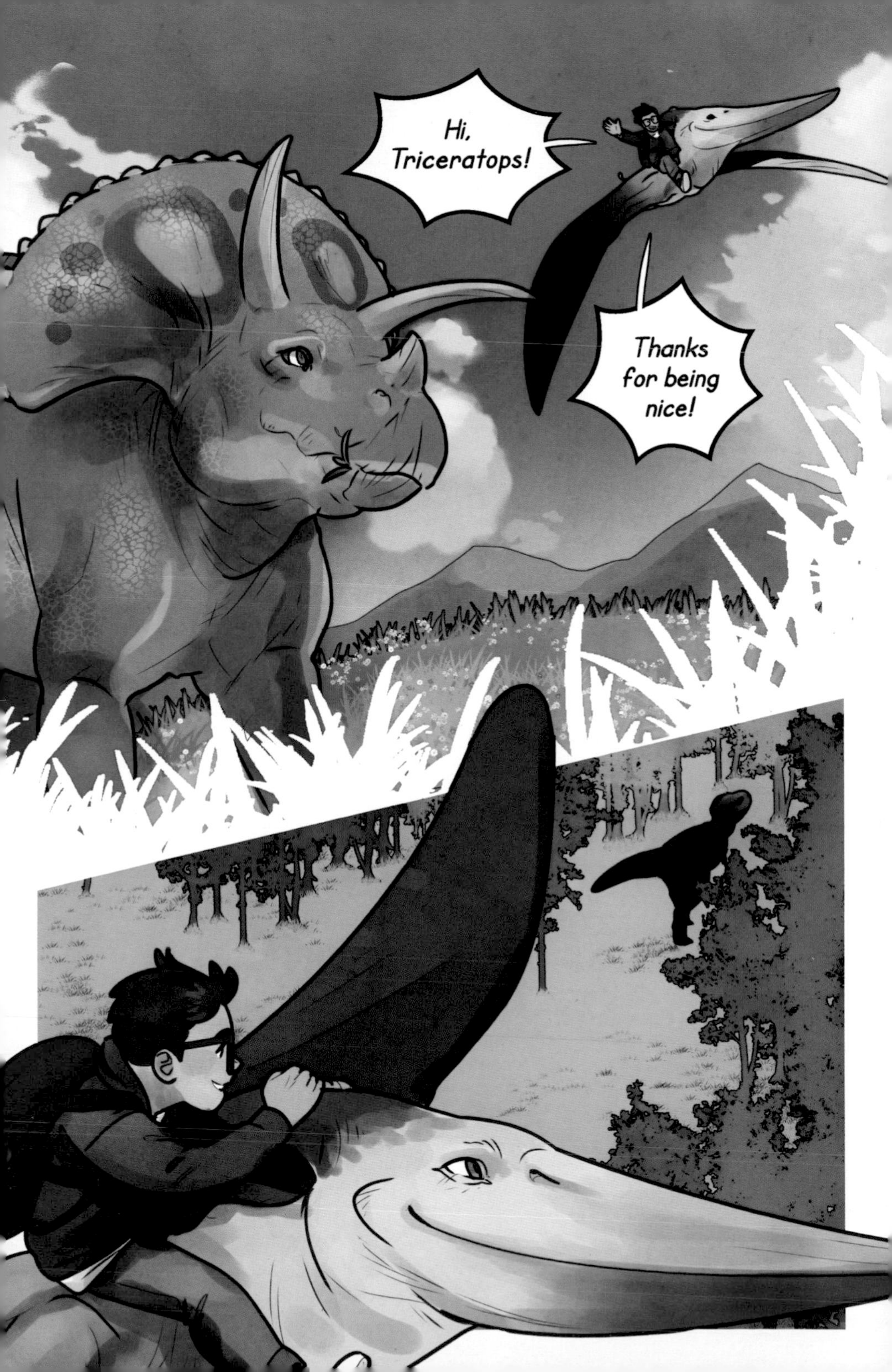
Hi, Triceratops!
Thanks for being nice!

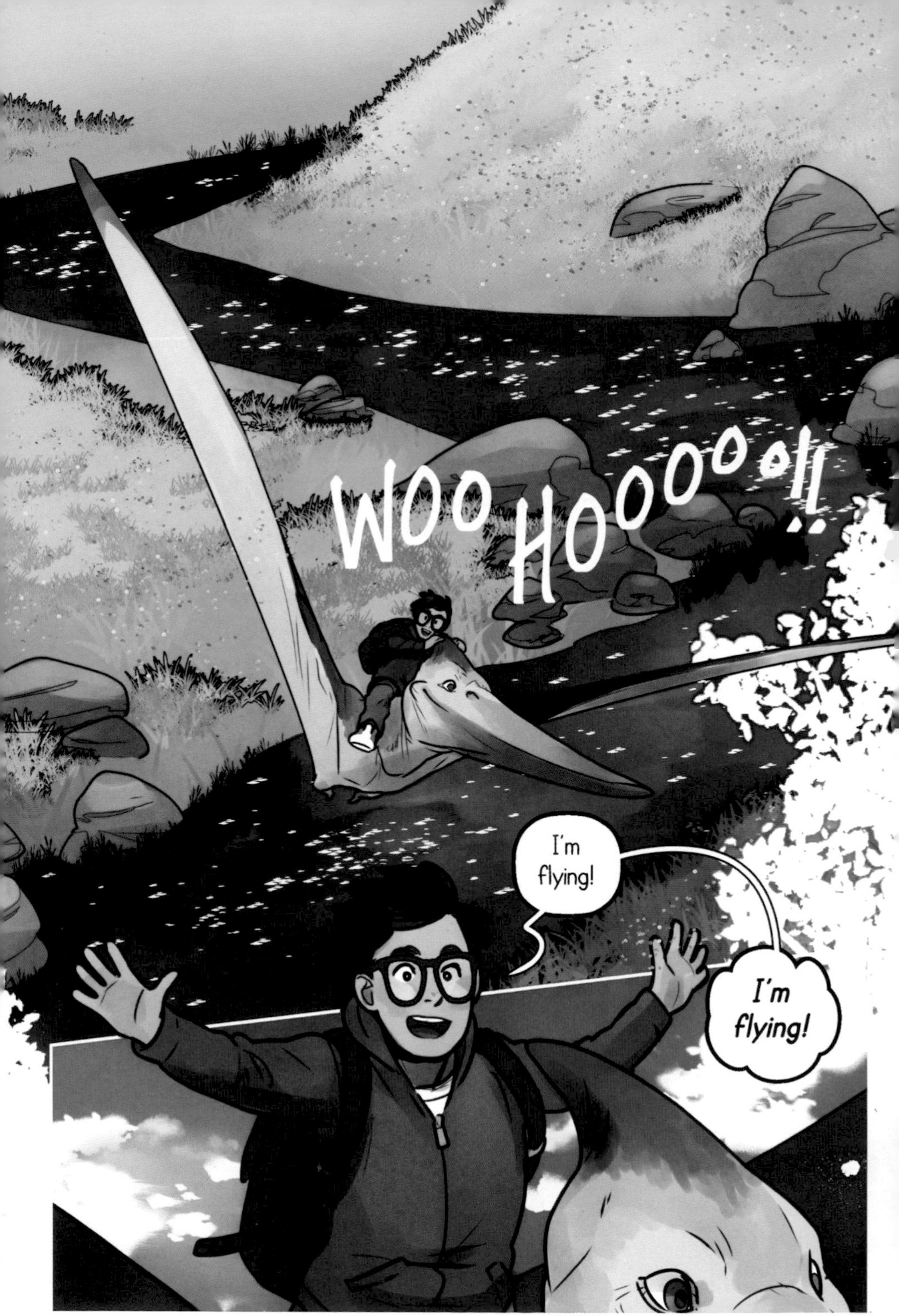
WOO HOOOOO!!
I'm flying!
I'm flying!

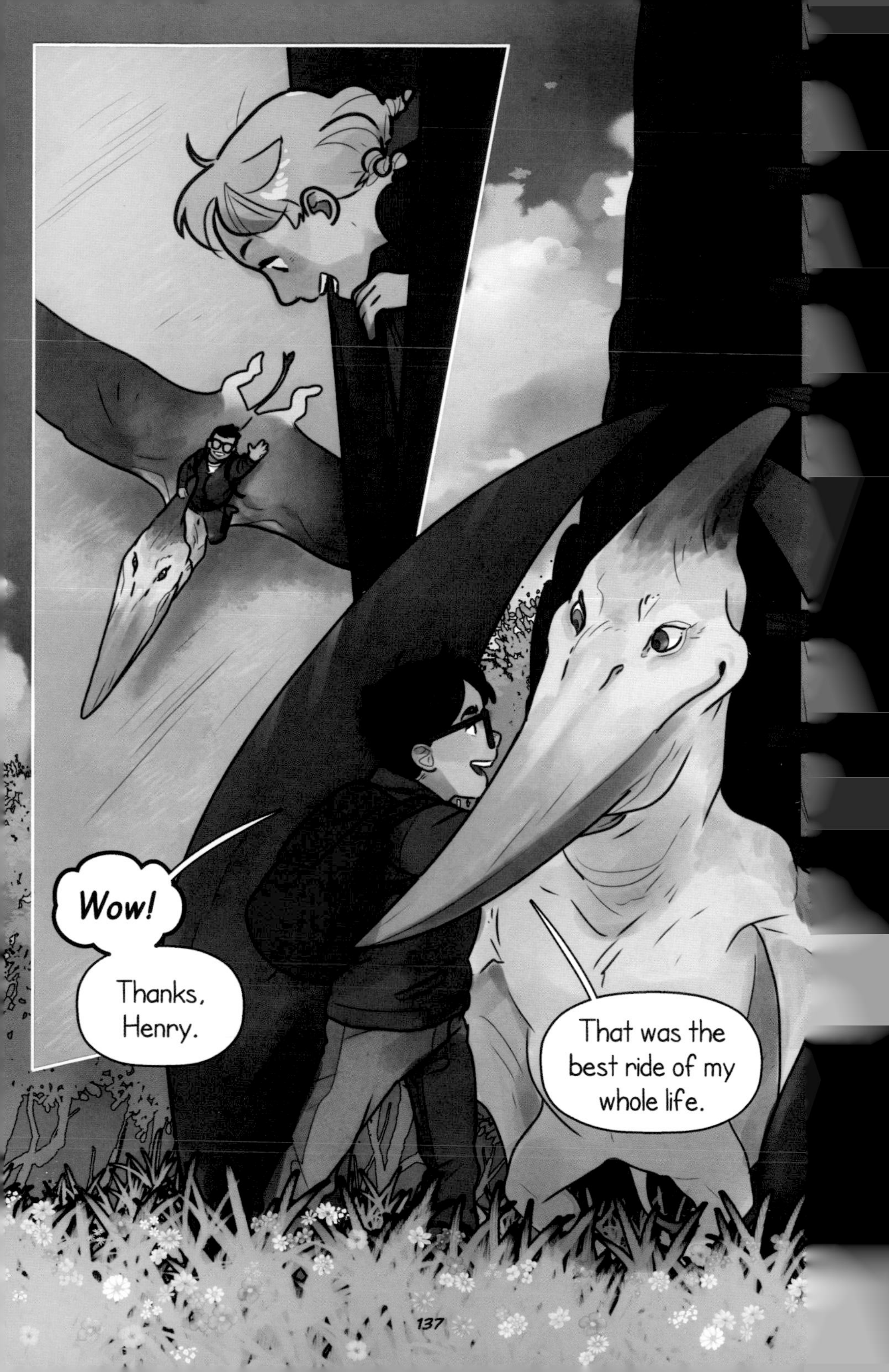
Wow!
Thanks, Henry.
That was the best ride of my whole life.

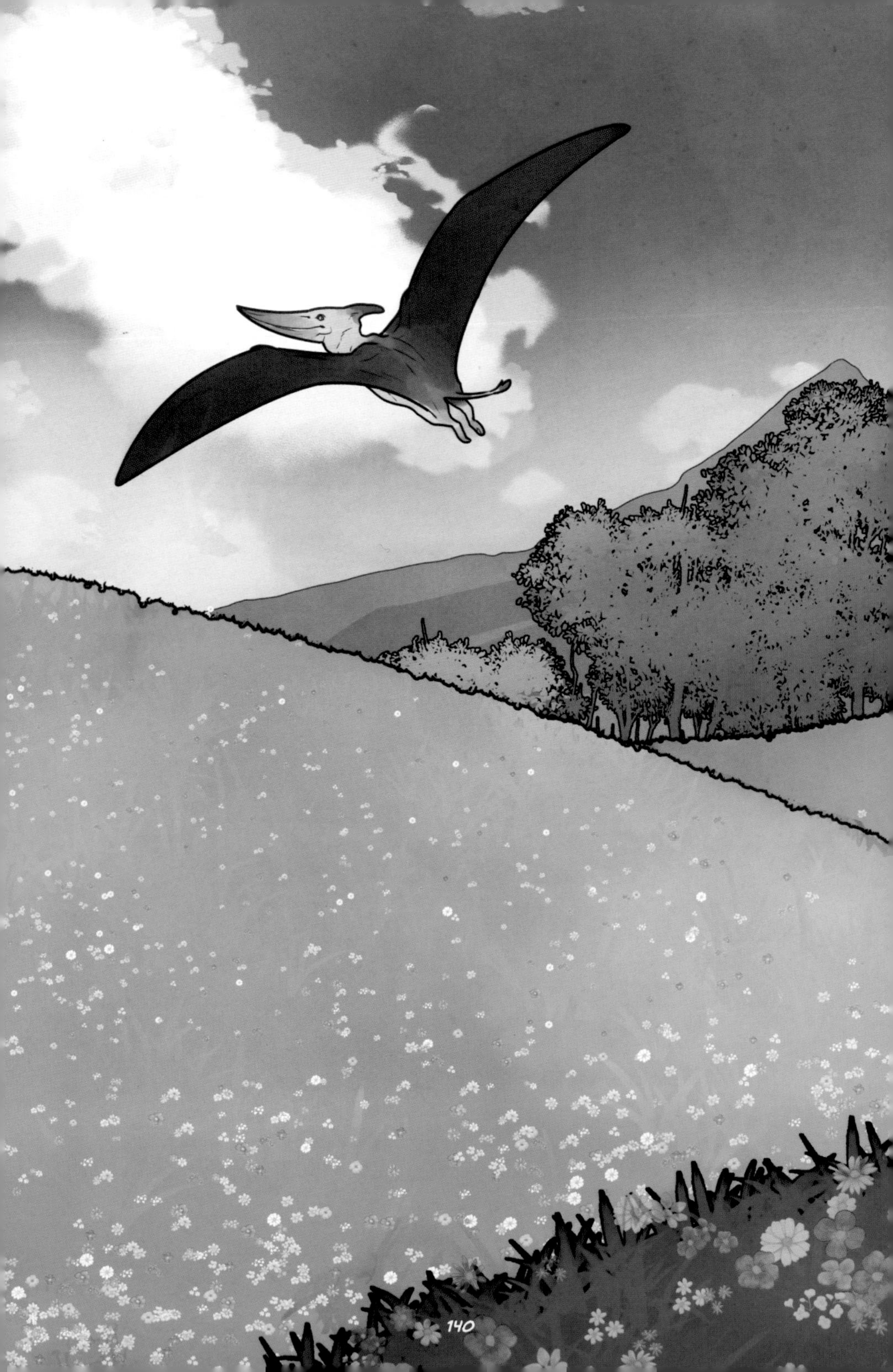

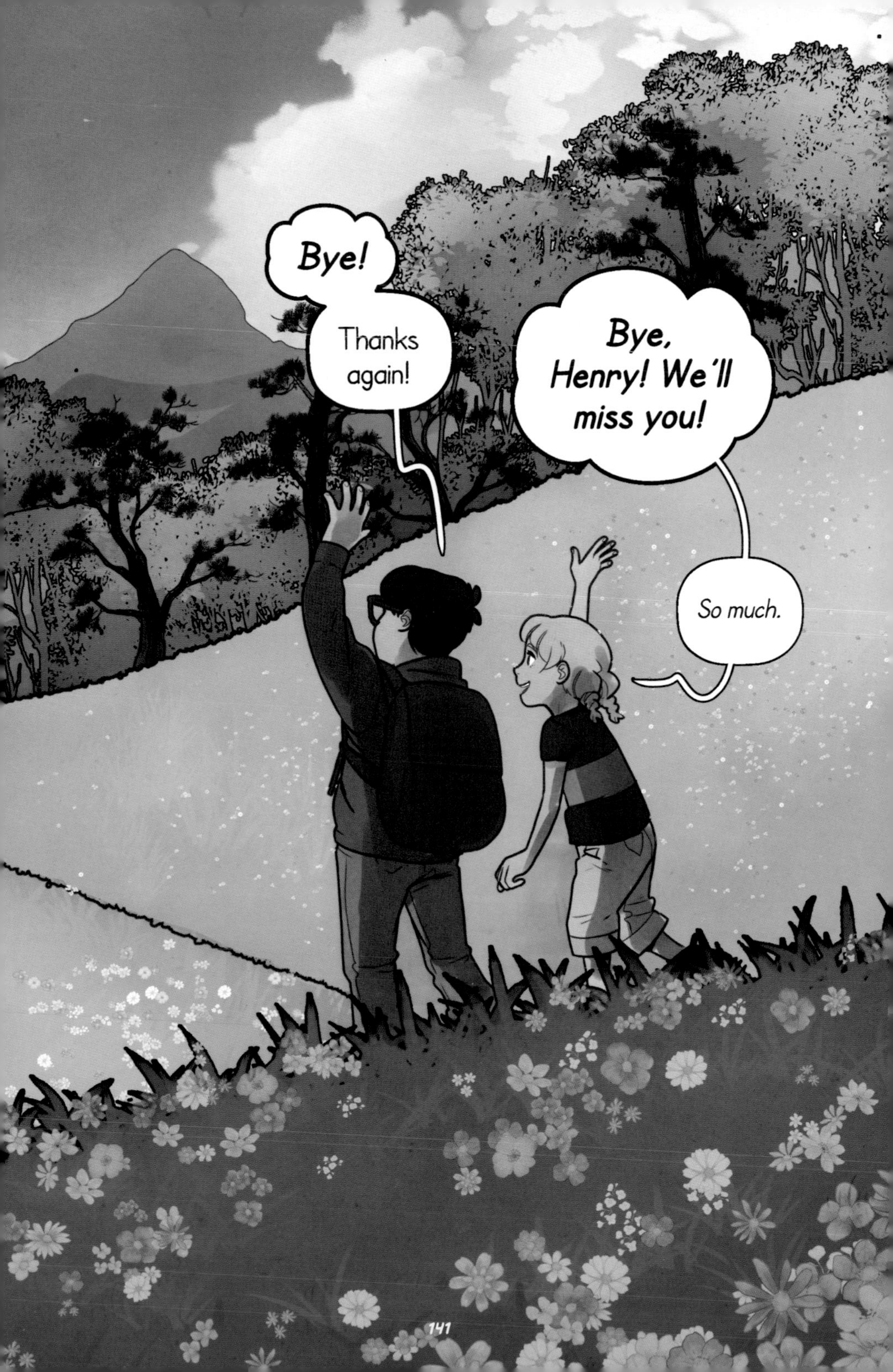
Bye!
Thanks again!
Bye, Henry! We'll miss you!
So much.

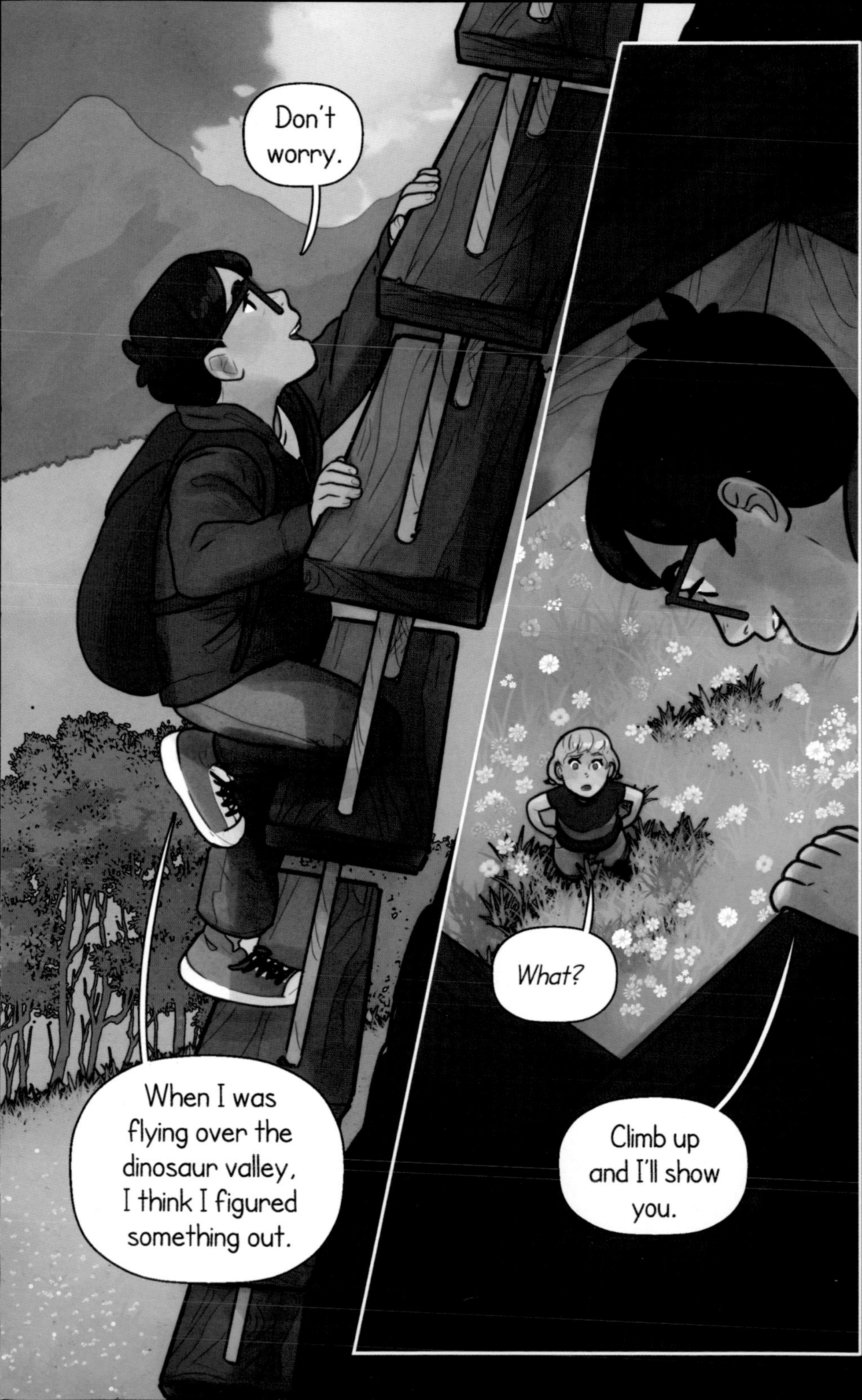
Don't worry.
When I was flying over the dinosaur valley, I think I figured something out.
What?
Climb up and I'll show you.

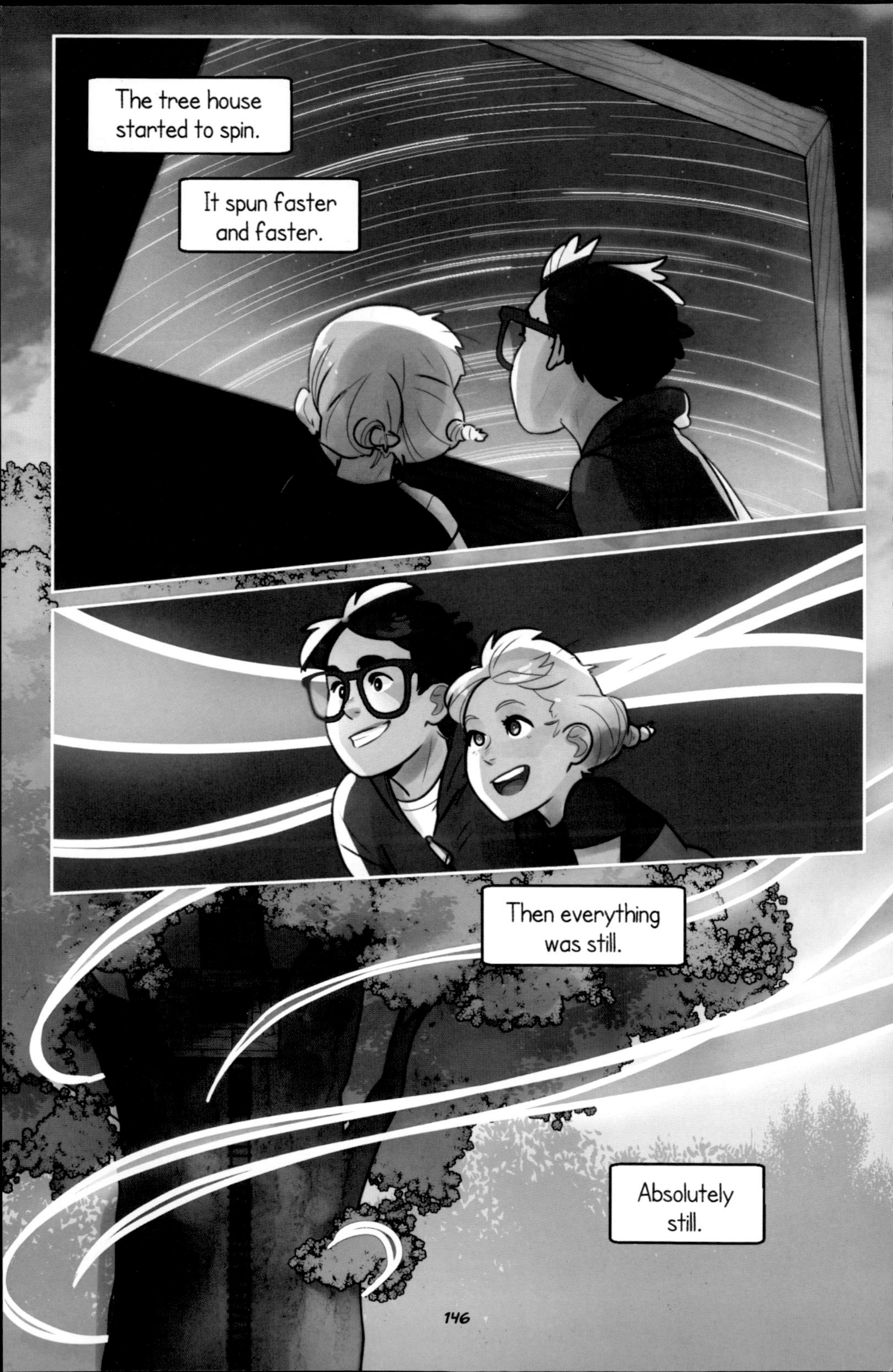
The tree house started to spin.
It spun faster and faster.
Then everything was still.
Absolutely still.

CHAPTER TEN

Home Before Dark

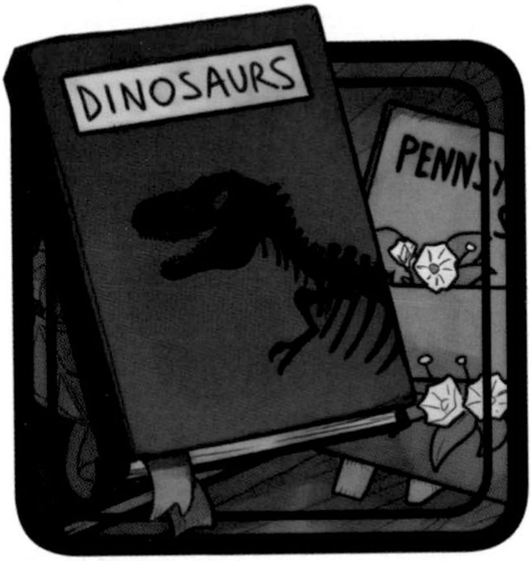
DINOSAURS
PENNS

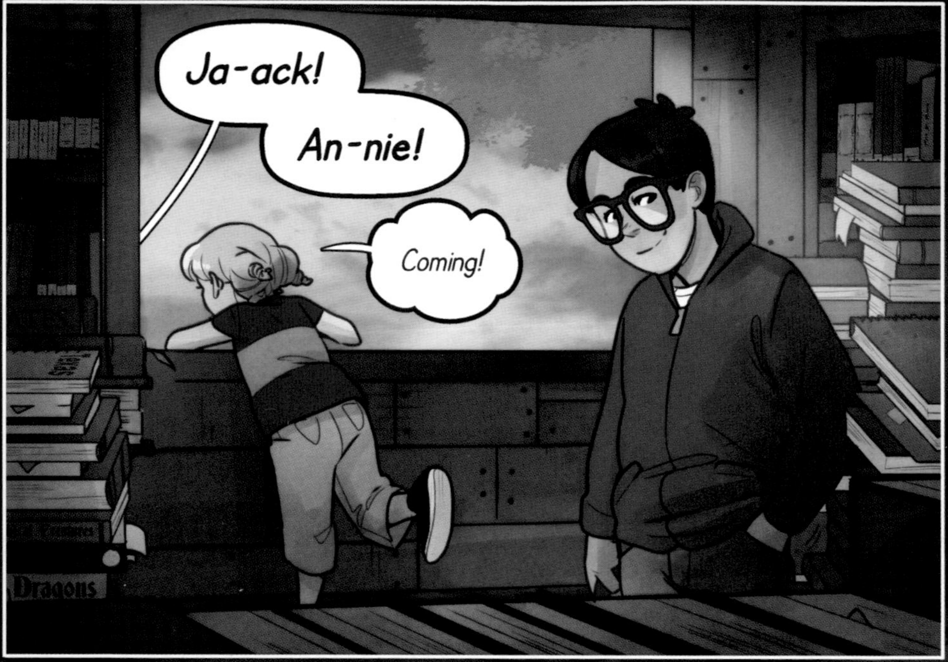
Ja-ack!
An-nie!
Coming!

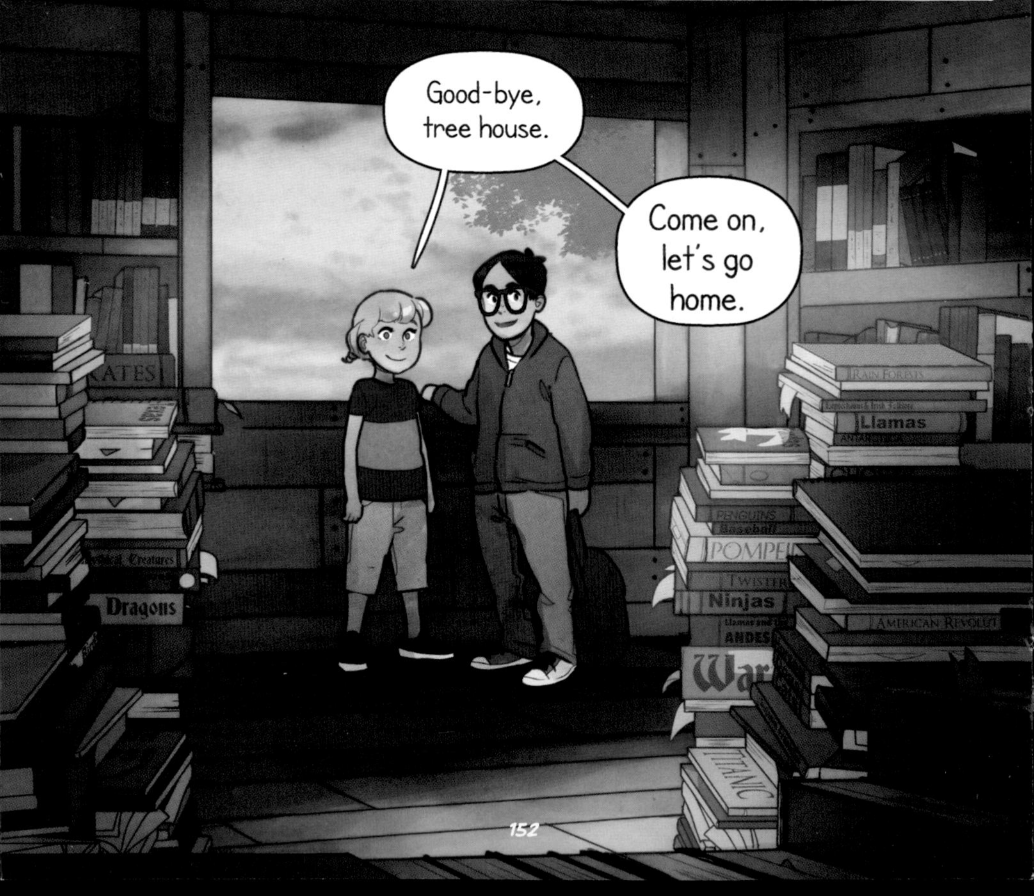
Good-bye, tree house.
Come on, let's go home.

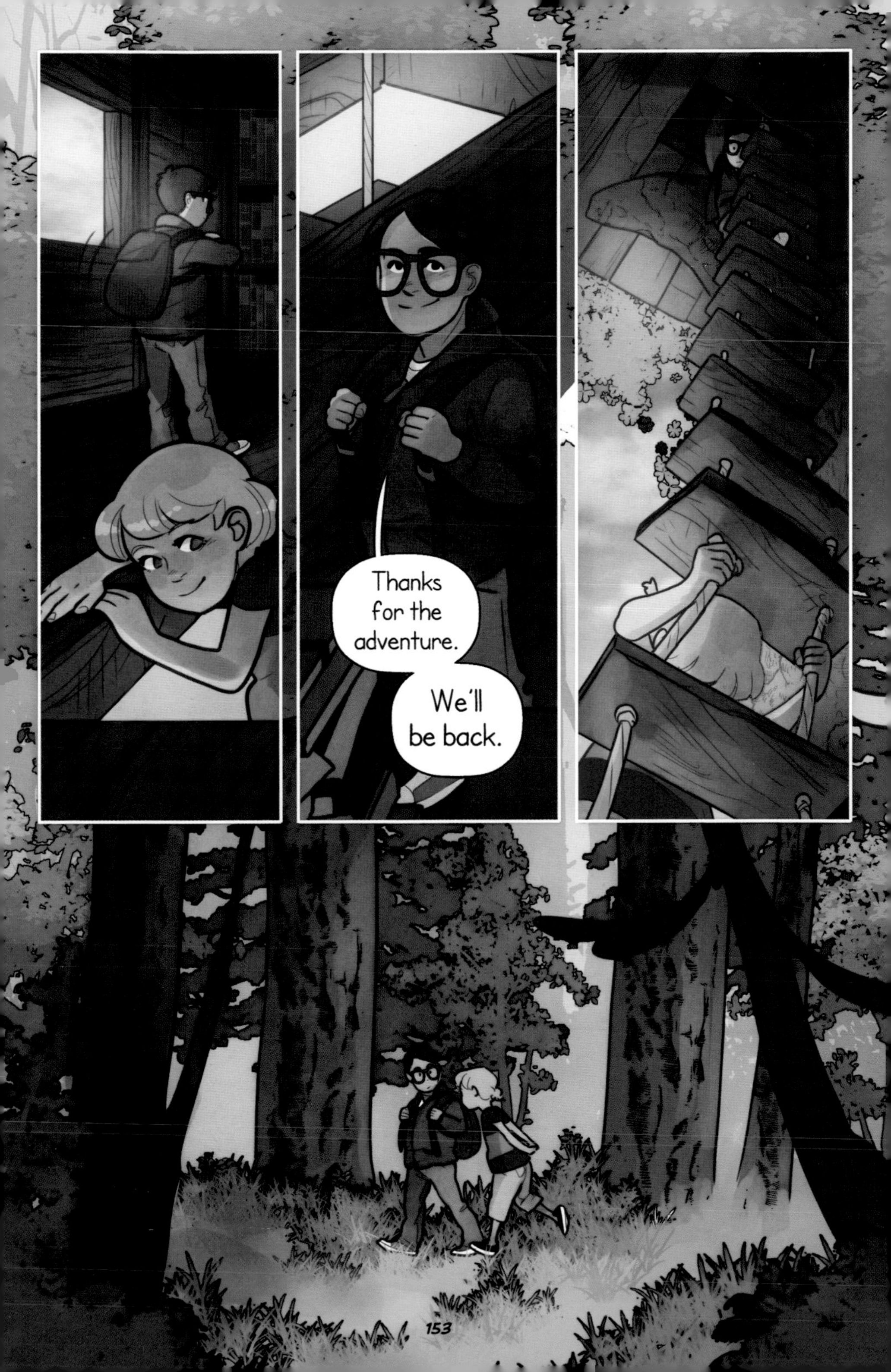
Thanks for the adventure.
We'll be back.

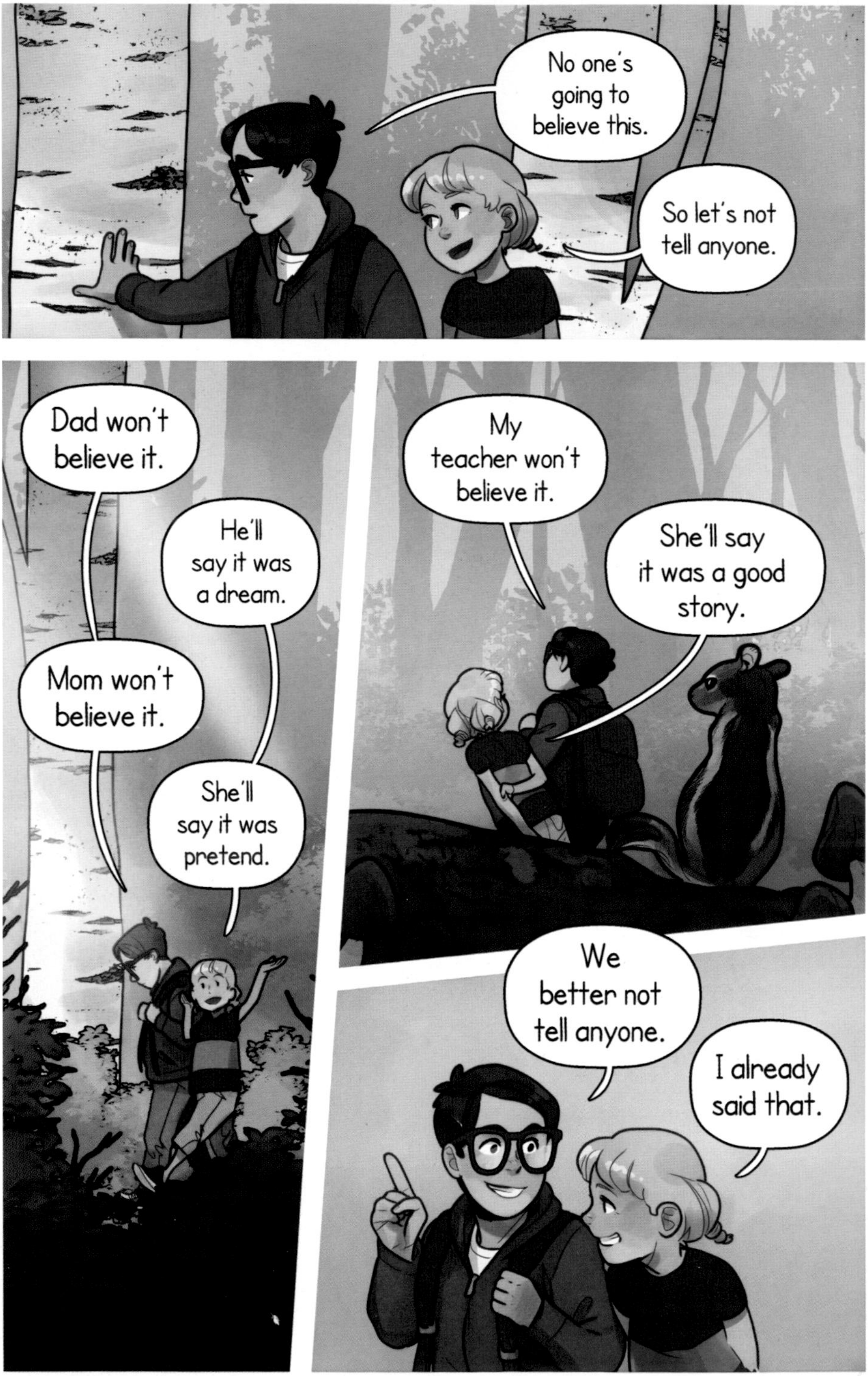
No one's going to believe this.
So let's not tell anyone.
Dad won't believe it.
He'll say it was a dream.
Mom won't believe it.
She'll say it was pretend.
My teacher won't believe it.
She'll say it was a good story.
We better not tell anyone.
I already said that.

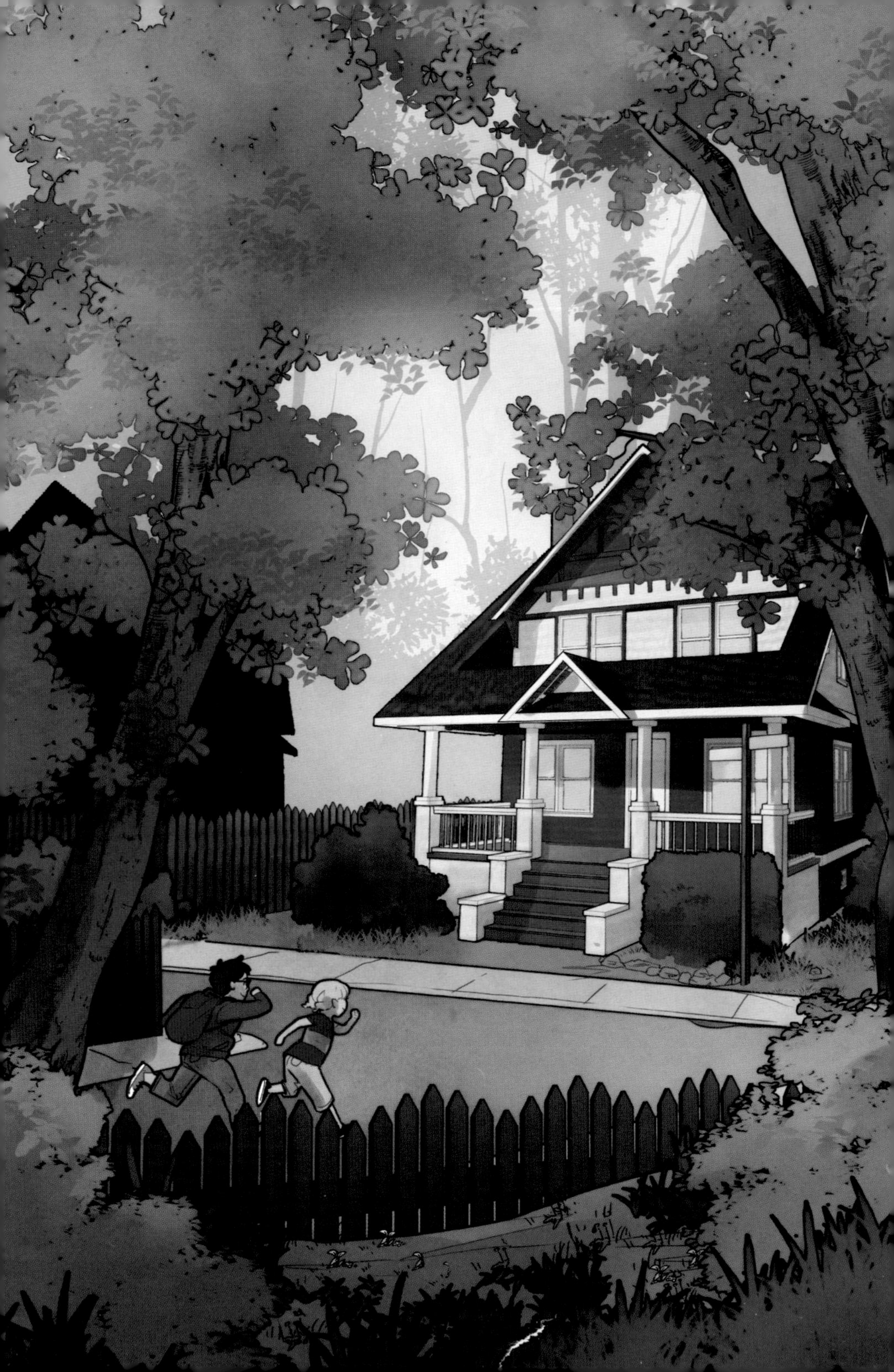

Don't miss the next adventure
in the magic tree house when Jack and Annie
are whisked away to the Middle Ages!

MARY POPE OSBORNE'S

MAGIC
TREE HOUSE®
THE GRAPHIC NOVEL

THE KNIGHT
AT DAWN

ADAPTED BY JENNY LAIRD
ILLUSTRATED BY KELLY & NICHOLE MATTHEWS

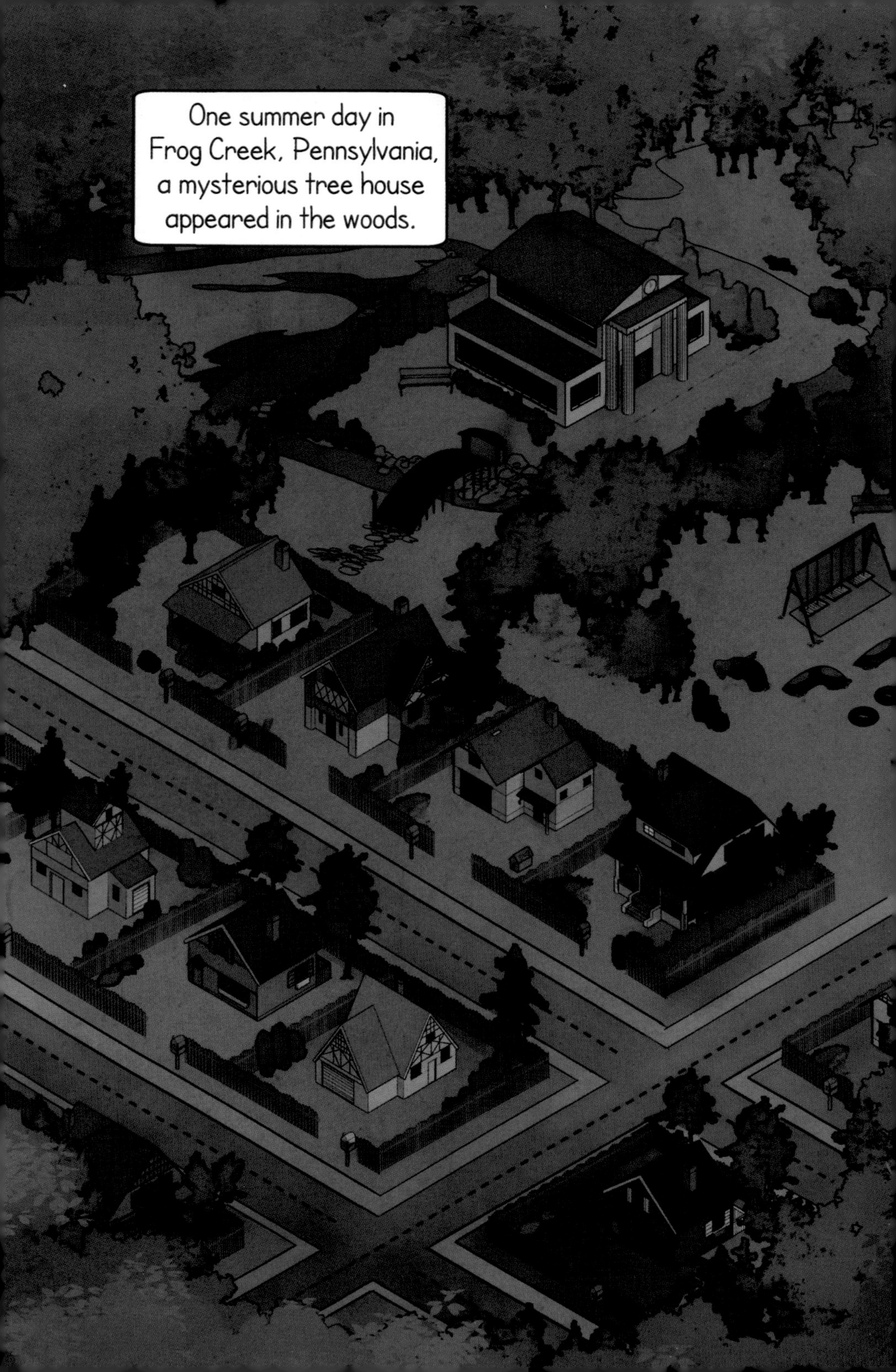
One summer day in Frog Creek, Pennsylvania, a mysterious tree house appeared in the woods.

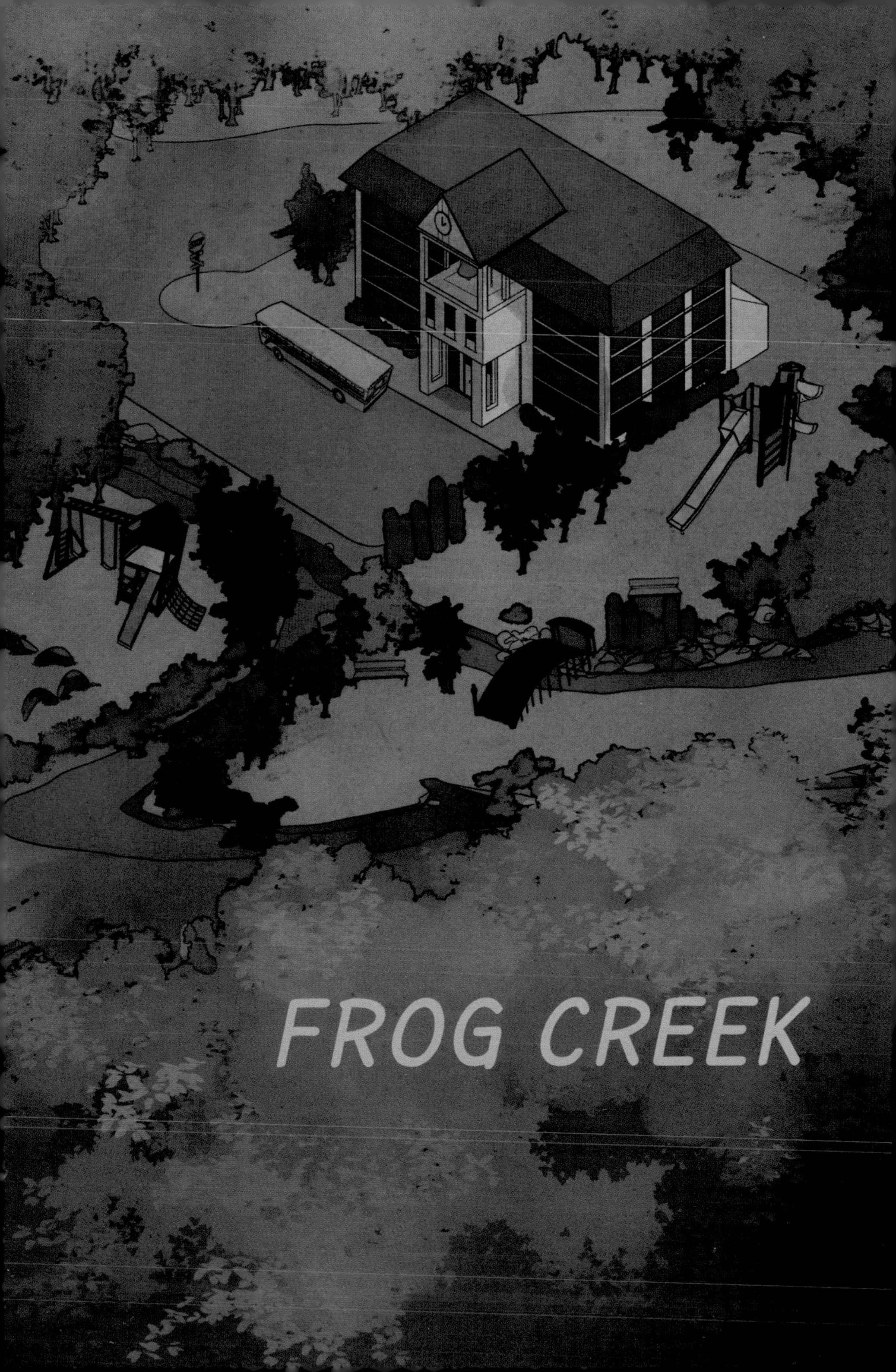
FROG CREEK

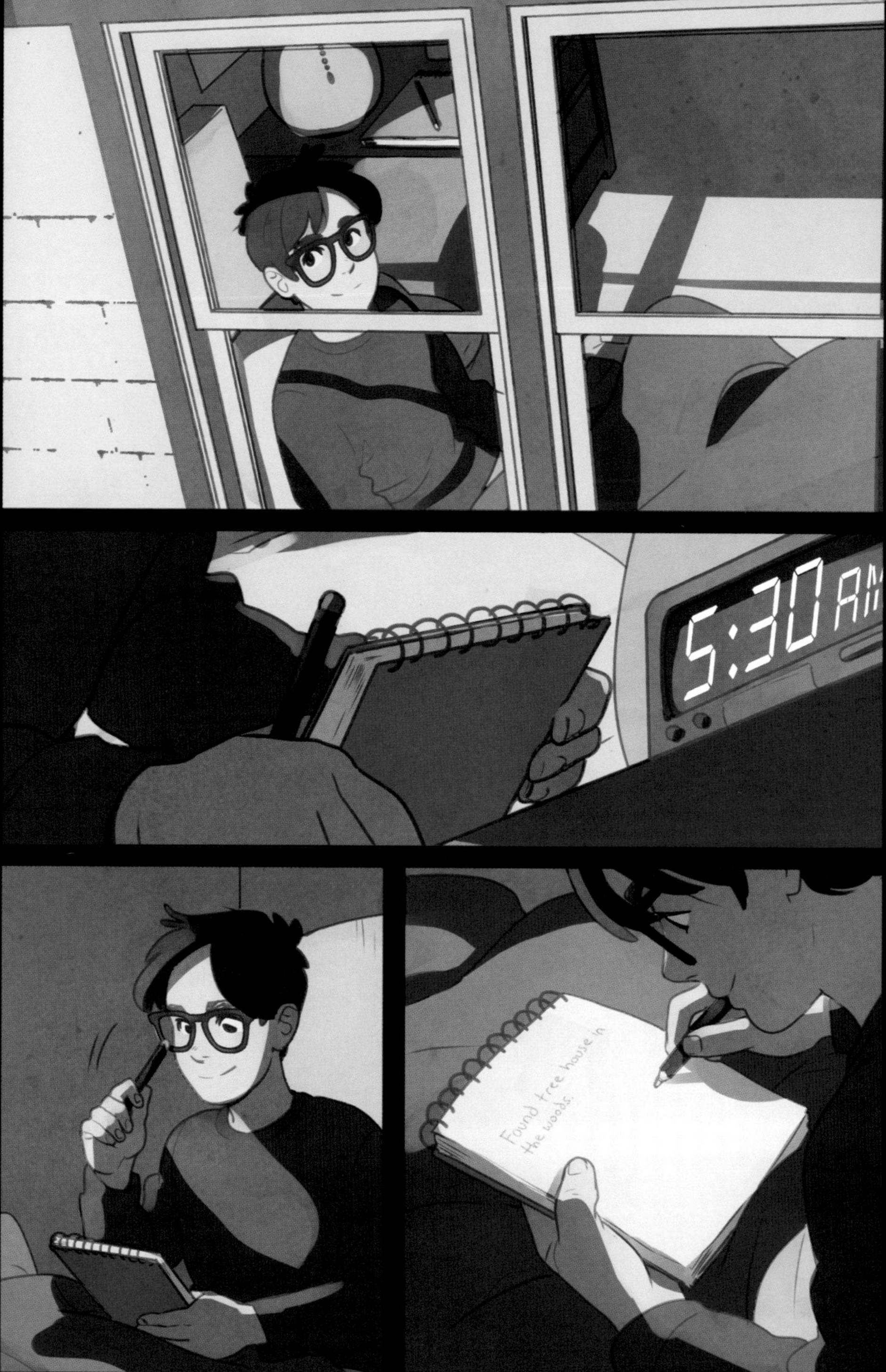
5:30 AM
Found tree house in
the woods.

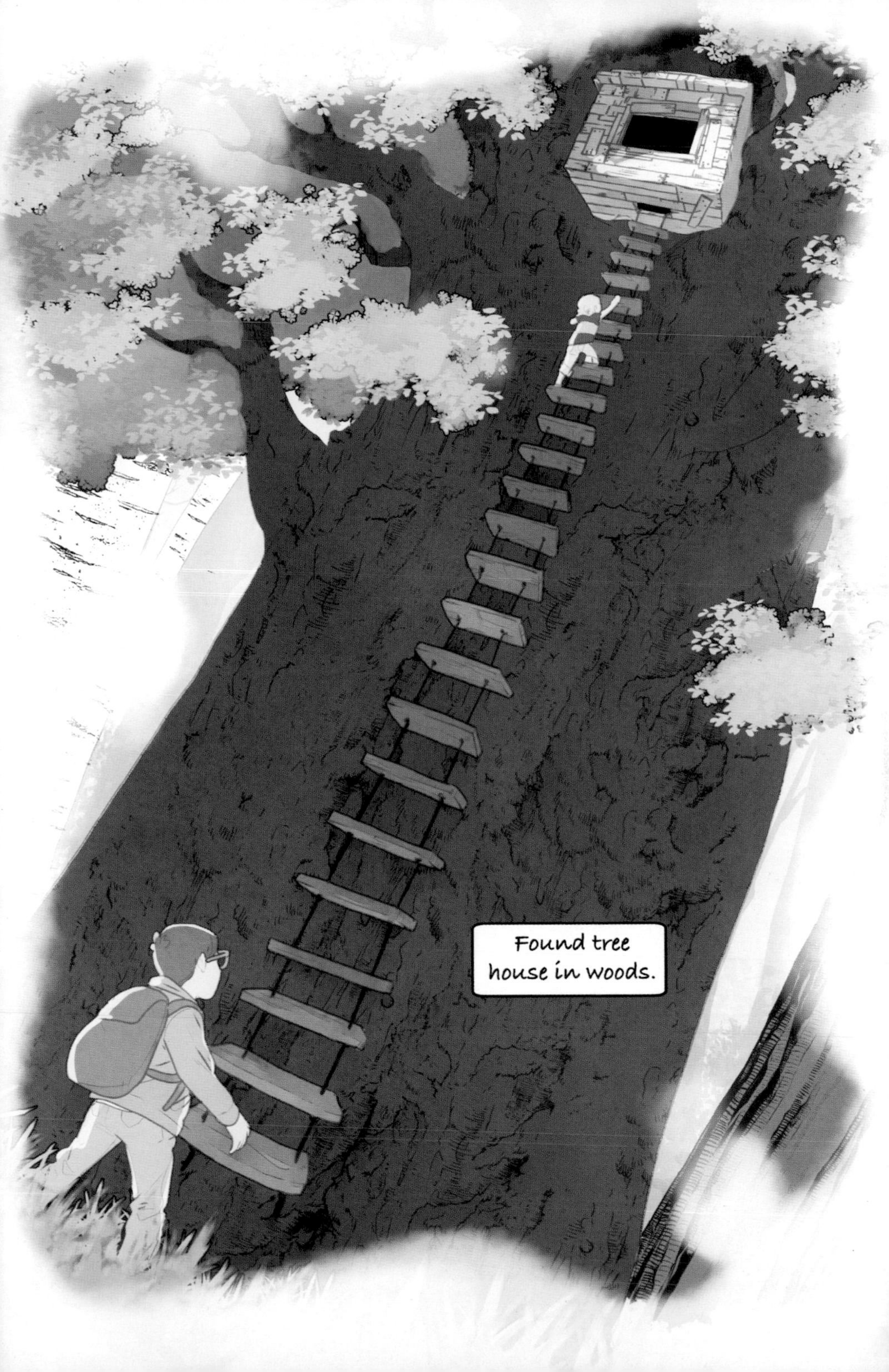
Found tree
house in woods.

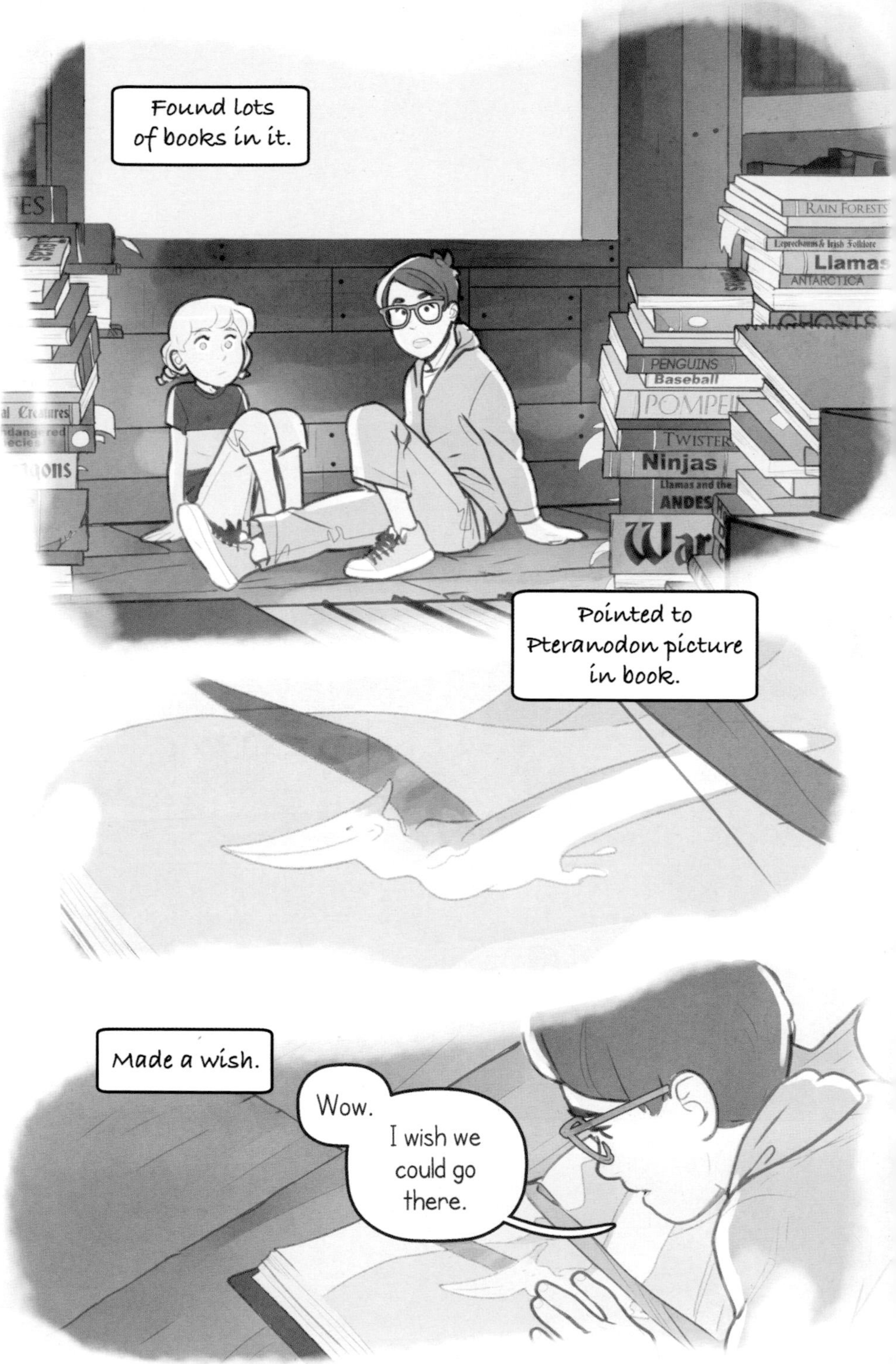
Found lots of books in it.
RAIN FORESTS
Leprechauns & Irish Folklore
Llamas
ANTARCTICA
PENGUINS
Baseball
Ninjas
Llamas and the ANDES
Pointed to Pteranodon picture in book.
Made a wish.
Wow.
I wish we could go there.

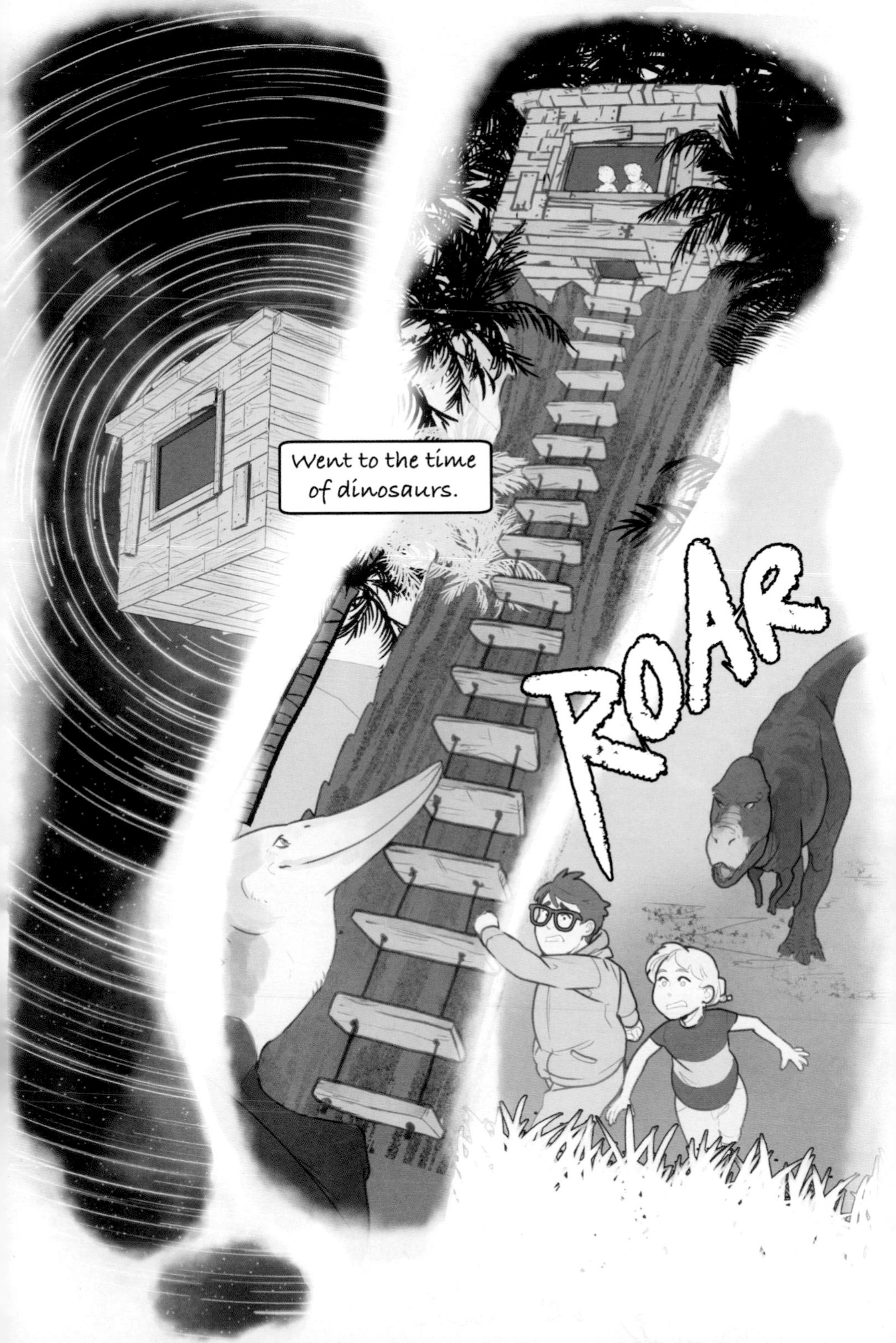
Went to the time of dinosaurs.
ROAR

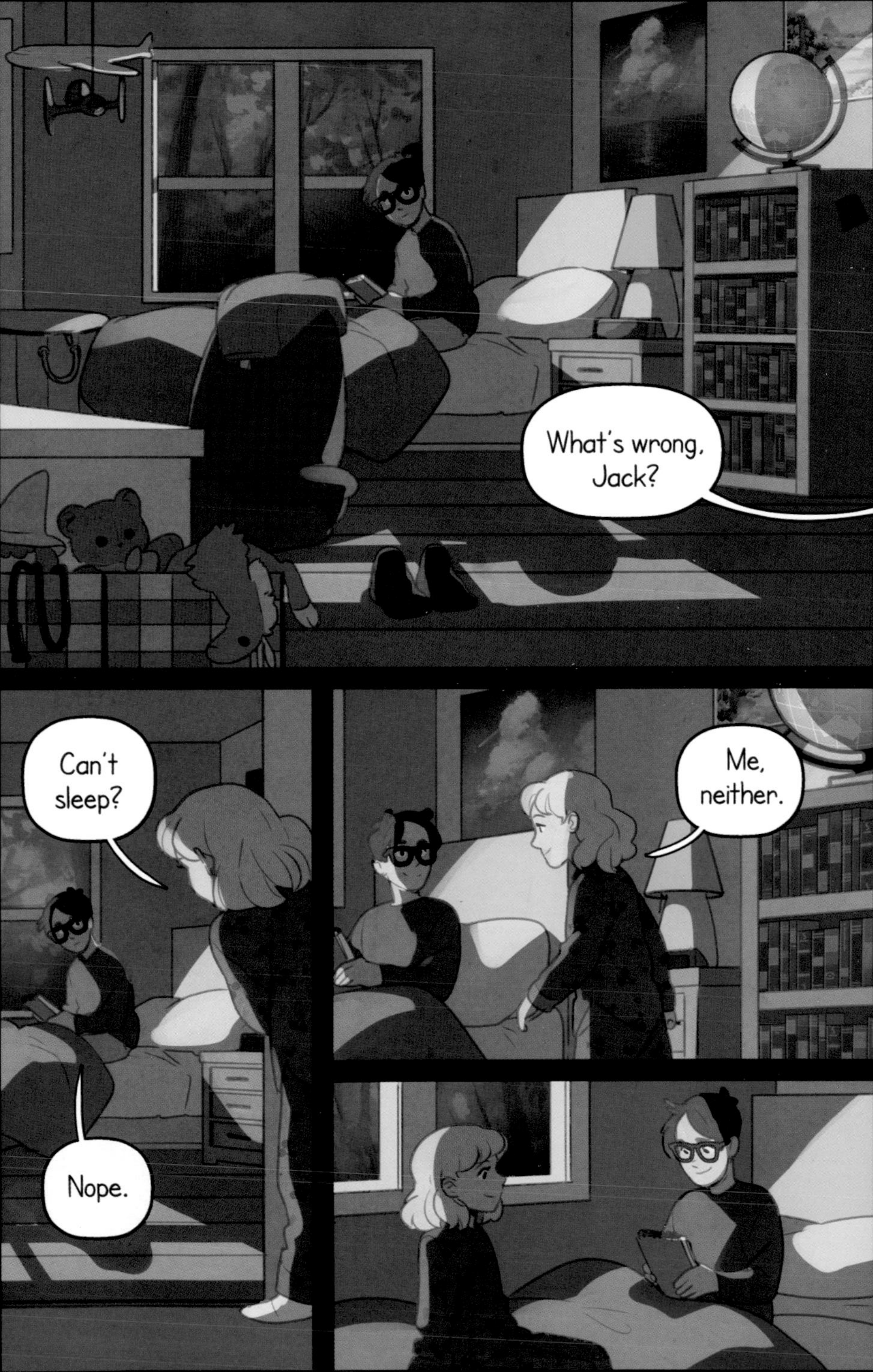
What's wrong,
Jack?
Can't
sleep?
Nope.
Me,
neither.

LET THE

MAGIC TREE HOUSE®

WHISK YOU AWAY!

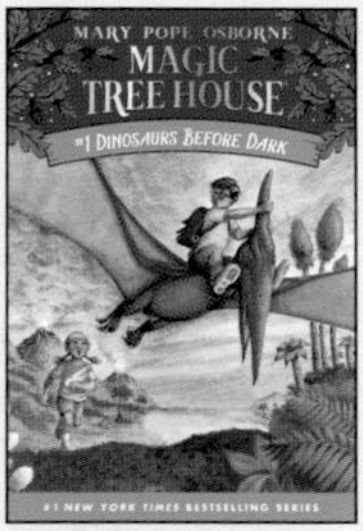
MARY POPE OSBORNE
MAGIC TREE HOUSE
#1 Dinosaurs Before Dark
#1 NEW YORK TIMES BESTSELLING SERIES

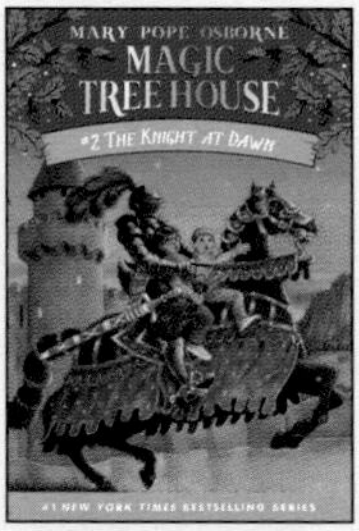
MARY POPE OSBORNE
MAGIC TREE HOUSE
#2 The Knight at Dawn
#1 NEW YORK TIMES BESTSELLING SERIES

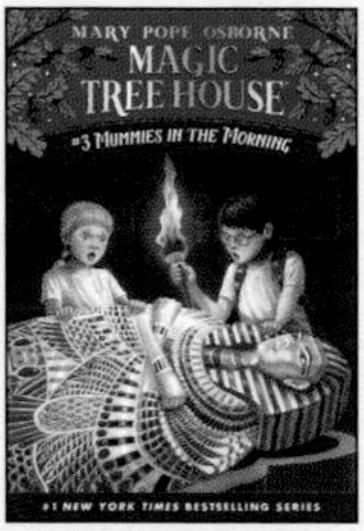
MARY POPE OSBORNE
MAGIC TREE HOUSE
#3 Mummies in the Morning
#1 NEW YORK TIMES BESTSELLING SERIES

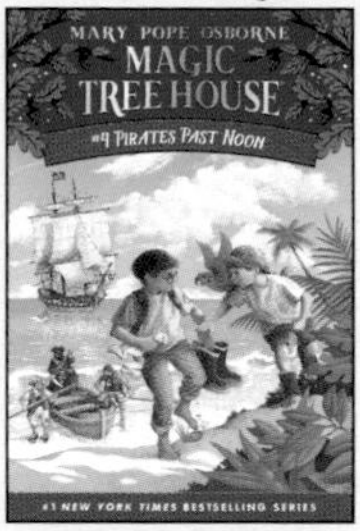
MARY POPE OSBORNE
MAGIC TREE HOUSE
#4 Pirates Past Noon
#1 NEW YORK TIMES BESTSELLING SERIES

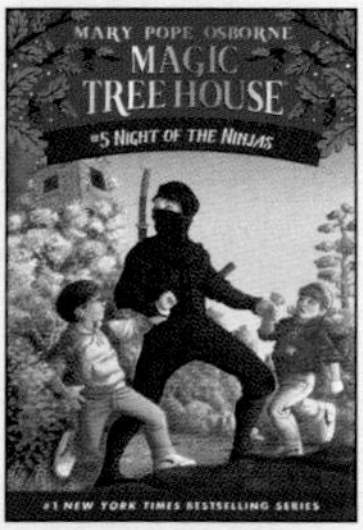
MARY POPE OSBORNE
MAGIC TREE HOUSE
#5 Night of the Ninjas
#1 NEW YORK TIMES BESTSELLING SERIES

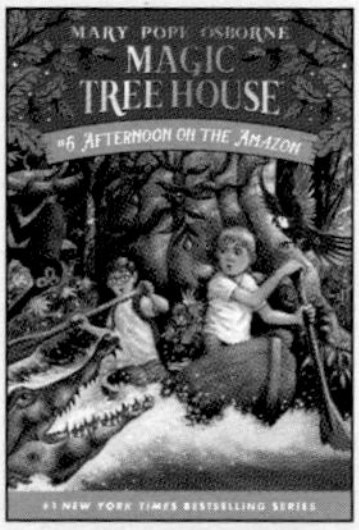
MARY POPE OSBORNE
MAGIC TREE HOUSE
#6 Afternoon on the Amazon
#1 NEW YORK TIMES BESTSELLING SERIES

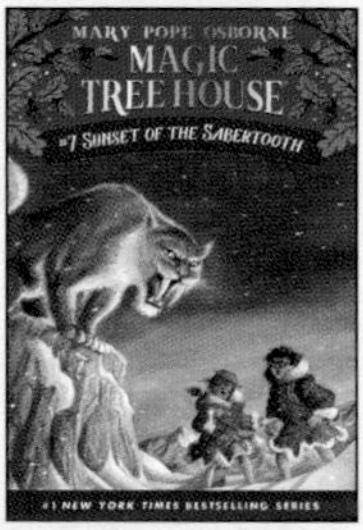
MARY POPE OSBORNE
MAGIC TREE HOUSE
#7 Sunset of the Sabertooth
#1 NEW YORK TIMES BESTSELLING SERIES

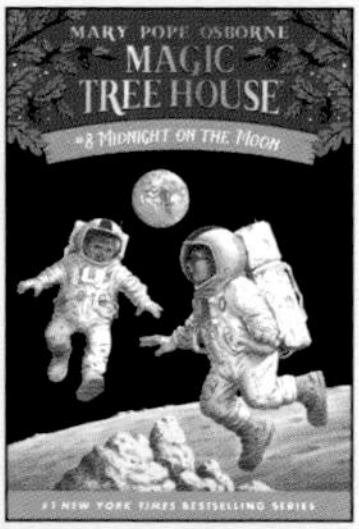
MARY POPE OSBORNE
MAGIC TREE HOUSE
#8 Midnight on the Moon
#1 NEW YORK TIMES BESTSELLING SERIES

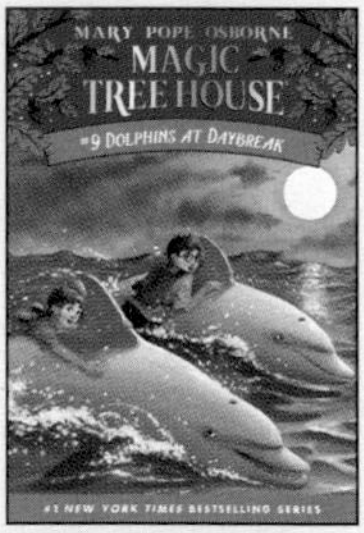
MARY POPE OSBORNE
MAGIC TREE HOUSE
#9 Dolphins at Daybreak
#1 NEW YORK TIMES BESTSELLING SERIES

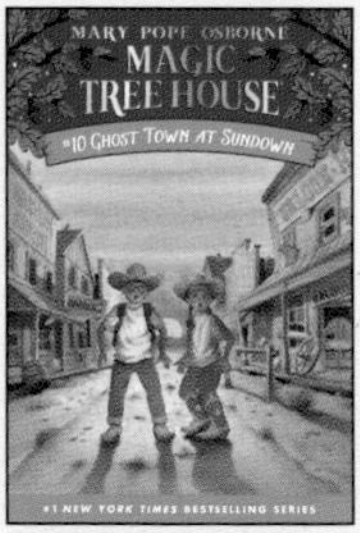
MARY POPE OSBORNE
MAGIC TREE HOUSE
#10 Ghost Town at Sundown
#1 NEW YORK TIMES BESTSELLING SERIES

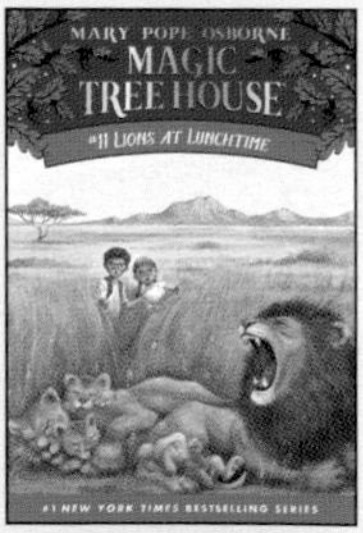
MARY POPE OSBORNE
MAGIC TREE HOUSE
#11 Lions at Lunchtime
#1 NEW YORK TIMES BESTSELLING SERIES

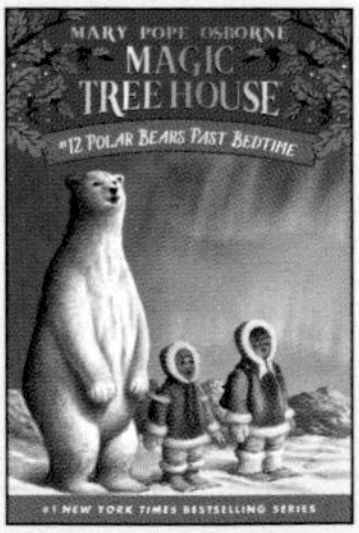
MARY POPE OSBORNE
MAGIC TREE HOUSE
#12 Polar Bears Past Bedtime
#1 NEW YORK TIMES BESTSELLING SERIES

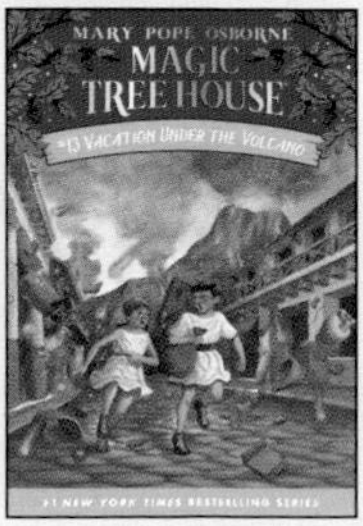
MARY POPE OSBORNE
MAGIC TREE HOUSE
#13 Vacation Under the Volcano
#1 NEW YORK TIMES BESTSELLING SERIES

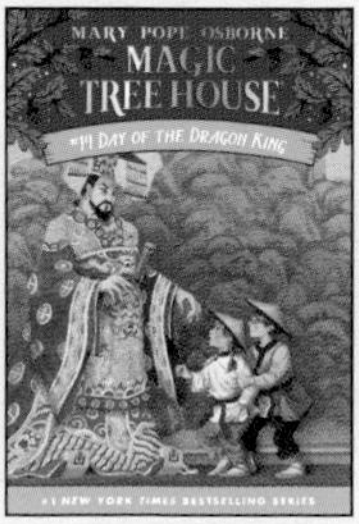
MARY POPE OSBORNE
MAGIC TREE HOUSE
#14 Day of the Dragon King
#1 NEW YORK TIMES BESTSELLING SERIES

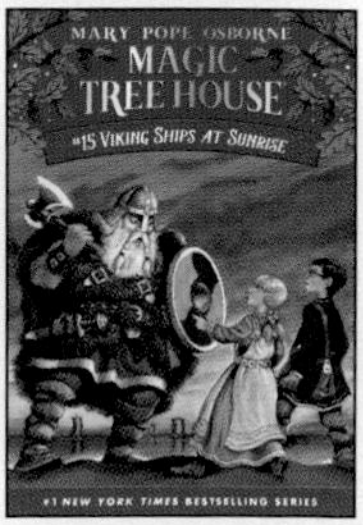
MARY POPE OSBORNE
MAGIC TREE HOUSE
#15 Viking Ships at Sunrise
#1 NEW YORK TIMES BESTSELLING SERIES

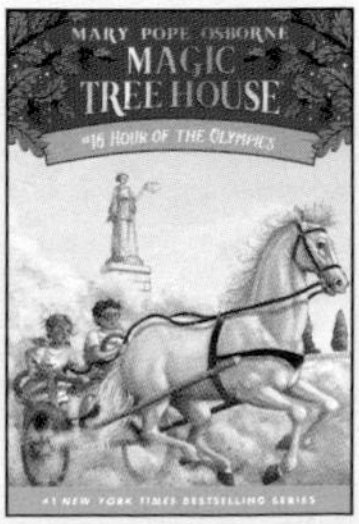
MARY POPE OSBORNE
MAGIC TREE HOUSE
#16 Hour of the Olympics
#1 NEW YORK TIMES BESTSELLING SERIES

Read all the novels in the #1 bestselling chapter book series of all time!

TRACK THE FACTS WITH JACK & ANNIE!

MARY POPE OSBORNE is the author of many novels, picture books, story collections, and nonfiction books. Her #1 *New York Times* bestselling Magic Tree House® series has been translated into numerous languages around the world. Highly recommended by parents and educators everywhere, the series introduces young readers to different cultures and times, as well as to the world's legacy of ancient myth and storytelling.

JENNY LAIRD is an award-winning playwright. She collaborates with Will Osborne and Randy Courts on creating musical theater adaptations of the Magic Tree House® series for both national and international audiences. Their work also includes shows for young performers, available through Music Theatre International's Broadway Junior® Collection. Currently the team is working on a Magic Tree House® animated television series.

KELLY & NICHOLE MATTHEWS are twin sisters and a comic-art team. They get to do their dream job every day, drawing comics for a living. They've worked with Boom Studios!, Archaia, the Jim Henson Company, Hiveworks, and now Random House!